Solitaire

Middle East Literature in Translation
Michael Beard and Adnan Haydar, *Series Editors*

For a full list of titles in this series,
visit https://press.syr.edu/supressbook-series
/middle-east-literature-in-translation/.

Solitaire

A Novel

Hassouna Mosbahi

Translated from Arabic by William Maynard Hutchins

Syracuse University Press

An excerpt from this novel appeared in *The Common*, no. 11, "Contemporary Arabic Stories," Spring 2016, as "Yunus on the Beach," 134–39.

This book was originally published in Arabic as *Yatim al-Dahr* (Beirut: Jadawel S.A.R.L, 2012).

First Edition 2022

22 23 24 25 26 27   6 5 4 3 2 1

∞ The paper used in this publication meets the minimum requirements
of the American National Standard for Information Sciences—Permanence
of Paper for Printed Library Materials, ANSI Z39.48-1992.

For a listing of books published and distributed by Syracuse University Press, visit https://press.syr.edu.

ISBN: 978-0-8156-1143-1 (paperback)   978-0-8156-5550-3 (e-book)

Library of Congress Cataloging-in-Publication Data
Names: Miṣbāḥī, Ḥassūnah, author. | Hutchins, William M., translator.
Title: Solitaire : a novel / Hassouna Mosbahi ; translated from the Arabic by William Maynard Hutchins.
Other titles: Yatīm al-dahr. English
Description: First edition. | Syracuse, New York : Syracuse University Press, 2022. | Series: Middle East literature in translation |Includes bibliographical references. | Summary: "Originally published in Arabic in 2012 as "Yatīm al-Dahr," this contemporary Tunisian novel encompasses a day in the life of Yunus—the self-proclaimed "Solitaire"—as he experiences an identity crisis upon turning sixty that mirrors the crisis in his own country"— Provided by publisher.
Identifiers: LCCN 2021037558 (print) | LCCN 2021037559 (ebook) | ISBN 9780815611431 (paperback ; alk. paper) | ISBN 9780815655503 (ebook)
Subjects: LCGFT: Novels.
Classification: LCC PJ7846.I6974 Y3813 2022 (print) | LCC PJ7846.I6974 (ebook) | DDC 892.7/36—dc23
LC record available at https://lccn.loc.gov/2021037558
LC ebook record available at https://lccn.loc.gov/2021037559

For Hanan
And Tunisia,
In hopes that they will regain
"Sense and meaning."

Every life is many days, day after day. We walk through ourselves, meeting robbers, ghosts, giants, old men, young men, wives, widows, brothers-in-love. But always meeting ourselves.

—James Joyce, *Ulysses* (1922),
episode 9 (Scylla and Charybdis)

Contents

Translator's Note

This experimental Tunisian novel is a deep dive into the life of the protagonist, a Tunisian intellectual. Its Arabic title is *Yatim al-Dahr*, which the author explains is the pen name adopted by the hero as a tribute to al-Tha'alibi's book *Yatimat al-Dahr*. This novel's title, in either al-Tha'alibi's original feminine form (with *at*) or the pen name's masculine one, can refer positively to a unique, precious pearl or gem but also negatively to fate's orphan—in other words, to a solitary, tragic, or pathetic figure. The closest English equivalent I have found is *solitaire*, which can be either a unique, precious gem or a solitary person or pursuit. This novel brings a letter in a bottle from a troubled heart rather than reportage from "over there."

The events of this novel occur on the hero's sixtieth birthday. A professor of French language and literature, he is a specialist in Gustave Flaubert, whom he describes as his master. At retirement, Yunus, who had by then separated from his wife, left Tunis, the capital, to settle in the Tunisian coastal city of Nabeul. Searching for solitude, he hoped to spend the remainder of his life among the books he loved. On his sixtieth birthday, Yunus plunges into a delayed midlife crisis that reflects his homeland's identity crisis. He embarks on an exploration of his past, recalling his life's most important way stations, starting with his childhood, when he was captivated by the Sufis and ascetics who lived in the nearby mountains and woods, and continuing with his youth, when he began to write short stories and tales under the influence of favorite, mainly French, authors. Yunus decided then not to publish what he wrote, however, because he deemed writing in Tunisia to be "sterile work." He recalls his stormy love affair with the girl who became his wife as well as a subsequent infatuation—when he was middle-aged—for a beautiful student, who loved "his lectures on Flaubert." Yunus proves to be a relatively reliable and sympathetic narrator despite a natural blindness to some of his own flaws, including his sexual assault on a maid.

During his journey back through time, Yunus muses about the lives of other people—like Gharsallah, a village dervish who strips naked to emphasize his spiritual message, and his friends Hisham and Béchir, who experience culture shock on returning to their homeland after long absences. Through the narrator's associations with various friends, the author explores not only a swath of Tunisian history and culture but conditions in other Arab countries: Algeria after independence, Libya in the Qaddafi era, and Lebanon during the civil war of 1975–90. The novel is set during the rule of Ben Ali, and that Tunisian autocrat's wife is skewered in it. The bravura portrayal of Madame Leïla Ben Ali, although extremely negative, adds a demonic feminine portrait to this overwhelmingly masculine novel. Without this portrait of her, the characters' motivation in the final chapter would be unclear. This satirical, elegiac, literary, and political novel touches on life and death, love and writing, male bonding, and the tensions between Tunisia's educated elite and the country's rulers, as well as between intellectuals and Islamist puritans and extremists in the contemporary Arab World.

From *Return of the Spirit* by Tawfiq al-Hakim and *The Cairo Trilogy* by Naguib Mahfouz, contrasting the microcosm of a family with the macrocosm of an entire Arab country has been an important way to write an Arabic novel. In *Solitaire*, the microcosm is Yunus.

I use italics for foreign words and also to set off interior monologue. There is at least one sentence in which two of these different uses of italics appear together, and I have then chosen to use roman letters for a foreign word in an interior monologue. (I do not use italics for an expression inside parentheses.) On at least one occasion when the narration switches from third person to first person, I have also placed the text in italics.

When an Arabic word is a technical term, I have tried to translate it each time by the same English word. When it is not, I have, at times, translated an Arabic word in various ways in English, both for the sake of variety and to capture different aspects of meaning of the Arabic term.

Since ellipses are more common in Arabic prose, as in this novel, than in English, I have suppressed them at times.

One strategy for dealing with a transliterated Arabic word in the text is to pair it with an English translation of it on the same page, but this book also has a glossary, containing brief explanations for specialist terms and most proper names, and endnotes for references. In this novel and other works Hassouna Mosbahi includes in his narratives both texts originally written in Arabic and texts he has translated into Arabic. Unless the English version is attributed to someone else in an endnote, the English translation is mine, usually (but not always) from Mosbahi's Arabic. The French originals of poems quoted in chapter 1 also appear in the endnotes.

I am happy to thank the two anonymous expert readers for Syracuse University Press for their perceptive and pertinent comments, almost all of which I have incorporated into my text. I also wish to thank my colleague Dr. Saloua Ben Zahra for her advice on Tunisian vocabulary and culture and to remember Dr. Béchir Chourou for the same assistance.

Solitaire

Prologue

When he woke at five that morning, he remembered a prayer he had repeated every morning as a teenager. It was a beloved prayer of the Sufis, whose sayings and maxims he once memorized. In his early years, he read their works zealously and followed the details of their amazing lives with all the yearning of a passionate disciple, hoping that he might become one of them. Then he would wear coarse wool, withdraw from human contact, live in a cave in the mountains, and spend his days and nights in devotions, while reciting the Qur'an and reading the life of the Prophet as well as the Sufis' maxims, poetry, and miraculous stories, which are filled with meanings, symbols, and riddles. This was the prayer:

> God, we praise You with our finest praise, invoking a blessing that, in its impact, will comply with and be commensurate with Your generosity. We praise you with words that we hope will meet Your satisfaction and merit Your forgiveness. We do not limit our praise for You but laud You with Your own words. We praise You, Master, as You have commanded and wished.

1

He knew why he stopped reciting this prayer. The period separating his adolescence and young manhood was marked by anxiety and agitation; questions intertwined and interlaced until he felt he could no longer direct his destiny or life. He sensed that he might continue wandering for a long time through a thorny desert with no direction or guide. This condition lasted for two full years, until he hit upon a plan he considered appropriate for his life, thought, and destiny. Then his agitation and anxiety decreased, and the questions tormenting him abated. He stopped reciting that prayer because he had become a man who made choices, not one controlled by divine decree. That prayer had restrained his imagination, suspended his powers, stifled his liberty, and turned him into a parrot that recited the same words all the time. His admiration for the Sufis did not end, though. Now he read their works not because they were the only ones worth his attention, but because they equaled other works of different ages, cultures, and civilizations in their merit and aesthetics, and in the values, thoughts, views, and illuminations they offered. Knowledge must be stripped of all barriers and chains. This had been his motto ever since. For him, everyone was equal. The only difference between a European, a Chinese, an Indian, an African, or an Arab was the quality of the work he created and the grandeur of the thoughts he fashioned and produced. Everything else was silly prattle and a type of knowledge that disintegrated into vapid clichés and was devoid of any human significance. He remembered he had recited that prayer while humbly closing his eyes to the morning light from the eastern plains that extend all the way to Kairouan, interrupted only by a mountain called Trazza and by Haffouz Hill. He never once prayed out loud because communion with God had to be secret and silent. God spoke to

2

the Messenger in the Cave of Hira. He did not speak to the Prophet while he mingled with groups of people in Mecca's markets and assemblies. Sufis and righteous saints of God practiced their devotions in secluded retreats, far from people. If someone approached, they would fuss and flee as if escaping from the devil, who sows discord and evil on earth. He did not think God loved people who boasted about their belief and recited private and ritual prayers within the sight and hearing of others, whose harsh voices spoiled the magnificence of silence and the dignity of humility. When sheikhs recited the Qur'an at funerals and religious gatherings, however, he experienced an amazing humility. The entire village became still and its worshipers and domestic animals calm—as did its earth, hills, valleys, and olive and almond trees. All of creation around him became bright symbols that glittered like the stars in the extraordinary, expansive summer sky. His uncle Salih, who had studied at Ez-Zitouna Mosque, would tell people, "Belief flourishes in the heart, not via some external show."

Now the order of the day was men with unkempt beards and black prayer calluses on their foreheads. Their harsh and crude voices grew even uglier when amplified by loudspeakers, night or day. Ritual prayers were conducted in the streets and public squares because mosques could no longer hold the number of people who sought relief from life's inferno, outrages committed by rulers, disasters and calamities that followed in rapid succession, and prayers transmitted on the hour by radios, cassette players, and television stations—like advertisements. Books discussing the torment of the grave were best-sellers from Indonesia to Morocco. Everyone wanted them—young and old, rich and poor, fortunate and hapless, men and women, contented people and malcontents, rulers and citizens, torturers and their victims—because prayers offered relief when despair, frustration, tribulations, and massacres were daily events. For this reason, voices were raised in markets, stores, train stations, offices, universities, schools, mansions, and huts, while silent, secretive prayer seemed a vestige of a distant past. Indeed, anyone who prayed silently would find the genuineness of his belief and of his love for God, His Messenger, and His Messenger's family and companions suspected and doubted. For this reason, voices should be raised in prayer; if not, the effort was null and void. Let us all pray together loudly, very loudly, as we repeat:

God, make our best days the last ones and our best deeds the ultimate ones. Make the finest of our days the day we meet You. God, if Your wealth is in the heavens, send it down to us. If it is in the earth, extract it for us. If it is distant, bring it to us. If it is nearby, deliver it to us. If it is in short supply, multiply it for us. If it is plentiful, bless us with it. God, release our necks from the Fire and grant us pardon, forgiveness, and robust belief. God, grant us victory over the unbelievers and chase away the Jewish people. Destroy their homes and deprive them of offspring. Make Islam the religion of the entire earth. Amen, Lord of the material and spiritual worlds.

Let voices ring out—very, very loudly—with all these prayers, until God, who is in the heavens, hears them. When we used to pray to Him secretly in silence, He abandoned us. Then we suffered all the disasters, tribulations, and devastation that we did and became the most miserable people on the earth—after starting as the best of nations. We were defeated by Christians and Jews, who plundered our goods, appropriated our land, and destroyed our cities and villages. They raped our women before our eyes and visited every conceivable evil upon us. Therefore, we must pray and pray and pray in loud voices—very, very loud voices—until God answers us. He will because He is the Forgiving, Compassionate, Cherished, Beneficent, Omnipotent, Mighty, Grand, and our Omniscient Guide to the straight path.

His friend Hisham, however, did not grasp what had occurred during his long absence from Tunisia and paid dearly for his ignorance. He had visited Tunisia once a year, but the short periods he spent with family and friends had not allowed him to analyze what had happened, both out of sight and in plain view, over the course of the forty years he lived in Paris. He had traveled there to study philosophy when he was twenty. Following graduation, he worked as a lecturer in France's universities. During his youth he kept company with the surviving Surrealists after the death of their godfather, André Breton. He was captivated by existentialism and then by Marxism. The Spring Revolt of 1968 enthralled him, and he participated in it enthusiastically. He erected barriers and barricades, thinking—like most of the other rebels—that the second Paris Commune would not fail and that its enemies would not be able to suppress it the way they had the first. But the second Commune also failed. Then Hisham sought refuge in alcohol, frivolity, and hijinks. During those days he fell in love with an Irish hippie and traveled with her to Afghanistan, which at that time fascinated people fleeing the inferno of the great European cities to search for simple, primal enjoyments. At thirty-five, he married a French-woman, and they had a daughter and a son. When, after he retired, his wife died of cancer, he could no longer bear life in Paris. So, he returned to his homeland, hoping to spend the remainder of his life in his family's home in the old part of the city of Neapolis, which he insisted on calling by its antique name, instead of Nabeul. He wanted to live quietly near the sea with his favorite books, music, and vintage wines. A few weeks after Hisham's return, the two men met in the Albatross Restaurant, which overlooks the sea in Neapolis. From their first meeting, they became fond friends. They began to meet there almost daily to discuss poetry, philosophy, and music—but not politics, which both men hated. Hisham, who was always nattily attired, was a cultured person and especially fond of poetry. He had memorized poems of the authors dearest to his heart—poets like Baudelaire. "Oh, Baudelaire?" he would say and then speak extensively about him. "He's always been my companion. I read him as a teenager. I read him as a young man, then as an adult, and here I am reading him as an old man. I've always felt that he is my favorite poet. That's why I never tire of reading him. Never! His poems reflect life with all its vicissitudes and visages, beauty and ugliness, roughness and suavity, joys and sorrows. Oh, Baudelaire! I'm crazy about everything he wrote. My wife was too. The day before she died, I recited to her stanzas from poems she loved. When I finished, she embraced me, weeping. Then she kissed me; that was her last kiss. Don't you love Baudelaire? Of course you do." Then he partially closed his eyes, his face shining with the gleam of his love for poetry and life, and recited from "L'Invitation au voyage":

My daughter, my sister,
Think of the sweetness
Of going there to live together!
Loving each other at our leisure,

Loving and dying
In a country that resembles you;
The dewy suns
Of those cloudy skies
Possess, for my spirit, the mysterious charms
Of your treacherous eyes
Beaming through their tears.[1]

Hisham would pause and gaze at the sea, where waves, driven by autumn's winds, clashed. He looked at the sea like a boy gazing at his affectionate mother. Then he recited a passage from "L'Homme et la mer," also by Baudelaire:

Free man, you will always cherish the sea!
The sea is your mirror; you contemplate your soul
In the eternal clash of its waves,
And your spirit is a whirlpool no less bitter.[2]

Hisham stopped again as sorrow clouded his features. He was now plunged into another world, one where only the author of *The Flowers of Evil* could disclose its magic and sway. Then, in a voice overflowing with presentiments about time, which devours lives, seizes our best friends and true loves, snuffs out the candles of joy and happiness, casts its dark shadows across the earth, and betrays people without them noticing, Hisham recited the final stanza of "L'Ennemi":

Oh pain! Oh pain! Time devours life,
And the obscure enemy, which gnaws at our heart,
Grows larger and stronger from our blood![3]

Yunus realized then that Hisham was joyously expatiating and that no one should interrupt him. For this reason, he allowed him to continue his monologue, which was spoken with the passion of someone who believes in ideas he knows do not appeal to other people—ideas that might in fact provoke and anger them. He merely nodded his approval of everything

Hisham said, since he would never disturb the delight of a person happily swimming alone in his own sea.

"Listen, my friend, you know very well that I speak sincerely. I love expressing myself out loud, fearlessly. This is what I learned in the West. That's why I allow myself to say that Arabic poetry doesn't appeal to me much. Adonis anthologized the most splendid work of the Arab poets, pre-Islamic or Islamic. That's why I return to them again and again. I have rarely read a poetry collection by an Arab poet from beginning to end the way I do those of poets from China, Japan, and ancient Greece, of contemporary Western poets, or of earlier Western poets like Virgil, Dante, and Ronsard. I may sound overly harsh when I tell you that I agree with Saʻid Aql, who once said that in all of Arabic poetry there are only about two hundred verses where we find true poetry, poeticism, and language that is fascinating and elegant. Saʻid Aql also said that he had not found a single perfect poem in Arabic poetry. Instead, he found many words and long poems, but most lines were merely verbal or metrical padding. A poem might harbor nothing more than poetic glimmers that sparkled in a verse or two, while the rest was stuffing that served no purpose. I realize that most people reject views like these in whole and in part because Arabs claim that, since antiquity, they have been the people of poetry. The problem is that the Muʻallaqāt, which they never stop bragging about, are as boring, arid, and monotonous as a trip through the desert. Arabs love to exaggerate and do not evaluate things on their merits. The poet they boast about, considering him the finest poet of all time—I'm referring to al-Mutanabbi—was slain by hyperbole, which he favored and used as ballast in his poems. He claimed that he was the sword, the spear, the paper, and the pen, that when confronted by his determination, blades break, that mountains testify he is a mountain and seas bear witness he is a sea. Uff! Aren't these silly, trite exaggerations that bear no relationship to poetry, directly or indirectly? Is it possible for a man to be a sword and a spear, a mountain or a sea? Exaggerations led to al-Mutanabbi's death because he told people who warned him not to travel through the desert where his enemies were lying in wait for him that he 'did not like people to say he needed any protection other than his sword.' He yelled at a man cautioning him, 'Is it slaves of the stick you fear might harm me?' In the end, he was killed in the worst possible way, along with his brother and companions. His thievish enemies, whom he had called 'hyena-and-jerboa eaters' divvied out his possessions, choice horses, mounts, 'select animals pleasing to see and read about,' his precious treasures, his women, and manuscripts."

Hisham continued rather acidly: "No, no, no! I hate panegyrics and poems that glorify majesty and pride—verse that issues from an inflated ego. What enchants me is poetry that arrives like the secret whisper of a dawn or evening breeze, that excites me like a lover's caress in a bed of love, that leaves me as ecstatic as little birds chirping in spring gardens, that awakens my sleeping senses to life like the strains of a guitar on the banks of the Guadalquivir, that intoxicates me like aged Italian wine, that perfumes my body like rose water, and that draws me from a state of stillness and reflection into one of ecstasy and beautiful insanity. Oh, my friend! Here's Ōtomo no Yakamochi's ancient Japanese ode, a brilliant poem I have never tired of repeating since my wife died:

> Before my house, flowers were blooming.
> I gazed at them,
> But my heart remained filled with grief.
> If my dear wife were still here,
> We would have gone together, like two ducks swimming in the water,
> To pick flowers for her.
> But man's body soon withers and vanishes
> Like dew or ice.
> My wife vanished like the setting sun.
> While I climb the rugged mountain trail
> I remember her, and then my heart misses a beat in agony.
> I cannot speak.
> No, I cannot describe my affliction.
> Nothing remains of her . . . nothing.
> What do you suppose I will do now?"

Hisham remained silent for a time; then, after he had drained the last of the Magon red wine in his glass, he said, "Ponder well, my friend, this simplicity, which is free of any affectation or exaggeration; then you will grasp the essence of poetry in the true, profound meaning."

Half a year after his return, Hisham began an insanely quick descent into the abyss. The first sign patrons of the Albatross Restaurant noticed was that he no longer took an interest in his appearance. He would let his beard grow for days and wore the same gloomy clothes for a week or more. He forgot to polish his shoes, although he had typically done that every day. His hair, which had been gray when he arrived, turned completely white, and bald patches began to appear on his scalp, showing that a lot of hair was falling out. His eyes sank into their sockets, and his cheeks became hollow. His teeth turned yellow, his voice sounded harsh, and his glances grew hostile. His expression revealed the alarm a man feels when constantly pursued. He abandoned the morning promenades he had enthusiastically taken on the beach. When he came to the restaurant, he collapsed into a chair, worn out, exhausted, anxious, and tense. Then he would start smoking and drinking avidly. Afterward, he would sink into the delirium of a tortured, frustrated soul. "Uff . . . returning seems to have been a fatal mistake. Oh! Why did I come back? Paris, which I used to love, no longer seemed tolerable, especially after my wife's death. Moreover, I had started to grow old and would die soon. I had begun to fear I would die alone, forgotten in an apartment on the seventh floor. From its balcony, I could see the Père Lachaise Cemetery, where my wife has her final resting place. I was afraid to go out on the streets of a city where I had lived the happiest years of my youth. Now that I'm a feeble old man, I walk and breathe with difficulty. I might faint and fall on the pavement or in a Metro station. Then strangers would carry me unconscious to the hospital. No, no, no . . . I could not stay there. Longing for my childhood home also swept over me forcefully. So I returned, hoping to live out my days near the sea—to enjoy repose, calm, sunshine, the enchanting Mediterranean light, music, and the books I enjoy . . . the way I once did, engrossed in contemplation and dreams, when I was a child seated beneath the lemon tree in our courtyard. But I seem to have made a mistake, and now I don't know how to rectify my error. Should I return to Paris? What would I do there—wait to die, while suffering the ailments of old age and its pains and sorrows? No, no, no . . . this is impossible. Impossible! My daughter lives in New York and sends me a text message now and then. She tells me tersely about herself and her life. Even her words are condensed to their essential letters. She says she is happy with her friend, the American painter she met in Paris, and that she will marry him shortly... perhaps next summer. The wedding will be there, of course. I may not attend for any number of reasons. This is how the times are. A person does what he wants and chooses. All a man can do is be patient and keep silent. My son, the doctor, is busier with his work than he should be. He's happy about his new baby, whom his wife named Sébastien; she says it's a name she has liked since childhood. He did not object. Why would he? 'She's free to choose whatever she wants.' That's what he'd say. I invited my son to visit me here, but he told me he won't be able to do that until the child is older. The boy is now eight months old, and that means I won't be able to see him for at least three more years. This is how things proceed in the normal course of events now. I haven't asked my daughter to visit me, because I'm sure she won't. She's crazy about America; her heart and spirit are there. I'm anxious and don't know what disaster this anxiety condemns me to. I say 'disaster' because I feel that things will end extremely badly. Uff! My friend? I didn't think history could reverse direction. But here I am, confronting this reality—a few months after my return. Before I emigrated, people used to look forward to the future and worked to change their lives, which were dominated by lethargy, ignorance, and puritanism. Now they want to return to the tyranny of the past, which is dead and buried. Even so, they are attempting to revive it by various means and methods: bushy beards that reach down the chest, black calluses on the forehead, baggy pants, Afghan gallabiyas, head scarves, burka veils, haggard, scowling, gloomy, rancorous visages, and jaundiced fatwas that forbid mirth, pleasure, love, music, shaking hands with women or wearing white socks, and that advocate sacred jihad against anyone who rejects these edicts and does not respect them. Prayers hardly ever stop— as if people were condemned to do nothing but pray. The Qur'an is recited on the hour and on all occasions—at weddings and funerals, everywhere, including public buses, shared cabs, and taxis. And the loudspeakers ... oh, the loudspeakers! They torment me night and day. They rouse me from my delightful, dawn slumbers and from my siesta. They ruin the moments of contemplation I enjoy in the evening. They keep me from reading and listening to music. They broadcast the call to prayer only five times a day, but I seem to hear it incessantly, whether I'm awake or asleep. I hear it when I'm walking on the shore and while I sit in the restaurant. Yes, I hear it all the time, summoning us to prayer as if calling us to a war that is about to erupt. When I complained about my situation to the imam of the mosque opposite my house, he grew furious and shouted, 'If you don't like the way things are, move—or return to the infidel land where you once lived!' I wanted to explain that I'm not opposed to prayer, but to the loud-speakers. He turned and walked off, muttering, 'To think I've lived long enough to hear sons of Muslims demand we curtail Islam's duties!' The next day, one of the congregants wrote on the door of my house 'May God curse you, heretic!' Now most of residents of the neighborhood have be-come my inveterate enemies, after they previously had felt respect, love, and veneration for me. They avoid looking at me or conversing with me. When I leave my house to walk in the streets, I feel all their eyes are skew-ering me like sharp, poisoned knives. It seems to me that all of them—adults and children, men and women—have me under surveillance and scrutinize my every step and gesture from behind their closed doors, shuttered windows, and high walls. Theirs are angry, rancorous eyes—the eyes of people who wish the ugliest and most hideous end for me. But why and how did all this happen during my long absence? This question per-plexes me a lot; I may never discover an answer for it. Prayers used to be performed calmly, silently, without any posturing or pretense, and people went to the Friday prayer as if attending a splendid party. The Qur'an was recited at specific times and places as people demonstrated an amazing humility and would perhaps weep because they were so touched by hear-ing eloquent verses that moved their hearts, settled their agitated spirits, and calmed their anxious minds. But all this has evaporated into thin air, vanished, and disappeared as if it had never existed. Prayers in this age are carnivals of pandemonium and clamor. People hasten to Friday prayer, crowding together as if heading to a ferocious battle. The Qur'an stipu-lates that people should listen to it at all times and places, but they're un-able to fathom its implications, glories, and meanings—now that it is drowned out by the noise pollution of daily life, with all its screaming and tumult." He sighed deeply. "My God, what has happened during my long absence? Now I don't know what to do with myself—with my tormented soul, which is suspended between here and there, a soul that is dangling in a terrifying void. One night, a neighbor, whose father was my father's friend, came to me, entering my home on tiptoe, glancing right and left for fear of being seen. I made coffee for him, and we sat in the living room. He was trembling he was so agitated. He remained silent, not looking at me. Then he told me in a low voice: 'My dear sir, I respect you and think very highly of you, and you know the esteem my late father cherished for your late father, but I suspect you have committed a grave error.'

"'What is it?'

"'You talked to the imam about matters that must not be discussed.'

"'But why can't they be discussed?'

"'Because that's how it is, sir.'

"'How's that?'

"'There are matters that must not be discussed.'

"I burst out laughing and continued guffawing, pounding my foot on the floor, while the poor man looked at me, stunned and horrified, as if he had suddenly found himself confronted by someone he now realized would offer him no opportunity to save his skin. I laughed longer than I had at any time since returning to Tunisia. When my bout of laughter abated, I noticed that the man had vanished into thin air. Perhaps he was already telling people I was crazy. So be it. I really am crazy. Why wouldn't I be crazy, when conditions in the Muslim world have turned it upside down and become the opposite of what they were in ancient times? When I was in my twenties, I traveled to Kabul in the company of a freckle-faced, redheaded Irishwoman named Virginia. We experienced the happiest times of my youth there, and perhaps of her youth as well. Oh . . . Kabul? How enchanting it was at that time! Everything was possible there. People were full of appreciation for life and its pleasures; they seemed to realize that difficult, dark times were coming. Afghan women wearing miniskirts chatted in coffeehouses about existentialism and Marxism and recited the poems of Nâzim Hikmet, Vladimir Mayakovsky, Pablo Neruda, Federico García Lorca, and Charles Baudelaire. People fleeing from the cold cities of the north and from depressing, gray ideologies found in Afghanistan simple, primitive pleasures that helped them forget the desolate inferno of consumer societies. They were seduced by this and hoped to remain there forever. Snow fell in large quantities on Kabul toward Christmas, and the mountains were white. Candles and lamps gleamed in coffeehouses and restaurants, and symphonies blended with the mournful songs of the Asian steppes. Freckle-faced, redheaded Virginia undulated beneath me, moist from the sweat of our lovemaking, while I was between her thighs, rising and sinking into her warm depths, wishing life would stand still and consist only of these moments of pleasure. Oh . . . Kabul? I didn't think conditions would change so quickly and that this fascinating country would degenerate into caverns and caves in which murderers hid to plot terrorist operations targeting innocent people in all parts of the world, or that devastation, death, and fear would spread through it. One day I read in a foreign newspaper that setting themselves on fire had become the preferred method for Afghan women to liberate themselves from their hellish life with the bearded ones. The article's author observed that even poor families had kerosene for cooking and matches, and that these simple commodities made suicide easy for girls rejecting a forced marriage and for wives suffering from harsh treatment. Women who attempted to flee were raped, stabbed to death, or shot. Women were even stoned to death in the presence of men who thought this outrage defended their soiled honor. The article's author recounted the story of a woman called Farzana, who, when young, had fallen in love with music and poetry and dreamt of becoming a teacher. When she turned twelve, her family forced her to marry. From day one, her husband beat and humiliated her, especially in front of her mother-in-law. That mistreatment lasted four years. Then, one day, Farzana calmly poured kerosene over her body and lit a match. She was consumed by flames as her two-year-old daughter watched."

Now as night settled quietly over Neapolis, Hisham's face seemed a dark slate that reflected wrinkles and scars as well the pains packed inside him. The twinkle of his eyes, which had sunk into his face, was extinguished. His lips were so dry they could have been a corpse's. His seafood omelet was cold, and he asked the waiter to reheat it. He probably had not touched it. The waiter walked away, leaving the cold *ojja* on the table as he had done repeatedly. Hisham drained his glass of Magon and continued his rant: "My dear friend Yunus—or 'Solitaire,' as you like to call yourself in the tracts you write and no one else sees—when I read Farzana's story, I thought I witnessed, burning before me, the bodies of the beautiful Afghan women I had seen in my youth in Kabul, which successive warlords over more than thirty years turned into one of the most desperate and desolate cities in the entire world. Uff! Is Islam this cruel and gloomy? I don't know what to do with myself these days. Occasionally my pain is so intense that I consider throwing myself into the sea one stormy night to let waves carry my body to some distant shore. I will be so mutilated no one will recognize me. At other times I regain my optimism and love for life. I laugh, amuse myself, and say, 'Live your life, Hisham, just as you always have. Ignore the hideous creatures around you.' Enthusiasm may get the better of me, and I may rise to the challenge. I see myself entering the mosque during the Friday prayer and interrupting the elderly imam's sermon to share with the worshipers what Our Master, Jalal al-Din Rumi said: 'Muslims, what's the solution when I myself do not know myself, for I am not Christian, Jewish, Zoroastrian, Muslim, Eastern, Western, land-lubber, or seafarer. I am not derived from one of the elements of the earth and nature, nor from the spheres and the heavens. I am not from the soil, water, air, fire, throne, floor, existence, place, India, China, the Bulgarians, or the Saxons, not from the people of the world, the people of the after-world, the people of paradise, the people of the inferno, the offspring of Adam or the descendants of Eve. I am not one of the people of heaven or of the Garden of the Elect. My place is where there is no place. My proof is where there is no proof. I am not the body and not the spirit, because I am the spirit of the spirit.'"

The month of Ramadan arrived, and the Albatross Restaurant closed for the duration. Hisham disappeared. Yunus, for his part, continued his walks along the seashore in the evening when the commotion had died down and the city emptied so completely it seemed to have been deserted for ages. He only returned home after the *iftar* meal concluded and people began to spill outdoors in great numbers, heading to the coffeehouses, markets, and streets, where they remained until just before dawn, when it was time for their *sahur* meal. As he usually did during this month, he devoted the night to reading and occasionally to writing. He set aside the greatest part of the day for sleep, only going to the market when he had to. Once the month of Ramadan ended, he hurried to the Albatross Restaurant, keen to see and converse with his friend Hisham. But Hisham didn't come—not that day, nor any subsequent one. Two weeks passed without any sign or news of him. Yunus felt very anxious and considered visiting him at his home because he might be ill, or perhaps his circumstances had deteriorated until he had decided to stay home and not leave by night or day. But as Yunus was preparing to quit the restaurant one evening, the waiter, a man in his forties and an enthusiastic soccer fan who could hardly stop talking about teams and national and international matches, approached and asked, "Do you know what happened to Dr. Hisham?"

He trembled with alarm and asked, "What's happened to him?"

His face clouded by regret, the waiter replied, "He's in prison."

"Why is he in prison?"

"Halfway through Ramadan, he had a severe nervous breakdown. Then he snuck into the mosque, intending to climb up the minaret to destroy the loudspeaker, but the worshipers grabbed him and beat him. Then they marched him to the police station. Now they say he spat at the imam, cursed what we venerate, and made ugly remarks about Islam."

The next day, Yunus went to visit Hisham in prison. The figure who stared at him from behind the bars was only the ghost of Hisham. In fact, he seemed an entirely different creature. He was an old man now, a broken man. His head had sunk between his shoulders, as if he feared a blow might end his life in the wink of an eye. He was very frail and thin. His bones protruded, and his cheeks were hollow. His face was totally devoid of any sign of the good health he had enjoyed when he arrived from Paris. He looked like one of the homeless people police officers round up at the end of the night and hold in jail until daybreak, when their identities can be sorted out.

"What have you done to yourself, Hisham?"

He did not reply.

Yunus asked the same question repeatedly, but Hisham's silence was glacial. He seemed to have bade farewell to life and to have lost all interest in the world of the living. Yunus finally departed, his eyes awash with tears.

Ten days later, Hisham appeared in court without an attorney. He wore a black suit, a black shirt, and black shoes. The judge read off the charges against him. When he finished, Hisham asked for a cup of coffee, a sugar cube, and a small spoon.

Displeased by his request, the judge asked, "Why?"

"So I can defend myself. I am appearing before you without an attorney."

His request was granted.

Hisham placed the cube of sugar in the cup of coffee and began to stir the coffee with the little spoon before the eyes of the startled judge while the courtroom fell silent. Soon the judge shouted at him, protesting angrily, "Enough! Enough!"

Hisham obeyed the judge's order and then smiled as if he had achieved a minor victory at the end of a battle that he had known from the start he would lose. He said, "Your Honor the Judge, you were upset by the ringing of a little spoon in a coffee cup, but ask me to remain calm when every night for two straight hours I hear the Ramadan prayer blasting from the loudspeaker of the mosque opposite my house . . ."

The judge sentenced Hisham to three months in prison. Two weeks later he was found dead in his solitary confinement cell. Next to his cold corpse was a piece of paper on which he had written in bold, black letters:

He returns after a life of absence to that spot of the earth where he was born, where he has always been, man and boy, a silent witness and there, his journey of life ended, he plants his mulberry tree in the earth. Then dies.[4]

James Joyce

2

That autumn morning, the heavy rain afforded his body, which was still a lump in bed, some of the delight he had felt when he was a boy in his village, where the residents feared drought as much as death. How splendid rain is when the fragrance of orange and lemon blossoms wafts through the air and the sea grows even more captivating and beautiful! This is when Neapolis again becomes the property of those who truly love it. The summer bustle recedes along with its dust, chaos, turmoil, and crowding. His back pain tormented him, however, and would perhaps become even more excruciating when winter arrived, the temperature fell, and the humidity rose. Then his resolve would collapse, and melancholy would overcome him. His ability to think or write would evaporate, and his solitude would become too harsh to bear. He was old now, and this chilly, dark, bleak time was chock full of anxieties, fears, apprehensions, and despair. Hadn't Montaigne said:

> Old age weakens us and makes us feebler day by day, hour by hour, and continues to affect us until death comes. It takes from us a quarter or a half of the man we were.[5]

Montaigne had died at fifty-nine, and Yunus was turning sixty today. He seemed destined to live many more years and confront the horrors of old age. Its complaints and maladies had long terrified him when he read or heard about them from people whining that they were afflicted by them. During his childhood and adolescence, old age had seemed the finest and most exemplary stage of life when a man's features glow with dignity, wisdom, and composure, and he adorns himself with patience and the forbearance to confront time's tempest and caprices.

People in his village respected old men, admired them, appealed to them in moments of turmoil, and solicited their advice to direct their affairs, resolve their problems, and overcome obstacles confronting them. No one dared raise his voice with them or oppose their opinions, since those were generally correct and beneficial. He had been fascinated by Sufis and was attracted to them at that early period of his life. They had all been venerable old men. Age enhanced their astuteness, genius, charm, radiance, rectitude of opinion, depth of insight, and love of goodness and virtue. Many stories were told about them and their feats. He had listened to these admiringly and been so moved that he occasionally contemplated becoming a Sufi sheikh to whom people hastened during hard times, seeking advice on worldly and religious matters. He would respond to their requests and provide counsel and advice to reassure them, calm their agitation, and relieve them of their fears and misgivings.

Stories about the righteous Sufi Ahmad ibn Sa'id enchanted and influenced him the most. This "Friend of God" had lived in his great-grandfather's time and died at the age of nearly a hundred. He remained in full command of his wits to his death and retained his powerful memory. He was thin and usually silent. He spoke only to utter some maxim or excellent exhortation. The glow of his countenance was constant, even in dire circumstances and severe crises. Not once had he embroiled himself in people's fights or disagreements. He preferred to serve as a referee, separating an assailant from his victim and awarding victory to those who stand defenseless against violence and tyranny. He would heal the ill, commiserate with widows and orphans, aid the poor and needy, and host wayfarers whom he sheltered in his house when they required refuge from the heat or the cold. Although he wasn't rich, God cared for him, and his household was prosperous and blessed, even during hard times, famines, and natural disasters. It was said that he never left his village. From time to time, however, especially during the holy months, he would leave his house and family for a retreat in a cave in a hill they called Snake Mountain because so many venomous serpents lived there. He would spend a week or longer there, sunk in his recitations of the Qur'an and in other devotions and vigils. Moreover, villagers who traveled frequently, getting about despite the dangers and travails of that remote era, swore they had observed him chanting the Qur'an in the courtyard of the great mosque in Kairouan. They had also seen him reciting the Qur'an at Ez-Zitouna Mosque in Tunis. Others claimed to have attended prayers when he served as imam in a mosque in Sousse. Pilgrims in Mecca reported that he circumambulated the Ka'ba with them and sacrificed a lamb with them on Mount Arafat. He himself did not comment on the stories told about him. People, however, heard him say once, "Only God knows what the Almighty's righteous friends do in the spirit world." Most of his discourse consisted of allegories and allusions; only a few individuals could decipher his riddles. When he received people, he liked to repeat Imam Sahnun's remark: "A small amount of knowledge in a righteous man resembles a sweet-water spring in good earth where the owner plants a crop and profits from it. Much knowledge in an unjust man resembles a trickling spring on land with a saline crust where nothing will grow, even if the water floods it night and day."

This righteous saint performed many feats and prodigies. His great-grandfather, for example, wanted to travel to el-Djerid to buy dates, but Sidi Ahmad ibn Sa'id came and told him, "I see massive bloodshed in a desolate wadi with more men falling victim than surviving the massacre." His great-grandfather realized that the righteous saint was warning him against the trip and abandoned the idea. His comrades who ignored this warning were attacked by brigands one night in a barren wadi. All their money, merchandise, camels, mules, and supplies were plundered, and five men were slain. The only two survivors returned to the village in tattered rags caked with dust from their disastrous trip.

During that year, which was referred to as "the year of strife," the Bey, at the behest of his grand vizier, unleashed his anger on Kairouan for sheltering one of the most virulent opponents of his rule. He demolished the city wall, obliterated its landmarks, slaughtered its most prominent citizens in broad daylight, and led others away to prisons and places of exile. Hunger and fear spread through both rural and village communities. The Bey wasn't satisfied with these measures and imposed punitive taxes on the citizens, sending his cruel troops to collect them. These soldiers conducted their filthy mission in the most hideous and repugnant fashion. They beat men and humiliated them in front of their wives and children.

They raped girls and compelled families to sell their possessions and most precious belongings, leaving them so indigent they had "no back to ride and no teat to milk," as Sidi Ahmad ibn Saʻid put it. He hid in his cave for two entire weeks. When he reappeared, they rushed to request his assistance, asking him to relieve their suffering and distress as best he could. He told them, "Never fear. Relief is nigh. The person who treated you in this way will die like a stray dog." Only a few months later, a report came from the capital that the Bey's grand vizier, who had engineered the ordeals that had afflicted Kairouan and its inhabitants, had been cut to shreds by swords as he entered his palace and that his corpse had been tossed in the street, where people attacked it the next day. They cut off the privates of the vizier who had ruled the land with his personal edicts without listening to anyone. Other people hacked flesh from his body to grill. The hands of angry, vengeful people took liberties with his corpse, which they dragged around like a dead ox, mutilating it. Later, when someone sought to wash the corpse, he found nothing left to wash and had to content himself with pouring water over bits of blood-smeared flesh.

In a year when drought and hunger were severe and anarchy was widespread in the country, the Bey's soldiers became even more vicious and cruel and started treating people like animals. Then Sidi Ahmad ibn Saʻid repeated to everyone who visited him, "The Bedouin will light a fire that will consume them." He repeated this consistently until reports circulated that the Awlad Majer Bedouins had rebelled against the Bey and were led by one of their outstanding men, someone named Ali Ben Gh'dhahim. Then anarchy knew no bounds in the cities, villages, and deserts, and disturbances spread through the entire country. People began to call openly for the downfall of the Bey and the trial of his corrupt viziers. Thieves and brigands exploited this troubled situation to attack the homes of prominent citizens, plundering and slaying without restraint. People from Yunus's village decided to join the rebels but changed their minds once they remembered the words of Sidi Ahmad ibn Saʻid, who remained silent and retreated to his cave in Snake Mountain to avoid the questions of anxious, terrified people. This bleak situation persisted until men arriving from the west passed through the village on their way to Kairouan. They told people that the Bey had apprehended the rebellious Bedouins, slaughtering and massacring them until his palace's courtyard was red with their blood. Their leader, Ali Ben Gh'dhahim, had been arrested and taken in handcuffs and leg chains to prison, where he awaited execution.

In the year of the famine, people were so hungry that they ate carrion, dirt, and dry plants. Dozens of people died daily until there was no place left to bury them. In the capital, too, a hundred poor people perished every day from extreme hunger and cold until there were no longer enough biers to carry them. For his part, the Bey was distracted by his personal pleasures—as if the calamities afflicting his people did not concern him in any way and the people dying each day might just as well have been his enemies, not his subjects. When people mentioned this to Sidi Ahmad Ben Sa'id, he sighed deeply and said, "This corrupt Bey will soon hand over the keys to the country to the infidel Franks." Two years before he died, the French arrived with their armies and canons. The Bey welcomed them in his palace and humbly signed the treaty of capitulation.

Gharsallah and the strange and wondrous stories told about this saint had also fascinated Yunus and continued to entrance him to the present day. It was said that Gharsallah's mother, Khadija, bore him when she was past forty. She was extremely perturbed by this pregnancy because some of her sons and daughters had already married and provided her with grandchildren. So, she decided to end the pregnancy to avoid a scandal. She gathered some herbs for this purpose, stewed them, and placed them in a bowl. When she was ready to consume this medicine, Hanuna Bint Abd Allah walked in on her. Hanuna was an elderly woman known for her wisdom and clear thinking, and her advice was respected by the villagers for this reason. When that old woman realized what Khadija intended to do, she gasped in astonishment, struck her thighs with her hands, and shouted at Khadija, "God has planted this seedling in your belly; yet you wish to tear it out, without knowing who it will be? It might be a prophet or a righteous saint, a wali!" So, she tossed out the herbs. Nine months later a boy came into the world, and they named him Gharsallah—in other words, God's seedling.

From the outset, this child's behavior proved amazing. He shunned play with his age mates and didn't associate or converse with them.

Instead, he spent many hours a day out of sight and only returned home at dark. His expression resembled that of a perturbed or anxious adult—someone preoccupied by a matter he did not wish to share with anyone, not even with close friends. He was satisfied with only a small amount of food. When nature was petulant, thunderclaps resounded, storms became violent, and their roar rumbled through the valleys and ravines, he would go to the open countryside, looking radiant, zealous, and defiant. This behavior left his family amazed and astonished.

At the age of six, Gharsallah began to learn the Qur'an. In only a few months he had memorized a large portion of it. Then he began to chant chapters from it in a mellifluous voice unlike any people in the village had ever heard. He also memorized al-Busiri's "al-Burda," and when he recited this poem people were so deeply moved, they wept. When he was ten, he began to visit the forest north of the village. There he would sit beneath a large tree with interlacing boughs. He would stay there for many hours, chanting from the Qur'an, reciting "al-Burda," and reading al-Jazuli's *Dala'il al-Khayrat*, which his uncle brought him from Kairouan. He later told his companions that, when he was fifteen, he came one cold winter evening to this tree, where he found a naked man who had inflamed eyes and sores and blue bruises on his back. He was praying and reciting passages from the Qur'an. Once he finished these devotions, he kissed Gharsallah on the forehead and told him, "You are my caliph." Then he died. That night, while sleeping, Gharsallah heard a voice call him: "Wake from your long slumbers and travel the earth. God, His prophets, and righteous saints will be with you always and forever." He answered this call and left the village in the dark of night, walking north, traversing mountains, valleys, and rugged trails. He avoided populated areas, which he only approached when he felt extremely hungry and thirsty.

He kept traveling until he reached the capital, drenched by the cold, winter rains. His feet led him to a vast square, where he found a man with his legs shackled. Furious and angry, this man was puffing to the right and left. A wrought-iron fence surrounded him, and he would occasionally stare through it at dawdlers who paused to look at him, feeling either astonished, compassionate, scornful, or alarmed. Two huge, ferocious dogs guarded this strange man, and a brown, middle-aged woman cared for him. Gharsallah did not know how he got inside the metal fence but found himself sitting beside the man, who suddenly calmed down, stopped huffing and puffing, and became as docile as a child. He then placed his shaved head on Gharsallah's knee and fell sound asleep. When the woman, who had left on some errand, returned, she was astonished and started to ask Gharsallah what he was doing there and how he had climbed over the metal fence and approached the man, despite the two dogs, but he did not reply. Then she asked who he was, where he came from, and where he was heading. He remained silent, as the man's head rested on his knee. The strange man was so still he might have been dead. Gharsallah said the woman stopped questioning him and seemed satisfied, as if she had accepted his presence there. Then he asked her to bring him a pitcher, tea, and some sugar. She obeyed his request. He prepared delicious tea that won her admiration and approval. When the strange man woke from his long sleep, he smiled and said with great delight and happiness, "Praise God! Finally, my dutiful son, whom I have long awaited, has arrived." Gharsallah realized the man was referring to him. He did not remember how long he had stayed with that man or how they passed their time together. He simply said he left the capital and headed on foot to Algeria, as the great powers began to plunge into a new world war. When tired, he sheltered in a Sufi *zawiya*. Once, in a *zawiya*, he found a deformed sheikh who claimed to be dignified and wise. Visitors put dirhams in his fez while he mumbled invocations and prayers, pretending he wished them only goodness and blessings. That charade upset Gharsallah, and he left this Sufi retreat, angry at this cunning swindler who lied to people and took their money in the name of religion. He continued his trip until he reached the Algerian-Libyan border. He later told his disciples: "Barefoot and naked except for a wool burnous, I walked forward, oblivious to nature's cruelty, serpents, vipers, and hungry wolves in the mountains and forests, brigands, hunger and thirst, and the English, Italians, and Germans, who were fighting in the desert, I kept walking. I observed my ego at every hour to check its forbearance and endurance vis-à-vis life's experiences in their cruelest and most bitter forms. As I walked, I learned about nature, about its manifestations, the true meaning of the distinction between night and day, between the different hours of each of them, between silence and clamor, laughter and weeping, sorrow and joy, calm and terror, and repulsive and attractive odors. I walked and learned about evildoers and the wicked, good people and pure, innocent souls, people who would snatch a piece of bread from your mouth, and those who go without bread to donate it for the sake of God, liars and cheats, as well as people whose tongues utter only verities and the truth and whom evil does not approach fore or aft. I continued walking and derived a lesson from everything I heard, saw, and sensed. So, I realized, even before I experienced it on earth, that life would be meaningless without its contradictions and distinctions."

During his tour of Libya, Gharsallah visited the *zawiya* of a righteous Sufi saint who had performed many feats. In Tripoli, a group of Muslims was fighting a group of Christians over a stone. Muslims claimed it came from a mosque that had been demolished and complained that Christians had used it as a column in their church. The Christians alleged that this rock had been theirs since antiquity and that the Muslims' allegation against them was false. When they appealed to this righteous saint to mediate, he told them, "Let's go to the rock," and they obeyed his demand. The saint stopped there, and the adversaries stood around him. They heard him say, "Rock, if you are what the Muslims say you are, fall—with God's permission and by His power. If you are what the Christians assert, rest firmly where you are." The column then tilted and fell to the ground, and the church corner it supported collapsed. Then the saint told the Muslims, "Take your rock," and said to the Christians, "Rebuild your church."

This righteous wali of God used to say, "What keeps us separated from Him, despite His proximity, is that He has not sought us yet. When He seeks us, He finds us, even if we aren't seeking Him. When we want him, we find Him only if He wants us." He also used to say, "Remorse is a person's best protection against false steps." He also said, "Much escapes a person who doesn't know how to obey God." He would say, "Avoiding goods and evils increases the radiance of the heart's knowledge of God." He said, "The more plunder there is in the world, the greater will be the number of those who are tranquilly oblivious to it." He used to say, "Every phrase that isn't based on reflection is dangerous, even if it leads to victory." Gharsallah memorized these maxims and recited them whenever they were relevant.

While he was sleeping near the shrine of this righteous saint in the
Libyan Desert, Italian soldiers fell on Gharsallah unexpectedly. In the
wink of an eye, they blindfolded him, bound his hands and feet, and
threw him in a vehicle, which may have been a Jeep. Then they carried
him away—he knew not where or why—without his understanding even
one word the soldiers shouted angrily at him. Hours later—he did not
know how many—Gharsallah found himself in a dark cell with only a
tiny skylight in the ceiling. The blindfold had been removed from his eyes,
but his hands and feet were still shackled. He spent a long time in the
dark, hearing nothing but soldiers' footsteps on the asphalt. When the
cell door finally opened, two soldiers led him to a spacious office where
a short, plump Italian officer sat smoking. On the wall behind him hung
a huge portrait of Mussolini, whose small, gray eyes gleamed with evil.
On the officer's right was a middle-aged Libyan who was dressed in the
traditional grab of Tripoli. He had a flat nose and large ears, perhaps—as
Gharsallah suggested—because he had trained for a long time to eaves-
drop on people. The officer's words sounded like the meow of a hungry
cat—according to Gharsallah's description—and this Libyan translated
them. Gharsallah grasped that he was accused of spying on behalf of the
French and of crossing an international border by an illegal route, and that
these were capital offences punishable by the gallows or a firing squad. For
a time, Gharsallah said nothing, then he burst out laughing. He continued
to laugh, laugh, and laugh while the short, plump Italian officer stared at
him with a mixture of anger and alarm. The snub-nosed Libyan with large
ears ordered the prisoner to stop laughing and warned that he was only
making matters worse for himself. But Gharsallah did not stop laughing.
Finally, he was put back into the cell. Gharsallah didn't remember how
long this stalemate lasted. From his frowning face and furrowed brow,
listeners realized, however, that he had been subjected to savage torture
during his interrogation. He did report that they took him one night and
threw him in a Jeep. Hours later they dumped him at the Libyan-Tunisian
border and shot back toward Tripoli without uttering a word. Gharsallah
would say, "In my many dreams in the dark cell, I saw that the man—
whose picture hung behind the short, plump officer—had been hanged
and that his corpse was dangling from the branches of a leafless tree.

People were laughing sarcastically at him the way I had scoffed while the Italian officer was interrogating me. I think this happened to him exactly two years after my release."

This was Gharsallah's version of his fugue. His family members, for their part, were alarmed by his sudden disappearance, and his mother grieved terribly. She wept night and day and said the jinn had spirited him away. Sa'id, his oldest brother, started searching for him and went to Kairouan. Then he continued on to Sousse and the capital. He didn't know how his feet happened to carry him to that spacious square where the odd man lived—his feet chained, guarded by ferocious dogs, and attended by a "good-hearted" Black woman, as he later described her. He recounted that this odd man noticed him standing outside the metal fence and then called the woman and mumbled something to her. The woman nodded her head in agreement and asked Sa'id to approach. So, he did. When he stood there, the odd man grunted something Sa'id could not understand, although the woman did. She told Sa'id, "He says the man you seek is traveling from place to place like migratory birds. Don't wear yourself out looking for him. Return whence you came. You will receive news of him in due time." Sa'id obeyed and returned to the village to tell his family what he had seen and heard during his exhausting trip in search of Gharsallah. They all calmed down, their alarm vanished, and their anxiety was assuaged. For her part, his mother stopped weeping and only mentioned Gharsallah infrequently. When they received reports that the great war had ended, people rejoiced and welcomed this good news, especially once some of their sons returned safely from distant battlefields. The village was preparing to celebrate the marriage of one of Gharsallah's brothers when at noon on one bright fall day, he appeared. He looked well and prosperous, and his white burnous and matching white jubbah diffused the fragrant scent people associate with a visit to the mausoleum of Abu Zama'a al-Balawi—Prophet Muhammad's barber—in Kairouan. Gharsallah said nothing about his life there after his return from Libya, but people surmised he had been a merchant during the war years and had traveled between different cities, concealing his identity by using an alias. He may have wished to increase his knowledge of people and of life's secrets and obscurities. His family assumed he had abandoned his former eccentric behavior, manifest in his spiritual tourism through the land—his feet bare, his hair and beard long, and his body covered only by an old, brown burnous. He had returned a normal man who wished to live as they did, according to their customs. He did not seem to have much to tell them. He merely mentioned to his mother that he wanted to marry his beautiful cousin Zaynab. She was slender, and her voice was enchanting. All the young men in the village wanted to marry her. Gharsallah's mother, who loved him more than her other children, was delighted by this request and praised God for finally guiding him on the right path of all God's pious worshipers. Everyone in his family rejoiced. Zaynab was overjoyed by his proposal, and her face shone with delight. The marriage was celebrated expeditiously during a cold, rainy period. The party was very subdued and low key, including hardly scarcely any of the typical joyous trilling, dancing, and singing. Gharsallah responded to his critics: "'You have your religion, and I have mine.'* I want to live as I wish—not the way you want." So everyone was silenced. His mother, who had hoped that her youngest son's wedding would be magnificent and in keeping with the family's status, suppressed her rage.

The night the wedding was consummated, Gharsallah refused to follow the custom requiring the bridegroom to emerge from the bridal chamber holding the bride's underpants wet with the blood of her deflowering, which his groomsman would announce. Then women would go trilling to the bride to bless and congratulate her. At first people met Gharsallah's refusal with intense disapproval, but they finally acknowledged that these rituals, which had been handed down from grandfather to father, had lost their meaning.

Within a few weeks of the wedding, Zaynab started complaining and grumbling to her mother, sisters, and girlfriends that Gharsallah left her alone at night and departed to unknown places. He would not return until daybreak, looking as if he had stayed up all night praying. Then he slept all day long or sat motionless and silent at the doorway. Whole days and

---

* A paraphrase of Qur'an 109:1–3 Al-Kafirun (The Unbelievers).

nights might pass without his uttering a single word to her or even looking at her—as if she weren't present!

Gharsallah's marriage to Zaynab lasted only half a year. One scorching summer day, when people were busy with the harvest, they saw him dressed as before, ready for more spiritual tourism—in other words: barefoot, his beard and hair long, and his body covered by nothing but an old, brown burnous. As if pulling a jenny, he led Zaynab by a coarse rope, which encircled her neck. She was barefoot, too, and wore threadbare clothes. She was weeping with all the bitterness and fury of an abused and humiliated wife. On reaching her family's house, Gharsallah told her father—who was motionless with rage and so paralyzed by shock that he didn't know what to do or say—"Here's your daughter. Today a rope binds her neck, but in a matter of years she'll be free, like all Tunisia's women." Then he marched off north at a deliberate pace. Their eyes followed him until he disappeared in the rugged forests. After she married a second time and had two sons and three daughters, women did begin to wear tight pants and preferred short hair to long hair that fell to their waist. Then Zaynab revealed for the first time that Gharsallah had occasionally ordered her to wear a man's shirt and pants, laughed sarcastically, and scoffed, "That's how you'll dress when you're liberated." After independence, the state issued edicts that outlawed polygamy and granted women the right to work and to receive an education. Then people remembered what Gharsallah had said when he returned Zaynab to her family; they proclaimed he had been the first to predict these laws.

Many years passed without anyone hearing a word from Gharsallah, exactly like his first period of spiritual tourism. This time, though, his brother did not search for him, and his mother did not shed a single tear. Instead, when asked about him, she responded, with the calm of a wise woman, "He's a wandering dervish. We hope God will return him to us safe and sound." Travelers recounted many different tales about him. For example, they claimed to have seen him in Kairouan wandering among the tombs in a cemetery called al-Janah al-Akhdar, where the first jihadis rest, or worshiping covered with ashes near the mausoleum of Imam Sahnun, in that same city. Others asserted that they had seen him in Sousse, looking exactly as he did when he departed, after returning

Zaynab to her family. They said that he had refused to speak to them; they even claimed that he had fled from them. One man from the village swore Gharsallah was working as a peddler and said he had seen him on the slope of Mount Oueslat. There, despite the ice and extreme cold, he was as naked as the moment he was born and looked like a statue carved from stone. Another man claimed to have encountered him in Algeria, in Souk Ahras. He had wanted to speak with him, but Gharsallah had chided him and disappeared in the crowd.

Then came difficult, black years when people grew fearful. Residents of the village were afraid to move about, travel, or go to the regional markets. They were even afraid to leave their homes, especially at night, because reports were circulating that the nation's war of independence had begun and that revolutionaries were attacking the French in the southern desert, the central forests, and the northern mountains. Elsewhere they were attacking colonists and French soldiers in their barracks, plundering their weapons and supplies. Armed, bearded revolutionaries wearing army boots passed through the village more than once. They requested water, food, and eggs, and then disappeared. People faced those harsh, alarming conditions in every season, both day and night, but then came an almost unprecedented winter, when heavy snow fell on the northern mountains between Kairouan and El Kef. The storms intensified, and cold rains brought traffic to a halt. Supplies began to dwindle in many homes, thievery and brigandage proliferated, and people feared for their lives. They barricaded themselves in their houses, which they left only to satisfy essential needs.

One night, when nature's fury was at its most intense, they saw a terrifying conflagration to the north, where flames rose high into the sky. After hesitating briefly, men raced there, armed with sticks, cudgels, and daggers. When they arrived at the scene, they saw something totally unexpected. Gharsallah, dressed just as he had been when he returned Zaynab to her family, stood there beside a huge pile of wood. Because people were awed by him and by the brilliant light the fire cast on his face, they did not dare approach or address him. This dramatic scene lasted for many hours while people felt warmth surge through their bodies, which the long, cold winter had chilled, and their strange awe spread a sense of security and contentment through their souls, allowing them to forget their fears and the many dangers that had been threatening them and ruining their lives. As dawn neared, the flames began to die down, and that bonfire was reduced to ashes. Then Gharsallah tossed his burnous far away and, without turning to face them, said, "Return happily to your homes. The war's fire has been extinguished." Then he stretched out naked on the hot ashes.

Early the next morning, Gharsallah walked the streets of the village, but contrary to their expectations, villagers saw no burns on his body. People were amazed and recalled Abraham and the fire that had become safe and cool for him.

A few months later, red flags with a crescent and star at the center flew in all the villages, towns, and cities of the country, and news came that Tunisia had won its independence and that the French were crossing the sea back to their own country.

Strange stories about Gharsallah started to circulate, and people began repeating them with anxious amazement.

The First Story

After returning to his village, Gharsallah chose to live in the hills and plateaus, especially at night. He never slept in low-lying places like the wadis, even though the hills swarmed with venomous serpents. All the same, he was never bitten or exposed to any danger—unlike other people who roamed those hills, especially during the summer. In winter, when the cold was severe, he lit a fire that could be seen far away. Then he sat near it and continued his devotions until dawn, when he stretched out, naked, on the hot ashes. He frequently visited the cemetery near Snake Mountain and spent hours wandering among the graves. He liked to sit beneath the juniper tree at the center of this cemetery. People noticed how much healthier and greener the tree had become since Gharsallah began sheltering beneath it—as if it had become his spiritual beloved, replacing women, whom he longer approached. Referring to the dead, he would remark, "There are more of them than of us living creatures. Thus we must emulate them and never forget them." During scorching, hot summer days that forced people to remain in their houses or in the shade of the olive trees, he liked to walk barefoot on the hot sand, traversing long distances at the peak of the midday heat—in other words, "when the sun stands on its tail," as the villagers put it. But people never once heard him complain about the heat or the cold. A villager said of him, "Gharsallah goes out in the wind, rain, heat, or cold; none of these have any effect on his body. He may be patience incarnate."

The Second Story

Muhanniya, the wife of Gharsallah's eldest brother, said: "Our village consisted of scattered houses and didn't have a weekly market. So, we were obliged to shop elsewhere. The closest was at El Alaâ, seventeen kilometers away. The farthest was at Maktar, which was thirty kilometers from us. Going to those markets was extremely difficult in any season. Of course, the village didn't have a school or a clinic . . . or a post office. Three years after independence, I wove a fine, white burnous I said I would give to Gharsallah because I felt sorry for him when, in the cold of winter, he wore his old, brown burnous that he wouldn't part with, despite all the efforts of his brother and mother. He would say, 'This worn-out burnous has been God's most beautiful gift to me. It's the burnous of truth and reality.' When I finished making my burnous, I took it to him. He was seated beneath the juniper; this was in the middle of autumn as I remember it. I placed the burnous before him and left without saying a word. The following day, while I sat in front of my house enjoying the warmth of the autumn sun, I saw Gharsallah at the center of the uncultivated land in front of our house; it was nothing but rocks and thorns. With sheep-shearing clippers, he started to cut the new burnous into long ribbons. That upset me. I leapt up to stop him, but my husband prevented me, saying, 'Let him do whatever he wants with the burnous. He knows better than we do what will come to pass.'

"When Gharsallah had finished cutting the burnous into long ribbons, he began to measure the area with it, as if he were planning to build a house or something else there. He stayed busy at that until night fell.

When he departed, the vacant tract was covered with those ribbons, and it truly was an amazing sight. Many years later I grasped the secret meaning of what he had done: that thorny tract of land became the site of the weekly market, and the clinic, school, and post office were built there."

The Third Story

Amin, who was one of the few people Gharsallah received and conversed with, said, "Gharsallah would pick the time and location to meet me, and I never once objected. I obeyed him blindly. Cold, heat, family chores, or whatever—nothing could delay or prevent me from going to him when he summoned me. Believe me when I say I went to him hungry at times, and he would offer me a glass of hot tea. Then I wouldn't feel hungry anymore. I would feel I had eaten an entire bowl of couscous with lamb. That glass of tea would shelter me from cold or heat and give me strength to chase off any chagrin or fatigue. Gharsallah spoke more sweetly than anyone else I've known. He would convey you from East to West and soar with you into the sky before bringing you gently back to earth. Occasionally he would drop you down hard, and you would feel a jolt that shook you to your core. You would lose your balance and imagine you had never existed and never would—as if you were at the edge of a bottomless pit. But that would only last a moment. Soon tranquility and contentment would return. He would also say strange things I didn't understand, although I memorized some. I don't know if these maxims were original to him or quotes from someone else. For example, I memorized: 'A Sufi is like the earth on which every hateful thing is spread but from which only pleasant things sprout. The Sufi is like earth on which both the godly and the libertine tread. He is like the cloud that shades everything and rain that waters everything. I shun the world, pray all night, and go thirsty by day.' Gharsallah understood that people were suspicious of him and asked me once, 'You occasionally harbor doubts about something I do or say, don't you?' When I vehemently denied this, he smiled. Then his expression turned glum, and he said, 'Listen, Amin. I resemble Abd al-Qadir al-Jilani. I was created in the Throne before my physical creation.' I went to him once when my late father was feeling sick, but this was nothing we thought would end his life in the next two weeks. Gharsallah greeted me with a gloomy expression and looked upset—the way he did whenever he had a presentiment of an evil turn of events. He made delicious tea for me as usual, without uttering a word. The weather on that autumn evening was atrocious, and the south wind had blown in some red dust that made nature appear even more forlorn and depressing. He did not speak for an hour or more. Then I noticed that he was staring at the ground. He seemed to have totally forgotten me for a long time. Finally, I heard him say, 'Now he is above the ground. Soon he will be beneath it. After that he will be in the sky.' A violent tremor shook my body, and I asked, 'Who, Gharsallah?' He did not reply and disappeared among the dark boulders of Snake Mountain." Then Amin added, "Gharsallah was the first person to predict the fall of the Soviet Union. One Saturday, which was the day of the weekly market, I was busy shopping for myself and my family when he sent for me. So, I left everything and went to him. I found him seated beneath an olive tree to the west of the village. Before I sat down, he asked me, 'Do you have any news about Russia?' His question surprised me because that country is far away and what little I knew about it I had learned during my schooling, which ended with the third year of middle school: It's an enormous country with plentiful resources ruled by Communists. I told Gharsallah, 'I don't know anything about this country. Why do you ask?' He ordered me to sit down and then he handed me a glass of tea. Next, he pulled a large map from the satchel in which he kept his books and basic necessities. Spreading out the map, he pointed to the Soviet Union and told me, 'Look at this vast country and remember that something totally unexpected will take place there.' Three years later, what was called the Soviet Union collapsed and Communism perished with it.'"

The Fourth Story

Mansur, another disciple of Gharsallah, said, "He frequently told us, 'Believers, you are responsible for yourselves, and I am responsible for myself. I am alone. Don't fear for me, because no one can harm or approach me, for I am not Tunisian or Arab, Eastern or Western, Black or white, yellow, red or blue. Everything we have dictated is a book.'" Mansur added, "After he turned fifty, Gharsallah began to repeat to me and the others, 'For eighty years I have endured two of the bitterest things on this earth: Poverty and old age.' Everyone was amazed to hear that and no one understood what it meant . . . until Gharsallah died, when he was eighty."

The Fifth Story

Salluha said, "My husband traveled to Maktar and planned to return in two or three days, at the most, but a week passed without me receiving any word of him. Travelers reported perils on the road between us and Maktar. I felt alarmed and was beset by fears and apprehensions that left me unable to sleep or eat. All my children were young and went to bed early. Then I would be alone, trembling with fear. That night—a cold winter night—my feeling of desolation became desperate, and I broke into tears. I was in this condition when Gharsallah, whom I hadn't seen or heard from for a long time, appeared before me. I was anxious because I wondered what could justify this sudden visit at such a time and how Gharsallah could have entered the house when I was sure the door was locked. He squatted before me and ordered me to light the fire and fetch the teapot. My weeping knew no bounds as I told him, almost choking on my tears, 'Habib Allah, my husband has been gone for a week, and I'm afraid some evil has befallen him.' He reassured me in an affectionate, paternal tone: 'He's on his way home. Don't be alarmed.' Fear slipped from me like a loosened cloth, and I saw Gharsallah's face shine like the full moon. I lit the fire and prepared tea while Gharsallah repeated that my husband would reach the house shortly. Then I went into the bedroom to attend to something. When I returned, there was no trace of Gharsallah, and my consternation and apprehensions returned. I feared that what had happened had been merely a dream, but then my husband arrived."

The Sixth Story

Al-Munji recounted, "I used to work in Libya, but suddenly the Libyan authorities decided to expel all Tunisian laborers in 1985, at the end of the summer. I returned to my village in terrible shape. The first thing I did was to visit Gharsallah, who was never stingy with advice for me in rough times. I went to him on an excruciatingly hot day when you would see a pond ahead of you, only to discover it was a mirage. I found him sitting on the slope of Snake Mountain with some men I did not know. He didn't greet me but asked straightaway, 'Have you heard about the planes that will bomb Tunisia?' I thought he was referring to the possibility that Libya might launch a military assault on Tunisia. When he realized that was what I was thinking, he said sarcastically, 'You've always been stupid and ignorant. The planes aren't from Libya or Algeria, but from some other country that I suspect is preparing to bombard Tunisia.' I didn't pay much attention to that warning because Gharsallah was always saying things we didn't understand. Two weeks later, though, Israeli planes bombed Hammam Chott, where the Palestinians live. I rushed to Gharsallah, who said nothing about the planes but commented, 'Bourguiba is demented. He refers to reparations from America but forgets about the dead.'" Al-Munji added, "Gharsallah gave a person only what he wanted, by his leave."

The Seventh Story

Sahra', the eldest daughter of his eldest brother, reported: "In 1969, a year our country experienced flooding that caused enormous damage, my grandmother, who was Gharsallah's mother, was almost ninety years old. All the same, she appeared to be in excellent health. Gharsallah, who— without showing it—loved her more than any other being on earth, suddenly changed, becoming morose and apprehensive. Weeks and months passed without him speaking to anyone or approaching other people. One day he came to us totally naked, his body coated with ashes and his face blackened with soot. Then he sat on the road that leads west to Maktar and east to El Alaâ. He replied to anyone who asked how he was, 'Don't ask. My heart is shattered.' He continued like this for a few days. When his mother died in her sleep, he vanished into the woods and did not reappear for forty days." Sahra' added, "My uncle Gharsallah was one of a kind. Whenever I felt wronged or lonely, I would find him beside me, whether I was asleep or awake."

The Eighth Story

Hasan related: "At the end of the 1970s, before the many wars flared up in the Gulf region, Gharsallah placed some barrels at the center of the village—no one knew where he had found them—and wrote on them in thick, red letters: DANGER. When people asked him about that, he replied, 'The Gulf is going to burn, and it will be difficult to extinguish the flames.'"

The Ninth Story

Shortly before his final illness, Gharsallah recounted to some of his disciples that, in a dream, he had seen an angel coming to him when he was on Snake Mountain. He was frightened, but the angel reassured him, saying, "Don't be afraid," and placed his hand over Gharsallah's mouth to warn him of the muteness he would experience before his demise. Then the angel placed a hand beneath his right ear and inclined his head to one side as an allusion to his death, which occurred eight months after this dream.

The Tenth Story

After Gharsallah died, something amazing happened to the juniper tree beneath which he liked to sit in the cemetery. Half of it remained bright green while the other half lost all its scale-like leaves—as if it had been burned or struck by lightning. Gharsallah had instructed people to carve on his grave this verse from the Qur'an: "Among the believers are men who honored their covenant with God. Some have redeemed their pledge, and others are still waiting—their resolve unchanged."*

---

* Qur'an 33:23 Al-Ahzab (The Confederates).

3

The rain stopped falling, and the clouds seemed to be dispersing because pale rays had started slipping into the bedroom through the blue curtains. He felt no desire to leave the bed, though, for many reasons. It was his favorite place to recall memories and put his thoughts in order, especially when he was waking up in the morning. Reading was pleasant there at this time too but also at noon, before he fell asleep, or when he suffered from sleeplessness and insomnia—and those bouts were frequent. He shouldn't forget to phone his younger brother, Jalal, who lived in the village and watched over the family's dilapidated homestead, to apologize for not visiting him tomorrow as promised. The problems of old age, which was quickly advancing upon him with its pains and concerns, had destroyed any desire he might have had to travel and move around. He could hardly bear to leave his own company and quit his solitude, which grew more pronounced every day. Solitude was now his ideal companion, his final sweetheart, and the equivalent of Gharsallah's juniper tree, but without its vigor or verdure. His solitude was dark and desolate—like a cell in some ancient prison. Even so, he clung to it because it was all he had anymore. Some months earlier he had visited his younger brother for Eid al-Adha. He reached the village at seven in the evening and found his brother, his brother's wife, and their five children waiting for him. He kissed them one by one, savoring the domestic warmth he had missed since his divorce. He stayed up talking with his brother until one in the morning. They discussed the country's affairs—the drought, which had pitched its black tent and didn't care to travel further; people's problems, which were becoming more virulent each day; the injustices inflicted on them; and the terrible suffering they were enduring. "Mouths are gagged, bellies are hungry, and

37

the massive anger, which is silent now, will explode one day." That was how his brother summarized the situation. As he retired to bed, he sensed that his country had become "poor in sense and meaning," and that the nation's rulers were again leading it to ruin and destruction. Sleep evaded him except for fleeting moments. So, he left the house before daybreak, as the bleating of frightened lambs rose from every house and every direction. Perhaps they had a foreboding sense of the slaughter awaiting them on the blessed Eid. Now they were raising their voices loudly to request assistance that would not come to them from the heavens or the earth. In nightmares he frequently saw blood staining the streets and squares of desolate cities and villages. The legends of the ancient Middle East had lost their symbolic magic and become mere pretexts for killing and slaughter. The present and future were now nothing but fuel for a past that refused to stay in the past.

He walked along the trails he had commonly followed during his childhood and adolescence. The lengthy drought had robbed nature of its beauty and splendor and had denuded the earth, which was bald now and looked ill, distressed, and encumbered by pains. As he walked along, he imagined he heard moans from the earth—the tormented, wounded earth that could no longer bear all its afflictions. Even the birds had migrated, except for some silent ones that refused to sing because of the desolate barrenness. On the slope of Snake Mountain, an elderly man was seated beneath a slender olive tree, gazing gravely at the dark boulders massed before him. He had wrapped himself in a faded burnous that revealed only his wizened face, which had been furrowed by suffering, loneliness, and the years. Yunus greeted the man, who then grumbled a reply, as if to protest his greeting. He paused and gazed at the sheikh, wishing to converse with him. When he had stood there for some time, the old man fidgeted with annoyance and asked in a hoarse voice, "Who are you and what do you want?"

When he introduced himself, the sheikh rose and said, "Oh . . . it's you. I haven't seen you for a long time, although news of you reaches me every now and then." After staring at him for some moments, he added, "You were a young man . . . and here you are now . . ." He may have felt awkward about completing his phrase.

He replied, "Yes, I was young and now am old."

The elderly man commented bitterly, "That's true, but what's regrettable is our inability to block perfidious time's march." They were silent for some moments. Nearby a bird with dusty feathers circled overhead and then disappeared behind the mountain's dark boulders. The old man said, "Many people ask why I choose to live in the wilderness. I guess you would also like to know. The truth is that since my wife died about four years ago, I can no longer bear to stay in my house. When I sleep there, I feel I'm sleeping in a tomb. That's why approaching it has begun to frighten me, especially if I'm alone. In any case, I'm always alone. My two sons live with their families in Sousse, where they work. They only visit the village once a year. My one daughter is married and lives in another village. She's fifty now, I think, and has three daughters and two sons. She suggested I move and live with her, but I refused. I prefer to live alone like this, in the wild. I pass the day roaming the fields and hills. Where I like best to sleep is in Gharsallah's mausoleum. I feel secure and content there and frequently see Gharsallah in my dreams. Before—like many others—I didn't understand what he said or did and used to think he was mad. How could an intelligent man who knew the Word of God by heart spend his life in the scrubland—barefoot, clad only in an old burnous, with no family or source of income? I may once have thought like the others that some saint had cursed him and that Gharsallah turned out as he did for this reason. That's why I didn't heed him and didn't care to approach or listen to him. Like many other people, I enjoy his blessings now that the wilderness has become my residence and solitude my companion." The sheikh stopped talking and looked at Gharsallah's mausoleum, which seemed suspended on the summit of Snake Mountain. Then he added, "In any case, I realize that Gharsallah left us many words of wisdom and lessons. If we study them, we will grasp the reasons for our evil conditions and the source of the dangerous crises we endure. Yes, my good sir, if you look around and listen carefully, you will see and hear more than enough to alarm and burden you with concern and distress. The drought has lasted for many years, leaving the earth so dry we see scarcely any crops or grass on its surface, and the sandstorms hardly ever cease. Hunger glares at us with its scowling face now as it did in the age of the Beys and in the colonial era. Countless injustices afflict us daily—too many for anyone to avert or confront. Fear inhabits every heart; paralyzes motion; destroys dreams, hopes, and delights; and our rulers do nothing but blab, blab, blab, for hour after hour, without ever satisfying their need to lie, deceive, and swindle. They assume people are suckers and idiots at a time when old and young, the wise and the simpleminded, know full well what's happening in this country. The realities and secrets the ruling clique consider private are the people's common knowledge. Tongues convey reports of the robbers and thieves who sit on comfy chairs, live in fancy mansions, and scoff at the disasters their corrupt deeds and ideas cause us. Yes, my dear sir, everything has been disclosed and published far and wide. But I'm sure something totally unexpected will happen shortly. When I pray in Gharsallah's mausoleum, I ask God to advance the hour of our deliverance."

He bade farewell to the sheikh, who was still trembling with ire, and returned to his brother's house. Would he be able to give up everything to live there in the wilderness, contenting himself with the barest minimum of sustenance and clothing? Eschew all of life's pleasures? Would he be able to do that? The idea was tempting and seemed especially attractive now after he had listened to the sheikh. Putting the plan into action would be difficult, though—in fact, impossible. But why impossible? Was an educated person trained to fail? Were weakness, hesitation, and cowardice about embarking on truly profound adventures ingrained in his character? Was he doomed because he was an intellectual? Yes, he had to admit that—if only because this confession diminished the burden of his guilt. The village was quiet when he reached his brother's house, and the air was filled with the aromas of Eid food; a person could smell nothing else. He ate only a little of the grilled meat and then slept until late afternoon. He and his brother visited Gharsallah's mausoleum before sunset. When they sat up together that night, Jalal began to recount some of his memories of the late saint. He did this with all the panache of the old-time storytellers who used to tour the countryside, where people received them with great ceremony and offered them the most delicious food. Then, their stories helped their hosts forget their poverty and concerns and alleviated the monotony of the life they lived—forgotten and abandoned in the scrubland.

Jalal said, "I don't know why, in the final years of his life, Gharsallah allowed me to keep him company, because he used to avoid people and wouldn't come near them, unless he was on some spiritual mission. Like many other people, I was captivated by him and his remarks, although I didn't understand his many riddles and allegories. Do you remember the Cave of the Patriarchs Massacre in Palestine? I think Gharsallah prophesied that before it occurred. Here's the proof: He sent for me one Friday. I found him sitting on the slope of Snake Mountain beneath the slender olive tree. Even though it was bitterly cold, he was totally naked, and a copy of the Qur'an lay open before him. He had placed a knife and an axe next to the Qur'an. He asked me, 'Why did it take you so long to arrive?' Without waiting for a reply, he inquired, 'Do you know what you're doing today? We will prevent people from praying. Yes, we'll do that. Come. Follow me!' So, we headed to the mosque and sat down near it. Then Gharsallah began to accost each person heading there and told him acerbically and angrily, 'It's forbidden to pray today!' When the prayer time neared, worshipers were congregated at the door of the mosque, but Gharsallah blocked them and stopped them from entering. We had rarely seen him so angry and excited. When I tried to calm him, he rebuked me: 'Do you think I'm stupid or crazy? I command you all to swear off praying today. If you want to pray, bring me a paper signed by every mosque official—the Friday imam, the weekday imam, the muezzin, and the Qur'an reciter—that they assume no responsibility for whatever happens.' Three signed, but the weekday imam refused. So a quarrel flared up between him and Gharsallah. Then Gharsallah's eldest brother began to weep, and the hubbub and shouting grew ferocious. Finally, Gharsallah allowed worshipers to enter the mosque. When the imam began his sermon, Gharsallah remarked, 'Those are the party of Satan.' Then he seized my hand and asked me to follow him. I walked tens of meters with him before stopping. Then Gharsallah realized that I wished to return to the mosque to pray and told me, 'Go and pray with them.' Placing a hand on his beard, he added, 'Hear my word: I swear by God that the first to die will be by the door and the last will be at the mihrab. If I have lied to you, never visit me again.'

"During the prayer service, I feared the roof would fall on us, and I didn't regain my composure until our prayers were completed. That afternoon I went to Gharsallah at his favorite place on the slope of Snake Mountain. Then he repeated the same remark he had made before I had left to pray at the mosque. That massacre occurred at the Ibrahimi Mosque in Hebron exactly a week later. As I watched television coverage of it, I remembered what Gharsallah had said."

His brother fell silent and took a sip of mint-flavored tea. Then he continued, "Before his death, I heard Gharsallah repeat, when others were present, 'Beware of another Purgation Day that will befall you when you're inattentive.' I've kept trying to crack the riddle of that statement but haven't succeeded."

A Purgation Day? Ibn Tumart, a native of the mountains of the Sous in southern Morocco, spent many years in the East listening to sheikhs and jurisprudents there. Then he returned to his country with nothing but a coffee pot and a walking stick. Wherever he stopped, he preached to people, emphasizing the need to command good and forbid evil. He kept that up until he reached Marrakech, the capital of the Almoravids, who were known as the Veiled Men. They were called that because they wore a black cloth that protected their faces from the heat and cold of the desert, although their women went unveiled in public. In Marrakech, Ibn Tumart gathered followers and disciples around him as he started to present his sermons. In the city's markets one day, he saw the Almoravid emir's sister in her convoy. Like the beautiful court women with her, she was unveiled. He was outraged and ordered his followers to discipline her. They obeyed his orders in sight and hearing of the people of Marrakech. The Almoravid emir was content to expel Ibn Tumart from the city, even though one of his viziers would have killed him, alleging that Ibn Tumart didn't wish to reform people but to cause civil strife. Then he went to the mountains of the Sous, taking his companions and followers with him. These men announced that the Prophet had proclaimed the glad tiding of a Mahdi who would fill the world with justice and who would appear in the far west. Ten of his devoted disciples rose and told him: "Only you possess the qualities of this Mahdi. You are the Mahdi." They pledged their allegiance to him as the Mahdi. From the mountains of the Sous, Ibn Tumart—now referred to as the Mahdi—began to fight the Almoravids. One of his disciples was Abd Allah al-Wansharishi, who at first appeared to be simpleminded, uneducated, and a numbskull. He seemed to have no knowledge of the Qur'an or jurisprudence, was filthy, and slobbered all over himself. Even so, the Mahdi paid special attention to him, honored him, and always seated him beside him. He would say, "There is a secret God will eventually reveal about this man." Apparently al-Wansharishi was secretly preparing himself for an important mission he would later undertake. Out of sight and hearing of the others, he studied the Qur'an, Hadith, and jurisprudence until he became proficient in all of them. The Mahdi may have been helping him and planning to use this man to eliminate any doubters and to blindside potential rebels. One dawn, when people came out to pray accompanied by the Mahdi, they saw near the pulpit a handsome man, who was sprucely dressed and smelled pleasantly of cologne. The man's eyes and face were luminous. The Mahdi asked him, "Who are you?" He replied, "I'm al-Wansharishi." The Mahdi seemed to doubt this and ordered some followers to investigate the claim. Once the sun rose, they saw that the stranger was in fact al-Wansharishi. When they reported this to the Mahdi, he asked that the man be brought to him. Then he asked about the secret of this transformation. The man said an angel had descended to him from the heavens the day before. The angel had cleansed his heart of the earth's filth and taught him the Qur'an, *fiqh*, and Hadith. Then the Mahdi wept, and people watched and listened—astonished and flabbergasted—because they had never witnessed a miracle like this. To prove his claim, al-Wansharishi started reciting eloquent verses of the Qur'an in a remarkable fashion. Then he demonstrated his knowledge of jurisprudence and Hadith. People praised him, and again the Mahdi wept. Next al-Wansharishi said that God the Exalted had given him a light by which he could distinguish the people of paradise from those destined for the fire and had ordered those destined for the fire to be slain. He asserted that God had positioned angels down a well, in a place he specified, to testify to his truthfulness. They followed him and the Mahdi as everyone wept. When they reached the well, the Mahdi prayed near its mouth. Then he cried out, "Angels of God, do you attest to the truth of what Abd Allah al-Wansharishi has said?" From the depths of the well, voices replied, "Yes, he spoke the truth." (Al-Wansharishi, at the direction of the Mahdi, had placed men he trusted in the well to testify on his behalf.) Then the Mahdi turned to the people and told them, "This well has become sacred since angels have descended to it. Therefore, it must be filled at once." So, he ordered that done. Then the witnesses who had perjured themselves were buried alive, and the secret of this conspiracy was buried with them. Next the Mahdi summoned all his followers to assemble at that place. When they did, al-Wansharishi proceeded to vet them. He would point to a man whom he and the Mahdi feared and say, "He's one of the people of the fire." He would order him killed and thrown off the mountaintop. Then he would point to a beardless youth and said, "He's one of the people of paradise," and order him to stand to his right. The culling continued until seventy thousand were slain. That was the original Purgation Day.

So Gharsallah died, warning people of another Purgation Day. He was right because there are many men like Ibn Tumart and his companion al-Wansharishi now, spread throughout all regions of the world. They are in large capitals and in small cities, in caverns and caves, on tall mountains, and in rugged areas that are difficult for modern armies to assault. All of them spread the glad tidings of paradise and encourage people to embrace jihad and martyrdom to guarantee themselves a place in heaven. Since the physical world is transient, clinging to it is forbidden. Ibn Khaldun pointed out how dangerous these men are, because they exploit religion to gain disciples from the masses. But they quickly renounce what they announced when they first appeared. Indeed, frequently their proselytism becomes a way to breed mayhem and spread anarchy, which "destroys mankind and corrupts civilization." Ibn Khaldun thought that most of those who adopt this approach are "delusional, insane, or possessed by demons." They want to rule and gain power. When they can't, their rhetoric becomes violent and stern, and anger seizes hold of them. Then they goad their disciples to kill and wipe out people, to plunder their properties, and steal possessions or rape their women. To confront these "sick men," as he termed them, Ibn Khaldun suggested some different approaches. The first was "treatment" if they are insane. The second was "making an example of them by executing or beating them" if they create strife. The third was "to mock them in public and rank them among the liars."

Yunus brooded about Ibn Tumart during the black years when a country neighboring Tunisia was plunged into civil strife and its victims daily numbered in the dozens, even in the hundreds at times. Massacres were committed in daylight or the dark of night and neither large cities nor small villages were spared, not even hamlets almost entirely cut off from the world. Cultured people and poets were the first victims of the civil strife that lasted for ten years. Some were slaughtered in their sleep, others as they sat at dawn looking at a blank piece of paper, waiting for the birth of a poem, or prepared to go off to work. Some were shot in front of their children and wives or slain while walking along the street at peace with the world. Instigators of civil strife there had been quick to do what al-Wansharishi had done: divide the inhabitants of Algeria into those destined for paradise and those destined for the fire. Based on this division, they began to kill old men, elderly women, and children. They raped girls and married women. Even herdsmen in the mountains were not spared their daggers and bullets.

His interest in Ibn Tumart inspired him to go to Marrakech, during one marvelous autumn. Light had never enchanted him as it did in that Red City, especially in the morning and before sunset. At these times, everything seemed to belong to the world of the imagination. In Jemaa el-Fnaa Square, people devoted themselves to games, magic, sleight-of-hand tricks, singing, and amazing storytelling. They seemed disinterested in the past, present, and future—with what had happened or would happen in the world. Instead, they were preoccupied by their own time, which was suspended in the space of Jemaa el-Fnaa Square, and only they could grasp its essence. The Red City was the capital of the Almoravid kings and had not lost its old magic and primal beauty. That's why it has begun to attract great celebrities—whether artists or businessmen—who arrive from northern countries, fleeing the inferno of contemporary life out of a desire to relax at the gates of the Sahara, immersed in an atmosphere like that of *The Thousand and One Nights*.

Before the creation of Marrakech, there was the city of Aghmat, which was situated on the foothills of the Atlas Mountains. This was the city of Zaynab al-Nafzawiya. She was the enchantingly beautiful woman whose orders were obeyed by the Almoravid emirs, who took no steps without consulting her. Amazing stories are related about her. It is said that she conversed with the jinn, who obeyed her requests immediately, no matter how impossible they seemed. Yusuf ibn Tashfin—the most famous of the Almoravid kings and ruler of all of Morocco—would never reject her advice or opinions and privately told his cousins he had conquered the country thanks to her advice. It is reported that when Aghmat became overcrowded with inhabitants who had moved there from all the tribes, the Almoravid emir Abu Bakr Umar ordered another city built. When he consulted his courtiers, they told him, "We suggest a desert location where no people, gazelles, or herds live and only jujube and colocynth grow." The emir rode to that location with the tribal leaders. After scrutinizing it for a long time, he said, "Build this new city." That city was named Marrakech, which is a Berber word meaning "pass quickly," because so many thieves lurked there.

Two days before Yunus returned from Morocco to Tunisia, he visited Aghmat, which he found to be a small, isolated village in the foothills of the Atlas Mountains. Where the massacres of Purgation Day had been committed, he found impoverished farmers, children playing in the dusty streets, donkeys, cows, and herds of goats and sheep. Nothing about this village indicated that it had once been a large city that linked the south of the country with its north, or that battles and events, which filled history books, had occurred there. The only vestige remaining was the mausoleum of the poet prince al-Mu'tamid ibn Abbad. It seemed out of place there in a spot that had been neglected and forgotten for a long time. On the tomb are inscribed verses that al-Mu'tamid ibn Abbad recited when he sensed that his time had come:

Tomb of a stranger,
May passersby offer you water.
You have truly claimed the remains of Ibn Abbad.
Yes, heaven granted me death
At its appointed hour.
When it granted me a rendezvous
Before the bier, I did not know
The mountain's advance over the tent pegs
Would be satisfied with the nobility entrusted to you.
May every glowering thunderstorm water you,

Weeping for its brother, whose downpour you banished.
Test him beneath the surface
With the tears of passersby,
Until tears of dew provide you a liberal downpour
From the eyes of flowers that
Are never stingy with a tryst.
May prayers to God continue in perpetuity,
For you who are interred here, in countless numbers.[6]

Beside the tomb of al-Mu'tamid ibn Abbad are those of his daughters and his wife, I'timad umm al-Rabi' al-Rumaykya, with whom al-Mu'tamid was besotted until the last moment of his life. She also remained faithful to him through years of sovereignty, plenty, and opulence in Seville, as well as years of hardship, humiliation, and captivity in Aghmat. He met her in Seville's gardens, which spread along both banks of the Guadalquivir. He liked to stroll there with his friend, the poet Ibn Ammar, who had once roamed Andalusia on his steed, composing panegyrics for princes and dignitaries and earning a living from his poetry. At the time, al-Mu'tamid ibn Abbad was still a youthful prince and infatuated with entertainment, poetry, and drinking with women entertainers and beardless youths. With his friend the poet, he would head out for an excursion in a disguise that made it hard for the people of Seville to recognize him. On that spring day, the two friends were strolling slowly through the gardens, where flowers shared their perfume and tree limbs danced to the birds' melodious songs. A gentle breeze was stirring the surface of the Guadalquivir River, rippling the water. In response to this enchanting scene, al-Mu'tamid improvised the first half of a line of poetry: "The wind turned the water into a rippling coat of mail . . ."

Not far from these two friends an enchantingly beautiful young woman was enjoying an outing with her girlfriends. She wore a plain dress that highlighted the charms of her delicate body, which bubbled with passions and desires. When she heard al-Mu'tamid recite this first half-couplet, she improvised a second half for it: "What a breastplate it would make if it froze."[7]

Al-Mu'tamid was amazed by her acuity and quick wit, and her beauty struck him like a thunderbolt. On the spot he invited her to accompany him to his palace, and she accepted without any hesitation. While conversing with her, al-Mu'tamid discovered her charm and refinement, her graceful manner of conversing, the delicacy of her singing voice, and the breadth of her knowledge of poetry and of music. So, he fell in love with her and married her. He was always ready to satisfy her every desire and to honor her caprices. If she wanted to see snow cover tree branches, he would accomplish that with almond blossoms. If she was keen to trade her life as a princess for that of the peasant women who frolicked barefoot along the banks of the Guadalquivir, he allowed her to do as she wished. Then she would renounce her fancy gowns and don simple clothing, returning to her former life, which was devoid of grandeur and luxury. With bare feet, she and her handmaidens kneaded "mud" prepared from musk, ambergris, and perfumes mixed with rose water while singing popular sentimental Andalusian songs. Other princes and courtiers scorned her and referred to her as "that ignorant peasant." They mocked her in their assemblies and spread biased stories about her. They accused her of having so corrupted their prince and severed his ties to the reality of the principality that he had little idea of its many, complicated problems. Since the mosques had emptied of worshipers, they launched fierce attacks against her, attributing responsibility for that to her as well because they viewed her as an impetuous, reckless, ignorant, and conceited woman, who was interested in nothing but play and mischief. Thus according to them, she was doing everything she could to plunge the prince into vice and depravity. She paid no attention to these comments or to the conspiracies clandestinely hatched against her. She frankly expressed her disdain for jurisprudents and sheikhs and paid no attention to their admonitions and sermons that goaded the people of Seville to cling to religion and to the precepts of the Shari'a.

Once al-Mu'tamid left Seville on a mission and, impatient at being separated from his beautiful wife, wrote her this poem:

When your person is out of sight,
She is present in my innermost heart.
Greetings to you as strong as my sorrows,
My tears, and my insomnia!

You, who are hard to reach, have seized hold of me,
And my affection cannot resist you.
I wish to be with you at every moment;
If only I could be granted my wish![8]

During that period, Andalusia experienced insurrections, wars, and struggles between the kings of the Taifas as each one of these kings strove—covertly or overtly—to conquer his rival's kingdom and demolish his army. Al-Mu'tamid was well aware of the enormous dangers threatening his kingdom, but his beautiful wife always succeeded in drawing his attention back to her. He enjoyed passing evenings with her, and wine tasted even more delicious when he drank it in her company as he recited love poems and erotic odes. She would deliberately separate from him from time to time until his love for her grew even more ardent. He would lament desperately, "I worship her name and am in love with every letter of it." Schemes and conspiracies multiplied as struggles and wars became more intense in Andalusia. Then anxiety seized the upper hand over people, who no longer felt secure or confident. Al-Mu'tamid was still distracted by his life of decadent pleasure and trying to find a way to forget the evil conditions surrounding him when he experienced a painful incident he absolutely had not expected. He discovered that his friend, the poet Ibn Ammar, whom he had known since adolescence and whom he trusted blindly, was secretly conspiring against him with his most dogged enemies and foes. His shock was severe. Once al-Mu'tamid managed to capture him, he started clubbing his head with an iron cudgel. Ibn Ammar died kissing his feet and begging for his pardon and forgiveness. Thus the tenderhearted king, the poet who was passionately fond of beauty and life, turned into a fearsome killer who did not know the meaning of pity and mercy.

When King Alfonso VI, who ruled northern and central Spain, realized that the Muslim Arabs were daily becoming more divided and weaker and that it would be easier than at any time in the past to attack them and finish off their kingdoms, which were engaged in internecine combat, he began to threaten al-Mu'tamid, demanding tribute payments. Alfonso VI soon mobilized his army to attack Seville. It set fire to the villages surrounding the city and destroyed the forts. Many Muslims were taken prisoner. When his army reached the shore of Tarifa, which is south of Seville and in sight of Morocco, Alfonso VI shouted cockily and boastfully about his victory, "Now we have reached the extreme boundary of our great country. Soon we will put an end to our enemies, the Arab Muslims."

The Andalusian principalities fell one after the other. Feeling that his kingdom was more threatened than ever before, al-Mu'tamid hastened to ask for help from the Almoravid king Yusuf ibn Tashfin, who had expanded his kingdom until its area extended all the way to the borders of Senegal. Al-Mu'tamid did this reluctantly because he was wary of the Almoravids, whom he regarded as hard-hearted, chauvinistic desert people, who were quick to kill and driven by a desire for vengeance against anyone who opposed them. All the same, he thought that asking them for assistance was unavoidable. He told his courtiers, "It is better to be a camel herder than a swineherd." Al-Mu'tamid became even more committed to this decision when he received a letter from Alfonso VI, who said sarcastically, "I've spent a long time in conference with flies and the heat is severe. Send me a fan from your palace so I can cool myself and drive the flies away."

Al-Mu'tamid replied defiantly, "I have read your letter and grasped your vanity and complacency. I will show you the fans of Lamti leather held by Almoravid armies. These will fan you away, not the flies from you, God willing."

In Marrakech, the Almoravid king Yusuf ibn Tashfin, who was a shrewd warrior although virtually illiterate, was keeping track of what was happening to the Arab Muslims in Andalusia. He received delegations who came to him weeping, complaining, and imploring him to help them before it was too late. When the delegation came to him from al-Mu'tamid ibn Abbad, he ordered his army to cross the straits to Algeciras, taking many camels. That was the first time the people of Andalusia had seen camels, and they stared at them with astonishment when the beasts bellowed loudly. The Andalusian horses were frightened and bolted, retreating because they had never encountered such creatures before.

In three campaigns, the battles between the Christians and the Muslims were brutal. At the end of each campaign, Yusuf ibn Tashfin would return to his country to resupply his army before crossing the straits again. Hundreds died on both sides in these battles, and the ground of

Andalusia was stained with their blood. Each battle left a legacy of devastation, destruction, and chaos. Every day, drums were beaten to announce war, and the earth shook and trembled as the horizons answered with echoes. As Yusuf ibn Tashfin's army advanced, Alfonso VI called on his people to fight. Then priests, monks, and bishops sallied forth, carrying crosses and copies of the Gospels.

Al-Mu'tamid ibn Abbad, who commanded the battles in person, recited optimistically:

> Relief must be at hand,
> Bringing you a wondrous marvel.
> Then you will soon return with the blessed conquest.
> Your happiness is God's, too,
> And a setback for the faith of the cross.

When the ascetic jurisprudent Abu al-Abbas Ahmad ibn Rumayla al-Qurtubi[9] told him he had seen in a dream the Prophet Muhammad, who had given him glad tidings martyrdom, victory and a decisive triumph, al-Mu'tamid ibn Abbad exulted and exalted God. He also sent a message to Yusuf ibn Tashfin to tell him about this.

But hopes of victory quickly dissipated, and al-Mu'tamid experienced difficult, dark days unlike any he had encountered in his previous wars. Christian spies spread the rumor that al-Mu'tamid was the torch that had lit the wars—their red-hot poker—and the man who had planned all of them. Therefore, he had to be done away with because the Saharans, even if they were keen on jihad, were not familiar with the country. Then the Christian armies encircled al-Mu'tamid's troops, and the war between the two sides stalled. He launched forays at numerous locations and received a powerful blow to his head that almost killed him. Blood flowed copiously from his body, which was covered with wounds. When he remembered his young daughter, whom he had left in Seville, he sought solace in poetry and recited:

> In the swirling dust, I remembered dainty you;
> That memory kept me from fleeing.

Al-Mu'tamid's army was retreating in defeat, routed by the Christian armies, when the army of Yusuf ibn Tashfin arrived. Then the earth shook with the grumbling bellow of the camels and under the hooves of the horses, and the day turned dark from all the dust of the fighting. Troops trudged through bloody mud. When their leader received a blow, the marks of which remained with him to the end of his days, the Christian armies retreated in defeat. Then the Muslims shouted, "There's no God but God!" and "Allahu Akbar!" They shouted to each other that they had won and wished Yusuf ibn Tashfin a long life. To top this all off, they built a minaret from the heads of dead Christian soldiers and offered the call to prayer from atop it. On that day while he waited, al-Mu'tamid wrote his daughter a letter in which he said, "I write to you from the battlefield on Friday, the twentieth of Rajab. God has fortified the faith and granted victory to the Muslims. He has provided them with a decisive victory and made the polytheists taste a painful chastisement and a mighty misfortune. So, praise to God for His pleasure in this huge defeat and great delight: the defeat of Alfonso, may God burn him in an exemplary hell and not spare him a mighty comeuppance with the plundering of his encampments and the continued eradication of all his heroes, troops, defenders, and commanders. The Muslims even made a minaret of their heads and offered the call to prayer from it. Praise to God for His beautiful deed. Thanks to God, I received only flesh wounds that hurt at first but later scabbed over. I have taken booty and conquered."

After the initial set of battles that he waged against the Christians, Yusuf ibn Tashfin discovered that the kings of the Taifas were selfish cowards who loved wealth and life's pleasures, to which they were addicted, leaving them oblivious to the dangers threatening them. From that time forward, he was furious with them and began to plot vengeance against them and the seizure of their kingdoms, which were threatened with downfall and extinction. When he stayed as a guest of al-Mu'tamid ibn Abbad in Seville, Yusuf ibn Tashfin was dazzled by Seville's beauty and the number of its gardens and orchards of olive and fig trees and grapevines. He was astonished by the splendor of the palaces erected on both banks of the Guadalquivir River. In the palace where he stayed, he found elegance and luxury that increased his astonishment and disbelief. When he heard some of his staff ask him to emulate al-Mu'tamid ibn Abbad and to take advantage of the opportunities sovereignty offered for enjoyment and pleasure, Yusuf ibn Tashfin, the ascetic desert warrior, who was raised in tents and had experienced a rugged life, grew furious. He told them, "Anyone who studies this man," referring to his host, "sees that he is squandering his sovereignty because the wealth that enriches him must belong to other people. Taking this much from them can never be just. He has seized this fraudulently and wasted it on these frivolous luxuries. This is the most atrocious form of depravity." Then Yusuf ibn Tashfin asked members of his staff how al-Mu'tamid amused himself. They informed him that there were no bounds to his enjoyments, in which he was engaged night and day. He also had no qualms about letting his beautiful wife share all of them. Yusuf ibn Tashfin bowed his head then and fell silent, but a fire flared in his heart.

Al-Mu'tamid was sitting with some of his drinking buddies, enjoying wines and various foods, when the servant told him that a stranger had asked to speak with him about an important matter. When he left his cronies, he found himself in the presence of a shabbily dressed man who was covered with the dust of a long trip and whose eyes sparkled with intelligence and cunning. When al-Mu'tamid inquired what he wanted, the stranger replied, "My lord and master, I find myself obliged to offer you the advice that a subject owes his king. I have heard from companions of your guest Yusuf ibn Tashfin that they consider themselves and their king more entitled to this good life than you. I have an opinion about this. If you would like to hear it, I will tell you." When al-Mu'tamid gave the man permission to continue, he said, "I think the desert king intends to harm you. Beware of him. He wants to seize control of your kingdom—in fact, of all of Andalusia. I advise you to seize him now and order him to command his army to return to the desert. In that way, you will be delivered from him and his evil and will have thwarted his evil schemes." Al-Mu'tamid liked the stranger's advice and bowed his head to consider it. Then a drinking companion, who had been eavesdropping, intervened and told the stranger, "Mr. Adviser, you know that our master al-Mu'tamid comes from an honorable family renowned for good deeds. He cannot treat his guest unjustly and betray him." The stranger replied,

"Treachery is justified against traitors. A man has a right to defend himself against a calamity that will leave him defenseless." But the drinking companion replied, "Suffering harm from being loyal is better than resolutely being rude." When the stranger inspected al-Mu'tamid's face, he felt certain that his own advice had been negated by the words of the drinking buddy. Then he thanked the king for receiving him and departed.

Yusuf ibn Tashfin began to take revenge on the Taifa kings. He attacked their cities and forts, and his army began toppling them one by one and sending them in chains to prisons in Marrakech. Those who refused to surrender were killed along with their children. When he was the only king left, al-Mu'tamid sensed his danger and regretted summoning Yusuf ibn Tashfin to assist him in his wars against the Christians. He was deep in thought about this when his desperate, enraged son Abu al-Hasan Abd Allah al-Rashid came to tell him, "My lord, you've committed a serious error because you brought us that huge scourge named Yusuf ibn Tashfin. You may remember that I told you from the start that this hard-hearted, scowling man from the desert—as dry as the earth he comes from—would destroy our realm and devastate our cities. But you refused to listen to me. Now we're confronted by an affliction we can't escape." Al-Mu'tamid remained silent for a time. Then he replied, "Son, caution will not forestall divine decree."

That night al-Mu'tamid retired with his wife. He still craved her beauty as much as he had when they first married. Perhaps, with her, he could forget the cares that kept him awake and tormented him. He began to caress her body, kissing her lips, neck, buttocks, and thighs, but she remained silent and still, as if she had never been the lusty woman who had excited his passion in the bed with her moves, kisses, and moans when their pleasure climaxed. That night al-Mu'tamid got no sleep. Even at daybreak he was still experiencing alarming nightmares, his eyes wide open in the dark, while his wife stirred restlessly beside him, releasing one sigh after another.

Al-Mu'tamid was preparing to confront the dangers encircling him and his kingdom when Yusuf ibn Tashfin besieged Seville. After he burned its fleet, he began to tighten the noose around the city day by day. That happened toward the end of 1090 CE. It was winter, but the cold wasn't too severe, and that fact helped the Saharan army achieve a quick series of victories. During this ordeal that afflicted him and his city, al-Mu'tamid summoned the people of his kingdom to fight. They fought hard, and he commanded them more bravely in the battles than any of the other Andalusian kings. Even so, some people in Seville grew alarmed and began to scale their city's high walls to surrender to the enemy. After a bitter siege that lasted until the beginning of autumn in 1091, the city surrendered, and the Almoravid army entered it. Troops spread through it, looting, killing, raping women, and robbing men, who fled their homes with nothing to cover their privates but their hands. Al-Mu'tamid continued to fight until he saw his son Malik fall before his eyes, smeared with his own blood. Then he cast his sword away and surrendered to his desert enemies as the screams and wails of his wife and daughters echoed through the large palace.

Al-Mu'tamid, his wife, and his daughters were led to Marrakech and then to Aghmat, where they found themselves in a desolate land. Before them were the High Atlas Mountains, and over the foothills circled crows and vultures. They were confined there in a poor excuse for a house. Yusuf ibn Tashfin dealt with them in a worse way than he had anyone before. He treated them like captured slaves and denied them anything that might shield them from the cold of winter or the heat of summer, both of which were unbearably severe. To resist the hunger that threatened the family daily, al-Mu'tamid's daughters spun thread for the people of Aghmat at a trifling price and did housework for its residents, as if they were simple maids. Despite the catastrophes that had devastated her and her family, I'timad retained some vestiges of her former beauty. Hers now was the beauty of the moon veiled by a delicate cloud, the magic of twilight at the desert's horizons, the charm of a flower just before it wilts, and the radiance of autumn gardens before a gloomy winter. She and poetry were all that al-Mu'tamid, whose heart was wounded, had to help him withstand the disasters that had buffeted his wealth and his glory and turned him into a lowly prisoner. He had recourse to his wife and to poetry whenever his wounds in his prison on the foothills of the Atlas Mountains bled severely. Al-Mu'tamid felt an aversion to daytime because by its light he observed time's slow march disfigure his features and those of his wife and daughters. By night, however, he found some peace of mind. When he lit a candle and surrendered to the seduction of poetry, which he had loved since childhood, he would continue playing with words until Aghmat's cock released its cock-a-doodle-doo to announce that day was dawning.

> Disasters have attacked me,
> And their swords have shredded my healthy body![10]

Of the fetters that tormented him in his prison, night and day, al-Mu'tamid wrote:

> My leg is enveloped by a serpent,
> Which coils round it, gnawing it with a lion's fangs.
> I am the man whom men fled,
> Entering heaven or hell by his sword.

On an Eid day, as his wife and daughters wept, he did too at their extreme subjugation, oppression, and humiliation. By candlelight he wrote:

> On past feast days, I rejoiced.
> In Aghmat, the Eid finds you imprisoned.
> If you cite your destiny as an example,
> Since destiny rejected, restrained, and held you captive,
> Anyone who becomes a ruler after you and rejoices in that,
> Finds delight in naught but dreams.

After four years of captivity, torment, and humiliation, I'timad died one gloomy dawn. Her death was tranquil and free of suffering. It was the death of someone who could no longer bear to live. Al-Mu'tamid could not stand to be separated from her and joined her a few months later. No one wept for him in Aghmat. In Andalusia, however, many did, and they continued to weep for him, generation after generation, until Christians expelled them and they scattered around the earth, carrying with them the keys to their houses in Seville, Granada, and Murcia and memories of a lost paradise.

He recalled the life story of al-Muʻtamid ibn Abbad while sitting in a wretched coffeehouse in Aghmat. Its only other patrons were still, silent, old Berber men, who gazed with expressionless eyes at the high mountains that rose directly before them. Neither the waiter nor anyone else inquired about his nationality or his reason for coming there. What was the use of that? Inevitably, others like him had come to Aghmat to visit al-Muʻtamid's tomb and had been treated the same way; in other words, they had been ignored. Perhaps the people of Aghmat were justified in this, because al-Muʻtamid had come to them as a stranger and died among them as a stranger. Those who visited his tomb were strangers too. Therefore, villagers were no more interested in them than they had been in him.

Late that afternoon, he boarded the last bus to Marrakech. On his way there he tried to imagine why Yusuf ibn Tashfin had punished al-Muʻtamid so cruelly and vengefully. Had the sole reason been al-Muʻtamid's delight in the pleasures of life, wealth, and luxury? He did not think so. There were other reasons associated with the history of the Almoravids, who were as puritanical, narrow-minded, and violent as the Almohads, who subsequently demolished their far-flung empire.

History says that the Almoravids were called the Veiled Men, that they were nomadic Bedouins who lived in the southern desert of Morocco and inhabited tents woven from camel and goat hair; that they owned horses, camels, and sheep and moved from one water source to another; that they were renowned for their guile, cleverness, and cunning; and that the person who popularized Islam among them was a stern jurisprudent, who favored application of the Shariʻa exactly as it came from the Qurʼan and the Sunna. For this reason, he did not hesitate to kill anyone who rebelled against him or disagreed with him. Motivated by their fear of him and panic, the desert's tribes responded to him. Then he became a military commander with an army that fought for glory more than for horses, and his troops obeyed him blindly, never refusing even one of his commands. He would tell his disciples, "When you obey me, you obey God and His Messenger." On raids against rebel tribes that refused to implement the Shariʻa of Islam, he granted license to kill them, to plunder their possessions, and to enslave their women and children. He was the person who named the Veiled Men "Almoravids" because they were so resolute in fighting alongside him in battles that he conducted to spread his teachings. It is certain that Yusuf ibn Tashfin, who experienced those battles when he was a young boy, was influenced by that jurisprudent's tenets, which remained his sole touchstone as he clung to them to the end. Therefore, it isn't odd that he disliked al-Muʿtamid's love for life, beauty, and poetry. This would explain the cruelty with which he treated him, his wife, and his daughters. In the end, nomadism won out over sedentary culture, and the puritanical desert warrior, who was almost illiterate, vanquished the sensitive poet who loved life and its pleasures.

With a reverberating laugh, his younger brother interrupted Yunus's memories and thoughts. Then he said, "Gharsallah did something else strange, five years before he died, and people still talk about it to the present day. During that autumn, which was dry, dreary, chilly, and dusty, Gharsallah made the rounds of the village, inviting men, women, and children to come to his favorite place on the slope of Snake Mountain for a joyous celebration, which would be held there. People were amazed and very curious because Gharsallah had accustomed them to expect surprises from him. When someone asked what the occasion was, he refused to reply, merely saying, 'Come see with your own eyes.' On the appointed day, many responded to the invitation. When they reached the slope of Snake Mountain, they found Gharsallah, who was half naked, and a jet-black donkey, its neck adorned with necklaces of beautiful colors. Two strangers were present too; one was drumming while the other played a mizmar. Gharsallah turned to the people and said, 'Look at this handsome donkey. In fact, he may be the most handsome in the entire Arab world. A month ago, he came to me and asked me insistently to host a party for his circumcision because he too would prefer to become a Muslim and guarantee himself entry into heaven. So now I am fulfilling his wish.' People burst into laughter. They laughed and chortled and guffawed until the distant horizons responded with echoes of their laughter. Like them, Gharsallah broke into laughter. Then he said, 'Laughter is the most beautiful thing in this world. Isn't it?' The joyous party lasted until early evening, and men and women danced, at Gharsallah's urging. It was the village's happiest day throughout that depressing, arid autumn."

His younger brother began to laugh again. Then, seriously this time, he commented, "I think Gharsallah wanted to show us by his actions that lousy conditions we experience should not keep us from laughing. We have a duty to laugh and laugh and laugh—at ourselves, at our destiny, at our rulers, at our history, at everything in this desolate Arab world, which feels as cramped as a cell in one of its prisons. Let us laugh, and may God help us all."

4

Breakfast: olive oil with two teaspoons of honey, warm bread, café au lait, orange juice. After breakfast he moved to the little room where he kept his favorite books. He spent three hours or more here each morning—reading, thinking, and writing down his reflections. At the beginning of the day, the mind is clear, and memory is at its best. His reading wasn't limited to one genre. At times poetry tempted him, and he would spend a week or two reading Arab and foreign poets, ancient and modern. After that he would turn to novels and devour new works that had received excellent reviews in papers and magazines, or he would reread books he always enjoyed and never tired of reading, like Proust's *In Search of Lost Time*, Céline's *Journey to the End of the Night*, Joyce's *Ulysses*, Malcolm Lowry's *Under the Volcano*, and all the novels of Henry Miller. Then he would set aside novels and read history books, like Ibn al-Athir's *al-Kamil fi-l-Ta'rikh*, al-Tabari's *History of Messengers and Kings*, and Ibn Khaldun's massive history. He found in Ahmad ibn Abi al-Diyaf's *Presenting Contemporaries the History of the Rulers of Tunis and the Fundamental Pact*[11] insights that helped him understand his country's history, especially during the nineteenth century, and grasp the injustices people were subjected to during the rule of the Beys and the continual catastrophes that upset their lives. In fact, this book furnished him an understanding of the present too, disclosing secret and covert aspects. He admired this author's mastery of major and minor points, his rare skill in narrating events, and his precise descriptions of the Beys, viziers, leading citizens, and common people. For these reasons, he read *The History of the Rulers of Tunis* like a novel instead of a history book. Ahmad ibn Abi al-Diyaf, for example, wrote in an exceptional, novelistic style about the execution of the Arab

vizier Zarruq, who committed atrocious massacres against coastal people
before the Bey disavowed him:

> On Tuesday night, the 13th of Safar (October 29, 1822) the Bey ordered
> the Arab Zarruq killed. Then Yusuf Kahiya brought Zarruq to the
> Pasha's residence after ten p.m. with armed men from the elite mamluk
> force in the palace. When Yusuf Kahiya released Zarruq from house
> arrest and took the road to the palace, Zarruq assumed he was being
> taken to the Bey. Yusuf Kahiya denied that, and Zarruq grasped the real
> plan and then strode forward, clasping a set of coral prayer beads. He
> continued walking in a dignified, calm manner. When he reached the
> dungeon, he walked alone to the execution spot, sat down on the mat
> there, and placed the strangulation rope around his own neck. Then he
> asked with amazement, "What have I done?" Yusuf Kahiya answered
> with his typical harshness, "You know what you've done." Zarruq shot
> back, "You're no one to talk, Mule Head!" Then Yusuf Kahiya executed
> Zarruq according to the will of God, and he departed, with others like
> him, into the distant past. The Bey sent Zarruq's corpse to his own cem-
> etery in Jellaz, where it was washed and buried, for fear fools would
> mutilate his noble body.

A week earlier he had reread chapters from Procopius's *History
of the Wars*, in a French translation. Once more he paused at this sentence, which almost attains the enchantment and charm of poetry, when
Procopius says: "Here I tremble and waver with the greatest hesitation,
conscious that what I write now will not be accurate or deserve to be
remembered for long." Procopius wrote his work under extremely difficult
circumstances—surrounded by spies who watched what he did (and did
not do), night and day. Had he ever been outed to the princes and kings
he supposedly served—although he slandered them in what he wrote in
secret, trembling from fear—his end would have been hideous. A second
passage that caught the attention of Yunus while he read chapters of *The
Wars* described the final days of Gelimer, the last king of the Vandals.
Procopius relates that Gelimer was reared in a royal family with a long
lineage and enjoyed power, glory, and strength. When decay and weakness
infiltrated his state, he fled from his enemies and, as an old man, endured

years of torment, fear, and misery. He was finally seized and taken to Carthage, fettered with iron chains. Confronted by his enemies, who gathered in large numbers to receive him, he burst out laughing and continued to laugh and laugh and laugh until his foes thought he had gone insane because of the loss of his might and glory. Procopius relates, however, that Gelimer exploded with laughter once it became clear to him that, in the final analysis, life doesn't deserve more than a resounding laugh, whether for its happy or painful events.

What would be the end of Arab tyrants seated on thrones of power for these many decades? He frequently liked to entertain himself by posing this question. When push came to shove, though, he was unable to answer it. Like many others, he had begun to believe that the Arab rulers would never renounce power, not even if they were forced to crush their peoples and torch their lands to remain rulers. Generations passed in succession, and the circumstances of nations and peoples changed, but the same tyrants remained in power. Their portraits, statues, and speeches greet people when they wake each morning and as they retire to bed. Even when they journey to the next world, they will govern from their graves, through their children or heirs, who inherit their same vicious natures, use their predecessors' same violent methods, and embrace their same greed for power and predilection for domination and tyranny in dealing with the affairs of their lands. This is a time-honored matter Ibn Khaldun affirmed when he remarked that Arabs "vie for leadership. One of them rarely relinquishes it to another, even if the other person is his father, brother, or his clan elder. In the few cases when power is transferred, that will be grudgingly and out of a sense of shame."

Ibn Khaldun also thought that the basis of rule among the Arabs was oppression of the citizenry. That was why he believed every land that an Arab governs is one where "the culture collapses and the resident is desolate." There, "the earth changes into something other than earth." What Ibn Khaldun said about ancient Arab rulers fits contemporary Arab rulers perfectly, and the countries these men rule appear to be extremely large prisons that are carefully monitored for a multitude of infractions and forbidden deeds. There is no tolerance for a sigh, a gesture, or any deviation from the principles decreed. All mouths are muzzled except those of eulogists, sycophants, and toadies. Even a person's innocent smile may have evil consequences. That's why people don't smile unless ordered to by the ruler. They don't rejoice except when he does—to celebrate his birthday or the anniversary of his assumption of power. He reminds them every day that they belong to him and that he can do whatever he wishes with them. They must be obedient and subservient to him. Anyone who disobeys becomes a lost cause. And so forth . . . From their excessive servility, Arab peoples have lost their desire for liberation from subjugation. They are certain they will travel to the other world without ever witnessing any change, not even the slightest change in this depressing and alarming scene. Uff!

He picked up the book he had begun reading the day before. It was a collection of intellectual and critical essays by a French author named Philippe Muray—a writer he hadn't known before. Articles he had read about him said that this writer had died at the age of sixty, without ever enjoying the fame he deserved. Only a very few people had recognized the greatness of his talent because this man had lived far from the footlights and had despised the buffoonish displays some people utilized to make themselves known and to attain glory and fame—people like Bernard-Henri Lévy. Muray had died relatively unknown, and the French had discovered him only when a famous actor read a text by him at the Odéon Théâtre in Paris. Since then, his works had begun to garner widespread acceptance with readers.

Most of the essays in Muray's book were profound in their ideas and significance. They reflected the author's intelligence, the scope of his learning, and his astonishing grasp of literature, philosophy, and new trends in the world. The essay that riveted Yunus even more than the rest treated the "copybooks" in which Flaubert recorded observations about his work as a writer. Nothing else distracted him from it—not family matters, friendships, occasional love affairs, the epileptic fits that afflicted him, or his hallucinations, which caused him to see a hundred thousand tiny flies "circling in the air like golden circles." Words were his ideal world, and he woke and fell asleep to their vagaries, puzzles, and melodies. His bitter daily struggle with them finally caused him to explode like a firecracker and drop dead when he was fifty-nine. For Flaubert, literature wasn't a part of his activities in life; it constituted his entire life. It pained him that he did not find around him anyone who treated literature as seriously as he did or who spoke about it in the same way. All his longtime friends married, became officials, went hunting in their free time, and danced and sang at soirées. He found no one among them who could spend half a day with him reading a poem. They all had occupations. His sole occupation was literature—just literature, nothing else. Flaubert wrote in his notebooks:

> Yes, literature impedes me to the greatest extent, but this isn't my fault. It's like a hereditary ailment for me, and there's no way to rid myself of it. I'm crazed with art and aesthetics, and it's impossible for me to live a single day without scratching this scab, which exhausts and torments me.

When he was fifty, Flaubert decided to compose what he called "The Dictionary of Received Ideas," wishing to include in this work the fruit of his absolute passion for writing, his life experiences, his knowledge of people, and a condensed version of research he conducted during his travels. Over a period of eight years, Flaubert continued to write, research, read, and copy texts, without feeling weary or bored. He did that while reviewing events of his past life—like other people who sense that their demise is near. Ultimately, a strange novel evolved from his Received Ideas: *Bouvard et Pécuchet*, although Flaubert died before completing it. This novel did not achieve any renown until the beginning of the twentieth century, when Joyce, Proust, and Kafka considered it the first modern novel in the true meaning of the expression.

Yunus believed that the only Arab author who resembled Flaubert in his total absorption in writing was al-Jahiz—that short, diminutive, misshapen, acid-tongued, and acid-penned man who devoted his life to writing and reading. Whenever a book fell into his hands, he would read it from start to finish. To the end of his life, he lived simply and never sought status or wealth, since literature sufficed—he needed nothing more. When someone asked him one day, "Do you have an estate in Basra?" al-Jahiz replied with a smile, "My household consists of me, a woman, a woman to serve her, a male servant, and a donkey." The Abbasid caliph al-Ma'mun loved everything he wrote and was enchanted by his elegant use of words and smooth articulation. He said of his style, "It's streetwise and royal, common and elite." When al-Jahiz was old, devastating ailments crippled him. One day people heard him tell a self-styled doctor who had come to inquire about his malady:

> On my left side I'm paralyzed, so that if I were cut by scissors there, I wouldn't feel it. My right side is so dehydrated that if a fly touched it, I would hurt. I have a kidney stone that makes it hard to urinate. And worst of all, I'm ninety.

He discovered Flaubert at the same time he discovered the other French writers who led him to worlds previously unknown. These worlds fascinated him, and he was drawn to them like an enthralled lover, forgetting the bleak, depressing rural area where he was born and the wretched, impoverished people among whom he lived. He now had many heroes with whom he discussed things and exchanged ideas. In fact, in his solitude, he attempted to imitate their characteristics and achievements, imagining he was one of them.

He was Julien Sorel who loved Madame Rênal and dreamt of wealth and status. He was Rastignac in the Père Lachaise Cemetery, challenging evil, cruel, hypocritical Paris, which had conspired against his dreams and ambitions. He was Antoine Roquentin, raving in the fog in Bouville as he fought off the nausea provoked by a world he could no longer abide. He was Meursault, who killed an Arab on the beach and claimed in court he did this to demonstrate his ultimate freedom.

He was the tormented and humiliated workers in *Germinal.*

He was Jean Valjean, the good-hearted thief, who fled as his enemies pursued him relentlessly but who died like a saint.

He was Madame Bovary, a farmer's Romantic daughter, whose monotonous marriage drove her to cheat on her spouse more than once. In the end, she killed herself in the presence of her dumbfounded husband.

It made no difference who he was. What mattered was finding in the books he read something that would open unknown worlds for him and transport him away from the monotony of life in the sad countryside, the suffering of the people around him, the storms of yellow dust, and the chatter of old men congregating at the mosque to recall their distant past. Now he was Madame Bovary. Why not? Before he read that novel, he had thought it wrong for a woman to cheat on her husband and right for people to shame her by walking round her after her head had been shaved as a warning to other women. Now all that seemed wrong. Madame Bovary wasn't to blame; her actions had not been consequences of her emotional outbursts. Instead, her dull-witted and coldhearted husband was to blame. After reading this novel, he would really have liked to discover an adulterous wife in his village and defend her by opposing any punishment allotted to her. He would launch a fierce attack on men who beat their wives, refused to dine with them, treated them harshly and roughly, never smiled at them, never spoke sweetly to cheer them and calm their doubts, and who brandished a stick:

> When their wives raised their voices in protest or anger,
> And when they were silent:
> Silently spinning,
> Silently weaving,
> Silently fetching buckets of water and carrying firewood on their
>   backs,
> Silently working in the fields and grinding grain.
> If they sang, danced, or smiled at a relative, they were considered
>   hussies.
> Every year their bellies filled, and before they turned thirty, they
>   were wilted and flabby. They were stooped and, from too much
>   breastfeeding, their breasts hung down like empty waterskins—all
>   this while they remained silent.
> Once their subjugation and suppression became too much to bear,
>   they wept.

At the age of seventeen, he started to write texts he signed with the pen name Yatim al-Dahr, which he chose because he admired al-Tha'alibi's anthology of Arabic verse titled *Yatimat al-Dahr*. But he soon tore up those scripts, after reading them more than once, since they seemed weak, superficial, and artificial. The best were merely lusterless imitations of books he read, and his texts, language, and style were stolid and insipid. He suffered for many months while his sense of failure increased drastically, day by day, until despair pervaded his soul and he did not feel like eating or speaking, even to the people he liked best. He spent most of his free time out in the countryside, roaming aimlessly, as his failure's pain and bitterness tortured him. One day, though, during his spring vacation, he found a copy of Flaubert's *Trois Contes*, which he read in a single day. It restored his hope of becoming the writer he wanted to be, and that evening he went into the countryside to plan his new texts. In *Three Tales* he discovered something he had not seen in all the books he had read previously. The protagonists of these stories, which Flaubert narrated in an exceptional style and terse, lyrical language, resembled people he knew personally. The atmosphere of these three stories did not differ much from that of the amazing tales he had heard as a child or those that storytellers, who traveled on the back of a weary donkey from village to village, told to entertain people, making people laugh and weep at the same time. Now the rural region did not seem as bleak as he had imagined it. In fact, it was filled with many stories he needed to record. In these texts, he would narrate real conditions and events he had experienced or heard about and describe people whom he had known or whom his family had told him about.

"The Tale of the Blue Man" was the first of these. He had experienced its incidents when he was five. Winter storms blustered angrily, the small village trembled through the cold night, and he was snug beneath a warm coverlet, listening to the winds' clamor with alarm—as if he feared they would bring the roof down on him and his family or break through the door to carry him far away, to a place where ghouls and other terrors lurked.

His father extinguished the oil lamp and told his mother, "The blue man passed through the village following the afternoon prayer, armed and carrying a knapsack over his shoulder. He was tired, and there were scratches on his face. He seemed to have participated in a battle today or perhaps yesterday. He requested bread, sugar, oil, and salt, which he placed in his knapsack. Then he headed off to the west, after thanking us and wishing us all the best. He was very calm and gracious. I didn't think he would be like this. Some people have claimed he is violent, insolent, ill-humored, and always agitated. They assert he never asks for anything but simply snatches it. I believe they weren't telling the truth; tongues frequently feel at liberty to switch facts and distort them. It's likely that, whether with his four comrades or alone, he attacks colonists' farms and police stations and the houses of local people who collaborate with the French. Until now he has killed one colonist, three policemen, and a man who was said to have been a major snitch for the French. That's why they pursue him night and day. They are determined to punish him, but he has always been able to elude them. That's miraculous! It's said that his bullet rarely misses its target, and that he's always on the move. He's in one place today and another, far away, tomorrow. This is what perplexes the French police. They travel in Jeeps, but he traverses these distances on foot or by mule. The four men with him are from his village and are devoted to him. He sends them to markets to gather news and scout areas that he's planning to attack. This shows why no one has succeeded in recognizing them yet; they are adept at disguising themselves and keep a low profile. This is the first time he has passed through our village, but I doubt he'll attack us—I read that in his eyes. Besides, why would he? We're all with him against the French, and there are no snitches among us, unlike some other villages. After he departed, we regretted not having invited him to eat with us. Why not? Anyone who eats your food will never dare harm you, especially without cause. Anyway, he's not that sort of man. His late father was a gallant, good-hearted person who wished the best for everyone. He hated injustice and wouldn't allow it. The French imprisoned him for a full year, humiliating and torturing him. Shortly after he was released, he died of grief. The dirt covering his grave had not dried yet when his son took up arms and set off for the mountains. May God help him and assist all those who defend the truth and prohibit falsehood."

"Amen," said his mother. Then all he heard was the wind's whistling.

A blue man? He had never seen a man that color. There were Black, brown, white, and blond people. Blue men he had never heard of. How could the man his father discussed be blue? Was he the color of the clear sky or of the bruises a stout stick leaves on a body? The color of the doves that frequented gorges and ravines and built nests there? Moreover, was this blue man real—flesh and blood—and not one of those legendary heroes people described, heroes he would never see? He hoped to meet the blue man in the village with his father and some of the other men. These ideas continued to cycle through his mind until sleep claimed him.

Early the next day, when he and a bunch of boys were heading to the Qur'an teacher's house on a frosty winter morning, he asked them, "Are there blue men?"

They laughed sarcastically at him: "No." They had never heard of such a thing.

"But I heard my father talking about a blue man yesterday."

A boy named Yahya, who was four years his senior, quickly warned him: "You mustn't mention him to anyone!"

"Why not?"

"Because he's dangerous . . . very dangerous."

The children stopped walking. Their noses were red from the extreme cold, and their bodies shivered inside their thick burnouses.

"Come on, Yahya, Champ: Who is the blue man? Why is he dangerous?"

"He fights the French, and they are chasing him in the mountains, where he has many hideouts. I've heard my father say that anyone who sees him and does not report him will be incarcerated for the rest of his life."

"Is what you're saying true?"

"True! By God, it's true. But beware: Don't mention this man to people. If you do, the consequences will be disastrous. When I mentioned him to my uncle, he threatened to cut out my tongue."

"But is he really blue?"

"No. I don't think so. People may call him that because he's courageous, valiant, and a champion—like the bulls that frighten us on the road and that our parents call 'blue bulls.'"

Every night, after the oil lamp was extinguished, his father would recount bits of information about the blue man. Almost all of them concerned him killing "snitches" or his repeated attacks on the farms of colonists and the police stations in Maktar, Haffouz, al-Waslatiyah, and Hadjeb el Aïoun. His mother blessed everything the blue man did, saying, "May God grant him and his comrades victory."

One night, when the storms had calmed, the frost had retreated, and the sky had cleared, his father returned home tired and sad. He ate supper quickly and silently, as if in a hurry. Then he started fiddling with his prayer beads, gravely and absentmindedly. Finally, Yunus heard him tell his mother, "Yesterday was a black one for the blue man. The gendarmes laid an ambush for him and his four men somewhere near al-Waslatiyah. Apparently, some snitch betrayed him. There was a fierce battle that lasted an hour or more. During it, two of his men were killed and the other two so severely wounded that it was easy for the French to capture them. He himself was able to escape, miraculously—as is typical for him." His mother began to weep. Then she uttered some words that he wasn't able to understand because she was choking on her tears.

Melancholy affected everyone the next week. He awoke one morning to find the village bathed in splendid light. He was overjoyed and contemplated skipping Qur'an instruction to roam the fields and look for birds' nests. His joy, however, lasted only moments because he noticed on his father's face the type of sad, pained sorrow reserved for funerals and rough times. For her part, his mother was weeping silently. From the distance, from villages scattered over the foothills of the western mountains, from the direction of Maktar and Kesra, wails of lament could be heard clearly at times and faintly at others, depending on the direction of the wind. What had happened? French gendarmes had slain the blue man the previous day. Reports circulated that he had spent the evening as the guest of a friend who lived between Kesra and Maktar. Then at midnight, when he wished to return to his hideouts in the mountains, he found that gendarmes had encircled the house. He fought with astonishing valor, killing one of the gendarmes and wounding two. Finally, he fell dead after shouting, "Long live a free and independent Tunisia!"

Yunus's second story was about Aisha the Blonde. Although both her parents were dark brown in complexion, Aisha was born blonde and blue-eyed, and her hair was the color of wheat in summer. This anomaly caught people's attention, and they explained this phenomenon in different ways. Some people believed that when Aisha's mother was a girl of fourteen, she had offered a soldier water when Germans were passing through the village during the war. Perhaps the image of that blond soldier had lain dormant in her memory until she became pregnant with Aisha at the age of eighteen. Others claimed that someone had prayed for something evil to befall her and caused Aisha to be born with the complexion of an infidel Christian.

Since childhood, Aisha had differed from other children. She spoke and walked earlier than any of the others. By the time she was four, she had begun to rouse people's astonishment, disbelief, fear, and anger with her comportment, behavior, exceptional intelligence, her tendency to perform bad and even demonic acts, and an extraordinary ability to wreak vengeance on anyone who treated her hostilely or attempted to harm or mistreat her. So, everyone—adults and children—were careful not to curse, hit, or mock her, to insult her complexion, or to threaten her. Unlike other children, she didn't fear the night. At times she even liked to leave her house when people were sleeping and wander the trails. When she was six, she did that barefoot in the cold of winter. She was seen more than once at this age prowling among the graves at sunset when her blonde hair glowed brilliantly, like a firebrand. Early in life she began to sing the most famous songs that adults performed and quickly memorized any song she heard. In her enchanting voice, she sang while nodding her golden head, with her blue eyes halfway shut. To classic Levantine songs, she also performed amazing dance routines. She moved so swiftly that people imagined she was flying through space and had vaporized in the air before she reappeared. She would turn and turn and turn like a flaming torch. When she sang melancholy songs, tears glistened in her eyes:

The eye laments separation from my gazelle.
Even sweet sleep isn't sweet for me.
What I experience at night is anxiety.
Misfortune has devastated me.
A fire flames in my heart,
Like a wildfire spreading through a grain field,
For my dark-eyed sweetheart, who has left,
Never to return.

Aisha the Blonde loved to provoke adults and to "play with their minds," as she put it. She wasn't ashamed to say or do in their presence things other children would never have dared. Once she stopped in front of the elderly imam, who was discussing the role of religion in life and standards of good and evil with some men. Then she said to him huffily and sarcastically, "It would be better for you to trim your filthy nose hair instead of haranguing people who don't understand what you're saying." The sheikh's dismay and rage showed on his face, but he remained rigid and still, not knowing what to say or do. The other men could scarcely restrain their laughter. Then the man rose, brandishing his stick and intending to teach Aisha the Blonde a lesson, but she had melted away like a jinn. When, one fiery midday, she was returning home, singing some of her favorite songs, a dissolute man smiled at her. She immediately raised her middle finger at him and shouted, "Ride this, Ape!" She was fascinated by filthy and obscene words and feared no one. If they scolded her for her lewd talk, she replied defiantly, "I learned all this from you. Why do you scold me for it?"

Aisha the Blonde shunned the company of girls her age, treated them harshly, hostilely, and contemptuously, and acted with them like an elderly, gray-haired woman whom life had robbed of affection and love, leaving her only a bawdy tongue and a hard heart. If they attempted to approach her, she shouted at them, "Quick! Return to the laps of your mothers, those harlots." She did like boys, especially ones older than she was. She laughed merrily when she spoke with them, and frolicked with them in the fields, hunting birds and searching for nests. She swam in creeks with them during summer's scorching days. In their company and under their protection, she slipped into orchards to steal almonds, figs, and apples. They obeyed her and followed her orders as if she were a favorite leader whose request was not to be rejected.

When she was ten, a rumor circulated that ruined her relationship with them. A herdsman reported he had surprised Aisha the Blonde with five boys in the wadi. She was naked and the boys were too. He said they were doing things with each other that the eye hated to see and the ear to hear. Men became furious and were all riled up, and women wailed and felt alarmed. The village had never experienced such a violation of its taboos before. At least one man threatened to slaughter Aisha the Blonde to punish her for this abominable deed. According to the men, and thus according to all the adults, she was the guilty party. The boys had been seduced by her when she tempted them into depravity and vice. This was only to be expected because she was born a demon and would remain demonic to the end. Therefore, it was necessary to plan a strategy to deliver the village from her evil before it was too late. Initially, Aisha the Blonde's parents retreated into silence, but when people surrounded them and insisted on hearing their opinion, her father remarked tersely, "My daughter says the herdsman is a liar who will soon be punished for his lie."

But where was Aisha the Blonde?

For two days, people searched for her without finding a trace. On the evening of the third day, the herdsman returned to the village covered with blood. Jackals had attacked him and slain ten of his sheep. Moreover, if the other herdsmen had not rushed to assist him, he would have perished as well. Then Aisha resurfaced—calm and silent. No one dared to approach or speak to her, and the village sank into a heavy silence. People felt gloomy now that their lies and strategies had been revealed. After this, Aisha the Blonde deserted the boys and never approached them again. She stopped singing and dancing and was seen frequently alone on the trails and out in the countryside, her golden hair cascading over her shoulders. Her blue eyes revealed the sorrow of a person whom people had betrayed and left in the lurch; she would never trust any of them again.

Once she turned twelve, Aisha's breasts grew round and firm and danced with every step she took. On witnessing her dazzling and dumbfounding beauty, many lost their equilibrium and stared at her as if she were an angel who had suddenly descended from heaven.

Then people began talking about Teacher Ziyad's insane love for Aisha the Blonde. This subject became a centerpiece of their gatherings, whether during the night or day, and preoccupied everyone—adults and children, males and females. Teacher Ziyad came to the village at the beginning of the academic year at the new school, which then had two classrooms, a small office, quarters for the teacher, and a toilet. He walked to the village from El Alaâ, which was approximately seventeen kilometers away. He brought only a suitcase, into which he had packed all his possessions: his clothes, books, and toiletries. He was exhausted when he arrived, his shoes were dusty, and sweat dripped profusely from him because of the early autumn heat and the daunting effort he had expended traveling that long distance, going up and down the hills. He was quite brown and also slender. He had curly hair and a thin nose, a light mustache, and a long neck. His narrow eyes had the determined, stubborn, self-confident look of a person who has succeeded in achieving his desired goal. People gave him a huge welcome, slaughtering a calf in his honor because they knew he would enlighten their children's minds and spread learning through the impoverished village, which was accustomed to living in dark ignorance. From the start, Teacher Ziyad appeared reticent. His was the reserve typical of loners reluctant to share their life's secrets. People noticed that he answered their questions concisely, hesitantly, and cautiously, choosing his words as if afraid of angering or harming someone. When he conversed with them, they also noticed that he used more than one accent; at times he spoke with a northern accent, then a southern, and finally a coastal one.

Someone asked, "Where are you from, sir?"

He replied, "From around Tunis."

"Do you mean from Tunis, the capital, itself?"

"No, I mean from the country of Tunisia."

"But we're all from Tunisia. We would like to know precisely where you're from."

Then Teacher Ziyad smiled enigmatically and replied, "I told you: I'm from Tunis."

That was enough to discourage folks from asking again. At the school, Teacher Ziyad's performance elicited people's admiration and appreciation because he was serious about his work and devoted his full attention to the pupils, whom he never shortchanged. He treated them like his own children and was affectionate and kind with them. He wasn't harsh, unless they were slack about their assignments or ignored the advice he gave them. He spent most of his free time in his quarters. Through its window, he could be seen lost in reading or busy correcting his pupils' copybooks. At night, his lamp remained lit late.

At the beginning of the school year, Aisha the Blonde was eleven. On the day students returned to school, the classroom was packed, and she sat at its rear. She brought with her a brown case in which she kept her notebooks and colored pencils. Teacher Ziyad scrutinized her for a long time. Then he walked toward her and asked, "What's your name, Miss?"

"Aisha."

"How old are you?"

"Eleven."

"We can't accept you in this school."

"Why not?"

"Because you're older than the legal school age."

"I don't know what you mean."

Teacher Ziyad tried to explain the meaning of "legal school age," but she interrupted him. "Sir, we built this school so we could learn. On the radio, I heard them ask fathers to send their daughters to school because it is necessary to instruct them. What's the problem?"

Nonplussed, Teacher Ziyad fell silent and taught the first lesson as if nothing had happened. That evening, though, he sent for her father, who arrived out of breath because he suffered from asthma.

"How old is your daughter?" he asked.

"I think she's eleven."

"Sir, the law says that elementary school only accepts children when they are six or seven. It may be possible to accept students who are eight with certain provisos, but with reference to your daughter, the law is clear and does not require any explanation."

"Have you explained this to her?"

"I tried, but she didn't seem inclined to understand me."

"Try again. Perhaps God will guide her to understand you."

"Why don't you?"

"I can't."

"Why not?"

"Because my daughter is used to making her own decisions without asking anyone's advice."

Aisha the Blonde continued to attend school regularly, and Teacher Ziyad didn't object again, never broaching the subject of "legal school age." Three months later, he sent for her father a second time.

"Sir, I would like to discuss an important subject with you."

"What is it?"

"Your daughter, Aisha, enjoys extraordinary intelligence and astonishing abilities."

"I know."

"She is far superior to the rest of the students in all subjects. Her writing is excellent, and her memory is powerful. Therefore, she must be helped
to catch up for the years she has missed, through no fault of her own."

"How?"

"I will volunteer to give her private lessons three times a week at the
end of the school day. I'm sure she'll be able to take the elementary certificate exam in three years at the most."

"Sir, you can do whatever you want with her, provided that she agrees."

"I've discussed the matter with her, and she is up for it."

"May God assist you and her and everyone else."

Was Aisha the Blonde's intelligence the only factor that motivated
Teacher Ziyad's offer of extra instruction? No! Never! It subsequently
became clear that he had fallen in love with her at first glance. That love
grew more ardent during the era of private lessons, even though Teacher
Ziyad was keen to avoid giving any hint of that. To forestall suspicion, he
repeated from time to time that Aisha deserved every success because she
was brilliant. He was certain she would be the first girl from the village to
obtain the elementary certificate with distinction.

The truth was that his love for her continued to torment him constantly, causing him pains, disturbances, and anxiety. It drove sleep from
his eyes, and he would remain awake all night long. He composed poems
for her and love letters moistened by his tears. Then he would hide these
and never send them. She did not reciprocate his love. Instead, she trifled
with his affections. At times she would let him touch her hand or neck.
Then she would quickly rebuff him with her demonic wiles and guile. All
the same, his love for her increased in intensity and ferocity.

Thanks to those private lessons, Aisha the Blonde dashed through all
the levels and after three years took the exam for the elementary certificate, earning honors. Delighted by this, Teacher Ziyad gave a party for
her at the school, and many attended. During this celebration, he gave
a brief speech in which he lauded her intelligence and asserted that she
would make the village proud. Like a princess wearing a diadem, Aisha

the Blonde rose to say she was indebted to her "dear teacher" for the great success she had achieved.

At the end of the summer vacation, Aisha the Blonde began her preparations for enrolling at the Institute for Girls in Kairouan. A day before she departed, she was seen with Teacher Ziyad in the classroom. No one knew what took place during that meeting, which lasted more than an hour. People noticed, however, that Teacher Ziyad's condition took a turn for the worse afterwards and continued to deteriorate day by day. His pupils were alarmed by the rapid changes affecting him. He neglected his appearance, lost his calm and composure, began to grow angry and lose his temper at the most trivial provocations. Then he would scream like a madman and inflict harsh punishments on them for no reason at all. At times he would stop teaching class and begin pacing around the classroom with his eyes fixed on the floor while his lips quivered. During his free time, he rambled through the countryside—stumbling, pale-faced, with wandering gaze. People who did not know him assumed he was a wretched vagrant who went begging through rural regions. The elderly school watchman mentioned that he had heard him scream at night more than once and weep, repeating the name of Aisha the Blonde.

The day before the winter vacation, Teacher Ziyad entered the classroom morose and silent and remained that way until the end of the period. Then he burst into tears and left the classroom, reeling like a drunk. The next day he disappeared, never to be seen again. People found in his quarters a pile of torn-up letters, all addressed to "my love, dear Aisha."

With the passing years, Aisha the Blonde's trips to the village decreased. Her parents visited her in Kairouan twice a year. When people asked about her, they replied simply, "She's fine, praise God." When they both died—in the same year and the same month—she attended each funeral. With calm silence, she accepted condolences and afterward stopped visiting the village. People forgot her, but when they did remember her, they referred to her as if she were the heroine of an ancient fairy tale.

Stories, stories, stories . . . one story leads to another, and life itself is a story in which laughter mixes with crying, sorrow with happiness, despair with hope, fear with courage, weakness with power, illness with health, and treachery with love. Shahrazad never tired of telling stories. She always knew how to begin and when to end. Enchanted by the magic of her stories, King Shahriyar relented, forgot his desire to wreak vengeance on cheating women, and became as meek as a child. People in the village were keen to hear stories that helped them forget their poverty, ordeals, calamities, and death. Apuleius, the first African novelist, proposed at the beginning of his superb book *The Metamorphoses* or *The Golden Ass* that he would recount a series of diverse stories to "delight with them the indulgent ear" of the listener.

But was it enough for him to narrate stories he heard, lived, or imagined? Yunus asked himself this after writing ten stories in a few months. He attempted to discover the answer from authors he admired. All of them agreed that a writer cannot be a true author without experiencing life, living it like an exciting adventure, mixing with people, and exploring the depths of the human soul. That meant that he was still on the surface, self-absorbed, apprehensive, and hesitant. Therefore, what he wrote would remain meaningless and overly bland and would quickly wilt and be forgotten. Flaubert, who devoted half a day, or the entire day, to writing a single sentence, had traveled through many lands to become acquainted with mankind, discovering the conditions of peoples and nations, studying their history, customs, and cultures, while recording in notebooks everything he heard, saw, and felt. Without all this, he would never have written his splendid works and would not have uttered his famous phrase: "Madame Bovary, *c'est moi*: I am Madame Bovary." It was high time for Yunus to leave the village and move to large cities, where life's clamor is found, and adventures, which would liberate him from his shyness, fears, and rural complexes, awaited him.

The next time he was in Kairouan he did not go to the great mosque and the mausoleum of Abu Zama'a al-Balawi as he typically had done on previous visits. Instead, he accompanied a cousin, who worked as a carpenter there, to a working-class bar to drink his first beer and smoke his first cigarette. At the end of the evening, he entered a brothel to find himself facing half-naked women, all of whom were talking dirty and acting flirtatiously and playfully. Flabbergasted, he retreated, wanting to leave, but his cousin shoved him forward forcefully, saying, "Pick a pretty one for yourself, and I'll pay." The youngest girl excited him. She was brown and of medium height, with jet-black hair that hung over her naked shoulders. Her face was round, and her black eyes retained some of their childish innocence. She had firm lips, and there was a slight hoarseness to her voice. She washed his organ with warm water and then stretched out on the bed, opening her thighs. So he threw himself on her and quickly did it with her. When he was pulling his underpants back on, she asked him gently, "Is this the first time? Never mind: God willing, next time will be better."

During that same summer vacation, he visited the capital and stayed with another cousin, who lived on a street near the Broadcasting Building. Almost every day he saw recording and theater stars: Sidi Ali Riahi with his magnificent linen cloak, his hair combed into a pyramid, and his broad, complacent face; Oulaya with her wide black eyes, her sweet smile, and her impetuosity that aroused desires; Naama with her dancing step, boisterous laughter, and irresistible flirtatiousness; Yousef Al-Tamimi with his country-bumpkin face, bushy mustache, and slow gait; Hédi Jouini with his Andalusian features, delicate mustache, lanky build, perennial elegance, and aristocratic grace; Hédi Semlali, whose face had developed wrinkles, whose eyes had lost their gleam, and whose chin drooped, thanks to late nights, alcohol, and smoking; and Abdel Aziz El Aroui, who had grown old and tired and drank coffee slowly while surrounded by admirers.

Each morning Yunus spent a couple of hours in the American Cultural Center, where he read novels by Hemingway, Erskine Caldwell, John Steinbeck, and Mark Twain, and stories by Edgar Allan Poe. After that, he toured secondhand bookstores. For a cheap price he bought (mainly French) books that appealed to him. After his siesta, he liked to drink a beer or two at the bars of the Lafayette District, where plump old Jewish ladies sat to play cards and drink *vin rosé* or *boukha* distilled from figs, while talking loudly nonstop. At the end of the evening, he would tour Bab al Bahr, which was full to overflowing with beautiful girls whose short skirts and tight pants showed off their charms. He never tired of following them stealthily with glances directed toward their boobs and butts. During the night he would conjure them up from his imagination and sleep among them, but now they all were naked. Occasionally he would penetrate the Medina by the narrow Jamia Ez-Zitouna lane, which was crowded with tourists. He would prowl the Medina's delightful markets for hours and leaf through elegant books in bookstores specializing in works of cultural heritage or sniff the fragrances of delicious, traditional dishes from the small restaurants. With every step he took, history manifested itself to him with its virtues and faults, victories and defeats, misfortunes and festivities, painful and happy periods, and through people who had left their imprints on it, whether they were extraordinary scholars, honorable reformers, oppressive or upright kings, cowards and brave people, or strong and weak. He could hear the voice of the historian discussing the Medina:

> Its ancient name was Tarshish, and then it was called Ta'nis and Tunis because it pleased anyone who visited it or resided there. Later it was al-Hadira because it was the "Hadra" or capital of the Hafsid sultans who improved its prosperity, built its markets, and expanded its footprint, making it the finest city in all Maghreb. It was also called al-Khadra' or the Green because it had so many olive trees, which stay green all year round. They are blessed trees.

Then he rode the train to the northern suburbs to spend an entire day there. Carthage was his first stop. He walked among its ruins, recalling its wonderful legends and bygone glories, the terrifying wars that it suffered in succession and that burned it down more than once, and the numerous raids that had been launched against it. The extreme heat forced him to sit beneath a tree that afforded luxuriant shade. He ate the sandwich he had brought in a small bag and then opened the novel *Salammbô* by Flaubert to the page he had reached the previous evening. He read:

> Carthage thus deployed herself before the soldiers now encamped on the plains.
>
> From the distance the soldiers could recognise the markets and the cross-roads, and disputed among themselves as to the sites of the various temples. Khamoûn faced the Syssites, and had golden tiles; Melkarth, to the left of Eschmoûn, bore on its roof coral branches; Tanit, beyond, rounded up through the palm-trees its copper cupola; and the black Moloch stood below the cisterns at the side of the lighthouse.

One could see at the angles of the frontons, on the summit of the walls, at the corners of the squares, everywhere, the various divinities with their hideous heads, colossal or dwarfish, with enormous or with immeasurable flattened bellies, open jaws, and outspread arms, holding in their hands pitchforks, chains, or javelins. And the blue sea spread out at the end of the streets, which the perspective rendered even steeper.[12]

All that remained of the scene Flaubert described was the sea's blue, which dominated all the other colors. It almost seemed that this was all there was—that there were no green gardens or white residences—everything was blue. The whole city was blue. He spent his siesta under the tree. When he grew tired of reading, he slept for an entire hour. Then he rode the train to Sidi Bou Said, and after that to al-Marsa, not returning to the capital until the beginning of the night.

In the filthy old bus that carried him back to his village, he sensed that his first visit to the capital had changed his entire life, deepened his experiences, opened his eyes to new worlds he had never been acquainted with, and liberated him from the monotony, coarseness, and stagnation of the rural areas. He would go far—very, very far—to where extraordinary words glittered like necklaces on the breasts of princesses, and the text he wrote, thanks to "a special approach to life," as his master Flaubert put it, would be something more than a thrilling tale.

5

During that period of research and experimentation, he read works by writers and poets of his own country. What attracted his attention was that even the finest had struggled against tyranny, bigotry, and despotism and had paid dearly for their efforts. They had died young—between twenty and forty—from heart disease, tuberculosis, or some other chronic disease or from neglect and ostracism by a society that crushed anyone who rejected its viewpoint and deviated from its laws and stern traditions. The one story he read by a writer called T. S. had shown a talent that differed in no way from that of the foreign authors who enthralled him. Even so, Yunus could not discover whether this author had died or was still alive. The story's hero, who was fast approaching middle age, fell in love with his beautiful Italian neighbor. She sold wine and milk, and her husband had been killed in World War I. This hero lived in state of constant tension that left him half crazed. His stress became even more pronounced when he heard the cock crow at dawn from his Italian neighbor's house. The cock's crow may have reminded him of her dead husband and interrupted his erotic dreams, plunging him back into his bleak reality, which lacked any stimulation because the Italian woman did not reciprocate his love and ignored him. In fact, she treated him as if he did not exist. In one paragraph, the man described his stress: "My nervous agitation keeps me from understanding what I want to do. Otherwise, why would the cock crowing bother me when I pass by the woman baker like a high-minded gentleman? Isn't death a mighty cock-a-doodle-doo in the face of life?"

On his second visit to the capital, while roaming through the ancient Medina, Yunus saw the author B. Kh. Elegantly dressed in traditional Tunisian attire, he was sitting in a small coffeehouse near Ez-Zitouna

Mosque. There was a jasmine sprig behind his left ear, and on the table in front of him sat a glass of hot green tea with mint, a small bottle of Safia mineral water, and the newspaper *al-Sabah*. He had discovered this author from a very short story, which was no more than two pages long. It described a sixteen-year-old girl who is forced to marry a man over forty. On her wedding night, without her or the groom's family noticing, she slips to the house's roof terrace to meet her boyfriend, who is her own age. There they melt into fervent kisses. Even when voices call her loudly and alarmed people search for her anxiously, she remains in her lover's arms, totally oblivious to everything.

That story had motivated Yunus to read other stories and novels by this writer. They were all marvelous in language and style, profound in their content and allusions, enjoyable and original in their subjects. According to a biography, B. Kh. left his birthplace in southern Tunisia when he was three to settle with his family in Tunis's Medina. When he arrived there after an exhausting trip on a slow train, the first things that astonished him were the many tall buildings, the extreme congestion of the streets, the absence of palm trees and sand dunes, and the tiles and electric lighting in their ancient house, which had white walls with blue doors and windows. All of B. Kh.'s short stories and novels, which reflected his life, alternated between the capital and his hometown. They painted an extraordinary portrait of the life of ordinary and marginalized people in the ancient Medina and in Tunisia's southern oases.

Feeling embarrassed, he approached B. Kh., greeted him, and asked permission to join him briefly. The writer graciously and politely agreed, saying, "Please do. I have a lot of time this morning." Yunus started by introducing himself. Then he expressed admiration for the author's short stories and novels he had read, especially the novel describing the lives of people in the south during the colonial period.

B. Kh. listened to him attentively and then commented, "You're clearly an excellent reader. Your comments are perceptive and reveal your knowledge of my works and of world literature too." Yes, he read a lot and liked French, Russian, and American writers. To demonstrate the breadth of his reading, he recited the titles of some famous works by these authors. Increasingly surprised by what he heard, B. Kh. said, "Ah . . . I'm happy to meet a youth like you because I was beginning to believe that young people today aren't interested in literature. Now I see I've been mistaken." As their rapport grew, his embarrassment and shyness faded, and he felt that no barrier separated him from B. Kh.—not the difference of age nor the extent of their respective experience with life and writing. Now they were two friends exchanging observations and thoughts about Flaubert, Balzac, Stendhal, Dostoyevsky, Gogol, and Chekhov. Then he asked B. Kh. about the writers and poets who had died young. He replied, "I knew all of them, some intimately and others only superficially. I attended some of their funerals. Their daytime was night and their nighttime day. What they wrote reflected their difficult lives, which were filled with pitfalls and stumbles, the instability of their difficult era, and the overarching troubles. Religious leaders hated them and fought them tooth and nail—exhorting people to renounce, despise, and shun them—even though they were the finest people our country has produced. Unfortunately, however, death carried them away in their prime. I learned to write from them. I am possibly one of the few to have escaped the serious illnesses that afflicted them. Unlike them, I did not plunge into the rowdy, wanton life they indulged in to escape from their bitter reality. Al-Shabbi was destroyed by his exuberant emotions and extreme sensitivity. I remember that my brother and I visited him in the hospital only a week before he died. He was pale and sad. When we said good-bye, he told us, 'I will definitely leave this world soon. What is tearing me apart now is that life won't let me achieve what I once dreamt of accomplishing.' He died at the age of twenty-five, but what he achieved in that brief time is beyond description."

When I mentioned the short story by T. S., his features showed his profound sorrow, and his eyes teared up. "Oh!" T. S. had been his dear friend, and they had met almost daily. "He was a torch of intelligence and perspicacity. You never saw him without a book. No matter what he said, it aroused people's attention. But life dealt him a losing hand and betrayed him."

"How so?"

"When he was ten, T. S. left Djerba, his island home, to join his older brother, who worked as a merchant in the capital. After earning his primary school certificate, he enrolled at al-Sadiqiya School but soon dropped out to work in commerce, although for a limited number of hours a day. He spent the remainder of his time reading and writing. A gracious companion and a person with exemplary morals and a honeyed tongue, he had a taste for life's pleasures, but not to excess. At literary gatherings, his comments astonished his listeners because he knew world literature, ancient and modern. He was also well versed in philosophy and history and was a keen observer of the mysteries of politics. He loved to talk about Aristotle, Plato, Saint Augustine, Ibn Rushd, Ibn Khaldun, Spinoza, Marx, and Freud and had a knack for transporting his listeners to the worlds of Goethe, Shakespeare, Dante, al-Ma'arri, and Abu Hayyan al-Tawhidi. Everyone profited from his vast knowledge and varied and diverse reading.

"When the story you just mentioned was published, we all felt even greater admiration for him and clustered around him because, with it, he had handed us a certificate that attested to his genius and his ability to produce wonders. Personally, I consider that story to be the first one that pushed our prose literature out of its traditional framework and beyond its imitation of other literatures into true, authentic creativity. The most awe-inspiring aspect of the story is the poetic mood that envelopes it from beginning to end, an ambiance we find in stories by Gogol, Chekhov, Edgar Allan Poe, and Maupassant. We waited for T. S. to publish other stories, but he didn't. When we asked why not, T. S. would reply with a smile, 'Anything beautiful requires time and patience. Haste only produces regret. Isn't that so?' He was reticent and rarely discussed his projects or writing. One day, though, he admitted to me that he was busy writing a novella set during the Spanish invasion of Tunis. The heroine, a princess, observed events from inside the walls of her palace and collected reports from Black servants she sent daily to the markets and mosques and to the Halq al-Wadi harbor, where the invaders' ships were anchored. When he finished writing it, he invited us to drink a beer at Bab al Bahr and told me, 'I think I've succeeded in writing the story I mentioned to you. I intend to publish it in the East, where there are real readers and critics, rather than in Tunis. You know al-Shabbi gained recognition in Cairo. Here he was treated harshly and disdainfully.' Later he told me he was writing a novel inspired by the tragedy of Habiba Msika, the Jewish singer whose lover torched her. Residents of the capital—Jews, Muslims, and Christians—marched in her funeral procession. I think T. S. had other writing projects too, not just short stories and novels. A friend told me he wrote a book called *Modern Tunis*. I remember that T. S. would disappear for weeks or days; we assumed he was occupied with his business or visiting his hometown. Subsequently we discovered, however, that there was another reason for these disappearances. As the nation moved toward independence, we realized that T. S. was active in resistance to French colonial rule and diligently attended secret sessions and meetings. He took charge of some operations to contact patriots in the interior. Consultations and negotiations about independence were taking place when a fierce struggle erupted between the two major nationalist leaders. T. S. backed one and began to distribute tracts in support and defense of him.

"The rivalry between these two leaders grew more intense and serious, dividing people, as the country hovered on the brink of a destructive civil war. The leader whom T. S. backed, however, was soon defeated and fled abroad. Then the victorious leader issued instructions and orders to liquidate his rival's supporters and pursue them throughout the country. Dozens were slain, and hundreds were sent to prisons and concentration camps, where they were subjected to savage torture, which killed some and left others with severe disabilities.

"During that black period, T. S. vanished. I searched for him in all his haunts but found no trace of him. When I asked his acquaintances about him, they either looked away or just said they knew nothing about him. What really upset me was that most of the literary figures who had close ties to him stopped talking about him—as if he had never lived among them. Finally, I yielded to the bitter reality and wept for my companion, convinced that he had been killed or incarcerated for many years.

"Five years later, something that I had definitely not anticipated happened. During the summer when the Bizerte War flared up, I returned to my house in the Medina one day at 1:00 p.m. When I was preparing for a post-lunch siesta, there was a knock on the door. T. S. appeared before me in shabby clothes, emaciated, with a dirty face—as if he had just emerged from the grave. We embraced fondly and sat in the small parlor, where he told me about his long absence. After the leader he supported fled, he was alarmed and destroyed many of his papers, documents, manuscripts, and books, leaving nothing to incriminate him. Then he left the capital to live out of sight, moving between various places. He spent many weeks and months without ever seeing daylight, speaking to people, tasting a hot meal, drinking aromatic coffee, or reading a newspaper or a book. Cigarettes provided his only relief during this ordeal, and he smoked dozens a day. His relatives knew nothing about him and thought he was dead or lost. The girl whom he had loved and who had loved him forgot him and married one of his longtime friends. In his hideouts, he lived in constant fear, conscious that at any moment, day or night, he might be arrested and thrown into prison like his companions in the struggle. Fear paralyzed his thinking and made it impossible for him to focus or record his observations and feelings. When he learned there was a general amnesty for supporters of the routed leader, he returned to the capital. The shock he experienced during the first hours after his return devastated him because during his absence his older brother had destroyed all his remaining papers, including his short stories and novels. The only story to escape this inferno was the one you mentioned. I suspect that this shock was responsible for ending my friend T. S.'s relationship with literature and writing. He subsequently devoted himself entirely to commerce. Every time I met him, I noticed that he avoided any reference to his past. He limited himself to recounting tales and anecdotes he had heard in the market or to discussing little problems he confronted in daily life. If I referred to a book I had read or a short story or novel I liked, he would jump up as if stung and leave, saying, 'See you soon, Friend.'

"T. S. married a divorcée, and they had a daughter and a son. Diseases finally got the better of him, and he died at the age of forty-five. Only his relatives and some merchants attended his funeral. None of the literary, educated people who used to evince affection and friendship for him came." B. Kh. was silent for some minutes while he gazed at the traffic on the street and smoked. Then he turned to me and said, "Listen, young man, it is an awesome thing to love literature. Perhaps you dream of becoming a writer or poet one day. But you should realize that writing in this country is a curse and a trial. So, you must beware of the devastating shock my friend T. S. experienced." B. Kh. took his leave and was soon lost in the crowd—a frustrated man with a wounded heart and spirit.

Since that time, Yunus had been writing, without publishing, under the pen name he had chosen: Solitaire. The many short stories, novels, and texts he had written over the last forty years were stuffed in a cabinet. He had occasionally considered burning or destroying them but had always postponed that to some unspecified time.

His cell phone rang. It was his daughter Maryam: "A lovely morning to you, Papa! Happy birthday and many happy returns of the day! Don't think I've forgotten you. I've been asleep and just woke up. And here I am calling you. By God, I wanted to visit you today and spend two or three days with you. But that seems difficult. I'll do it soon . . . very soon. I promise. Listen, Papa . . . I only have five hundred milliemes left on my phone. Can you call me?"

He phoned her back. "How are you, dear Maryuma? I really, really miss you." She did too but felt anxious. Her nerves were shot. She couldn't think straight. She didn't fall asleep until late at night. It was hard for her to concentrate. That's why she had stopped attending lectures at the university. Occasionally she went with girlfriends to drink coffee at Bab al Bahr, Sidi Bou Said, or El Menzah. She watched videos of old films, but when she picked up a book, she could read only a few lines before she tossed it aside. She didn't know why.

"Perhaps you're in love, dear Maryuma?"

A loud laugh. "No, no . . . definitely not! By God, Papa!" She didn't trust today's young men, most of whom were superficial and interested only in silly, trivial things. None of them were capable of uttering a lovely Romantic phrase. She was a Romantic and loved Romantic men. But to escape from the disturbing condition that had afflicted her for weeks, she was thinking of going to Paris. She had an awesome friend who studied there. She could stay with her. She had visited Paris twice but could never get enough of it. The only museum she had visited was the Louvre; she wanted to visit all the other major museums to cleanse her eyes of the filth of Arab cities. "Ha, ha, ha! Isn't that right? You're the one who told me this when you gave me a book of the most famous paintings in the Louvre. Remember?" Yes, he did. She was thirteen then. She remembered too that he always used to tell her about Paris, to show her pictures of its boulevards and gardens, the Eiffel Tower, the Cathedral of Notre Dame, and the Palace of Versailles. Oh! How beautiful those days were! Yes. They really were beautiful.

"Papa, do you still love Paris?"

He did not know. He no longer knew what he loved or hated. Everything seemed on a par to him.

"Is that because of your age?"

"Perhaps."

But Paris really was the City of Light, and life was good there. All it would take for her to forget the anxiety tormenting her now was an excursion along the banks of the Seine in sunshine, rain, or snow. She had to go. Had to! She might do that during her winter break and spend Christmas there. Her girlfriend had assured her that Paris was amazing during the final month of the year. Candles and dances, presents and invitations to fine dinners, and other amazing things. Her mother had promised to buy her plane ticket. The rest would be up to him . . .

"Oh, Papa, you're always super! You've never let me down." But how would he celebrate his birthday?

It would be an ordinary day. He would go for a walk on the beach, as he did almost every day. At the end of the evening, he would go to the Albatross Restaurant for a drink with his friends. Then he would return home to watch a TV show or a video.

But she couldn't believe he was sixty!

"Does that frighten you?"

Silence . . . then: "No, no . . ." Silence again. Then: what mattered was that he still enjoyed good health. She had noticed lately he seemed younger than his chronological age. Perhaps that could be attributed to his having left the capital to live in a quiet city by the sea. Life in the capital was intolerable now . . . an unbearable inferno! People were nervous and violent . . . stressed out all the time! "You politely ask someone to let you pass or anything like that, and he curses you and your parents. If you're offended, he punches you, spits in your face, or calls you the worst possible names. You're a hillbilly snob, troublesome vermin, or a stray dog. Night and day, unemployed youth attack riders on the light-rail Metro or in public buses and steal their money and cell phones and rip off women's necklaces and handbags. Yes, dear Papa, there are incidents like these in the capital every day." She made a point of returning home before dark. It was true that her neighborhood was quiet and its residents respectable, but who could say? That was why one needed to be careful and take precautions and avoid nasty surprises. She wished she could leave the capital and live with him in Neapolis, but necessity had its own rules. "Isn't that so, Papa?" Yes, she was right in everything she said. Silence. Then: "But what about my master's thesis? Do you still want me to devote it to Céline, as you previously suggested? But dearest Papa, this writer terrifies me. He's like a tsunami that sweeps away everything in its path." She didn't deny that she liked him a lot, but his world was frightening. No other author resembled him. That's why she would rather devote her thesis to Jean Giono. "What do you think, Papa?"

"A splendid writer, no doubt."

"Yes . . . a splendid writer." She had read many of his novels and liked all of them. Now she felt he was the writer closest to her and her temperament. His world was simple and original at the same time. It contained forests, shepherds, beautiful peasant women, simple folk, wise old women, birds, the murmur of brooks in the mountains, nights studded with stars, a fire in the woodstove, and thrilling tales, which seemed endless. That was why she wanted to devote her master's thesis to this author. So be it. That was what she ought to do; he would help her and give her important texts for Jean Giono. She might benefit from them. "Thanks, Papa!"

Silence. Then: "You know I love you very much, Papa, but occasionally you hurt me." How could that be? He never asked about her mother. How was she? Terrible. She was a tortured soul, especially nowadays and suffered from suspicions . . . had terrifying nightmares every night, extreme attacks of nerves. Goes without food. Repeated absences from work. Bouts of weeping and screaming. Almost constant depression. Fear of death. Always visiting clinics. Physicians claimed her health was excellent. She just needed a long rest or a trip, inside or outside the country. But she rejected their test results and said consistently that some malady was devouring her body—that it had to be discovered before it was too late. She did everything she could to calm and reassure her mother. She sat with her every day and tried—with stories and anecdotes—to make her laugh the way she once had. But her mother remained silent and morose.

Finally, she would flee to her room, where she burst into tears. She didn't know what to do. She was exhausted and couldn't bear to watch her dear mother wither away before her eyes—to age and slowly descend into the abyss. "Oh, Papa, if you saw her now, you wouldn't believe your eyes. She is a shadow of her former self." She was very worried about her mother. "What can I do, dear Papa?"

He did not know. She knew full well that her mother did not want to even hear his name. Since he had left the house, she had worked hard to erase every trace of him—as if he had never existed. So how could he help? She would need to be patient and wait. Perhaps her mother's condition would improve. She did not think so. In any event, he couldn't do anything. It was a sorry state of affairs, but that was the truth.

Silence. Then: "Dear Papa, perhaps I've upset you by talking about this on your birthday. I apologize for that."

No, no, she didn't need to apologize. She knew his heart was always open to her, no matter what. "Isn't that so?"

"Yes, that's true. Thanks, Papa. Happy birthday again."

"Thanks, dear Maryuma. You must visit me before you leave for Paris."

"I will."

"Until we see each other in Neapolis."

Once this conversation ended, he felt as exhausted as if he had just performed a taxing chore. He lay down on the sofa in the living room, and memories of his divorce five years earlier returned.

A cold downpour . . . the smell of overflowing storm sewers that the torrents had flooded . . . intense congestion . . . the loud roar of vehicles . . . insults, curses, and obscenities colliding in the air. The city was as dreary and gloomy as if a disaster had struck it. There was no trace of the city's two dominant colors: white and blue. The only hue was dirty gray. People were discussing floods inundating poor neighborhoods in the city. Bridges and overpasses were destroyed, and houses had collapsed on their inhabitants' heads, leaving heavy material losses and many victims—no one knew how many because the media was not much interested in the loss of human lives. They were also not disposed to discuss material losses because that might harm the nation's reputation for safety and security and prompt tourists to consider alternative destinations. Vested interests might exploit such reports for base goals that could shake the country's stability and stir civil unrest. Therefore, a deft, quick mention of such incidents was preferable, without going into details or being too precise about results or consequences. Besides, what could be done about nature's fury and fluctuations? Nature might grow angry and appear mercurial anywhere in the world—even rich, developed countries weren't spared. Had people forgotten Noah's flood? Besides, what were these floods compared to the disasters and calamities experienced by other countries that were plunged in civil wars? Atrocious massacres took place daily and didn't spare young or old, women or men. When the media went to pains to ignore reality and conceal the facts, people resorted to rumors, which spread through the country like an infection through a body.

A filthy torrent of rain . . . he was walking aimlessly amidst a dense, unruly crowd that emitted clashing waves of the curses, insults, and obscenities people of his country favored. They were past masters of these and performed miracles with them. Without them, their joy and anger would have been meaningless. They would not have enjoyed life and wouldn't have experienced passionate love or exchanged jokes and information. They wouldn't have drunk or eaten, walked or worked, screwed their women or expressed their feelings, emotions, and opinions. Aroused by them, women became more excited and lustful in bed. For this reason, such words were always present in their lives . . . to the point that they almost constituted their identity.

Under dirty, heavy, chilling rain, he continued walking, oblivious to the number of hours he had slogged along or to the distance he had covered. His clothes were soaked, and his shoes were wet, but he didn't want to stop, not even momentarily. The intensity of the inferno inside him could only be diminished by plodding through torrents of rain.

As he walked, his wife's shouts echoed in his ears and, at times, even drowned out the city's clamor: "You're an ignoramus, a coward, a pathetic failure, a liar, a hypocrite, a cheat . . . two-faced! No, ten-faced! All bad qualities unite in you; you don't lack a single one. Get out of the house right now! I can't bear to see or hear or smell you any longer! Go to hell and have a miserable life! You and your culture, your books and your fantasies! I hate you! I hate everything about you! I hate the way you talk, the way you eat, the way you treat me and other people. Uff! My God! How have I put up with you for thirty years? How could I have wasted my youth and the best years of my life with a vile man like you? How could I have done this to myself? Oh! That's my mistake. No, it's my inexcusable crime that has caused me to suffer all these pains and agonies now. What did I ever find attractive about you? What made me love and marry you? Why has it taken me all these years to open my eyes to the bitter truth? No, the deadly truth! Go! Leave the house! Leave now or I'll kill you or kill myself. It will be your fault in either case. I'll erase every trace of you and live the remaining years of my life in peace and tranquility. I'll try to mend what is rent and to restore what has been spoiled. I still have the energy to do that. Yes, I still have some energy. Oh, what curse descended on me? Did I commit some evil that deserved such painful punishment? No . . . no . . . no. I've never done anything wrong! No, you're to blame. Yes, you're what's wrong! You are the evil! You are responsible for all the devastation afflicting me. Get out of the house! Do whatever you want, but don't ever return here. Ever! Because I can no longer bear to live with you under one roof! No, no, no, I won't accept that! Will not! Have you heard me clearly? Wretch, have you understood me? You libertine! You smelly drunk! Get out! Scram! Go!"

Maryam had watched the sad scene silently. Then she burst into tears and disappeared. He put some clothes and books in his bag and left the house at 10:00 p.m., pursued by his wife's screams. He spent the night at the Grand Hotel de France, where his master Flaubert stayed during his visit to Tunis in 1858. He was only able to sleep an hour. At daybreak he left the hotel and wandered through the city, which was drowned by torrential autumn rains.

Her outburst did not come as a surprise. For years, warning signs had threatened an eruption at any moment. His wife had set the stage in various ways. Weeks—even months—passed without her exchanging a word with him. A thick, cold silence spread melancholy and gloom throughout the house, which grew desolate and depressing, as if it had been abandoned. Maryam would try to break the dreadful silence by telling jokes, relating anecdotes, offering some comment on what was happening in the country, or discussing problems she had with her courses. Eventually, though, she would dash to her room in tears. Relying heavily on rejection and evasion, his wife would conduct herself at home as if he were not there or his presence was undesirable. She would express her displeasure with ugly grimaces and twitches, by breaking dishes and glasses, with ferocious temper tantrums over trivial matters, by raising her voice to curse matrimony and to complain about the vile and crafty nature of men, by refusing to sit with him at the table for breakfast, lunch, or dinner. Four years earlier she had quit the conjugal bed and taken her former office for her bedroom. On feast days and festivals, she would set out for unknown destinations—ones he would learn weeks or even months later—always from Maryam.

He had responded patiently, silently, and calmly to these serious and fast-breaking developments in his marriage. Occasionally he would endeavor to mend the rift by speaking graciously to his wife or asking her advice or opinion on some matter, but then she would become even more hostile and contemptuous. Eventually he grew convinced that all his attempts to mollify her were meaningless and pointless and even added more fuel to the fire. So, he had stopped trying while he waited for the devastating tempest to erupt. Now it finally had. Painful and bitter as this was, he felt a sense of relief and liberation because waiting for the storm had oppressed and enervated him, distorted his thinking, and frozen his feelings and emotions. The life he had been living had consisted of monotonous, arid days—in slow, tedious succession—that shoved him down a dark, brackish pit where death seemed the best way to liberate himself from his pains and worries. But who was responsible for what had happened? Was it his wife? No, no, no! Was he responsible? He wasn't to blame either. It was time. Oh, time . . . time, which betrays and cheats everyone.

Time had unexpected consequences. It destroyed beauty, deformed bodies and souls, ruined minds and relationships, turned criminals into innocent people and innocent people into criminals, a king to a slave and a slave to a king.

Time withers love, which dwindles so quickly that it seems never to have been a flame that once scorched lovers' hearts. It separates brothers, lovers, and friends. It sinks mighty, dread empires in the wink of an eye, and turns conjugal life into an unbearable hell.

Yes, time was to blame.

Anyone who wasn't on guard against time would come to a disastrous end.

He had begun to sense the effects of time's treachery when he approached the age of fifty. He had felt the effects of time not only on his body, not only in the changes that started to appear in his thinking, emotions, or attitude to life, but in the way other people viewed him, in the way they treated him. He also sensed it in the stern aversion with which young women rebuffed him when he tried to flirt or chat. One girl had even raised her voice when his gaze lingered too long on her charms: "Oh! What does this shithead want? Isn't he embarrassed by his gray hair?"

His wife did not seem to understand the effects of treacherous time, or perhaps felt them but not as a devastating blow. Possibly for this reason, during the last few years she had become a humorless, obstinate, stern, ill-tempered woman who grew angry and burst into tears for the most trivial reasons. She certainly felt some vertigo and terror when she contrasted the splendid, dazzling image of the past to the hideous pains those splendors had led to.

For his part, he had yielded to time, allowing it a free hand with him, and was content to recall beautiful memories now and again.

He had loved her at first sight. It had been a *coup de tonnerre* as the French say—a thunderbolt. One rainy autumn morning he had observed her drinking coffee in the cafeteria at the university. Her face and green eyes looked pure and innocent in a Romantic way that was irresistible. This romanticism resembled the Romanticism that fascinated him in books, although he had never found a real-life equivalent before. When she finished her coffee, she walked across the courtyard through the rain without opening the umbrella she held in her left hand. Once she disappeared beneath the porticoes, he felt he had witnessed a marvelous scene in a romantic film set in some gray, northern city. The poem by Jacques Prévert about Barbara beneath the rain in Brest ran through his mind.[13] This romantic scene took on added brilliance and enchantment as he spent the rest of the day remembering it—oblivious, or nearly oblivious—to his classes, lectures, and friends' remarks.

In a few days, he gathered some information about her. He learned that her name was Hadiya and that she was a history student. He also learned that she lived in the capital, in the Medina. Her friends at the university agreed she was extremely shy and tight-lipped about her personal life. All the same, they liked and respected her. They mentioned her graciousness, equanimity, calm, and intelligence, which her professors had praised more than once.

He made a point each day of sitting in a distant corner so he could watch her sip her coffee deliberately or flip through her notebooks, totally oblivious to her surroundings. Matters continued in this fashion for more than two months without his finding the courage to approach or speak to her. Even so, he kept repeating like a beloved refrain: "She will be mine, and I will be hers." A trip to Chott el-Djerid was organized for winter break, and he signed up for it. He was happily surprised to find himself seated next to her on the bus, which left Tunis at dawn. She wore black trousers, a red pullover, and brown athletic shoes, and had wrapped a blue shawl around her neck. When the bus started moving, she closed her eyes and dozed off. Meanwhile, he was brooding about a way to start a conversation with her. His heart was pounding rapidly. It was a long trip, and he had to tear down the wall of silence between them because talking while traveling makes a journey seem shorter, abridges the distance, and brings hearts closer together. A conversation might even produce unexpected results.

But how should he begin? What excuse could he use? She was sleeping or pretending to sleep, possibly to keep him from disturbing her world with his words or gestures because—as her classmates affirmed—she was extremely introverted. He had never seen her with anyone else either in the cafeteria or the porticoes. She rarely spoke to other students or walked with them. For all these reasons, he would need to be cautious. If he messed up now, his loss would be enormous, and the Chott el-Djerid trip, which he had long anticipated, would become extremely exhausting, sad, and painful.

At daybreak the bus drew in sight of Kairouan—which is situated on barren plains—with its dust-colored walls and venerable mosque. Shivering in the cold of the winter morning, she opened her eyes and began to observe the ancient city with delight as they gradually approached it. He thought this was a golden opportunity he should not neglect.

"Have you visited Kairouan before?" he asked.

She looked at him suspiciously, as if wishing to make him feel that she hadn't noticed his presence until that moment. Smiling wanly, she replied, "I've visited it many times."

"Do you like it?"

"It's one of the most beautiful Tunisian cities I've visited. Each time I come I love it even more."

She fell silent but then added, "I visited it for the first time when I was nine—with my grandmother, who loves to attend commemorations of the Prophet's birthday. We toured the city by night: lights, colors, hymns, joy on people's faces, fragrant incense in the shrines, the magnificent markets, winding alleys, and women in a white haik, their wide, black eyes peering out. I felt I was experiencing a marvelous, novel dream. This all remains clearly etched in my memory even now. I observed the salty plains surrounding the city and their dense thickets, which were full of wild animals and vipers before the Muslims arrived."

Then she asked, "How about you? Have you visited Kairouan before?"

He came from a small village that lay eighty kilometers to the west of Kairouan. Since he was a child, he had been fascinated by this holy city, which had become his spiritual home. On every visit there he made a point of returning to the places he cherished: the mausoleum of Abu Zama'a al-Balawi; the Great Mosque; the Aghlabid cisterns; the Barrouta Well, which a camel with blinkered eyes circles; the old covered markets; the mausoleum of Amor Abbada, the eccentric wali who smoked hashish in public and created amazing items from wood and iron on which were inscribed verses of the Qur'an, prayers, cryptic phrases, and poems praising the benefits and merits of hashish. He was said to have been the first person to prophesy that the French would occupy Tunisia. Other saints were no less strange. Some were considered retarded or insane but would surprise people with statements and actions that displayed their genius, experience of life, and intuition. Yunus was interested in the lives of these saints and had also read many books about the history of this holy city, which had experienced might and glory in the age of the Aghlabids. Then the famished Banu Hilal arrived from Upper Egypt and destroyed it. Ever since, the city had experienced misfortunes attributable to that invasion and had never recovered. Ibn Khaldun, however, had discerned another reason for its devastation: the fact that the Arabs had built it in a wasteland with no concern for the building blocks of civilization. Their sole concern had been with grazing lands for their camels. The great historian thought that cities built in arid deserts like this, far from the natural location for a city, would quickly fall to ruin.

Her face beamed with admiration and satisfaction, but she did not comment. When their bus stopped in the square opposite Bab el Jalladin, the trip's organizer—who was, like him, a student in the Department of French Literature—announced a half-hour rest stop. The two seatmates entered the Medina by Bab el Jalladin and walked toward Bab Tunis. He started repeating to himself calmly and slowly, "She'll be mine, and I'll be hers." Calmly and slowly the holy city was emerging from a long winter night. Under the influence of the sun, which was starting its journey to the west in a sky virtually free of clouds, the chill of this December morning lifted, and activity picked up in the streets and markets. A necrologist started to inform people of the day's funerals by making the rounds of the coffeehouses. The two travelers drank orange juice and ate some pastries before continuing their leisurely walk. Pointing to an ancient structure that time had reduced to dust and desolation, he told her, "This was the most famous hotel at the beginning of the century, and many Europeans stayed there. The great German poet Rainer Maria Rilke was one of them. He visited Kairouan in 1912 and spent one of the worst nights of his life in this hotel because mosquitoes kept attacking him and drinking his blood until daybreak. In a letter to a girlfriend, he described Kairouan as a city surrounded by the dead, alluding to the cemeteries spread throughout its districts. Other writers visited here: Montherlant, Maupassant, André Gide . . ."

"Oh . . . André Gide too?"

"Yes, he visited a number of times."

"What did he write about it?"

"He complained about the number of flies and the excessive fertility of the seed of Abraham . . ."

She burst out laughing. "Was that all he said about it?"

"He wrote about the heat, the dervishes, and the Asiatic music in the mausoleums and mosques. He remembered it when he visited the Turkish city of Konya, which is also a city of dervishes."

"Where did he write this?"

"In his *Journals*."

"I don't know this book."

"What have you read by Gide?"

"I've read his *Immoralist, If It Die*, and *La Symphonie pastorale*—I like that last one a lot and have read it more than once."

"It's great that a history student is interested in literature!"

She stopped walking and asked, "How do you know I'm a history student?" There was an apprehensive look in her green eyes.

"I also know that your name is Hadiya."

She blushed, and her lips trembled. "Have you been spying on me?" she asked, smiling.

"No, never. Merely curious."

"Why curious?"

"Don't know."

"This is amazing," she said, blushing even more.

Just then, he felt certain that she would be his and he would be hers.

The bus continued south. The students sang, told each other jokes, and then laughed loudly at them. He conversed excitedly with her about Chott el-Djerid, the characteristics of its people, and Sahib al-Himar— that short, peevish teacher.

"He wore a wool cloak, a white skullcap, and prayer beads around his neck and taught boys in Tozeur. Then he mounted a gray donkey and traveled around the country, fomenting unrest and setting fires wherever he stopped. He used to say, 'The life and property of anyone who fails to join my jihad are fair game.' His supporters mutilated men by cutting off their hands and members and cursed women, slit their vulvas, and split open their bellies. In every place they stopped, they didn't leave a single habitable dwelling. Afraid of their brutality, people fled from them, barefoot and naked. After Sahib al-Himar and his followers devastated Kairouan, Sousse, and Tunis, they besieged al-Mahdiya. People's suffering there became so terrible they ate carrion, beasts of burden, and dogs. The siege lasted for many months. After that, Sahib al-Himar and his followers headed to Kairouan again and then on to Tunis, without ever stopping their spree of killing, setting fires, and wreaking havoc. Finally, this 'Master of the Ass' was slain. He was flayed, and his skin was filled with straw. People exchanged congratulations, and peace and security returned to their souls."

He spoke and she listened attentively and admiringly, oblivious to the racket the other students were making with their laughter and songs. Sensing that she was focused solely on him, he continued to speak about Chott el-Djerid and its people, as if recounting a thrilling narrative. As the bus neared Tozeur, he asked, "Do you know about Gustav Jung?"

"A famous psychologist . . . isn't that right?"

"Yes, the famous psychologist."

"What about him?"

"He visited Chott el-Djerid in 1920."

"Oh, I didn't know that either. Did he write about it?"

"Yes, in his autobiography.[14] Sousse was his first stop. The moment he set foot there, he detected a strange smell, which he quickly discovered was the smell of blood—the blood of an earth where three civilizations in succession were buried—Punic, Roman, and Christian. In Sousse, Jung spent many hours in a coffeehouse watching people's gestures, trying to grasp their emotions and feelings from their facial expressions. From Sousse he headed to Sfax, and from there to el-Djerid. After visiting Tozeur's oases, where he discovered some homosexual relationships among the men, he set off for Nefta on the back of a mule, accompanied by a guide. En route he passed a mounted Bedouin, who wore a white burnous and turban and had prayer beads around his neck. He rode a black mule that looked dignified and distinguished. Even though this Bedouin did not offer him any greeting or even glance at him, Jung was much impressed. Jung continued his journey, enchanted and fascinated, fancying him to be the opposite of the European man who, in Jung's analysis, had become a slave to time and to his own progress—as represented by trains, planes, automobiles, rockets, and so forth. The farther he went into the desert, the more Jung felt time's speed decrease. In fact, time even seemed occasionally to be running backward. Beneath the fiery rays of the sun, Jung felt that he was experiencing a strange dream in this expansive yellow void. He didn't wake from this dream until he entered the Nefta oasis and saw its houses. Early the next morning, the square in front of the house where he had spent the night filled with large groups of people and camels, donkeys, and mules. Many were rushing to and fro, kicking up a thick cloud of dust, and waving their hands in the air. At first, Jung thought they were quarreling, but his guide told him that they were preparing to conduct a religious celebration that noon. Masses of people attended, carrying green banners, dancing to the music of drums and pipes, and shouting loudly in the midst of all that dust. A venerable sheikh with a white beard and a saintly expression made his way through these throngs on a white mule, and the crowds applauded him admiringly and respectfully as he delivered occasional exhortations. After observing this religious celebration, which did not end until night-fall, Jung concluded that the mighty crowds of people he had witnessed were responding to instinctive, primitive emotions and influences. He also concluded that the ego in Eastern lands does not enjoy autonomy—unlike the Western ego. The night before he embarked for Marseilles to return to his homeland, Jung dreamt he saw himself in a square Arab city, set in the center of a vast plain. This city had a casbah inside it and four gates in the walls that surrounded it on all sides. A wide moat filled with water encircled the casbah. In this dream Jung saw himself standing in front of a wooden bridge that crossed the water and led to a dark horse-shoe gate that was open. Wishing to see inside the casbah, Jung began to cross the bridge. When Jung was halfway across, a handsome, brown-complexioned Arab peered out at him from the portal and then headed toward him with stately, almost regal, steps. Jung recognized this youth as the man in the white burnous and reflected that he must live in the casbah. As he neared, this youth assaulted Jung and tried to throw him to the ground. The struggle between the two men became increasingly fierce and intense. During their ferocious battle, the two collided with a railing and fell into the moat. The Arab tried to drown him, pushing his head under the water, but Jung protested: 'No! This is going too far!' He retaliated by shoving his foe's head down, trying to drown him. Although he succeeded, he felt great admiration for the Arab. He had not meant to kill him—just to forestall his attack. The scene of the dream changed then, and Jung saw himself with this Arab youth, inside a spacious, domed, octagonal chamber with white walls, in the middle of the casbah. Despite its simplicity, the room looked astonishing. Jung noticed a book open in front of him with black calligraphy of extraordinary beauty on milk-white parchment. The lines were not in Arabic script but resembled the Uighur script of western Turkestan. Jung recognized the script but did not understand the meaning. He merely sensed that what he saw before him might be the book he had finished writing. He asked the young man, whom he had just defeated and who was sitting on his right, what the book said, but the youth refused to reply.[15] So Jung made him, using a combination of patience, gruffness, and fatherly good humor." He wanted to offer her Jung's interpretation of this dream, but she interrupted him: "When did you read Jung's book?"

"I finished it two days ago."

"Did someone recommend it to you?"

"No one . . . just chance."

"You read a lot. Isn't that so?"

"It is."

An apprehensive look glittered in her green eyes again. "You frighten me."

"Why?"

"I don't know," she replied. Then she looked away and fell silent. He felt he had just been stabbed in the heart.

The bus stopped in front of their hotel, and the students shoved past each other to get out. Hadiya picked up her bag and left the bus without speaking to him or even glancing at him. He saw her in the lobby, standing alone, paying no attention to her surroundings—the way she acted at the university. After receiving her key, she headed to her room, ignoring him. When it was his turn, he took his key, found the room, and then dropped exhausted on the bed, cursing himself for being a dunce, a flop, and a chatterbox. He had spoiled everything with pointless talk about matters that meant nothing to her. He should have discussed Gide with her—not Jung or the crimes of the disgusting Sahib al-Himar. Right! He shouldn't have done that. It would have been better to let her tell him something. She might have opened her heart to him and spoken about herself, about her life, which she kept under wraps. Instead, he had rattled on until she grew bored and could no longer bear to listen to him. Uff! What a conceited fool he was! He paid no attention to other people. He didn't listen to them. He wasn't interested in their feelings or ideas. Consequently, he reaped only failure and a guilty conscience. Now he was humiliated, contemptible. She must be mocking him in her room now, laughing at him and saying, "That pathetic guy—who does he think he is? He made my head ache with his senseless chatter and bogus ideas, preventing me all the way here from admiring nature. Oh! I should have stopped him from addressing me from the outset. How could I have known he was so boring, nosy, and forward? That's why I won't allow him to come close to me again during the three days of this trip. If he tries, I'll give him an earful. In fact, I may even slap him. He deserves it! He ought to learn some manners and how to restrain his long tongue from trite talk."

Oh, he would not be hers, and she wouldn't be his.

What a catastrophe! Should he return to the capital at once? Perhaps. But, not so fast . . . slow down. He ought to wait until morning. Then he could reach an appropriate decision that would spare him further suffering and humiliation.

He had meant to ask her to watch the sun set over the oases. Now he felt that he did not dare leave the room—that other students might be whispering to each other: "Poor dope . . . why did he fall into the trap and speak to her? Doesn't he know she's a secretive girl who flees from anyone who tries to approach her? He must be an idiot. Otherwise, why would he upset her with idle chatter during the entire trip? She finally left him and went up to her room, as if he had never existed." Oh! What a disaster! What a scandal!

When night fell, he still lay crumpled up in bed, feverish and tormented. He went down to the restaurant at 9:00, chose an isolated corner, and ate his dinner, carefully avoiding glancing at anyone's face. Then he headed to the bar and ordered a beer, which he downed in one go. He ordered a second and a third. His body started to feel looser, and he regained his composure. She could go to hell! A superficial girl who wasn't worth thinking about in the first place . . . He was sure she suffered from some serious psychological disorder. If not, why did she treat people so cavalierly, hostilely, and evasively? He hoped she would keep on like this. Then she would become an old maid, a spinster ignored even by contemptible men. She could go to hell! He had made a mistake when he spoke to her. He should have left her to her scruples, complexes, and the tedious desert road. Moreover, why had his words frightened her? It was clear that she loathed educated men and preferred superficial ones—effeminate lads who would accept being her lap dog. He needed to forget her. She didn't deserve all this attention from him. He shouldn't allow the trip to el-Djerid, which he had long anticipated, to be ruined by her. Moreover, why focus on her alone? Many other girls were on the trip, and most of them were his friends. They would all be at the dance that began in the hotel at ten. Why shouldn't he erase the image of that troubled girl from his memory by looking for one of the other girls?

When he had knocked back his fourth beer, he made his way to the ballroom. As he approached the door, she stepped before him. She had dressed for the occasion and wore a traditional silver necklace, a blue dress that highlighted her attractions, and elegant black shoes.

"Where have you been? I've been looking for you a long time," she said, smiling.

"You looked for me?"

"Yes, I did."

"Aren't you going to the dance?"

"I don't like the commotion and loud music. Come, let's sit in that corner."

They sat down. She ordered coffee with milk, but he didn't order anything.

She asked, "Are you angry at me?"

"Why should I be?"

"I may have hurt your feelings on the bus when I told you that you frighten me. I chose my words poorly. I meant to say that your vast erudition astonishes me and makes me conscious of how uneducated I am."

"You . . . uneducated? That's not true! Your classmates praise your brilliance and your profs. do too. Isn't that so?"

"Oh, you seem to have collected a lot of information about me. What else do you know about me?"

"I know you live in the Medina."

She appeared happy with what she heard. "On what street? What's the number of the house?"

"I'll soon learn that."

She burst into laughter.

"You're different, Mister . . . what's your name?"

"Yunus."

She held out her hand and said, "I am happy to meet you, Yunus."

"Same here."

They lingered in the lobby until midnight, talking about French authors and poets they both admired: Baudelaire, Verlaine, Hugo, Flaubert, Camus, Jean Giono, and Colette. She told him that after she graduated she planned to write a thesis on the fall of the Ottoman Empire because the period before any great empire collapses is important—just as important as that preceding its birth. Sultan Abdul Hamid's personality also appealed to her a lot; he personified the Eastern despot.

"What about you? What are your plans?" she asked.

"I'm going to write a thesis about my favorite author, Flaubert. In my opinion he counts as the first modern novelist. Every great twentieth-century novelist agrees on that."

"All I've read by him is *Madame Bovary*."

"I recommend reading his unique work: *Three Tales*."

"I'll do that when I return to the capital."

Before heading up to her room, she suggested touring the oases early the next morning. He agreed, prancing in his imagination with extreme happiness.

He returned to the bar and drank his fifth and sixth beer while repeating, "She will be mine. I will be hers."

The pale sun rose from the desert's void. Soon its rays were dancing through the palm fronds and spadices, sweeping away the cold of a long winter. Rejoicing in the light, birds released their trills through the expansive oasis. Amid this genial scene, the gurgling of waterwheels echoed like mysterious music performed by desert angels. In response to these melodies, the farmers of the oasis began to move about like ghosts. Nothing marred the calm of this awe-inspiring morning . . . a calm that precluded speech and instead invited surrender to the stillness.

They walked silently down the sandy paths in loose desert garb. She looked like a Bedouin princess who had slipped into the oasis for an early morning tryst with her lover, sneaking away from her tribe. He started repeating silently to himself: *Is she mine now? Am I hers? But I must not utter even one word for fear of ruining the grandeur of this stillness. Didn't the ancients say that silence is wisdom? But how enchanting she is in these desert clothes! Her beauty is matchless. Her eyes are palm oases undulating in the morning light. Oh . . . if only I could take her hand and lead her to a thicket! There I would embrace her and whisper to her, trembling: "I love you, my Laila, my Persian beauty Ayn al-Shams Nizam, my Beatrice, my Elsa, my blooming oasis in life's bleak desert!*[16]

Suddenly, she broke her profound silence to ask, "What are you thinking?"

He hesitated a little and then asked in reply, "Should I tell you the truth?"

"The truth and nothing but the truth."

"I'm thinking about you . . . just you."

"Why are you thinking about me?"

He stepped closer to her and took her hand; she didn't protest. They continued walking, hand in hand.

"You didn't answer my question."

He squeezed her hand.

"I can't," he protested.

"Why not?"

After a few minutes of silence, he asked, "Do you want the truth?"

"Yes, the truth . . . and nothing but the truth," she replied with a smile.

Trembling, he responded, "Because I love you."

She stopped and studied his face for a long time. Then she objected, "You're in too big a rush!"

"No one can put out love's fire once it bursts into flame."

She blushed.

"How can you love me when you don't even know me?"

"All true lovers fall in love at first sight."

"Don't you know that to let yourself be guided by emotions without regard to reality is dangerous?"

"For your sake, I'm ready to confront all dangers."

On the way back to the capital, she told him about herself. She really did live in the ancient Medina, on a narrow street near place Halfaouine. Her father sold vegetables and fruit and was an affectionate, jolly man who told witty, barbed jokes. He loved music and had a remarkable singing voice. During happy, companionable hours, he would sing songs of Umm Kulthum, Abdel Wahab, Farid al-Atrash, Sidi Ali al-Riahi, and Hédi al-Jouini. Even in hard times he retained his composure and good humor, making sarcastic jokes. He always advised people not to take life too seriously—otherwise its pitfalls and upheavals would crush them. Her mother was reserved, diffident, and extremely thin-skinned. She wept easily, laughed easily, and became angry easily, although her anger wouldn't last long, for its bubble quickly burst. Her parents were extremely devoted to her and always told her the house felt desolate and empty when she left, if only for a few days. She had one brother, who was five years older. He was married and worked for a bank. Her relationship with him was problematic—at times cold and stiff, and at others extraordinarily affectionate. Why? She didn't know and didn't care to find out.

After their trip to Chott el-Djerid, the two became virtually inseparable. They were seen together in the university cafeteria, in the city's streets, coffeehouses, literary societies, cinemas, gardens, and on its northern shores. Other students their age were preoccupied by revolutions, demonstrations, and slogans advocating freedom, justice, and resistance to tyranny and imperialism. They did not object to any of that and indeed approved of all these initiatives. They themselves, however, preferred to observe this scene from a distance, since they had agreed to establish a little world just for themselves, a world that no one else was allowed to enter or explore. He read her some texts he had written, and she urged him to publish them. He, however, refused, and eventually she accepted his position and no longer raised the subject.

They graduated the same year and finished their theses in the same year too. Hers was about the fall of the Ottoman Empire, and his on his

master, Flaubert. After they were offered positions as lecturers at the university, they married and spent their honeymoon in Istanbul. This city
had served as the capital of the Byzantine Empire, the Latin Empire, and
then the Islamic Ottoman Empire, which had marched far enough west
to lay siege to Vienna. Istanbul's residents appeared disinterested in its
rich historical legacy, clutching instead at the present with all its problems,
concerns, and fears—leaving the past to tourists, Orientalists, and archaeologists. The city resembled an ancient temple of Janus that sheltered a god
with two contrasting sides to his face—one that looked East and the other
West. The tense relationship between the two encouraged convergence at
times and rupture at others.

During their honeymoon, he read stories by Aziz Nesin, selections
from contemporary Turkish poetry, Yashar Kemal's novel *Memed My
Hawk*, and a book about the life of Jalal al-Din Rumi. For her part, Hadiya
read two tomes about Sultan Abdul Hamid, her hero, who was—as she
put it—"ill-starred," since he ruled in a period of decline when various ills
teamed up against the empire, which had once struck fear into peoples'
hearts, East and West. Then the Ottoman Empire seemed more like "an
old wooden wagon careening down a rutted, winding road." The farther it
went, the more parts broke. Finally, its wheels flew off, and the people who
were attempting to fix it were tossed into the abyss of history.

When Maryam was born two years after their wedding, her parents
grew even more attached to their little world and clung to it because they
assumed it could protect them against the world's woes, calamities, and
sorrows. Yunus and Hadiya didn't distinguish between the successive
wars in the Middle East; racial, ethnic, and religious conflicts in various
parts of the world; natural disasters; epidemics; earthquakes; and terrorist operations—whatever appeared on television and was printed in the
newspapers. By contrast, their little world was characterized by calm, harmony, love, tranquility, concord, and an unusual happiness of a kind that
many other marriages lack. All the same, like a hungry mouse, time had
started gnawing on their little world, creating holes that began to grow
larger, without them noticing. By the time they became aware of these, the
damage was already irreparable.

The first clue to the harm that time had secretly done was the death of Hadiya's father and mother during the same year—the same month even. Her father succumbed to cardiac arrest during a hot siesta. Her mother proved unable to withstand this blow and followed him two weeks later. During the days and nights prior to her demise, she sank into a dreadful silence and remained entirely motionless. She continued in this state until she took her last breath, just as the muezzin gave the dawn call to prayer. The calamity of death wreaked havoc on Hadiya—like the first autumn storm that attacks a green tree, strips it, leaving its branches bare, and confers on it the look of mournful, dark winter. Within a few weeks, Hadiya lost her bloom, charm, and splendor. Wrinkles dug into her face, the gleam of her green eyes dimmed, her hair became streaked with gray, and blue veins appeared on her neck and legs. She was now a middle-aged woman, and also enervated, devoid of willpower, wilted, despairing, scared, hostile to the outside world, and more introverted than at any time before. This introversion differed from the shyness for which she was known at the university when she had been a dreamy, romantic student. This was the introversion of a person whom time had robbed of life's enjoyment and deprived of every hope or aspiration. Once Yunus's little world collapsed, his only refuge was his own tortured, anxious, and fearful soul. Hadiya no longer cared to travel, inside the country or abroad, although she had enjoyed voyages in the past. Similarly, she began to refuse to frequent coffeehouses and restaurants. She went to work as if compelled to. Speaking with people, even those closest to her, became severe torture. The only thing that appealed to her was visiting the shrines of the saints every Friday. Perhaps she found, by spending an hour or two there among other afflicted women, some consolation to lighten the burden of her grief.

Yunus lost his parents too, as well as some other relatives, and began to see time's distortions, wounds, scars, and brutality clearly. Convinced that the little world he had constructed with Hadiya could no longer shelter him, he returned to the outside world he had frequented in his youth. There he sought protection from the dangers that stalked him and something to quiet the fears devastating his body and spirit. Since the house had become forlorn and devoid of life's joys, he started spending more time in coffeehouses and restaurants, lingering there and staying up late with former classmates, who like him were fleeing from the drabness of married life. He frequently stumbled home drunk late at night and slept in his clothes in the living room. Eventually he began looking surreptitiously at coeds, registering thrilling details that helped restore the warmth of lost youth to his frigid body. He noticed a dreamy, fleeting look, black eyes moist with the dew of desire and hungry for pleasure, a smooth neck that might stretch forward in anticipation of a desired kiss, breasts surging in preparation for a tryst, the curve of a waist, two dimples dancing in the lecture hall, the ring of a laugh that stripped resigned middle age from a body and rekindled the fire of desire in it, a prancing step, the nonchalance of hungry eyes, a boyish haircut that suggested irresistible lust, a crafty smile of feminine seduction, crimson lips that parted slightly to kiss him to honor his awesome probity, a soft hand that slipped toward him, trembling, to caress him in the warmth of a bed, a sweet voice like a strong current that sweeps a person to a garden of desirable pleasures, and that splendid feature visible between thighs once tight pants open, waiting for someone to water it with a drizzle of crazy love.

After he ended his lecture on the aesthetics of Flaubert's *Three Tales*, while his students rushed toward the door and he gathered his papers, she stopped before him. It was very cold outside and raining hard—the beginning of December. She wore a black coat and had wrapped a rainbow-colored scarf around her neck. He didn't know why, but looking at her face, he was reminded of the French actress Juliette Binoche in *The English Patient*, which he had seen a few days earlier.

"Professor . . . I want to say that you impressed me a lot today," she said, smiling.

"Haven't I impressed you before?"

"That's not what I mean. You always impress me, but today you were brilliant; extremely marvelous."

"Thank you very much."

"Do you know, Professor, that because of you I've become addicted to reading Flaubert?"

"That's splendid, but I advise you to avoid taking your addiction to an extreme, because other writers deserve your attention too."

"Right now, I'm in love with Flaubert. Perhaps I'll change my mind in the future."

He started toward the door, intending to leave.

"Professor . . . I would like to talk to you about something."

"Go right ahead."

"No, not now."

"When?

"Do you have time over the weekend?"

He considered a little.

"Yes, I do. Would you like to meet here at the university?"

"I'd prefer to meet somewhere else."

He thought a bit more.

"Will the issue require a long discussion?"

"Yes."

"Then it would be best to meet in a restaurant."

"Great idea!"

"Do you know the restaurant called Dar El Jeld?"

"That's near place du Gouvernement."

"Yes, we'll meet there Saturday, at 1:00."

"Thank you, Professor. See you then."

Anticipating Saturday, he trembled like a teenage boy preparing for his first date. While walking, he thought about her. While eating, he thought about her. While speaking to his daughter and his friends, he thought about her. While drinking, he thought about her. But what did she want to discuss? Was it something to do with Flaubert? No, no, a topic like that would not require them to meet outside the university. What did she want to discuss with him? Uff! Was he now such an old man that he could no longer guess what was passing through the minds of young women? Perhaps she was experiencing heartache and wanted . . . but was he a shrink? Besides, why would such a matter involve him? If she did present it to him, he would advise her to deal with it herself because the world of emotions is extremely complex; outside interference only complicates matters. Moreover, he didn't believe she would dare broach such a topic with him because they really did not know each other outside of their professor-student relationship, which did not lend itself to such confidences. But why was he so preoccupied by this? He should just be patient and wait. Wasn't it marvelous to be meeting such a sensitive, beautiful girl? She was a Flaubert fan, and he would be alone with her in the restaurant, conversing with her, far from curious eyes. It had been a long time since he had scored like this. Fidelity to his wife for thirty years had kept him so isolated from the world of women that he no longer knew anything about them, and a man who did not know women did not know life. Indeed, he did not even know himself. He needed to reacquaint himself with his ego to discover what had become of it and what future it might have.

On Saturday, the weather fluctuated between sunny and rainy—a veritable "wolf's wedding," as his fellow countrymen would say. She arrived in the same coat, but the rainbow scarf had been replaced by a lavender one. They selected a corner table suitable for an intimate luncheon. As she removed her coat, her body exploded with a femininity that awakened his repressed desires. She ordered fish soup and a plate of sea bass with *tastira*. He ordered a Tunisian salad, lamb with steamed vegetables, and a bottle of Magon red wine, as well as a bottle of Ayn Qarizi mineral water.

"What are you drinking?" he asked.

"May I split the bottle of Magon with you? I love red wine," she said with a smile. He filled her glass and his. Then they drank to their health. They talked about the unsettled weather and then about the war in Afghanistan against al-Qaeda and the Taliban.

She asked, "What do you think of bin Laden?"

"Islam's history is filled with men like him," he replied tersely. He was eager to discover what she wanted to discuss with him. She ate calmly and elegantly while he stole glances at her charms, laying them bare in his imagination.

"I don't pay attention to politics or politicians," she admitted.

"Same here," he replied.

When she finished her fish soup, she said, "The truth is, Professor, I've wanted to talk to you for months, but I'm not sure why. I really don't have a clue. We don't actually know each other; in fact, you don't even know my name."

"The time has come to learn it. Isn't that so?"

She said, "My name is Hind." Then she continued, "Yes, I don't know what has made me consider speaking to you. I hesitated a lot but finally thought I would. Many things have bothered me for a long time—things that relate to my life, emotions, and ideas, and the changes I have experienced and still am suffering. I wanted to discuss them with a friend I've known for a whole year, a guy my age who studies in the French Department with me, a nice young man, who is very polite. We've gone to the movies, studied our lessons in the National Library, and roamed the city together. In fact, I've accompanied him more than once to the small flat he shares with a friend in the Lafayette District. But we didn't do anything, because he is very timid and always embarrassed. For this reason, our relationship never progressed beyond swift, light kisses. I finally broke up with him since he approaches life like an innocent child and treats me like his mother or big sister. After that, I thought I would open my heart to a close friend who studies in the Law School. When I discovered that she is conservative and clings firmly to tradition, however, I changed my mind. I have continued looking for a person I feel comfortable with—a mature, resolute individual to whom I can disclose my heart's convulsions. You were the only one I could finally think of. Perhaps your marvelous lectures about Flaubert convinced me that you're the only person who could understand me because I feel I'm a typical Flaubert heroine. I have a lot in common with Emma Bovary. It's true that her social life differs from mine, but I feel very close to her. In fact, she's my dearest friend."

She drank half a glass of wine and continued, "I come from Neapolis, from a middle-class family long resident there. My father is a carpenter, who is an extremely nice, pious man. He obeys my mother, who was a very beautiful woman and still retains traces of her former beauty. When I was eight, I discovered that she was regularly cheating on my father. Once an elegant, handsome man, who looked like the Egyptian actor Hussein Fahmy, came to our house. My mother claimed he was there to repair something and asked me to go play in the street with other neighborhood children. I obeyed, but soon returned home because I had my doubts about this man, whom I had never seen before. Approaching the living room door on tiptoe, I heard my mother moaning, quivering, and talking dirty—using words I had definitely never heard her use before, not with me or anyone else. I crept close to the door, which wasn't shut all the way, and through the narrow crack saw the stranger's butt rising and falling. My mother's legs were spread and raised in the air. This scene shocked me, and I raced back to the street panic-stricken. My head was spinning and turning. In fact, the entire world was revolving around me. I wanted to weep and call for help but couldn't. My father came home from work early that evening—tired as usual. I thought I would tell him what I had seen, but fear got the better of me. Instead, I started to shake and weep. My father was amazed to see me that way because I would almost always greet him with happy delight and sit on his lap. Then he would pet me and tell me charming stories. My mother intervened immediately, took me hastily to my room, and gave me a piece of chocolate. She told me, 'Go to sleep, dear. You'll feel better in the morning, God willing.'

"The stranger's visits to our house were repeated. As the days passed, I began to treat the matter as routine. In fact, I started to collude with my mother because I derived a strange enjoyment from watching what my mother did with her lover through the crack by the door. The obscene words that she and the stranger used no longer offended me. I might not have kept the secret had my father not been so subservient to my mother. He never raised his voice to her or refused any of her requests. He never once expressed any concern about her conduct and always treated her as if she were the most virtuous woman in the whole world. She was very beautiful and elegant and had exquisite taste. She was also a superb cook and pastry chef. She excelled in her management of the household and everything else. My mother, who may have guessed I knew about her private doings, treated me ever more tenderly and indulgently. She pampered me more than before and gave me lovely things. She honored my every request without any hesitation and praised me a lot to my father, our relatives, and the neighbors.

"A cousin, who was twenty-five when I turned eleven, loved me a lot and coddled me. Ever since I was three, he took me to the sea in the summer and prowled through the city's markets with me. He bought me presents for feast days and special occasions. In short, of our entire family, he was the one I loved best. For this reason, I was very affectionate with him, but something happened that summer. I went to my maternal uncle's house by myself one day, but my uncle, his wife, and the other children had gone to a wedding in Hammamet. My cousin was clad only in a blue swimsuit. The sun had tanned his skin, making him look even more handsome. I noticed that he was drinking beer. Before him sat a plate of sardine salad. Delighted to see me, he sat me down beside him and invited me to share his food. A moment later he drew closer and kissed me on the lips. This was the first time he had done that. I told him disapprovingly, 'Don't do that to me again!' He asked, 'Why not?' I replied, 'Because you smell bad.' He laughed loudly, and I laughed too. He drained the glass of beer and approached me again. He hugged me to him and began to kiss my lips fervently. I tried to push him away but could not. Finally, I surrendered to his kisses and caresses, feeling a pleasure I had never known before. The house was still; indeed, the entire world was. I closed my eyes as if dizzy. Then he took my hand and began to run it slowly over something solid and warm. He kept doing that until my hand became wet. I opened my eyes to find that my hand was coated with a white, viscous liquid.

"I shouted at him in alarm, 'Marwan, what have you done to me?'

"'Nothing, dear Hind. Nothing,' he said, looking exhausted and fatigued.

"Then I realized that what my cousin had done to me was comparable to what the stranger who looked like Hussein Fahmy did to my mother. After that experience, I began to crave meetings with my cousin. I liked to close my eyes as he kissed me, fondled my body— especially my breasts once they developed—and rub my hand over his warm, solid thing until that sticky, white liquid spilled out. I liked this so much that I couldn't bear for a week to go by without meeting my cousin. This continued until I was fifteen. Then one beautiful spring day, after my morning lessons, I returned to our house to find it deserted and so desolate that I felt terrified. When I asked a neighbor woman about my mother, she said she was at her brother's house because Marwan had died in a traffic accident two hours earlier. I raced to my uncle's house, ululating like a mad woman.

"Marwan's death in that horrible wreck was the most atrocious disaster I've ever experienced. After that, the world seemed deserted and sad. I felt I was an orphan who had lost all affection, love, and hope—everything.

I wept inconsolably when I saw his picture, people mentioned his name, or I remembered his hearty laughter, lazy voice, strutting walk, and his hair, which was always neatly combed, and what he smelled like during our secret meetings. Then I was overwhelmed by a feeling that I was to blame . . . that I was a loose, fallen slut, a nasty, dirty, low-life girl who had led him to that disastrous end by her foul deeds. This feeling grew and increased until my life became a putrid, stagnant swamp. I looked around for help and support. Then a girl from our neighborhood sprang to my rescue, but I couldn't reveal anything to her because of her narrow-mindedness and cold nature. She was the first girl at the Institute to wear hijab; she defended it vehemently in public, unperturbed by the disciplinary measures taken against it. Even now, I don't know why I allowed that girl to come so close to me. Perhaps it was from despair or fear . . . I don't know which. The point is that I started meeting her almost daily. I didn't confide my secrets to her. Instead, I gave her the impression that I felt tortured, didn't sleep well, suffered frightening nightmares, hated myself, loathed myself, couldn't bear myself, and felt I was about to tumble into a black, bottomless abyss. That vile girl began to advise me—mentoring me the way an experienced, worldly wise, mature woman would shepherd a fickle, wayward, naïve girl. I obeyed her advice and accepted her instructions without any hesitation or resistance. Under her influence I adopted hijab, performed the five prayers diligently, recited extra invocations, read yellowed books discussing what is permitted and what is forbidden, tribulation in the grave, red-hot hell, and woman's evil and corruption. I also grew addicted to the religious channels on TV, focusing especially on talks by Sheikh al-Qaradawi and Amr Khaled. I remained in this stupor for three years. Then I began to feel restless again and sensed that I had forced myself to bear more than I could and had darkened my spirit. So, I distanced myself from that girl. When she tried to approach me, I would put her off with various excuses. One afternoon during winter break in 1998 I placed jeans, a sweater, and a pullover in my sports bag and went to the beach attired in hijab and religious attire. I walked for an hour. The sea was calm, and the weather was almost warm. I was the only person on the beach. Before dusk, I withdrew to a remote area, stripped naked, and swam for half an hour. Then I donned the jeans, pullover, and sweater and returned home without hijab. My psychological pains abated, and I felt cleansed of all my agonies and suffering as if I had been born anew. Yes, I really felt born anew."

Hind fell silent. Then she clinked glasses with him and said, blushing, "Professor . . . I'm happy that you heard me out."

"I'm happy you chose to confide in me so candidly and spontaneously."

"I think I guessed right when I chose you."

He took her hand and started to caress it gently.

"Professor, do you still have time?"

"Yes, I do."

"I'd like to invite you for a drink in my apartment on Marseille Street. My roommate is away and won't return until Monday . . ."

"Why not?"

The small, sparsely furnished apartment was clean and tidy. She prepared two coffees. Then they drank two glasses of whisky silently while the city's clamor increased to a distant roar. When he approached and embraced her, she yielded to him.

He did not return home until shortly before dawn.

He was madly in love with her. Nothing else mattered in life. He even ignored his daughter. Hind gave him everything he wanted and acquiesced in everything he asked of her during intercourse, liberating him from the chill of a long marriage. He loved to pester her from behind when she was leaning forward in the kitchen. He became even more aroused when he heard her talk dirty as he drummed on her thighs. He dissolved into intense delight when she licked his member and grew ecstatic when her tongue caressed him in sensitive areas.

During the summer holiday of 2004, Hind returned to Neapolis, promising to phone him. Two weeks passed without a call. He couldn't think straight and didn't know what to do. On the street, he looked like any other drunk or tramp, no longer like the luminary professor whose specialty was Flaubert. Halfway through the third week his patience wore out, and he phoned her. The automated response was: "This number has been disconnected." He tried the number several more times, but the response was always the same. He drank himself into a stupor in a miserable, working-class bar and then burst into silent tears, to the amazement of the other patrons. The summer holiday ended, but there was still no news of Hind. She didn't return to the university at the start of the academic year. When she didn't appear as anticipated, he made inquiries about her and learned that she had traveled to France, where she planned to finish her studies.

Over winter break he went to Paris and made the rounds of all the universities, asking about her, showing her picture to Tunisian, Algerian, and Moroccan students, claiming to be her uncle, saying she had disappeared without informing any member of her family, but found no trace of her.

He returned to Tunis two days before the year's end, raving like an old man who had lost every hope in life and now thought only of death.

6

Sensing that writing would be his destiny, Flaubert also chose solitude so he would not be distracted from writing by life's pleasures, history's upheavals, painful or happy experiences, love affairs, traveling or travel adventures, friendships, family or conjugal duties, or any other eventuality. Until death struck him down while he was writing a new chapter of *Bouvard et Pécuchet*, solitude remained his favorite world. He dreamt, danced, sang, created, and wrestled with words there—as if struggling with predatory beasts. The choice of solitude came early for Flaubert. When he was in his twenties, he wrote, "Tomorrow I will be alone . . . I will not visit anyone . . . I'm a bear." Even when he married, Flaubert continued to cling to solitude like an Oriental sultan clinging to power: "I live alone, completely alone. I embrace solitude even more." My parents have died, and my friends "have given up on me or changed."

Dogs were his only companions in his endless solitude. He treated them like dear friends and his brethren in good and bad days. They were present when he lunched or dined and accompanied him on his rambles when he needed a break from writing. He may have discussed with them topics that preoccupied him. He talked about his dogs with admiration and affection in letters he sent to his lovers and friends. In a letter to his close friend Louis Bouilhet, he wrote:

> I spent an entire week alone like an ascetic, as calm as a god. I submitted
> to an insane discipline. I woke at noon and went to sleep at four in the
> morning. I dined with Daco.

Daco was his dog. He loved his other dog, Giulio, so much that the fleas afflicting it seemed of more importance to Flaubert than three-quarters "of the human race." For Flaubert, solitude was that of an animal with no company but its own. Therefore, he referred to it by the name of the lair for the animal to which he likened himself, according to his desires and the psychological and creative situation he experienced at each stage of his development. It might be a lion's den, a burrow, a cavern, a cave, a hole, or a lair. From time to time, he also liked to compare himself to a particular animal. While writing *Sentimental Education* he wrote to George Sand, "I live like an oyster and my novel is the rock that holds me fast." When George Sand criticized Flaubert's propensity toward solitude and called him a seal, he replied, "I feel a great desire to be a seal, as you say." Then he added, "There's no place left in the world for people of refined taste. We must withdraw to solitude the way the rhinoceros does in *Waiting for the End*." Flaubert also fancied being an ant lost in the desert, a bear living alone on the ice, or a camel mulling over its thoughts and ideas in a thorny wasteland. Shortly before he died, he wrote: "It seems to me that I'm traversing infinite solitude to proceed to an undetermined destination while I am at one and the same time the desert, the traveler, and the camel."

What about Yunus? What was the essence of his solitude? A void and waiting . . . waiting for what? The end that no one can escape. All he could hope for was that his end might be without pain or suffering—while he was sleeping, roaming the seashore, leafing through a book, listening to a favorite symphony, lost in thought, recalling memories from his happy past, or lying on the bosom of a beautiful woman. That last choice would be the best, no matter how impossible it was.

Void? Oh, the void! It was frightening, dark, and weighty. All his reading, writing, walks, conversations with his new friends at the Albatross Restaurant, and other activities and endeavors did not fill even a little of the alarming void in which he resided. When he chose to settle in Neapolis, he thought writing might be more beneficial than at any previous time. Therefore, he had decided to devote himself to it seriously, thinking that might relieve him of his torments and pains and restore his serenity, vitality, and hope. But whenever he picked up a pen and brought it toward a white piece of paper, words fled from him like birds from a hunter. Then he would be overwhelmed by frustration and despair as he tumbled into the void again. If there were an animal he wished to identify with, it was the donkey—that emaciated donkey he had seen frequently when he was a child: a donkey standing out in the open, in the scorching sun, morose and sorrowful, while persistent flies danced around the sores left by all the loads it carried each day.

But had he written anything that deserved attention? He frequently asked himself this, and he knew he ought to respond. In one of her fits of anger before their separation, his wife had shouted at him: "You call yourself a writer but refuse to publish what you write because you say this country offers opportunities to become prominent, succeed, and achieve renown only to fakes, self-promoters, and hacks—people with no talent whatsoever. Truly creative writers are destined to being marginalized, ignored, dismissed, scorned, and tormented until the end of their life. This is your opinion, which you never tire of repeating. Isn't that so? Of course it is! But you're lying to yourself, to people in general, and to me in particular—me, who has agreed to live under the same roof with you for all these many years, putting up with every type of trouble. Now, let me tell you frankly what I haven't told you before: Everything you write is twaddle, silly twaddle, lies, claptrap that hurts the head and the heart, the ravings of a man who has failed at every level, a fart from a diseased belly, words that lack sense and savor, produced by a mind that is corrupt and ruined. Shit, yes, shit: s-h-i-t! Uff! How could I have believed that you are a writer and that what you pen truly deserves respect? What an idiot I was! How naïve! Even stranger than all this is that you boast shame-lessly that Flaubert is your master! But how could the mighty Flaubert, who wrote books like *Madame Bovary*, be a tutor for a person of your ilk? What hypocrisy! How fraudulent! May all God's creatures realize, as I do, that this fellow is worthless." She had stopped and bowed her head, with its thinning hair, thoughtfully toward the floor. When she raised it again, her eyes were gleaming with an even more intense anger than before and her pale, slender finger was pointing at him. Then she continued her rant: "Do you know what my advice for you is? I advise you to burn all that sacred crap in the cabinet as soon as possible. I'll be happy to see a blaz-ing inferno consume all your lies before my eyes, turning them into a pile of ashes. Yes—before these eyes that can no longer stand the sight of you. After that, each of us will go our own way."

His wife might be right. Perhaps what he had written until then was twaddle and more twaddle. Then, if burning them was appropriate, why did he insist on retaining his manuscripts? Was he contemplating stunning posthumous fame—like that of Kafka and others? *Not so fast! Not so fast, Yunus. You've already succumbed to enough fantasies that have led you astray and caused you to lose your moral compass. Be realistic and courageous. Free yourself from all these trivial matters that no longer help you in any way and that ultimately have led you to the disgusting and humiliating situation with which you struggle now. Will you do that?*

Yes, he would.

When? When? When?

Uff! It was hard to set a date. But he certainly would. Ah . . . another postponement! That meant he would never do it. No, he wouldn't. Yes, he would.

But would he dare burn what he considered the most beautiful thing in his life? The issue was extremely difficult. Wasn't that so? Therefore, if he decided to set fire to everything he had written, he should also set fire to himself. That would be a dramatic end, in the Greek sense. Afterward, someone might search in any papers that escaped the flames for signs of his talent and elevate his status when he was rotting bones. That was possible, since it had happened to some previous authors, people who had lived craving one single grape and then were handed an entire cluster after their demise, as someone once said. *Stop it! Enough dreams, fantasies, and ravings, Yunus! You're sixty now and need to be realistic and resilient, to grasp the facts of your life, which has quickly begun to approach its conclusion.*

He went out to the small garden. It was a clear autumn day. The clouds had dispersed, leaving only white streamers to decorate the blue sky. The mountains and the hills were resting in the warm sunshine. The scent of the rain that had poured down early that morning mixed with the smells of the sea and of lemon and orange blossoms. From his neighbor's radio came the voice of Sidi Ali Riahi singing, "I'm like the bird; we sing in my nest." Yes, that's how that vocalist had lived: a wild bird that never tired of soaring in the sky and singing, oblivious to everything else. He had loved art since childhood, but his family—a family of prominent citizens, jurisprudents, and judges—had shunned it. Even so, he challenged them and left his family to become what he wanted to be. He set off to sing in praise of beauty, love, and life, with its vagaries and creative flow. He sang for the drowsy lake beneath the summer moon; for the beautiful woman gazing down from a blue window at her lover as he inhaled the musky smell of jasmine on a spring evening; for the beautiful woman who caused him to taste the anguish of banishment; for the brown, barefoot Bedouin woman who filled her jug from a well in the field while her night-black hair flowed over her shoulders; for blue, white, and green Tunis bathing in the waters of the Mediterranean; for the freedom of the artist in a society that considered art a sin deserving the harshest punishments. He sang and sang until he fell dead on the stage of the Municipal Theater of Tunis while singing, "I'm like the bird; we sing in my nest."

The telephone rang. It was the maid, Sulaf.

"Good morning, Professor."

Her sweet voice made him feel good, and sensitive parts of his body warmed. His organ moved, wishing to dance for a time between her tender thighs and swim in the viscous fountainhead of pleasure. That's how he had always felt with her since the first time he had had sex with her. When he heard her voice on the phone or in the house, his desires became inflamed, and he would be incapable of suppressing or restraining them.

"Professor, forgive me. I won't be able to come today."

He replied somewhat sharply and emotionally, "But there's a lot of laundry, and the kitchen is in despicable condition. Dust is accumulating on the living room furniture."

He was lying; the house was clean, and the kitchen was spotless. There were only two shirts and a few pieces of underwear to wash, but he wanted to start his sixtieth birthday with her. In fact, he might not allow her to do anything besides have sex with him.

"My mother's ill, Professor. I must take her to the doctor in an hour. The poor woman hasn't eaten for three days. Last night she was moaning from pain." Then she continued in a sad voice that he found even more seductive than before: "I fear for her, Professor. I have no one but her in the world. My mother's everything to me . . . more important even than my son and daughter. If she passes, we won't know what to do."

"Fine. When will you come?"

"God willing, tomorrow, Professor."

"You'll need to come early because I have appointments at noon."

"First thing tomorrow morning I'll be with you, Professor. I'll make your house as immaculate as a bride, God willing."

God willing. Inshallah. *God willing. How sweet her mouth is!*

Early the next day she wouldn't do anything until he'd had satisfied his lust with her. She had to come to him while he was still in bed, perfumed with solitude's and night's desires. He would mount her and begin to strike while she wailed beneath him until his organ slackened and was unable to achieve another erection. When she had first come to the house, a month after he settled in Neapolis, he hadn't paid much attention to her looks, and her voice hadn't enticed him because he had a preconceived idea that maids are pushy. This preconception inspired, indeed confirmed, the idea that they are vulgar, mercurial liars motivated by primal, animal instincts. Thus it was necessary to treat them with enough condescension and caution to keep them from crossing red lines. Based on this preconception, he had decided, when she first entered his house, to guide his interactions with her by rules he had sketched in his mind. He would give her orders seriously and sternly and then withdraw to his study, which he would not leave until she finished her work. He would pay her and then escort her to the door, where he would reply to her good-bye with a faint grunt. But once he had needed a cup of coffee and surprised her in the kitchen when she was hard at work, her face toward the wall. Her dancing hips, her bare neck, the spread of her back, the harmony of her body parts, the boyish bob of her hair, which was tinted with henna, and that plumpness favored by Middle Eastern women had all struck him like a thunderbolt. He froze in place, thinking that he was in the presence of some other woman—not Sulaf, the maid. Sensing his presence, she turned, and he was confronted by her honey-colored eyes, which shone with a femininity that he found hard to resist, a radiant face that shone with youth and enchantment, two firm lips that were slightly open as if preparing for feverish kisses, and a pert bosom that seemed to desire fondling and caresses, for fear it would explode from waiting too long for love.

He remained standing there without speaking or moving.

"Would you like something, Professor?"

Stammering, he requested a cup of coffee and returned to his study, but his desires were as rowdy as the street during celebrations or angry, massive protests.

She placed the cup of coffee before him.

And remained standing there.

Out of the corner of his right eye he saw her gaze at the books, enchanted and attracted.

What does she want? Why doesn't she return to the kitchen?

"I love books . . . I don't know why," he heard her say, like a child suddenly confronted by a toy she has long desired.

"Have you read books?" he asked, without looking at her.

"No. Never. But I love books!"

Should I order her to return immediately to the kitchen?

He decided to do it, no matter what.

He rose and approached her, his throat dry and his heart pounding. He took her hand, and she didn't object. Her lips were trembling, and her breasts projected toward him forcefully, not to fend him off but for an embrace. Her eyes gleamed with the sparkle of feverish desire. Her body was in a state of turmoil, apparently with no restraints.

He embraced her, and she did not object. He led her silently to the bed, and she submitted to him totally, as if this turn of events did not surprise her at all!

Since that time Sulaf had been his secret lover. Her body enchanted him. Her moans enraptured him. Her surrender to his desires and insane whims aroused him, as did her expertise in satisfying them. Not once did she ask about his private life. For his part, he was satisfied with what he knew about her: a mother of two who lived with her aged, ailing mother. Was she married? Divorced? This did not interest him at all. What mattered to him, quite candidly and frankly, was the woman herself, nothing else.

She was diligent and obedient at work and playful and lusty in bed.

♦

He returned to the study, to read newspapers on the internet. Prominent National and Cultural Figures Implore His Honor the President to Accept Nomination Once More.

Nomination again?

That meant the president would remain in power until . . . until Yunus turned seventy? But would he live that long? He would probably die first. *That southern poet, the one accused of heresy, was right when he wrote that we are destined to live with one god, one messenger, one book, one party, one flag, one national anthem, one first lady, and one president for as long as we live. Therefore, it is impossible for you, fine, noble people to escape from the grip of any of these. You are imprisoned in a cage, shackled with chains, forbidden to disobey or even to express your opinion on the simplest matters. (But do you really have an opinion?) You are forbidden to lift your head, to strive to affirm your existence. You are forbidden to express your feelings. (But do you truly have any feelings?) You are forbidden to violate our excellent laws and maxims, and it is impossible for you to doubt or abuse them. Thus it will be best for you, gracious, good-hearted, innocent, well-behaved, hospitable, generous, noble, obedient, servile, and craven people sapped of volition and life, to bow and yield, because the knife rests on your necks. If you attempt to wiggle so much as the width of a finger, your jugular vein will be severed and your life will end, without you having aroused the mercy or compassion of anyone, near or far, whether on earth or in heaven.*

All the legal shenanigans devised during the last twenty years had been exhausted. Therefore, it was necessary to coin a new stratagem: to urge the elites to implore him now, quickly, to remain in the seat of power five more years. Then it would be easy for the people to be led, since the deep-rooted elite groups that steered the country's affairs and that knew everything big and small had initiated this request. Huge crowds would immediately fill the streets and squares in the cities and villages to demand—with roaring chants, the tunes of *mizmar* flutes, the beating of drums, and the trills of women—that he remain in power for five more years. Indeed, perhaps forever! Because he was the savior and the architect of mighty projects; he was sacrificing his health and comfort for the good of the country; he was the friend of the poor and wretched; he was the guarantor of the future of the coming generations; he was the shield protecting the nation and a zealous defender of the rights and freedom of women. In brief, he was a safety belt against all dangers. Once more, then . . . once more . . . once more, please, Mr. President . . . please! *People, you will never grow weary,*

you will never feel afraid, you will never despair, and you will never die. In
fact, you will feel proud and happy, and your children and grandchildren
will be happy too. Adjure him, then. Implore him!

◆

Here was an article about Mao Zedong as a great symbol for members
of his generation and for young people of the 1960s and 1970s. The title
was "Years of Hunger and Death." On its first page was a picture of Mao
Zedong seated on a fancy chair, with one leg crossed over the other. He
wore summer clothing: a white shirt and gray trousers with athletic shoes.
He seemed to be in excellent health. To his right, dazzled male and female
students gazed at him with smiling, radiant faces—as if looking at a god.
They clearly were gleaning every word he spoke as if it represented a divine
pronouncement. The only one of them who looked dubious and apprehensive was a male student wearing glasses and standing at the far edge
of the photo. He was gazing quizzically at the revered Great Leader. The
picture may have been taken during the years of the Cultural Revolution
when Mao Zedong unleashed the Red Guard and students in all parts of
China and asked them to revive the Great Leap Forward and to wipe out
the bourgeoisie, reactionaries, and agents inside the Communist Party.
The article said, "We must not deny that Mao Zedong was the father of
the Chinese people because he did unite the country, knew how to rescue
it from the destruction threatening it, and then returned it to its place
among nations. The final thirty years of his rule, however, were alarming and calamitous. In the name of 'cleansing the party's path,' massacres
were committed. Those massacres began in the 1930s when Mao Zedong
retreated to Yunnan after the Long March. During the Hundred Flowers
and the Great Leap Forward campaigns approximately thirty-five million
died of starvation. The concentration camps that were established to 'reed-
ucate' antisocial elements and critics housed nearly fifty million, including
educated people, physicians, engineers, merchants, and renowned university professors. Only half of them survived. All this was achieved under
the heading of Agricultural Reform. Even sparrows did not escape the
atrocious massacres committed during that black period of Chinese history; they were accused of eating grain and therefore were killed to protect

agriculture. Mao Zedong and his comrades forgot, however, that sparrows also feed on insects, which found themselves free, in the absence of predators, to wipe out the crops. In 1966 Mao Zedong launched what he called the Cultural Revolution, asserting that he wished to create 'great anarchy under heaven' in order to revive a 'tremendous regime,' although in the end all he achieved was anarchy because schools and universities were closed. He sent hundreds of thousands of educated youth to the countryside. As a result, there were waves of suicides, arrests, floggings in public places, and mass killings." The author of the article concluded by asking, "But who was Mao? Merely a library assistant who hated educated people and specialists. He was a failed artist and poet and a repulsive creature with yellowed teeth. Despite having syphilis, he did not shower. Instead, he preferred to bathe in the bodies of his young lovers."

◆

"Marrakech Is a Paradise for Pederasts"

The author of this article said that a great number of French and European homosexuals and pederasts head to Marrakech, not to enjoy its Arab/African beauty, to wander through its unique, covered markets, or to watch the magicians and listen to the storytellers in Jemaa el-Fnaa Square, but to search for pleasure and enjoyment in the company of boys and adolescents. Jawad, a fifteen-year-old adolescent, related the story of his life. He said, "For the last two years I've sold my body to men seeking sexual pleasure—Europeans for the most part. I don't care how old they are, if they smell bad sometimes, or what their foul sexual caprices are. All that matters to me is making money. The favorite place is the upscale quarter called Jiliz, where there are fancy cafés, restaurants, and hotels. Usually contacts start in fast-food restaurants, and the sex is conducted in the gardens, far from sight; in automobiles; or in hotel rooms. The cost of each job is three hundred dirhams. The first person who led me to this world was a Frenchman in his fifties. He took me to his hotel room and sodomized me for one thousand dirhams. That was a bigger sum than I had ever dreamt of." Jawad continued: "My father has been unemployed for years. I have three brothers and a sister. My mother is sick most of the time. I'm the family's sole breadwinner. No one asks me where and how I make the money."

♦

"The Inferno of Somalia"

In this essay, the French journalist said that thousands of Somalis—including men, old men, women, old women, and children—are fleeing to Kenya on account of drought, starvation, the wars that have raged unchecked for years, and the brutality of the Islamic militias that rule the largest portion of the country and that impose their laws by force, brutality, violence, and terror. Describing the groups of migrants, the French journalist wrote: "They emerge like phantoms, walking like robots along a road dug into the dust-colored earth. The scorching sun pounds them, and they are weighed down by the possessions they carry on their backs and by the calamities they have endured. An old man leans against a cart transporting flour, a mattress, and cooking utensils. Not far from him, a woman walks bent over by the weight of the food she carries on her back. The children are not crying. All the migrants are sweating profusely under the merciless sun. They once owned camels and goats and sheep, but these perished during the long drought." The French journalist also discussed a Somali named Muhammad Abdi, who was forty-two. He had lost his two-year-old daughter because he had not been able to provide enough food and milk for her. He had been forced to bury her by the road. One Somali told the French journalist, "We're not just fleeing from drought and starvation, but from al-Shabaab as well. If you don't support them, they cut off your hands and feet and do whatever they want to you. If you have a wife or a beautiful daughter, they snatch her from you. They also seize children and adolescents to send to the battlefronts or to utilize for certain missions." Another Somali related his story in approximately this way: "Al-Shabaab came to me and asked me to lob a bomb at innocent people. When I refused, they shot my right foot, causing a deep wound. Some days later I returned to my house to find they had killed my wife, son, and daughter. Since then I don't sleep at night; if I slept, I would dream about my wife and two children. When I woke up, I would find myself alone. Now I live in constant fear. I'm afraid of dying alone in a spot far from my birthplace."

◆

"De Tocqueville among the American Indians"

This column was about a book called *A Fortnight in the Wilderness* by Alexis de Tocqueville, who wrote the famous book *Democracy in America*. This young French judge arrived in the New World in 1831. When he decided to interrupt his studies of democracy, he set off for the American West in hopes of discovering "savage virtue." Thus he spent two weeks in a desert with white Americans, who had moved to that area, and red Indians, who crowned their heads with feathers. He wrote, "I doubt that I ever felt a more total disappointment than I experienced when I witnessed Indians for the first time." De Tocqueville added that the Indians had loud voices, lean limbs, gleaming hair, and very wide mouths. During his tour of the desert, while surrounded by strange and amazing scenes that he described with "an imagination afflicted by a high fever," de Tocqueville witnessed the "methodical destruction of the primitive Indian culture." Befriending the Indians caused him to shy away from "the whites' language," which in his opinion sanctioned "deceptive trade practices," and failed lamentably to "express the natural sentiments closest to the heart."

◆

"Bloody Explosions Shake Baghdad and Numerous Other Iraqi Cities with Dozens of Victims"

"Sectarian Strife Grows More Intense between Sunnis and Shi'a"; News reports like this had become extremely common. One heard them almost every moment; now they didn't enrage or upset him. In fact, they might not make any impact on him. They quickly dissolved in the deluge of news reports that poured down at every moment. These articles barely distinguished between wars, athletic competitions, famines, victims of the deathtrap ships in the Mediterranean, scientific and medical discoveries, the scandals of artists, political summits, and so forth. It was the

responsibility of the listener, viewer, or reader to digest it all quickly . . .
yes, with extraordinary speed, because time is precious and can't be
wasted on meaningless stuff. If he didn't adopt this approach, he would
need to retire from life in the present-day world. In any case, violence,
despotism, civil strife, wars, grudges, and lethal hatred had a long history
in the land of the two rivers, the Tigris and Euphrates. Most of those who
had ruled Iraq from the Assyrians and Babylonians to the present time
were bloodthirsty tyrants who were past masters at slaying and torture.
They felt the same passion for chopping off heads that a lover feels for
plucking flowers to offer to his true love. Perhaps the legendary beast, the
Zabzab, still lives in the land between the two rivers. If it disappears for a
period, it will quickly return to spread terror, crime, and strife. Legends
say that this phantom scares the people of Iraq when it appears. At times
they see it only as a shadow or a black bird circling over the rooftops and
above the surface of the Tigris. It eats children and cuts off men's hands,
feet, and penises. It mutilates the bodies of women and rips open the bellies of pregnant mothers. It plucks off the breasts of virgins and snatches
beautiful women from their husbands and lovers. It spreads murderous
epidemics that kill dozens of people daily, planting death in the markets
and public places, snuffing out the candles of joy, happiness, and hope and
spreading a thick, dark shadow over the whole land. Welcome, Zabzab,
once more, since there is no way to escape from you and since the people
of Iraq, exhausted by a succession of wars, calamities, and disasters, have
no ability to confront you or to avert your atrocious massacres and the
hideous deeds you commit against them in broad daylight and the dark of
night, in spring's radiance and winter's gloom, in summer's extreme heat
and autumn's romantic mood.

◆

**"The Arab States, Especially the Gulf States, Currently Experience
Anxiety and Alarm Because of the Determination of the Islamic
Iranian Republic to Enrich Uranium to Produce a Nuclear Weapon"**

The flame of the ancient enmity between the Arabs and the Persians—
which also has a religious dimension—will never be extinguished and

may burn brighter because the Persians from the beginning chose to enter Islam as heretical Khawarij. Even before Islam, the Persians attacked the Arabs from time to time, killing many of them and destroying their means of livelihood. At that time, the Arabs were Bedouins—uncouth, barefoot, destitute, hungry desert people who ate beetles, scorpions, and snakes. They wore cloth made from yarn they spun from camel and goat hair and wool. Each tribe fought the others and practiced female infanticide. Hatred was a staple they could never have enough of, and disagreements were settled by the blade of a sword; pity and mercy were unnecessary luxuries. Their ambitions did not extend to a lust for status or sovereignty.

When the violent and brutal Shapur II—known to Arabs as Broadshouldered Shapur—learned that Arabs were causing havoc and destruction and plundering people at the boundaries of his kingdom, he readied a mighty army and ordered his troops to slay every Arab they encountered. The army advanced and proceeded to shed blood until it poured down like rain. The Arabs fled from death's terror but found nothing that could protect them from the evil of this attack. Then they turned back to let swords tear open their bodies, and the Iranian troops did not pass a water source they did not fill or an oasis they did not burn.

Before Persia fell to the Muslims, Khosrow dreamt that he saw his lofty palace cleft asunder and flying off in pieces. Early the next day, he summoned the many astrologers and sorcerers in his service. Among them was an Arab called al-Sa'ib, who was an expert astrologer. He was rarely wrong in his prognostications. After Khosrow related his dream, the soothsayer bowed his head sorrowfully and said in Farsi, "*Shah bishakest*: the king is broken." Then the king ordered his astrologers and sorcerers to investigate the matter. They left his presence anxiously, and each one sequestered himself somewhere to solve the riddle of the king's dream. Al-Sa'ib went off on a dark night to a hill and stood on its summit, thinking and considering. At midnight he witnessed a flash originate from Hejaz in the west. Then, in the wink of an eye, it streaked to the east, traversing all of Persia. At daybreak he found at his feet a green meadow that undulated in the sunshine. He told himself, "I think a king will emerge from the Hejaz and extend his rule over this land." When the other astrologers learned what he had concluded, they were alarmed and afraid. They told each other, "If we tell Khosrow this, he will grow angry and kill us all. We must devise some strategy to protect us from this calamity." After consulting with each other, they went to Khosrow and advised him to build a new palace. "Perhaps the current palace has some design flaws." He accepted their advice and devoted considerable resources to this project. Once the building was completed, he asked to sit atop the wall on a luxurious carpet. The wall, however, collapsed suddenly, and Khosrow escaped death only by a miracle. Muslim legends and history books say that Khosrow was sitting during the hottest part of the day in his private lounge, where no visitors were admitted, when a man surrounded by light appeared by the emperor's head, holding a stick. Khosrow heard this man say, "Khosrow, will you surrender or shall I break this stick?" Khosrow replied, "Go away! Leave me alone!" and the man disappeared. Khosrow was angry and yelled at his guards, "Who let that stranger in?" They informed him that they had not seen anyone. A year later, at the same time and place, the incident was repeated, and the stranger declared that unless Khosrow surrendered, he would break the stick. When the Iranian emperor refused, the man immediately disappeared. Again, Khosrow summoned his guards and gave them a tongue-lashing: "Which of you permitted this stranger with a stick to disturb my rest during the heat of the day?" They denied seeing anyone. The next year, the stranger appeared for a third time in the same place, stood by Khosrow's head, and asked him, "Will you surrender, or shall I break the stick?" Then Khosrow replied, "Leave me alone! Go away!" This time the man broke the stick and disappeared. "Afterward, the Persian king was broken: *Shah bishakest.*"

◆

"Two days ago, a renowned cleric issued a declaration denouncing plans for the new airport in the capital of his country." This religious leader said that the project—which he claimed resembled an erect penis about to penetrate a woman's vagina—was a screaming assault on religious taboos and on his country's sanctity. This cleric added that infidel Westerners had prepared the plans and that this clearly revealed their foul, evil intentions and proved once more that their crusader propensity still haunted and motivated them to the present day. Now they were attempting to express and embody it in different ways, even with the plans they had drafted for the airport of an Islamic Arab country. The cleric demanded that the government renounce the plans. If it did not, the consequences would be "disastrous," as he put it.

◆

The telephone rang again. It was his friend Samir.

"Good morning. Happy birthday, my dear friend."

"Thank you very much."

"You're celebrating your sixtieth birthday today. I will celebrate mine in about a month. We're in the same cart, my friend. But no one knows who will fall first."

People discussed death more than life, and here it was peering down with a glowering face, preparing to pounce. "Death stomps its hooves forcefully on the ground, impatient to enter." *Who said that? Who? Kundera? Yes, Kundera.*

"Can you hear me?"

"I hear you fine, my friend." (As a matter of fact, he hadn't heard what Samir had said.)

"I asked: What are you doing today?"

"Oh . . ." He didn't know. Perhaps he would go to the Albatross Restaurant as usual.

"For the past several years, I have also stopped making plans to celebrate my birthday as I once did. We've grown old, my friend. Such matters no longer retain any significance or meaning. What happiness does a man find in celebrating his birthday when he knows there's not much left of his life? Isn't that so?" He fell silent for a time and then continued, "The fact is, Yunus, I don't believe we're turning sixty. Not so long ago we were young guys—dancing, singing, and carousing, oblivious to the cares or problems of the world. When an old man walked by, we would glance at him with regret and pity because wrinkles had creased his face and furrows his brow, fatigue showed clearly in his expression, and his gait was so slow and uncertain that it seemed he might fall with any step. His hands trembled and his back was bent, and the black moles sprinkled over his bald head showed that his departure to the next world was imminent.

Why cling to life? I believe we will soon be in that old man's condition. He looked at us young men and women crossing the street as if we were superfluous creatures who ought to proceed at breakneck speed to avoid missing the delight of life and the bloom of youth. Don't you agree?"

Samir was right.

"I'll call you back in a few minutes," Samir said, "because I hear the doorbell."

His relationship with Samir dated back to their university days. Then it had matured into a firm friendship because they held similar views about literature, music, and other things. They had graduated from university in the same year and then had enrolled in doctoral programs. Samir traced his roots to a village in the south, although Yunus could never remember its name. Four years before he was born, his family had settled in the capital. He had spent his childhood torn between the capital and the desert, since his father, who was a merchant in Souk el Grana in the Medina of Tunis, was keen on sending him back there for every school holiday: "So he won't forget his roots." Once his father died, Samir stopped going to the village and never referred to it, not even in passing. One time when he was inebriated, he said, "I'm a child of the capital. I love its clamor, prostitutes, thieves, and riffraff. I hate the desert, which is a place favored by lazy people, sorcerers, swindlers, and idiotic romantics. I can't stand sand dunes, oases, or coarse, cunning Bedouins and their lies about courage, honor, and generous hospitality. They are servile cowards and even stingier than the people skewered in *The Misers* by al-Jahiz." Samir married twice, but these marriages were flops. His first wife accused him in court of beating her and forcing her, during intercourse, to perform disgusting acts she preferred not to mention. The second fled from him after only three months. In court, as tears flowed down her cheeks, she said, "I want nothing from him but a divorce because he's a savage in the true meaning of the word." After that divorce, Samir chose to live with his mother who, despite being over eighty, enjoyed good physical and mental health. She was the person he loved best in the whole world, and she preferred him to her other four sons. She treated him as if he were her baby boy who needed all her affection and care. She may have been delighted by the failure of his marriages because she couldn't bear for him to be far from her. She would console him and observe from time to time, "Women today, my dear son, don't seem to be good enough for you. You'll need to be patient until God brings you a decent girl, who will make you and herself happy because you're a generous, good-hearted fellow. Any virtuous woman would want to be your wife." But Samir stopped thinking about marriage, especially once he turned forty and began to satisfy himself with whatever brief, transitory couplings chance afforded him.

The telephone rang. It was Samir again.

"Sorry. My older brother came to visit my mother. He does that at the end of each month. God bless him in any event! The others only visit her during holidays and the Eids. But this doesn't concern you. Oh, before I forget: I'm going to Bizerte to visit the father of our dear, lamented Béchir. Will you come with me?"

He couldn't.

"Why not?"

Attending Béchir's funeral had devastated Yunus psychologically. It would be difficult for him to see, again, the poor father who had awaited the return of his prodigal son for thirty years, only to have death snatch him away four months after his return.

"As if he had returned to die!"

"Yes, he returned to die."

"My mother—may God prolong her life—says the spirit of an émigré prods him to return as quickly as possible to his homeland once he senses that his death is imminent, even if that means traveling to the ends of the earth." He fell silent but quickly resumed: "I will go, my friend. Someone needs to console his wretched father. Besides, we're the only two friends Béchir had in this country: you and me. Isn't that so?"

"True." All the same it would be a jolt for him to go to Bizerte.

"Fine. I'll phone you when I return. Then you'll have to come to the capital. I miss you a lot."

Why didn't he come to Neapolis?

"You're right. I need to visit you. It's been a long time since I've done that. I love the city and your soirees at the Albatross, but I'll be busy this week. Next week I'll come and spend two days with you. Would that inconvenience you?"

"No, not at all, never."

"So, until then, and take care of yourself. Don't drink too much, the way you did on your birthday last year. Do you remember?"

"Yes, I remember."

"Be careful then. You're old enough that you shouldn't drink or do anything else to excess."

◆

The sea had been rough, and waves were breaking angrily over each other on the way to the shore. The sky was full of thick, black clouds, which were pierced by lightning from time to time. A deluge of rain was falling heavily. Bizerte was miserable and distressed. The old quarter was groaning with agony and the pain of separation. Faces were gloomy, and the gloomiest face was that of Béchir's miserable father. He stood in the bitter cold, accepting condolences. His parched lips mumbled muffled words no one understood or heard clearly. The calamity had transformed him into a dark ghost that now belonged not to the world of the living but to the land of the dead. Béchir's brothers and family, who were still and silent, were also accepting condolences. Their expressions suggested that they did this coolly and nonchalantly because most of them were grown, and some had married and had children. The only trace of the deceased during his long absence had been his name, which had been mentioned occasionally by his father or mother. Over the years they had perhaps begun to feel that this stranger was no longer one of them and that they were no longer related to him. This feeling became more ingrained in them at his mother's death, when he did not attend her funeral and did not inform them how her demise affected him. Even his father mentioned his name less frequently after that. He may have decided that his son, who had left the country when he was twenty-two, would never return, and this meant that he too would die without seeing his son again. In his rare, infrequent letters, Béchir talked about himself or his private life only tersely. He merely inquired how members of the family were. He never asked about the state of the nation or what was happening there. These letters came from different places: Paris, Rome, London, Madrid, Beirut, Cairo, or Damascus. Reports that émigrés brought back contradicted each other and were confused; it was hard to judge their accuracy. These reports said Béchir worked for major Arab newspapers and magazines and had married a French or Lebanese Christian woman. Some affirmed that they had seen him in Montmartre in Paris with two children who might have been his sons. He looked well-off and seemed prosperous and happy. In letters he wrote replying to his son, the father never dared ask even once about his personal life. Instead, he limited himself to telling Béchir he wanted him to return, missed him very much, and did not wish to die without seeing him again.

Thirty-four years after his departure, Béchir sent his father a letter in which he said he would soon return to the country—in about two weeks. When he received this happy, unexpected news, the father remained still and silent, plunged deep in thought. Then his family saw him prostrate himself in prayer seven times to thank God for His grace and affection for him after an extended period of forgetfulness and neglect. Soon he began to make the rounds of the quarter—now the frown that had shadowed him for many years had vanished—inviting young and old, friends and enemies, to attend the grand party he would host to celebrate the return of his son whom he hadn't seen for thirty-four years. "Everyone, come! Come! I'll slaughter a lamb. There will be a joyous party unlike any you've ever experienced." When he said this, his face shone, and a smile illuminated his countenance. This old man, whose back was bowed by the weight of his years, suddenly stood erect and began to traverse the quarter with the agility of a man in his forties. Béchir's brothers and other family members were skeptical: how could someone far away announce he would return in two weeks without specifying the day, the hour when he would arrive at the airport, or even the flight number? If he had been serious, he would have done that, like all other expatriates and travelers arriving from abroad. Moreover, the country had changed a lot. Even those who had lived there all their lives no longer recognized it. He said he would return in two weeks but hadn't asked for a family member to be at the airport to meet him and handle any problems that might arise. He might not be able to find the house, for example. That was conceivable. No, no! One needed to be wary. That was necessary. This absent family member who was far away also had a history of being opaque and had avoided all references to his private life in his letters. Thus they scarcely knew anything about him. The one fact they knew was that he had left the country suddenly when he was twenty-two, interrupting his study of philosophy at the university, and had roamed the world. Now he was in the West; then he was in the East— exactly like a migratory bird. No, no, one could not trust what a distant traveler announced. One couldn't. The only ones who shared the father's delight at his son's return were the young children, who were enjoying the final weeks of their summer holiday. They accompanied him on his tours of the quarter, whether in the morning or the evening. When he sat down to rest, they surrounded him and asked him to tell them about his son whom he hadn't seen for thirty-four years. At night, before falling asleep, each child would try to sketch a mental profile of this man. What would he be like? Ugly or handsome? Charming or rude? Taciturn or garrulous? Plump or thin? Good-hearted or cold-blooded? Tall or short? Haughty or humble? Generous or stingy? Brown-haired or blond? Perhaps he would be blond, since he had lived in those worlds with Europeans . . . yes, that was likely. Didn't the adults say that a person who imitates a group comes to resemble them? He might be like one of his brothers. But which one? The eldest? No, no . . . he was always scowling and hated children. He beat them for the most trivial reasons. He also beat his wife. The middle brother? He too was not much liked in the quarter. He was always sequestered in his house and rarely spoke to people. He didn't mingle with folks and acted as if he lived on his own private continent. The youngest? Oh . . . this one was always laughing. He was bright and loved children. He was devoted to major soccer stars like Pelé, Maradona, Beckenbauer, and Zinedine Zidane and told amazing stories about them. He also loved the cinema. All the girls in the quarter were fond of him. If this distant stranger resembled him, all the children would be happy and become his loyal friends when he arrived.

Two weeks after they received that letter, a yellow taxi stopped in front of the family house in the old quarter of Bizerte. Out of it stepped an elegant, dignified man with gray hair. He wore a beige suit and light brown shoes. His dark glasses were of a fashionable brand, and his suitcase was of medium size. Over his right shoulder, he carried another bag. *Who can this stranger be? Who is he?* the father wondered as he sat at the doorstep.

His heart almost stopped beating. The stranger smiled. Then the father leapt up to throw himself into the man's arms. Weeping, he shouted, "My son! My son! My dear son has returned! He's back!" The uproar quickly spread through the entire quarter, and men, women, and children shoved against each other to kiss the revenant and congratulate him, his father, and his brothers. Celebrations lasted three entire days, during which the family home was never empty of well-wishers—not in the morning or the evening, not during the day or the night. When the commotion diminished, and the number of visitors decreased, the son sat with his father and informed him that he had decided to settle permanently in Tunisia, and that living abroad was now a thing of his past. Once more the father threw himself in his son's arms and wept loudly.

◆

He was sitting with his companions in the Albatross Restaurant one autumn evening when the daylight had begun to fade and the veil of a light fog was preparing for the night, which had started to blanket the hills and the western mountains. The coast was enjoying this stillness and calm—like a lover surrendering to the kisses of a sweetheart. A refreshing breeze pursued the last remnants of summer's heat. He and his comrades had finished their second bottle of wine and ordered their third. The waiter soon brought them a plate of broad beans, Tunisian salad, and grilled sardines. They were discussing what to discuss. Should they talk about Arab republics that were preparing themselves to become kingdoms with a dynastic succession of power? Then a stranger approached and asked graciously and politely if he might join them. They glanced at each other. None of them knew him. He might be a boring curiosity-seeker who would spoil their evening. No . . . not really. His appearance did not suggest that. His gentlemanly, urbane, dapper appearance belied that assumption. Who was he, then?

The stranger smiled. "Fine. Sorry. I seem to have disturbed you. Isn't that so?"

"No, no . . . not at all." But what did he want?

"One of my dear friends is sitting with you, but he seems to have forgotten me."

"Who?"

The stranger pointed to him and said, "Professor Yunus."

Me?

"Yes, my dear Yunus. Don't you remember me?"

No, he did not.

"Look carefully at my face and you will. You will certainly recall me."

No, he didn't remember him.

"You're right. You haven't seen me for thirty-four years and . . . perhaps have heard nothing about me."

Who was he?

"Yunus, I'm the fellow you used to call 'that naughty boy.'"

"'The naughty boy . . . the naughty boy?' You're not Béchir?"

"Yes, I am Béchir: that crazy, naughty boy!"

He jumped from his chair to give his friend a long, fervent embrace in front of his astonished drinking buddies. Then he turned to them and explained, "Dear friends, please excuse me from your distinguished company because this naughty boy needs a private tutorial!"

He chose a remote corner on the restaurant's balcony so they could enjoy the beauty of the sun setting over the sea. Each man began to scrutinize the other's features to discern the effects of the long years of separation.

"Do you know, my dear friend, that you've always been on my mind," Béchir said. "You've always been on my mind. Most of my old friends, my university friends, have been obliterated from my memory, but not you or Samir. You, in particular. Wherever I went, I remembered you. I thought of you in the alleys of Cairo, in the coffeehouse called Havana in Damascus, in the bars of the Latin Quarter in Paris, in the gardens in London, in the restaurants of Tangier and its hostels. I always thought of you and remembered our tumultuous days at the university; our nightly discussions about Flaubert, your favorite author; and Nietzsche, my favorite philosopher. By the way, is Flaubert still . . . ?"

"Yes, he still is."

"I'm the same. Nietzsche is still my favorite philosopher. I'm always rereading his works without ever feeling bored or dissatisfied. I say: Friend, you've always been on my mind. I would ask myself from time to time, 'What do you suppose that Bedouin Yunus is doing? Has he finally accepted that he should publish what he writes? But you seem to have stuck to your original decision because I've scouted the bookstores of Tunis and Bizerte and haven't found anything you've published. Before I returned, I told myself: I must see Yunus. When I went to Tunis, ten days after I returned, Samir's face was the first of the old ones to shine at me in Bab al-Bahr. I recognized him easily, but he had trouble determining my identity . . . exactly like you. He's the one who gave me your telephone number and told me you live in Neapolis and sit in the Albatross Restaurant every evening. I didn't want to phone you and preferred to surprise you in your excellent hangout."

He truly was happy with this delightful surprise. He too had thought of Béchir from time to time and asked himself: "Where do you suppose that naughty boy is? What country has snatched him from his friends? What is he doing and how does he like his exile?" Once, in Paris, Yunus met an old friend who informed him he saw Béchir at times in the Saint-Germain-Des-Prés Café in the company of beautiful women.

"Ha, ha, ha. Always in the company of beautiful women! That's something from my distant past, my friend. Now I'm accompanied by nothing but the vagaries of old age, my ailments, and my concerns."

He too!

"We're in the same boat," Béchir said. Then he laughed briefly and nervously.

"Come on. Tell me about yourself. How did you spend your years abroad?"

A light cloud of sorrow shaded Béchir's face. "My story . . . is long . . . very long, my friend."

He lit a Gauloises and looked at the sea, which reflected the colors of the sunset. Then he added, "You and I belong to a generation of fantasies and dreams, my friend, and many of us have paid a high price for that. Yes, this is the truth. As you know, I was an extreme devotee of Nietzsche—a rebel against the culture of malice, banality, and hypocrisy, against the politics of fear, deception, opportunism, and despotism. At the university, nothing appealed to me. The lectures were exasperating, disgusting, and nauseating. The professors were superficial and had all the attributes of civil servants whose minds had been dumbed through growing accustomed to obeying and bowing and to the politics of the big stick. The distinguished ones were restricted and placed under surveillance after Michel Foucault was thrown out of the country on the charge that he organized lewd soirees and parties in his house in Sidi Bou Said. Actually, he was expelled because he sympathized with the left-wing students. I thus found myself studying with stupid instructors, who repeated the same words every day. They got on my nerves so badly that at times I wanted to throw my shoe at them or to spit at their faces, especially when they discussed Nietzsche. I couldn't stand the other students in the Philosophy Department either. Most of them accepted the silly and superficial lectures presented to them, with no criticism or protest—as if they were heavenly revelations. They digested them as happily as donkeys eating hay in winter stables. You will recall that when Bourguiba wasn't satisfied with having his pronouncements broadcast on the radio and TV more than once a day he began to visit the law school and deliver lectures in an attempt to counteract the students rebelling against him and his regime. In these, he would laud his own struggle and his battles. He would expatiate about his times in prison and in exile, his mother, Fatouma, and his one testicle, which had allowed him to sire a son who was his spitting image. Disgusted by all this, I decided to leave. I traveled light, taking only one small suitcase, in which I packed my books by Nietzsche, a French dictionary, some clothes, and a few toiletries. My family thought I would not be gone long and said good-bye to me casually. My mother did not shed a tear, and my father didn't suspect my intentions. The country of a million martyrs was my first stop, but after only a week there, I felt even more suffocated in Algeria than in my own country. It became obvious to me that the Algerian regime's lies were even more atrocious and loathsome than those of our own. The media there never stopped praising the tremendous accomplishments the revolution had realized and would realize. But I encountered nothing but devastation and the distortion of everything true, beautiful, or authentic. I witnessed honor and conscience bought and sold, intellectuals terrorized, an expanding expertise in deceit and misinformation and in the betrayal of the martyrs. In the name of the Agricultural Revolution, fields were ruined, and estates and orchards neglected—while farmers went hungry. Agricultural workers began to move in great numbers to the capital and other large cities, where they crammed into shantytowns and a surrounding belt of poverty. Later on, in those areas, the spark of the bread riots ignited and propagandists for puritanical extremism and civil strife established themselves. They would eventually plunge the country into crime and blood and slaughtered educated people and poets as if sacrificing sheep. The condition of that country of a million martyrs alarmed me. So only a month after my arrival there, I left it with no regrets for the country of the Green Revolution.

"The moment I entered its capital, Tripoli, I was met by huge pictures of its leader—posted everywhere—in different poses. Here he was in a tent, reading the Qur'an—dressed in desert garb, drinking camel milk, or in a military uniform with medals all over its shoulders and chest, standing in front of his beautiful bodyguards, whom he selected from all the different Libyan tribes, and shaking hands with a Bedouin deep in the desert. He was giving a speech in Green Square, waxing almost hysterical, or with his mentor, Gamal Abdel Nasser. Every day, students left their universities, pupils left their schools, civil servants left their offices, workers left their place of employment, and the unemployed left their slums. Why? To descend into the streets in massive groups, which were led by angry men with frowning miens and fists held high in the air, to shout for the victory of the Green Revolution and for death to America and Israel. When those groups tired of chanting, shouting, shrieking, threatening, and menacing, they congregated in Green Square, where in the most extreme states of anger and fury they began to burn 'poisoned books,' pictures of agents and reactionaries inside and outside the country, and the flags of countries hostile to Arabism and Islam. All this occurred with the blessing of the leader who had unleashed a cultural revolution throughout the country, like Mao Zedong. He claimed to have invented a new style of governance, one the world had not known before. He called it the Third Way. Like Stalin, he used to say in his orations, which were as long as the Nile, 'Seek even the devil's help if that benefits the revolution!'

"I left the country of the Green Revolution, while it was plunged in alarming anarchy, and took a plane to the Land of the Cedars. At first, I felt I had reached a safe haven where I could live freely, with hand and tongue unrestrained. I could do what I wanted and say what I pleased. So, I threw myself into its capital the way a man throws himself into the sea after crossing a long expanse of burning sand in a desolate desert. Other educated Arabs settled there after fleeing from their countries' regimes. Like me, they were looking for freedom and adventure. They wanted to write without censorship and to think without being threatened by the cudgel of a policeman or the fatwas of an imam. In the coffeehouses and clubs, evening discussions lasted until morning in an extremely cordial atmosphere. Even when conversations were rowdy or heated—whether about poetry, religion, or politics, which were dominant topics at the time—they would always end with hugs, apologies, and brotherly handshakes. Everyone accepted the possibility of difference. The Nasserist or the Baathist talked with the moderate or extreme Communist without growing angry or agitated, and vice versa. A person defending Islam would listen to everyone else magnanimously without attempting to impose his views on the others or trying to act like God's own caliph on earth. In short, concord prevailed. I lived in Beirut with a clear conscience, like my own boss. I would sleep when I wanted and write articles in which I attacked, acerbically, the regime in my country as well as others, made fun of religion, or presented my ideas about Gramsci, Jean-Paul Sartre, Camus, Herbert Marcuse, or members of the Frankfurt School. I translated the poetry of Lautréamont, the plays of Beckett, and erotic texts by surrealists. I read books banned in my country and listened with enjoyment to the speeches of leaders of the Palestinian Revolution. In their zeal, they pictured themselves as capable of liberating not just their country but all the occupied countries in the world. That night I had sex with my friend Marie-Rose, who enjoyed having sex after a late night because that helped her sleep for a long time; she wouldn't wake until late the next day. Then I went to the kitchen to have another glass by myself. When I heard gunfire from the city's outskirts, I assumed it was the Palestinians, who customarily celebrated the success of their operations against Israel and their other enemies in this way. But the gunfire became more concentrated and it soon spread to other areas, until the whole city began to shake from the gunfire. I wanted to tell Marie-Rose, thinking she might help find some explanation for all this, but I discovered she was sound asleep—like a small child worn out by playing on the sandy seashore. So, I returned to the kitchen. The clock showed that it was three in the morning. I sat drinking and smoking while I listened to gunfire, which became increasingly ferocious, and to muffled voices from the distance. In the morning, news came that bloody battles had flared up between the Palestinian Resistance and Christian Phalange Party forces. I heard an important political figure say on the radio that the Land of the Cedars would plunge into another civil war, which would last longer and be more destructive than the civil war of 1958. Thus in the wink of an eye, beautiful dreams turned into alarming nightmares, and the city lying between the sea and the mountains, a city I had considered a paradise amid Arab devastation, became a theater for fires and daily massacres as death and terror patrolled it night and day."

The sea was black now, and the sky was resplendent with its stars. There were few patrons left in the restaurant. Béchir fell silent. He lit a cigarette and filled his glass. Then he launched again into his narration of his memories of his long exile. "That prominent political figure was right; a destructive civil war exploded in the Land of the Cedars and brought vipers out of their lairs, savage beasts from their black grottoes, and demons from their secret hiding places. They revealed what had lain hidden in people's souls and hearts: grudges, hatreds, or strife between the different factions, parties, and organizations. Killing people for their sectarian identity or political affiliation, became very easy . . . as easy as drinking a cup of water. Those men who had spent pleasant nights debating justice, liberty, equality, socialism, Arab unity, and universal brotherhood sloughed off their comity and began to fight each other savagely and ferociously. Each was now the other's enemy. Each wished to see his foe slain in the worst possible way: his corpse charred, disfigured, separated from its head, without hands or feet, its belly slashed open, or rotting in the sunshine as armies of blue flies swarmed over it or stray dogs circled it to finish off any remnants. In a few weeks, the savage, primitive instincts of the Middle East emerged to pulverize everything I had considered progress, civilization, nobility, love, and human values. Possessed by savage instincts, fraternal enemies proceeded to devise the most lethal and destructive means of murder against each other. In every location—whether in our homes or the coffeehouses, a shop, in the street, or on the beach—death stalked us, especially after the appearance of booby-trapped cars. To wreak vengeance on the Land of the Cedars, which had been a luminous candle in the Arab darkness, that country's great neighbor goaded its soldiers and spies to increase its devastation, to infect its wounds, to kindle the strife between feuding brothers, and to turn the country into a battlefield for internecine combat and a struggle between internal and external factions—until it was impossible for a person to distinguish friend from foe. Once again, I awoke to grievous news: a prominent journalist, whom I liked and respected and whose editorials I had read because they illuminated the concentrated darkness surrounding me, had been slain in his office. It was clear that his killers had used their expertise to torture him before polishing him off. They had cut off his ears and nose, gouged out his eyes, and broken his fingers to punish him for what he had heard of their weighty secrets, what he had sniffed out of their dreadful plots, what he had witnessed of their slaughters and massacres, and what he had written about their violence and savagery. Finally, they placed his pen in his anus and departed tipsy and content with what they had done to "the perfidious journalist and agent." I didn't leave the apartment that day. I smoked and drank, to the music of the gunfire and successive explosions, until night fell. Early the next day, I awoke to find I had slept fully dressed on the kitchen floor. A week later I was able to escape in one piece from that inferno. Then I was in Paris. For some time, I could not sleep. If I fell asleep, I had alarming nightmares during which I heard the commotion of that distant war—the reverberations of explosions, the pop of gunshots—and saw flames consume people and buildings, corpses stacked one on top of the other, the broken fingers of the great journalist and his pen stuck up his ass when morning dawned glowering, frowning, and haunted by the calamity of death and the repulsiveness of crime. But Béatrice restored my composure, peace of mind, and calm. Like me, she patronized the Cluny Café in the Latin Quarter. There she secluded herself in a corner and devoted her time to reading after she enjoyed a snack. Her face and eyes channeled the beauty of girls in paintings by classical artists; I was fascinated by her. She may have realized that I devoted a lot of time to looking at her because she smiled at me—when Paris was welcoming autumn with its yellow leaves, the joyous school *rentrée*, the tumultuous resumption of cultural and literary activities, the return of feverish speed to daily life and crowds to the streets, cafés, and restaurants—and I smiled back. After hesitating briefly, I approached her and asked permission to sit with her briefly.

"Please," she responded, smiling, as she pointed to the chair opposite her with her right hand. The way she said this word spread through me a desire to kiss the lips that had uttered it. I told her about myself and, when I said that I had come directly from the inferno of the civil war in the Land of the Cedars, she moaned and said, "Oh! That's the country in the entire Arab world that my grandfather loves best! He was a diplomat who was posted to Morocco, Egypt, and another Arab country I've forgotten, but the country from which he retains the most beautiful memories is the Land of the Cedars. He's now in his eighties. When I visit him, he talks about it a lot and shows me pictures he took there. The last time I went to see him, I found him sad and confined to bed with gout.

"He told me: 'I knew they wouldn't leave this country in safety and peace, and now they are finally lighting the fire of war in it so successfully that it will sink into the abysmal condition they desire for it—a wrecked, devastated country, where anarchy, terror, and death thrive on a daily basis. It's not possible for Lebanon to enjoy security, stability, or peace, and what's true for it is also true for most of the countries of the Levant.'"

She also told him about herself. She was from Toulouse, but her family had settled in Paris when she was six. She studied philosophy at the Sorbonne. Spinoza was her favorite philosopher: God was on earth, not in the heavens. He was in everything. That idea had attracted her to him. "Our discussion lasted until nightfall, when I invited her to a small Tunisian restaurant, where we ate couscous and drank a bottle of Bordeaux. Then we toured the cafés of the Latin Quarter. Late that night, I found myself in her small apartment in Montparnasse, and her body opened for me like a flower opening to welcome the morning light.

"I loved Béatrice and she loved me. We married after she graduated and spent our honeymoon in northern Spain. Four years after we married, Béatrice gave birth to our first child, whom we named Adam. Then we wanted a second child, and that happened. We named him Amin. I was working for Arab newspapers and magazines and translating books from French to Arabic. Our life was calm and simple. The years passed swiftly without our noticing their effect on our countenances, thoughts, feelings, and every other aspect. Then suddenly our life began to deteriorate and go from bad to worse, day by day. Quarrels flared up between us and intensified until neither of us could stand the other. In the end, we separated. One morning I woke up after a night on the town and found myself looking at a stranger's face—a face carved by wrinkles and marred by furrows, with bleary eyes, a swollen nose, a pendulous chin. Gray was advancing through my hair along both sides of the part.

"I felt alarmed. How could I have grown old so quickly? That evening, my son Adam visited me. I asked him, 'My dear, has your father changed?'

"'Yes, he's changed a lot.'

"'How?'

"He looked at me almost with pity and replied, 'Father, you've become an old man.'

"'Really?'

"'Yes.'

"Adam was twenty then, and I scrutinized his face in search of the young man I had once been, but the reflection of my face in the mirror thwarted my effort. I began to mutter, 'I'm an old man . . . an old man . . . an old man.'

"'What are you saying?' Adam asked me, somewhat dismayed.

"'Nothing. Nothing, my dear son.'

"'You're talking to yourself like old men I see at times in the street . . .'

"His words pierced my heart like a needle. Had I truly started raving like old men Adam saw in the street while hugging his new girlfriend, whom he might switch out a week or month later, like athletic shoes. That was possible, very possible.

"I wanted to change the topic, so I asked Adam about his studies, but he cautioned me, 'Take care of yourself, Father. You're growing old so fast that it frightens me and Amin.'

"I had wanted to invite Adam to dine with me but changed my mind. I was afraid of going out, of walking in the street, as if I were afflicted with some disability that would attract the attention of passersby and incite in them feelings that ranged from compassion and pity to aversion and repulsion.

"Adam said good-bye, grumbling angrily at me. I rushed to the kitchen and opened a bottle of wine, polishing off half of it in a few minutes without eating anything. Rain had begun to fall in torrents. I went to the window and looked out at the street. At the bus stop across the street, a young man and a young woman were trading kisses as their bodies melded. The scene alarmed me. I seemed to be a dead man granted a chance to observe the joy of life from the darkness of the tomb. The glass escaped from my hand, and shards of its glass flew across the kitchen floor. I did not hear the laughter overflowing with love that a smashing glass had inspired in a poet—it may have been Apollinaire, Éluard, or someone else. What I heard was my spirit splintering like the dry bough of a green tree. I left the kitchen and went to the bedroom to curl up in bed. I closed my eyes, wishing to flee from my black soul to another world. At some moment, a different vision of my country dawned on me—not the vague, gloomy one I had grown accustomed to harboring as an expatriate. It came to me with the radiant light of a Mediterranean morning on the beach at Les Grottes in Bizerte, green and fragrant like the vineyards and the orchards of figs and almonds in the spring at Raf Raf, dreamy like sunset in the oases of el-Djerid, and white and blue like the houses in Sidi Bou Said. I leapt out of bed happily, like someone who had long misplaced something and found it again after despairing that he ever would find it. So, I returned to my fatherland."

Béchir spent that night at Yunus's place. In the morning, before departing, he said, "Please, Yunus, visit me in Bizerte as soon as possible because I need you . . . you and Samir. You are the only two friends I have in this country, where I live now as a stray foreigner."

At the beginning of winter, he visited Béchir in a house he had rented in Bizerte on the Corniche. The weather was cold, and the sky was cloudy. The sea was unsettled and gray, especially late in the day. They dined at El Khyem Restaurant on the Corniche: sea bass, Tunisian salad, a plate of spaghetti for each of them, and two bottles of Magon. Béchir seemed depressed and preoccupied. He looked unhappy and disappointed. He spoke slowly, with a tired voice. No trace remained of the enraptured man who had returned after a long absence, the man whose face had sparkled when he visited Neapolis. They returned to the house at eleven that night, and Béchir collapsed on the sofa, lit one Gauloises after another, and launched into a long, sad monologue.

"Listen, Yunus, my dear. We, who were born in the middle of the last century, have entered the twenty-first century as orphans in every sense of the word. We have entered it with our hands and feet flayed, our powers exhausted by the lengthy distances we have traversed during what now seems an Empty Spring, when our dreams and hopes have been demolished and buried alive before our eyes, with no mercy or compassion. We were born in a time of national independence movements. In those days, our fathers raised flags high, and our mothers trilled to celebrate new leaders who promised to transform our arid, impoverished countries into Gardens of Eden. In our schools, we sang, with tear-filled eyes, ardent anthems in honor of the martyrs of Algeria, Bizerte, the Suez Canal, and Deir Yassin. We celebrated the revolution that toppled the monarchist regime in Iraq, without paying any attention to the massacres committed in its name. With the ardor and delight of youngsters, we listened to the orations of Abdel Nasser when he promised Arabs 'from the Ocean to the Gulf' that he would return ravished Palestine to its people. At the thresholds of adolescence, we—unlike youngsters today—paid no attention to new fads in clothing and music. We were satisfied with hand-me-down clothes from our older brothers and with the small amount of money our mothers allocated for us from the family's daily budget. We bought books from the old bookstores and enjoyed reading Rousseau, Voltaire, Sartre, Camus, Aragon, Gorky, Mayakovsky, Taha Hussein, Naguib Mahfouz, Tawfiq al-Hakim, and Khalil Gibran. Even though the nationalist leaders betrayed the promises they made before independence (and after it) and institutionalized violence, tyranny, and corruption, our dreams continued to grow day after day. But suddenly, there came the first shock that was so cruel its pain still torments us: on the television sets that had begun to enter our impoverished houses we saw 'our fearless soldiers' reduced to rotting corpses scattered in the Sinai Desert or wandering in groups beneath the scorching sun. We also witnessed Israeli tanks seize control

of Jerusalem, Sinai, and the Golan Heights. In the wink of an eye, our
dreams were reduced to a giant heap of ashes. When, thunderstruck, we
took to the streets to vent our anger, 'our fearless soldiers' sent us packing,
and any demonstrators who refused to obey were imprisoned and labeled
'misguided gangs' by the media. Then young people in Europe revolted
and erected barricades in the streets of Paris, Berlin, and London. The
vertigo that had afflicted us on the defeat of our armies diminished, and
we returned to our dreams and hopes, searching for deliverance. Under
their influence, we went into the streets again, chanting for freedom, but
'our fearless soldiers' met us with live ammunition, tear-gas canisters, and
heavy cudgels, driving us back, defeated and broken. When we turned
thirty, wars flared up in different parts of the Arab world. Then cities
and villages were burned, and many of their inhabitants were forced to
flee. Others were obliged to go into exile far away, in search of deliverance. From these successive wars, calamities, and defeats, bearded thugs
erupted like dead men popping out of their graves. With scowling faces
and frowning expressions, they spread through the earth to promote a
culture of hatred and death, threatening with death and painful torture
those who didn't obey them blindly and did not implement their many
fatwas, because such slackers were infidels and destined for hellfire. 'Their
eyesight is blackened; their minds are gone. Each of them has a head like
a dome, a body like a mountain, blue eyes, and hair like stalks of grain.
They don't have a death they die or a life they live. Each of them has a skin
with seven layers of fire. Inside them swirl serpents of fire; they hear these
roar, like wild beasts. They are encircled by chains and shackles and beaten
with sharp implements, which also slash their faces.' What this means is
that Arabs are destined to endure hell's torment in the physical world *and*
in the world to come. Because of these bearded men, all the peoples of
the world have started to regard us as suspect terrorists, until evidence to
the contrary is produced. Thus they are wary of every word we utter and
every action we take. In this way, we have reached old age with souls as
bitter as toxic oleander and with sick hearts, after the reservoir of dreams
and hopes we had in childhood and old age has been drained. Uff! How
cruel history has been to us! I returned dreaming that I would find—in
my country's light and from its sea and fragrant orchards—something to

restore vitality, rapture, and joy to my life. Instead, I've found nothing but this morass. I've found an exhausted country weakened by its wounds, a country that fears the present and the future, a country writhing with pain beneath the cudgels of rulers and the fatwas of bearded men, not knowing when the hour of deliverance will arrive. Here dangerous ailments are nurtured: lying, hypocrisy, servility, passivity, fear, unbridled egotism, malice, mutual loathing, internecine combat, corruption, and bribery. I believe there is no place for me now in this country to which I have returned after spending thirty-four years abroad. When I walk the street, roam through the market, or take a taxi, people address me as Hajj, although this title was once used only for people who had completed the Islamic duty of pilgrimage. Now it is applied to anyone whose hair has turned gray and who looks old. When someone addresses me with this title, I sense he is hastening my demise and wants to make me feel that I no longer belong to the world of the living but to the world of the dead. Uff! I feel so tired and sad, Yunus! I don't know if I'm capable of remaining here or whether I should go back where I came from. My longtime friend, I don't know! No horizon beckons me now. Yesterday I broke down and wept like an orphaned child. It had been a long time since I last cried. In fact, I hadn't since I heard the news of my mother's death. But yesterday, around midnight, I found myself weeping audibly; I didn't stop for about half an hour. You—you're the only person I can confide in because you're a dear friend!"

The next morning, they roamed the beach at Les Grottes and did not talk much. Each man was preoccupied by his own thoughts. Suddenly, when they were walking down a narrow trail, Béchir fell and experienced great difficulty rising. He looked pale, and his eyes were bleary. He may have felt that his tumble had demeaned him and robbed him of his dignity, because he remained silent until they reached his house. That evening, Yunus said good-bye to Béchir and returned to Neapolis.

Two days before the new year began, Samir phoned him around noon. Audibly struggling with tears, he told Yunus that Béchir had died in his bedroom of cardiac arrest.

7

In the living room, he opened the journal he had been compiling diligently since he settled in Neapolis and began to read back over some of
the entries.

October

The day is calmly fading. The magic of a Mediterranean autumn is
barely noticeable because too much of the summer's brutal heat lingers
on. Little birds, whose names I don't know, are twittering in the small
garden. They do this at dawn and twilight—welcoming birth and death
with the same songs. In any case, I'm happy to live here in this quiet
house near the sea. I moved here after the turbulent tempests of my divorce. Here I enjoy tranquility and try to heal some of the wounds of
the past years, when I experienced pain, anxiety, and unending quarrels
with my wife.

October 31

Indian summer continues to wield its influence throughout the country.
Because of the unseasonal heat, the ground has dried out, again, after
the rains at the end of September. Tourists are on the beach in swim-
suits. During my walks along the shore or through the city's streets, I
hear most European languages: French, German, Italian, English, Spanish, Swedish, and some Eastern European languages as well—especially

Czech. The music of these languages is splendid! I await, with intense longing, autumn's heavy downpours and winter's gales.

November 2

At the ceramics market, I saw a woman from my village. She was accompanied by two children and a man who might be her husband. I recognized her at once. Is first love ever forgotten? I remember that her marriage seemed a tragic event for me because she was the only girl who had captivated me and kindled love's fires in my heart. I would frequently meet her far from prying eyes. Then I would kiss her, fondle her breasts, and caress her thighs while trembling feverishly. We did this most often on summer nights or during hot siestas. When I heard she had accepted the proposal of a young man from a neighboring village, I was very sad. I went to ask to speak with her but was sent packing. I was as sad as a bird that finds its nest destroyed and flutters aimlessly through the countryside. When I was returning to our house that evening, I noticed that my uncle Salih's spotted dog was chasing me. So, I sped up to keep him from attacking me. Once I reached our house, I told my mother. She gasped in alarm and said, "It may have rabies. During a wedding party, a dog bit two of my relatives. One of them, Faraj Allah, was a renowned dancer, singer, and drummer in our region. The men went out with their rifles to kill the dog once they had determined it really was rabid. Destroying it took a lot of effort. In the meantime, two of my relatives traveled to Sousse to be vaccinated against rabies. Faraj Allah made light of the whole matter and continued to dance, sing, and drum at weddings that summer. Forty days later he died."

November 5

A gray depressing morning. The light drizzle ended a few minutes ago. In the public bath near my home, four men in their forties were discussing the Sunday soccer matches. Suddenly they switched to religion. One man, who had a thin mustache and small, narrow eyes, said, "Guys, may God grant you all His guidance! Everything is found in the Qur'an, including the atom bomb. Did God Almighty and Exalted say, 'He who commits an atom's worth of evil will see it'?* The other three immediately agreed and said, "Yes, you're right. Everything is found in the Holy Qur'an."

Same Day, 5:00 p.m.

In the taxi to the Albatross Restaurant, the driver, who was wearing a gray cap, observed, "The drought continues unabated, and the economic downturn affects everything. Nothing is the way it should be. People are fearful. Ramadan, the return to school, expenditures for the summer—these have all burdened them financially. Now people have begun talking about a lamb for Eid al-Adha. Uff! Why don't we celebrate the sacrifice symbolically? In every city or village, we slaughter sheep to honor custom and religion—that's the point. Wouldn't a more symbolic sacrifice be an excellent, beneficial idea and make sense economically? But if I said this, many folks would call me an infidel. How about you? What do you think?"

"I totally agree with you, 100 percent!" I replied.

"I'm happy to hear this response from you." After a brief silence he added a bit acidly, "Does it make sense for Muslims to turn their religion into nothing but a string of banquets?"

November 8

"Israel commits a new massacre in the Gaza Strip."

International TV channels show the victims' bodies—especially those of women and children. On one channel, an aged, angry, disgruntled Palestinian woman asked, "Where are you, Arabs? Where?" I think the Arab memory of Palestine has dimmed. Otherwise, this poor old woman wouldn't need to voice this appeal. The Arabs have been and continue to

---

* Qur'an 99:8 Al-Zilzal (The Earthquake).

be oblivious to the calamities and disasters that have afflicted and continue to strike this woman's people since the 1948 Nakba right up to the present!

November 22

Yesterday, I dreamt rain was falling heavily on the orchards of Neapolis. Today, I felt autumn's shivers for the first time. Clouds. Cold wind. But no rain. When will the rains come to drown the economic stagnation affecting all regions of the country?

November 24

"To hell with music, poetry, and all the arts that I have practiced without learning from life, from my soul, or at least without garnering any 'substantial, essential, spiritual' sustenance from them."

This is what the poet Lorand Gaspar said. He lived for a long time in our country and wrote beautiful pages describing its natural characteristics, cities, and desert, but most of our poets know nothing about him. I doubt they would be capable of grasping what he meant in this sentence because they live an empty life that is superficial and impoverished in every sense. For this reason, when they discuss poetry and the various other arts, they never say anything—not a single sentence—worth memorizing.

The Same Day

The Palestinian people confront death and hunger daily, and the Palestinian organizations—especially Fatah and Hamas—compete for what may be called the "ministries of control." This confirms again that the tragedy of the Palestinian people is not merely that they have been the victims of an oppressive, persistent occupation for more than sixty years, but that their ruling elites are dominated by narrow personal ambitions and desires. They are enchanted by rhetoric and vacuous slogans and consequently afflicted by a chronic inability to deal with the concerns and requirements of the palpable reality.

December 17

During the last two days, rain has fallen in torrents throughout the country. This has afforded me great delight. I might as well be one of the impoverished farmers who live on whatever the earth provides them. I traveled yesterday to the capital to deal with some matters at the university. Everyone in the shared taxi with me seemed quite joyous and happy. One—a portly, middle-aged man in his forties—said, "The economic depression has become unbearable. Tourist hotels are almost empty. Only these rainstorms can restore hope to our hearts."

December 18

Yesterday on the Arte channel I watched—for the second time—the film version of Tolstoy's renowned novel *War and Peace*. The film is not as good as the novel but still provided me with an enjoyable evening. Henry Fonda is splendid in his role, and Audrey Hepburn—once described by a film critic as "the Morning Star"—played Natasha Rostova, the dreamy romantic girl, in the most brilliant way. The film closed with Tolstoy's famous statement: "The most difficult thing—but an essential one—is to love Life, to love it even while one suffers, because Life is all." Intoxicated with this thought, I went to bed happy and slept soundly.

December 25

The tension in our country may not resemble tension anywhere else in the world. When you watch how people act in the street and in public places, you feel that we are experiencing a silent civil war. People quarrel and exchange blows and nasty words, usually for trifling reasons. This is true even for the educated elite. Scarcely a day passes without ferocious scuffles in the restaurants and coffeehouses they frequent.

December 26

The situation in Somalia reminds me of Afghanistan when the Taliban first took control of it. Somalia's Islamic courts, which are run by bloodthirsty terrorists, differ in no respect from the Taliban's courts. Both groups force people to pray at gunpoint, compel women to adopt hijab, close cinemas and music clubs, and prevent people from watching international soccer matches and other athletic events. All these policies may improve conditions in a country that has been plunged in a destructive civil war since the beginning of the 1990s. They may provide bread, a decent living, and security for people, most of whom live below the poverty line. Some leaders of those Islamic courts have appeared on television, and all are repulsive with unkempt beards they dye with henna to hide the white. They have scowling faces and resent anything in life that offers enjoyment, happiness, joy, beauty, and love.

January 29

Drought again. My garden is mournful now all the little birds have deserted it. They no longer wake me in the morning.

February 14

Four a.m. I woke and became absorbed with reading the journal of Bulgakov, who wrote *The Master and the Margarita*, a stellar work. In his journal he describes, precisely and with great lyricism and stinging sarcasm, conditions he experienced during the first years after the Bolshevik Revolution. In one splendid paragraph, Bulgakov discusses his daily travails and the sufferings he met in the shadow of Soviet rule. On Friday, October 26, 1923, he wrote:

> Writing is difficult at the moment. With my views, expressed as they are voluntarily or involuntarily in my works, it is difficult to get published and earn a living.
> And being ill under such circumstances is extremely unfortunate.[17]

All the same, Bulgakov remained optimistic. That same entry continued:

> But I must not get depressed. Have just finished *The Last of the Mohicans*, which I recently bought for my library. What old-world charm this sentimental Cooper possesses! Just like a David singing and singing his psalms and inspiring in me thoughts of God.[18]

On January 5, 1925, Bulgakov wrote:

> The weather in Moscow is something quite extraordinary: in the thaw everything has melted, and the mood among Muscovites precisely mirrors the weather. The weather suggests February, and there's February in *people's hearts*.
> "How's all this going to end?" a friend asked me today.
> Such questions are asked in a dull, mechanical way, hopelessly, indifferently, any way you like. Just at that moment there was a group of drunken communists in my friend's apartment, in a room right across the corridor. In the corridor itself there was a foully pungent smell—one of the Party members, my friend told me, was asleep there like a pig, completely drunk. Someone had invited him, and my friend hadn't been able to refuse. Again and again he went into their room with a polite, ingratiating smile on his face. They kept shouting to him to join them. He kept coming back to me, cursing them in a whisper. *Yes, right: somehow this must all stop. I believe it will!*[19]

Toward the end of his diary, on Wednesday, February 25, 1925, to be precise, Bulgakov wrote, "I'm facing an insoluble problem. / That's all!"[20] This intractable problem seems to have been the Bolshevik Revolution, which claimed among its victims many illustrious, creative Russians. Bulgakov was one.

March 14

The birds woke me with their splendid warbling. So, I rushed to the little garden to welcome this spring morning. I stood gazing at the clear sky, listening to the little birds and my internal complaints, which frittered away and disappeared.

The rain that fell last week brought beauty back to the earth and hope to the people. Will we enjoy a beautiful spring? Afterward, I entered the office and opened a book of selections from world poetry.

William Blake
So Man looks out in tree & herb & fish & bird & beast
Collecting up the scattered portions of his immortal body.
Into the Elemental forms of every thing that grows[21]
* * *

. . . . wherever a grass grows
Or a leaf buds The Eternal Man is seen is heard is felt
And all his Sorrows until he reassumes his ancient bliss[22]

Pablo Neruda
Here I Love You.
* * * * * * * * * * * * **

My loathing wrestles with the slow twilights.
But night comes and starts to sing to me.
The moon turns its clockwork dream.
The biggest stars look at me with your eyes.
And as I love you, the pines in the wind
want to sing your name with their leaves of wire.[23]

March 26

I don't know why I fell for the trap and attended a poetry soiree in Neapolis, only to find myself confronted by soi-disant poets who recited trivial poems in which they wept as one person over Iraq and Palestine—even praising Saddam Hussein. Clearly these poets, who strutted like peacocks before the sparse audience, had not been able to pierce the façade to see the "living flame" behind it, to use Adonis's expression. A poet doesn't reach this living flame until he can create: "A picture more beautiful than man and his struggle," because a poem, as Adonis also says, "Isn't an event or a reality [like the tragedies of Palestine or Iraq] but the flame that is concealed inside them or that discloses them." A poem "doesn't shrink" into the event or reality but "envelopes and surpasses it." The essence of poetry is consciousness and political expertise; it isn't a tool for consciousness-raising or governance. It is itself an action—not a call to action. Therefore, Adonis says, "When we insist on poetry being subservient to political action and the practice of politics, we insist on abolishing it as art, which has its own special character and independence." Had the poets who came to Neapolis read this manifesto, or do they only read their own work?

April 22

A small bird that has built its nest in the kitchen woke me up with its excellent trills at dawn. I'm happy to have this bird share my solitude.

The Same Day

I have been busy for some days reading Borges in the Pléiade edition. This morning I spent a long time with the paragraph he devoted to Flaubert:

> Milton, Tasso, and Virgil consecrated themselves to the composition of poems; Flaubert was the first to consecrate himself ... to the creation of a purely aesthetic work *in prose*. In the history of literatures, prose is later than verse; this paradox was a goad to Flaubert's ambition. "Prose was born yesterday," he wrote. "Verse is the form *par excellence* of the literatures of antiquity. The combinations of metrics have been used up; not so those of prose." And in another passage, he added: "I can say the novel awaits its Homer."[24]

This statement applies to the Arabs now because they are no longer the Nation of Poetry as they claimed long ago. Poetry written in Arabic today is weak and hackneyed, for the most part. Only attention to prose can restore beauty, freshness, and splendor to the Arabic language. Was al-Jahiz the last to undertake this project? I see no one who equals him today in the Arab east or the Maghreb.

September 7

I have returned to reading *Kitab al-Aghani*, which is one of the greatest books in the Arab cultural tradition—according to me, of course. In it we read about kings and princes, tribal chiefs, poets major and minor, jurisprudents, religious and linguistic scholars, male and female singers, women entertainers, eunuchs, and the marginalized. In this book and in the works of al-Jahiz, I find enough to save me the effort of reading numerous other books, ancient or modern. The first truth we derive from reading this book is that there can be no true or original literature unless audacity and reality influences all aspects of it—whether these references are murky or luminous, obvious or concealed, disclosed or hidden. A second is that no true literature can exist in the shadow of censorship— whether political, moralistic, religious, or other. Books like the mighty *Kitab al-Aghani* or the works of al-Jahiz, al-Tawhidi, and Ibn Arabi—as well as *The Thousand and One Nights*—have been threatened with burning by narrow-minded people who have accused them of being "a shrill attack on religion and morality." The odd thing is that such critics find a rapt audience today among young people, despite the fact that they know nothing about these books.

September 8

Kitab al-Aghani says that Aisha bint Talha, an extraordinarily beautiful woman who captured the hearts of many of the Arabian Peninsula's military commanders, never veiled her face. When her husband, Mus'ab, criticized her for this, she replied, "God the Blessed and Exalted granted me this beauty. I want people to see me and to appreciate my superiority over them. If I concealed it, by God, I have no blemish by which anyone would remember me!"

The author of *al-Aghani* mentions that the Hadith reporter Abu Hurayra, on seeing a veil fall from the face of Aisha bint Talha, remarked, "Praise God! What excellent nourishment your family has provided you! You look as if you had just emerged from paradise!" She replied, "By God,

I'm a better sight than a fire at night for the chilly person's eye." It is hardly amazing that "jurists of darkness" today should call for burning books like *Kitab al-Aghani*!

September 15

In a short work about Verlaine, Stefan Zweig discussed great creative geniuses who at a certain moment of their lives found themselves rejecting the world, their age, and the way of life to which they had become accustomed until then. He wrote:

> We find Wagner, who served as choir master for the royal chapel, rushing off to the barricades and then finally fleeing. Schiller fled from Karlsruhe. In Karlsbad, when he held a cabinet post, Goethe suddenly decided to climb in his carriage and head to Italy in search of freedom and independence. Shelley as well. Byron rushed off to Greece. When Tolstoy was in his eighties, he fled from his manor house. Ill and feverish, he rushed alone into the winter night. Each of these great men suddenly renounced the luxury they enjoyed—as if quitting a cell in which they had been imprisoned—to head toward freedom—oblivious to everything else—toward the eternal horizons, where they would view the world as if on another planet.[25]

Few Arab creators are capable of embarking on an adventure of rebellion against their age and of exodus from it. In fact, such figures are extremely rare. This perspective helps us explain the paucity of artistic and literary creativity at present.

October 14

Daily dedication to reading has saved me from the psychological stress the month of Ramadan would otherwise cause me. It has allowed me to escape to the world of imagination and thought. Each morning—and occasionally at noon—I walk on the shore and then return home with a keen hunger for reading. At night, I watch the excellent films shown on Arab and European channels. I reread pages from *Conversations of Goethe with*

Johann Peter Eckermann and Henry Miller's *The Books in My Life*. I have thoroughly enjoyed reading the novel *Immortality* by Milan Kundera and Calvino's *The Uses of Literature*: primarily lectures he gave at American universities. Now I believe that my "tank" has been filled as full as it needs to be. So, will I be able to start writing a new text to add to the others piled in the cabinet?

October 23

This morning the Arab papers bring news of the death of the Iraqi poet Sargon Boulus, whom I long hoped to meet and converse with. I was devastated. Since the 1970s, through avant-garde magazines, I have followed the career of this poet, who spent the greater part of his life in exile in San Francisco but died in a cramped room in Berlin. I believe he is one of the rare Arab poets to understand the true meaning of modernism. His poems are distinctive and reflect his profound experience of life and his reading. I pulled some collections of his poems off the shelf and began to read his delightful verse. Then I found I was weeping. I felt I had lost a dear friend with whom I had shared sweet and bitter moments, bread and salt. Sargon, from what region of calamities did you hail? To which region of calamities will you travel? And how can "the darkness be recapped," as you expressed it in one of your poems?

October 24

What is certain is that there have been serious disturbances in the Gafsa Mining Basin. These have led to fatalities, casualties, and layoffs of workers and youth. Why? Anger against the regime. The region is rich in phosphates, but only a few people enjoy the profits. The overwhelming majority of the region's citizens endure penury, deprivation, unemployment, and neglect. The official media outlets are silent about all these events, as usual when it is a question of such serious events. Instead, they constantly assert that everything is just as wonderful as could be. Angry people are described as "a small, aberrant group hostile to the nation's interests." When the official media are silent about serious events like these, rumors multiply and grow enormous. Then anger flares in souls and hearts, even though it is a silent, hidden anger. What destiny awaits those who ignore and scorn it—when it does explode?

October 31

He always arrives alone and then sits by himself at the Albatross Restaurant. He speaks to no one, except the waiter, to order. He seems a person forcibly denied a good life—at least his expression suggests as much, with its blend of grief and rage—perhaps against those responsible for his ordeal. He drinks a bottle of Magon slowly while gazing at the sea or lost in his thoughts. When he finishes, he pays and leaves, shuffling his feet.

One evening he downed his bottle of Magon quickly and very nervously. Then, his eyes red and his features scrunched up, he rose and shouted at the other diners: "Everyone, listen to me carefully. I don't give a damn what happens to me, because cowards don't deserve to live! This country and everything in it have become the private property of one family. They act as if they can do as they please with it—protected and supervised by the head of the regime himself. Do you hear what I'm saying? Fine! Now I wish you a good night's rest. I hope I haven't upset you with my short speech." Then, his head held high, he departed with a firm stride—as if he had just defeated secret enemies.

November 20

Fruit for this morning: some lines by García Lorca:

> I do not want to hear the weeping,
> But from behind the grey walls
> Nothing is heard but the weeping.[26]

These verses describe my current psychological state. I would really like to shutter my window because I'm not ready to hear the atrocities and painful events in my country and in the other Arab countries, but I always fail;

wails penetrate my walls and assault me, even in the bathtub, in bed, or when I am between the maid's thighs.

December 31

Alone on New Year's Eve. Candles. Symphonies. Mozart. Tchaikovsky . . . and Baudelaire's *Fleurs de Mal*. These are my companions for celebrations that will last until 1:00 a.m.

Yunus returned his journal to its place, donned sports clothes, and headed out for his daily stroll on the beach.

8

He walked down the beach; a few tourists were scattered along it. Two nights earlier Yunus had experienced a dreadful nightmare in which he found himself on the coast of a polluted sea with black, viscous, stagnant water. Many dead birds—large and small—littered the beach, where frightened, naked children with blood-smeared faces ran around. Women dressed in mourning slapped their faces and wailed anxious laments. Men with hands and feet shackled by chains stood with their backs to the sea. He had retreated, wanting to flee, but a man of about thirty, wearing swim trunks, stopped him and said acerbically, "Look carefully at this scene. This will be our destiny if matters continue the way they are in our country."

Perhaps the nightmare reflected his fears, which had recently grown more acute in response to the situation's rapid deterioration, which left him feeling that the country was sitting on the lip of a volcano and that a terrible explosion might occur at any moment. Everywhere he went, he heard news and rumors of other black clouds massing at the horizon. On the faces looking at him in the markets, in the streets, in coffeehouses, and along the shore, he detected anxiety and dread that reminded him of the difficult, black years the country had experienced thirty years earlier when rebellions, upheavals, and explosions had increased exponentially. The aged president had been barely sentient then, and around him rivals for his succession had hatched vile conspiracies. Would his country once again become "poor in sense and meaning"? What an eloquent phrase! Ahmad ibn Abi al-Dayyaf, the personal secretary for the Husaynid Beys in the nineteenth century, had used it to describe the country's condition in that difficult, gloomy period, when tyranny intensified, corruption prevailed, and the Bey was distracted by lust and private pleasures with Mustafa, the handsome boy whom the Bey's obedient servants brought from the Medina's Suq al-Balat, where he had worked as a barber's assistant. If Mustafa absconded for a day or two, the Bey would grow depressed, grieve, become feverish, spurn food, lie awake, and refuse to receive his ministers and advisers. Once this handsome youth appeared again, health, well-being, and happiness would return to the Bey, who loved to welcome the fresh flesh of boys in the royal bed. Conscious of his standing with his master, Mustafa, who had blue eyes and a slender build, became obstinate and evasive. Then the Bey became even more attached to him and wept audibly when Mustafa prolonged his absences. Once he ascertained that all his demands, even preposterous ones, would not be rejected, the youth began to devise one plot after another, until he banished from the palace everyone who wished to reform the country's affairs, resist corruption, and alleviate the people's humiliation and abasement. The only opinion the Bey ever heard was Mustafa's. One morning, the kingdom's citizens woke to find that the comely youth was the grand vizier, and the country soon sank into crises and debts. When the French invaded, the corrupt Bey handed them the keys, without any remorse or pangs of conscience. His grand vizier fled to Istanbul, where he lived as a beggar, depending for daily sustenance on benevolent folks with compassionate hearts. Eventually, one cold winter day, he was found dead on the sidewalk. Will the fate of the people who have landed the nation in its current disgraceful conditions, leaving it "poor in sense and meaning," mimic the handsome lad's? This seemed likely, given that the end of tyrants and corrupt people is typically dreadful. These individuals, however, do not seem aware of this and do not appear to realize that history may repeat itself.

Here they are—building magnificent villas on the shore of Neapolis and in other beautiful places, depositing their riches and gold in foreign banks, looting the country's wealth in broad daylight, and residing in the finest hotels of Rome, Paris, London, Vienna, and Toronto. They buy real estate in Dubai and help themselves to other people's possessions with no scruples. They spend their summer holidays on their yachts, which call at the islands of the Mediterranean. They feel relaxed and self-confident because no laws restrain them and no one can curb their ambitious drive

to garner wealth and status or to help themselves to the enjoyment of pleasures. They have nothing to fear from the citizens. Oh! People who have
been miserable, cowardly, submissive, and servile from the most ancient
eras—who cares about them or their feelings? The First Lady, who like the
handsome youth was once a hair stylist and who, like him, grew up in the
ancient Medina, sanctions all this and in fact encourages it, doing everything in her power to assure its success. Her husband, the general, fears
her, is afraid of her, and obeys her blindly, humoring all her requests. By
bearing him a son who is his spitting image, she increased her control over
him until he is little more than a ring on her finger, as she likes to tell the
ladies of the new, velvet society—in the elite club she has opened on the sea
as a showcase for her beauty, eminence, and regal taste. In it she displays
her temerity, power, and might. Why shouldn't she? She is now the First
Lady in every sense of the phrase. Photos of her take pride of place on the
front pages of papers and magazines, and news of her and her activities
begin radio and TV newscasts. Cabinet ministers and advisors at the Carthage Palace obey her orders, and the top officers in the army and security
forces bow obsequiously before her. At national and world conferences, she
presents herself as the foremost defender of the Arab woman's rights. Yes,
she is the First Lady, and anyone doubting that pays for their poor judg-
ment dearly, very dearly. Her husband, the general, boasts proudly that she
has mastered the arts of hosting official receptions, of public speaking, and
of conversing with ambassadors, diplomats, and business executives, even
though she came from a poor family, grew up in a working-class neighborhood, and left school at fifteen because she was doing extremely poorly
in every subject. She treats him like the ring on her finger—as she tells the
ladies of the new, velvet society during the extraordinary soirées she hosts
in the elite club. These feature plates of exquisite sweets and glasses of hot
tea—served with pistachios, hazelnuts, and almonds—and cups of coffee
flavored with rose water. At first, conversation focuses on the country's
political situation as viewed by the First Lady, who possesses all the secrets
and all the background information. Then it progresses to the First Lady's
latest and forthcoming forays to conferences and meetings that she has
convened or will convene. Then they discuss the benevolent organizations
she has established or plans to. Eventually, they reach the latest trends in

fashion, coiffure, and fine perfumes. When the voices of the ladies of the new, velvet society become subdued and whispers, glances, and winks multiply, the conversation turns to revelations of the latest sexual scandals and stories of new romantic escapades in elite districts. Then the First Lady leaves her revered but inattentive and frivolous guests for her private wing, where she gazes for a long time at her comely figure in the wide mirror. She downs a glass of gin with lemon, which has been her favorite drink since she was young. When, radiant and merry, she returns to them, their laughter rings out loudly: "Ha . . . ha . . . ha . . . ho . . . ho . . . ho . . . hee . . . hee . . . hee. . . . Ooooh, how lovely the First Lady is! How bright! How powerful! How gracious! How bountiful and generous! Ha . . . ha . . . ha . . . ho . . . ho . . . ho . . . hee . . . hee . . ." The women of the new, velvet society love to laugh like the First Lady, smile like her, grow irate like her, furrow their brows like her, rejoice like her, and relax like her at their own parties. They hold her every gesture and pause sacred. Hasn't mimicking the First Lady assured them entry into the new, velvet society? "Ha . . . ha . . . ha . . . ho . . . ho . . . ho . . . hee . . . hee . . . hee . . ." The First Lady fills the spacious, elite club with her effrontery, beauty, and authority, which everyone has begun to fear, as they make a thousand and one calculations. Those who most fear her are people with wealth, status, and influence. For one of them to criticize, ignore, or challenge her is virtually impossible, we could say. Anyone who touches a hair of her head, as our people put it, exposes herself to substantial dangers—like losing the fortune, prestige, and all the physical and immaterial distinctions she enjoys. She will become an abject, contemptible person, who walks, delirious, in the street like a madman. Anyone who is rude or unruly is thrown in prison. There are specialists who know how to fiddle expertly with laws and to manipulate them to find "legitimate reasons" for placing the suspect in solitary confinement and to prevent even his wife and relatives from visiting him. He will never escape punishment, unless he is able to flee abroad through some fiendish scheme. Even then, he will need to live out of sight because everywhere she has agents who are fully capable of pursuing him and dealing with him. A man went behind her back once, contacted her husband, the general, and began to spend delightful nights with him in secret venues with underage girls (the greatest beauties in the land of Hannibal) but eventually received the punishment he deserved. He lost his high rank and was stripped of all the distinctions he enjoyed. The court sentenced him to prison for many years, and he was unlikely to emerge from there alive. On learning about his secret adventures with the general, the man's alarmingly hysterical wife threw herself off the roof of the airport terminal, after revealing her reasons for killing herself to the large crowd who had gathered. Watch out, then, beware, because the First Lady governs by her own rules, and no one can buck that. In Carthage Palace, she conducts herself like the real ruler of the country. No cabinet minister or advisor—no matter how high his standing is with the general—can hold onto his post without her approval and consent. Many a minister and advisor has found himself discharged from his duties when he woke or prepared to head to his office. Orders from Carthage Palace would state that it was incumbent upon him to remain in his house for an unspecified length of time. If he accepted an invitation to dine with friends one evening, they might find themselves targets of the First Lady's suspicions. He was also exposing himself to the chance that an accident staged by anonymous agents would cost him his life or leave him bedridden for many weeks or even months. Therefore, everyone needed to be on guard because the First Lady had morphed into a lioness, ready to slay any foe who dared to attack her lair or touch her interests, those of her family, and especially those of her brothers. How many of them were there? How many?

Eleven brothers? Yes, eleven, because their mother was fertile and their father a stud. All the same, blindness and deafness are the fate of all those who feel jealous, envious, or rancorous about blessings God bestows on anyone He wishes among His righteous worshipers. Benefiting from the protection and care of the First Lady and the docility of her husband, the general, the eleven brothers spread their hands across the land to wreak havoc and corruption and to plunder it until nothing of value remained safe from them, not even Phoenician, Roman, Islamic, Berber, or other artifacts. Anyone who dared restrain or oppose them, whether in public or private, would soon find himself hanging upside down, divested of every means of protecting or defending himself. Ah! Such was his fate, this dog, this son of a bitch, because the eleven brothers—poke a stick in the eye of the envious person—were reared in the old city's lairs and in its dark, narrow alleys, where many thieves and vicious criminals lurked; these were people who saw no difference between killing a fly or a human being. The eleven brothers learned from neighbors martial arts of all types and forms, including the use of swords and daggers. In this school for thugs, they grew proficient in malice, meanness, ignominy, iniquity, brutality, cruelty, and frivolity, becoming past masters of the arts of deception, cunning, deceit, feinting, and maneuvering until they were fully capable of pulling the teeth from a barking dog. The years of poverty and deprivation they experienced in the ancient, dilapidated house turned them into predatory beasts capable of imposing the law of the jungle to protect their interests and to satisfy their hunger for wealth and their limitless appetites. Thus in a few years, they succeeded in establishing a near-total monopoly over the country's wealth because they had a hand in tourism; import-export trade; large banks; television, theater, and cinema productions; in tourist agencies arranging trips for pilgrims and other religious travelers; and in . . . and in . . . and in. . . . Foreign investors could not initiate any scheme without their approval, and this approval could not be obtained until an investor agreed either to share the profits with them or to pay them a bribe commensurate with their stature. They dominated the labor market, and young graduates from the universities were forced to seek their assistance if they wished to escape the rampant, persistent unemployment. Even all this did not suffice. No, they deliberately deprived people of their livelihoods and seized other people's possessions, especially those of people who dared to compete with them for wealth and status. Using their astounding fortunes, which they had amassed with little effort or difficulty, they built fancy villas in the capital and in the most beautiful resort cities. In these mansions, the great artists, who are invited by the Ministry of Culture to perform at the festivals it sponsors, play at parties celebrating one of their birthdays or the circumcision of one of their sons. They appear without remuneration because the eleven brothers all agree on grabbing money rather than expending it, accumulating wealth not dispersing it. They also purchase private planes, elegant yachts, and fast cars they drive without a license or registration papers, since the minister of the interior has informed security officers in all parts of the country to turn a blind eye to any infraction or violation they commit. Haven't they become the lords of the land ever since their dear, precious sister slipped into Carthage Palace? Therefore, everything is pardoned, permitted, and licit for these eleven brothers. In the spacious, elite club, which overlooks the sea, the First Lady boasts of her brothers, of their great abilities, astuteness, and sagacity in managing their affairs, of their skill at seizing golden opportunities for success, of their victories and triumphs over rivals, and of their dedication to the service of the dear nation . . . the very, very dear nation. Why would it not be close to their hearts? It has lavished all these blessings on her eleven brothers after poverty scowled at them daily when they were crammed into that ancient, dilapidated house, awaiting the return of their father, who spent the entire day pushing a vegetable cart from one alley to the next before returning home exhausted at the end of the evening with enough profit to allay the hunger of his large family. But God is benevolent and compassionate to His righteous devotees, and the gates of an all-encompassing wealth opened wide for the eleven brothers, allowing them to join the lords of the land—in fact to become the lords of the land! Their dear, precious sister, whose husband, the general, now seems like a bangle on her wrist, does everything in her power to assure they continue to climb high, very high, until the name of this poor, humble family flutters in the heavens like the nation's flag—in fact higher than the nation's flag. Ha . . . ha . . . ha . . . ho . . . ho . . . hee . . . hee . . . hee . . . hahahahaha! The First Lady is certainly brilliant at managing the country's affairs from behind the curtain. Without her advice, her husband, the general, would never have been able to chop off the hands of his enemies, who are eager to reach the presidential chair on which he has sat for twenty years. She is wise, the First Lady—in fact wiser than anyone else. Ho . . . hee . . . ha . . . ha . . . hahahaha!

Night falls. The cherished guests leave the spacious, upscale club, and the First Lady enters her private wing. She needs to be alone—to collect her thoughts and prepare not just for the coming weeks and months but for the coming years, especially by anticipating any nasty surprises they may bring. Her enemies, and there are many of them now, lie in wait for her, watching for an opportunity to pounce on her and her eleven brothers—to crush and flay them and to rub their heads in the dirt. Any false step by her would allow those rogues to execute their schemes. So, she must be cautious and take everything into consideration after spreading her influence over the entire country, having the first say in the decisions of her husband, the general. Recently, a despicable French journalist, who looked like an ill-omened owl, as one of her girlfriends described him, published a book "exposing her black past," as he put it. Her secret enemies had certainly provided him with the documents, which were all counterfeit! At first, she suffered a severe shock and kept to her bed for many days without eating—sleeping only a little. The only member of her family she saw was her younger brother, who was responsible for increasing her influence with her husband, the general. Even he knelt before her out of reverence and respect for her huge accomplishment. Why shouldn't he? Hadn't she granted his ultimate wish? That was to be granted the title "Father of Girls" because he was afraid of passing from this world without leaving behind an heir to remind the country's citizens of his mighty feats, deeds, and accomplishments. She remained in bed while her warm tears flowed profusely. Since this vile French journalist's book had caused her massive pain by virtually stabbing her in the heart of her glory and honor, what would stop this birdbrain from taking an interest in the scandals of the country's First Lady, a fashion plate who offered her body to a new lover every night? Her vile enemies were behind all these disgraceful deeds. Thus it was necessary for her to take revenge on them preemptively and prevent them from implementing their machinations and vicious conspiracies against her. She would have to . . . Suddenly her husband, the general, entered her room, slipped into bed beside her, and began kissing, fondling, and comforting her—whispering words as sweet as honey. He swore fierce oaths to take vengeance on the vile French journalist and the traitors who had furnished him the forged documents. He also informed her that he had ordered the embassy in Paris and the consulates in various other French cities to purchase all the copies of the book they could—and leave none on sale. It was inconceivable that the journalist would be able to enter the country. In a speech he would deliver on the twentieth anniversary of his assumption of power, the general would announce to the masses that the true aim of such actions was to detract from the country's honor and prestige and to besmirch its reputation. Before leaving her room, he bent over to kiss her as she wept with fervent emotion.

Her cell phone rings. It's her husband, the general. She won't answer . . . She won't! She acts this way when she needs to pressure him to be more flexible—to satisfy all her requests and desires. Now she wants him to allow one of her eleven brothers to assume control of one of the country's most renowned banks. She will leave him on tenterhooks for several days, even for several weeks—until he collapses before her, kissing her hands and legs, asking for her forgiveness, telling her endearingly with tears in his eyes, "I love you. I obey you. Everything you want and desire will come to you in the wink of an eye, my dear, my darling, my assassin, my princess—no, my queen. Men and the jinn are at your service. So, ask for whatever you desire. Ask for anything!"

Five years earlier, furious and enraged, he had entered her chamber—when she was preparing to bathe before retiring to bed—to tell her that he was very upset with the conduct of her eleven brothers, who had crossed some red lines. The people's complaints about them had become so vociferous that protests were starting to threaten his regime. She left him shouting, retired to her private wing, and locked the doors. First thing the next morning she flew to Paris, where she stayed many months. He tried to contact her dozens of times a night and as often during the day, at different numbers. She, however, did not respond to any of the messages he left and didn't return until her spies in the presidential palace informed her that her husband, the general, could no longer focus on his work and instead passed sleepless, agonizing nights. He had canceled the weekly cabinet meetings; indeed, servants had discovered him weeping like a child who could no longer bear the absence of his affectionate mother. When she arrived, he threw himself into her arms, begging her pardon and forgiveness. Oh! It was necessary to be stern at times. Quite necessary . . . Moreover, by denying him entry and holding herself aloof, even when she had no requests, she kindled the flames of his love and attachment to her. The past summer she left him alone at the Palace of Hammamet and stayed with her son at a hotel in Hammamet South. When he could no longer bear her absence, one night when he was intoxicated, he shot off in his car and crashed into a sapling. But for God's benevolence, he would have died. Denial and evasion were necessary. Necessary . . . The sorcerers and witches she consulted unanimously agreed that—to assure the success of her schemes and to win her many battles—evasiveness was the best way to dominate him and to keep him at her mercy forever and a day. Therefore, she does not respond to his message until he passes a night enflamed by her evasion as he suffers and laments. After bathing, she prepares for an intimate evening, the secret nature of which is known only to God. The First Lady stands before the broad mirror and proceeds with smug infatuation to scrutinize every portion of her body. Praise the Lord, praise the Lord for what He created! And a stick in the eye of the critic! The First Lady remains beautiful even after fifty, and her hair has retained its body. Her eyes are wide and clear, and their brows arch like the crescent moon. There are scarcely any wrinkles on her face, and her lips grow even more seductive when they open. Her neck rises soft and tall. Her thighs . . . Oh! Her thighs are like twin columns of polished marble, rising and falling without the least flabbiness or crookedness. Blessings to God! Bless God! How beautiful the First Lady is! How bewitching she is! How enchanting she is! The first person to alert her to her body's beauty had been that elderly masseuse in the bathhouse—near the family's ancient, dilapidated house—she visited once a week with her mother. When she was thirteen, that old woman, whose forehead was adorned with green tattoos and who had handled thousands of female bodies of all ages, stared at length at her figure, pausing especially at the girl's breasts, waist, and lower reaches. One time she whispered to her, "Blessings to God for you, my daughter. Praise the Lord for this excellence, this figure, these breasts, this crotch! My Lord has granted you the best He has. But watch out, my daughter! Be careful while you're young and don't understand life. Times are harder than before, and there are many evil men now. Be wary with them. They will eat you with a ladle, court you, and toss you aside like a bone. By the time you turn thirty, you'll be an old woman like me. Beware, my daughter. They are rough fellows, and the devil rules over them." Then she turned to the girl's mother and warned her, "Na'ima"—that was her name—"my Lord has granted you a little girl as beautiful as a gazelle. Watch over her as best you can. She doesn't belong to filthy butchers. This daughter of yours belongs in Bab al-Bahr, Carthage, Sidi Bou Said, and al-Marsa. Get her out of here before these wolves attack her. Let her stroll about in those other areas where the elite spend their time—men whose pockets are full and whose eyes and laughter are benevolent. If you leave her here, you will gain nothing from her—nothing! Naʿima, this girl will be make your fortune. Mark my words!"

Like a bucket of cold water that awakens a person who is sound asleep, the elderly masseuse's words had roused her from indifference to her body and beauty. Then she mixed less with the girls and young men in her neighborhood and started to stare at her face and figure in the mirror many times a day, and at night too, especially before going to sleep, because she liked to admire her charms, which were visible through her diaphanous nightie. Playing with her breasts and fondling sensitive parts of her body excited her a lot as she stood before the mirror, slipped beneath warm covers in the winter, or flung herself bare-assed naked across her bed on summer nights. She would continue to fondle her body very slowly until she shrieked with delight and the entire world assumed a crimson tint of enjoyment. In school, she daydreamed and ignored the lessons while wandering in her imagination through the rosy worlds awaiting her. Teachers would scold her for being lazy, dim-witted, and gravely deficient in math, natural sciences, and Arabic—indeed in all subjects—but she paid no attention to them and ignored their counsels. In fact, she privately mocked her teachers, saying, "Oh . . . what mules these teachers are! Why don't they look carefully at me and understand that I don't need their lessons and diplomas? They can go to hell and have dreadful lives! I know I'll climb to the highest realms while they scurry beneath me like nasty, frightened mice. May God help that elderly masseuse and grant her a long life! If not for her, I wouldn't have recognized my potential and wouldn't have discovered my body's value." Her mother was as focused on her beautiful daughter as if she had been her only child. She coddled her and gave her special treatment in everything. She deliberately served her only *al-mammu*—in other words, the most delicious and nutritious food. From the large family's meager daily budget she squirreled away enough to purchase for her daughter dresses befitting her beauty and graceful figure. Each week she took her to the tombs of righteous saints and to Sidi Mehrez, Sidi Belhassan al-Shadhili, and Abu Zamaʿa al-Balawi in Kairawan on the noble Prophet's *mawlid* or Laylat al-Qadr. Perhaps the door of matrimony would open for her and save the family from its poverty and destitution. At every shrine the mother spread out her palms and, in a whisper, implored God, His Prophet, and His righteous saints to protect her beautiful daughter from the mischief of the evil eye, to guard her from the cunning of envious and rancorous folks, and to spare her being harmed by enemies who hid behind false smiles. "Amen, Lord of the Universe."

During this period, the beautiful girl, with help from her mother, also began to take an interest in witchcraft, relying on women, most of whom were elderly or at least middle-aged. They were skilled and success- ful practitioners of sorcery and connoisseurs of its secrets and mysteries. She loved to sit with these women, who had stern visages, pursed lips, and harsh gazes, as they spoke at length about the benefits, virtues, uses, and extraordinary wonders of sorcery. Under their influence she started to believe that magic could produce prodigious marvels and miracles. Thanks to it, the powerful became weak and the weak powerful, the rich became poor and the poor rich, a macho man became a docile eunuch with whom his wife could do whatever she wished (without harming him), while he remained oblivious. A giant might succumb to a sudden illness that prevented him from moving or speaking or that might kill him in a few days—indeed, in a few hours. An astoundingly beautiful woman might turn into a hideous she-ape, whose former lovers mocked and shunned her. An incurable invalid might rise to her feet and walk away laughing and happy, as if nothing had happened. An extraordinarily astute and cunning person might turn into a simpleminded numbskull who didn't know the difference between black and white or between past and pres- ent. That old woman, who kept poking snuff in her nostrils, affirmed that if a deserted, abused, and disgraced woman placed a chameleon in her husband's food, the next day he would be her abject slave, kneeling at her feet. Oh! Sorcery had its rituals, secrets, and arts. All this was easy, but only for those who could adorn themselves with the patience to master and practice it. This had to be done covertly, in the dark, because, if the matter were disclosed, the effect of the sorcery would be ruined. Beauty and a pretty figure by themselves weren't enough to allow a girl to realize her ambitious hopes or for her and her family to quit the ancient, dilapi- dated house and its filthy, impoverished district to dwell in the area and residence that her captivating beauty deserved. Magic was also necessary. Ah . . . it was a necessity. Thus she refused to renounce it, even when she became First Lady. Indeed, she clung to it and gravitated toward it even more. She sought its aid to consolidate her control over her husband, the general, his cabinet ministers, and his advisors—in fact, over the entire country. She brought sorcerers and witches to Carthage Palace from Marrakech, Senegal, and the Sudan to prepare "medicine" for her schemes, which were countless. She also relied on sorcery to search for treasures hidden in the belly of the earth, in grottos, caves, and tombs left behind by the Phoenicians, Romans, Carthaginians, Vandals, and Arabs—the successive generations of the country's inhabitants since antiquity. When she entered Carthage Palace, after expelling the general's former wife and his daughters from that marriage, she established special groups of operatives whom she dispatched throughout the country, especially to archaeological sites, to dig for treasures.

Standing before the mirror, the First Lady continues to gaze with admiration and fascination at her body's beauty now that she is over fifty. She reflects on her early years before her swift, if clandestine rise, toward Carthage Palace, from the time she turned sixteen and left school with no regrets. She had met a girl named Amal, whose friends called her Ammula. That short, slightly plump girl, who was three years older, wasn't pretty like her but was an expert at relationships and setting traps for men. She could plunder their minds and wallets without them noticing as she laughed playfully and displayed a naïve innocence in everything she did and said. Accompanying her, the beautiful girl began to visit the restaurants, coffeehouses, and hotels of Bab al-Bahr and the capital's northern suburbs frequently. She smoked premium-brand cigarettes and avidly drank gin and lemon, which remained her favorite drink even after she entered Carthage Palace. In a few weeks, she acquired renown and status with men looking for a good time and "dames," as the locals put it. They began to race after her breathlessly and to hover around her, devouring with their glances—which were hungry for pleasure—her swelling bosom and her dancing rump, which was clad in jeans, and other highlights of her body. Each man compared her to his favorite film star or artiste—the royalty of sexual attraction. She was either Claudia Cardinale, Gina Lollobrigida,

Soad Hosny, or Nadia Lutfi. She *was* Marilyn Monroe! This beautiful girl from the ancient, dilapidated house mastered the art of playing hard to get with astonishing speed and didn't grant a kiss to anyone who fancied her until he had bowed humbly before her, trembling like a chilly bloke on a bitterly cold night. She enjoyed having a lover race, day after day, through the city searching for her without finding any trace of her. Then, when she appeared a week later, he would throw himself into her arms, complaining and weeping. To humor her, he would drive her in his elegant new automobile to the most renowned hotels in Hammamet, Sousse, or the island of Djerba, because the capital had started to cramp her ambitions and aspirations. Her sphere of action had to broaden, expand, and increase in length and breadth before the beautiful girl could realize for herself and her family, which was crammed into that ancient, dilapidated house, what they desired and pined for. The one man who achieved with her what he wanted without abasing himself or chasing breathlessly after her like all her other suitors was a florist in Bab al-Bahr. He was about forty and as handsome as Alain Delon, who was her favorite actor at the time. Both loved the songs of the Tawny Nightingale—in other words, Abdel Halim Hafez, and those of the Thrush, as Sabah was known. He had a way with words like no man she had met. Oh! What an enchanter he was! One beautiful spring evening when Bab al-Bahr was noisy with chirping sparrows soaring over the trees, he offered her a jasmine garland and said with a smile, "Beauty, I hope you will accept this trifling gift from me." The moment she held out her hand to receive the flowers, she felt attracted to him and wished to rest her head on his broad chest and its hair, which showed through the opening of his thin, white shirt. The following day, he invited her to drink gin with lemon on the fifth floor of the Africa Hotel. The third day, they went to al Hamra Cinema to see the Egyptian film *My Father Atop a Tree*, which starred Abdel Halim Hafez and Nadia Lutfi. In the dark cinema, while most spectators had their eyes glued on the screen as the Tawny Nightingale performed songs about love and desire with a voice as smooth as silk, his hand found its way to her breast and then down between her thighs. His caresses left her so giddy that she closed her eyes and abandoned her lips to his. Before the film ended, they raced to his small Paris Street flat, where they made love until dawn.

Next Ammula led her to a hair salon patronized by socially mobile, middle-class women; divorced women; young widows; and girls her age, who obtained contact information there for men looking for a good time, either Tunisians or foreigners. She began to work in that salon as a hair stylist and became skilled at it. The beautiful girl discovered societal situations, conditions, secrets, and clandestine matters that had never previously come to her attention. Now she knew from A to Z the names of girlfriends of the pillars of the state, of powerful men in sensitive government agencies, of wealthy men who came from the Gulf Region or from Tunisia's oil-rich neighbor. She also knew the precise details of the places and times for assignations for love and passion whether in the capital, Hammamet, Sousse, Monastir, Tobruk, Libya, or elsewhere. With the assistance of her new lover, who was an expert at executing contracts and deals—small or large—on the black market, the beautiful girl now became skilled at acquiring wealth, which was easier and quicker through illegal channels and methods, via Paris, Rome, London, and Istanbul, importing banned and forbidden goods of every type and variety. She did this without exposing herself to any danger. She relied on her alluring smiles and the sweet words of a voice, which from white nights, premium cigarettes, and gin with lemon had acquired a huskiness that men loved, to charm customs officials into letting her pass like an angel, immune to harm from any source. All the same, one customs agent, who was close to retirement and was renowned at the airport for his fidelity to the laws and careful enforcement of them, stopped her on her arrival from Rome one night at 10:00 and asked her to open her bags. She smiled once, twice, five times, ten, but the portly customs agent, who had difficulty breathing because he suffered from asthma, remained stolidly at his station, oblivious to her smiles, beauty, and elegance. When she eventually obeyed his orders, he led her to the airport security offices, where her passport was seized and she was threatened with prosecution for violation of multiple laws.

Feeling forsaken and crushed, the beautiful girl returned to the ancient, dilapidated house and slept for only two hours. The next morning she rushed to her lover and woke him with great difficulty because he had only gone to bed at dawn. When she told him what had happened, he yawned and replied in a hoarse voice, which was raw from late nights, alcohol, and smoking, "You have nothing to fear. It's a minor problem that I'll fix quickly today."

"How?"

"Don't you know that my cousin was appointed director general of national security? That means the Ministry of the Interior is within his grasp. Just let me finish sleeping. I'll contact him before noon."

She sighed profoundly as her fear and agitation lifted. What an idiot she was! She had forgotten that her lover's cousin had become one of the regime's most powerful men after the bloody events of Black Thursday, when dozens of people were killed and hundreds were wounded in the capital and other cities. The elderly president had himself commended the man's "qualities" and "superior patriotism" and extolled his "resolve" and "courage" after he used bullets, metal truncheons, and tear gas against the trade unionists who threatened the regime by organizing the first general strike since the country obtained its independence. Now all the trade union leaders were in prison, and the courts had handed down harsh sentences for them. The whole country, near and far, was trembling with fear because the new director of security was a military man known for his brutality and severity. He was ready to fire live ammunition at anyone who attempted to demonstrate in the streets again. The elderly president warned citizens in an official address: "Yes to the regime! No to anarchy!" The new security chief wanted to implement this with actions, not just words. Oh! She wouldn't have spent a night racked by doubt, if—when she stood before the elderly, asthmatic customs agent—she had remembered that her lover's cousin decided who was released from prison and who got locked up—not just for the Ministry of the Interior but throughout the entire country. Praise God for her safe deliverance! Two days later her lover came to tell her, gaily and happily, "You're in luck, Darling! Very lucky! Very!"

"What do you mean?"

"My cousin wants to hand your passport to you in person!"

"Really?"

"He expects you tomorrow in his office at 4:00 p.m. So be on time because my cousin is very punctilious about appointments—like the Americans he studied with."

Svelte and elegant, she set off for the important appointment, the most important of her life until that moment. Her heart betrayed her apprehensions and terror from time to time by its pounding. What could the security chief want with her? Did he fancy her because of her passport photo? But that picture did not do justice to her beauty! What did he want from her then? Was he curious about the reason for her trips abroad? Or what? She just had to wait and hope for the best, because the security chief would not have scheduled an appointment for her had he wanted to harm her.

The security chief greeted her warmly, ordered coffee for her, and began to converse with her so graciously and affectionately that he seemed to have known her a long time. She felt at ease with him but replied to his questions about her private life with equivocation and vagueness. When their meeting ended, he gave her his private number and said, "Contact me in two days, toward the end of the evening. I want to see you again!"

She left the Ministry of the Interior and headed to Bab al-Bahr. She felt disconcerted; for the security chief to receive her in such a friendly way and converse with her so graciously, to be so affectionate when first meeting her—there must be some secret behind this. There had to be. But what? All the same, she had noticed that he had occasionally seemed embarrassed while speaking with her. He had stammered, even when attempting to appear dignified. Perhaps this suggested he had fallen in love with her. That would be love at first glance . . . or even before? If her hunch was right, many doors would open for her in the future. She would ignore the rumors about the security chief's harshness, about the trade unionists he had tortured and thrown in prison, and about all the blood that had been spilled on Black Thursday. What interested her was success—to rise to the top echelons by any path and any means!

Their second meeting was in an upscale restaurant in the northern suburbs—in a private booth away from curious eyes. On this occasion, after he drank two glasses of whisky and she consumed a glass of gin with lemon, the security chief confessed his love for her. He told her in a whisper that he had admired her passport photo and had been keen to meet her, to discover if she was prettier than her picture.

She replied with a smile, "There's no doubt about that!"

Yes, she was beautiful and captivating, and he wanted her to be his alone. For that reason, she would need to renounce his cousin and all the men she had known previously. His high and sensitive rank made it necessary to deny malicious tongues any opportunity to fleece him or sully his reputation. She was to be his alone, and he would open doors for her. She accepted these conditions without any hesitation. Over the course of approximately two years, she remained his alone, and no one else shared her body. He was eager to satisfy her desires and to obey her demands— even costly and questionable ones. Through her good graces and her lover's, her eleven brothers acquired a lot of influence in the black market, after previously serving as nothing but obedient pawns of major players.

The country was soaked with blood again, however. Armed men attacked a city in the south of Tunisia in hopes of toppling the regime, assuming that the citizens, who were angry about the events of Black Thursday, would support them. But they failed and were executed in less than a week. To challenge them, the elderly president toured the oases, accompanied by his wife. To media representatives who asked what he thought about these events, he attempted to reclaim his prestige of former days, when people had lifted him on their shoulders amid resounding cheers of "Glory and praise to the Greatest Liberator." So, he claimed, "The people love me. Anyone who wants to harm me, harms this country and will meet the same fate as those traitors." As soon as he returned to the capital, however, the elderly president fired the security chief and named him an ambassador to a distant country, hoping that "my dear people" would therefore believe that democratization was imminent.

Even so, her rising star did not set, because she had become an authority on high society's secrets and clandestine activities. She was soon able to forge a romantic liaison with the prime minister's son-in-law—yes, his son-in-law—who was in his forties, tall, and muscular. He had dark blue eyes and a fair complexion; he was always elegant and loved life's comforts; and he was blessed with good taste, delicacy, sensitivity, and a graciousness that differed from the security chief's brusque crudeness. Thanks to his assistance, the eleven brothers received new opportunities in the black market and, with his protection, she continued her ascent to the top echelons. She felt comfortable with her new status, and the image of her former lover, the former security chief, had already faded in her mind when the Bread Revolt exploded. Once more the country endured dark, critical days that forced the elderly president to recall quickly the former security chief, who had demonstrated that he was the only person capable of safeguarding the regime. His return frightened her, and she disappeared from sight. She stayed in bed, following breaking news on TV. The security chief, however, soon sent for her. He greeted her with great fanfare and gave her an assortment of fine perfumes that he told her he had purchased for her at the Frankfurt airport. During that same hour he took her to his office, giving not the slightest hint that he had learned about her recent affair. A few months later, though, she woke to the agonizing news that her former lover, the prime minister's son-in-law, had died in a dreadful automobile accident on the road linking the capital to Bizerte. Rumors spread that the accident was planned, but by whom? No one dared to answer this question publicly, because the security chief had consolidated his position and enjoyed the unqualified confidence of the elderly president. Therefore, one needed to be wary and circumspect. Before uttering a word, people had to determine whether it might harm or injure them or their family, because the security chief would not hesitate to impose severe penalties on anyone who attempted to challenge him, treated him insolently, or doubted his "probity" or "superior patriotism."

She returned to the arms of the security chief, whose influence increased day by day—especially once plots and conspiracies regarding the succession overwhelmed the nation. To decisively demonstrate his mad love for her he gave her a beautiful villa in the capital's northern suburbs and a red Volvo. He sent her to Paris more than once to purchase all the clothes, jewels, and fine perfumes she wished. In this way, she began to live like a high-society lady. She whispered to her mother one night, "Soon we're all going to leave this ancient, dilapidated house and this miserable, wretched neighborhood." Her mother offered a prayer to God to thank Him for His grace and benefactions. She remembered that the elderly masseuse had told her, "Na'ima, your daughter is your fortune."

Then events began to unfold so swiftly they made people's heads spin, affecting spirits and hearts. Serious rebellions and protests rocked the country and caused its citizens to feel they should expect an explosion that might send them to disaster. Oblivious to all this, the elderly president continued to cling to power, changing cabinet ministers like a man changing shirts on a hot summer day. He appointed the security chief first as minister of the interior and then as prime minister. What happened next? The citizens of the country awoke to an unanticipated event: the former security chief, who had served as minister of the interior and then prime minister, had removed the elderly president from power and taken his place!

When she heard the news, she trilled with joy at her lover's triumph. The doors of Carthage Palace swung open wide for her. The girl who had suffered privation, misery, and humiliation in the ancient, dilapidated house became First Lady of the land of Hannibal.

The clock indicated that it was 2:30 p.m. He bathed and donned his black suit, which he customarily wore on formal occasions, and a matching shirt of the same color. He also wore black shoes. In this mournful garb, he rushed off in a taxi to celebrate his sixtieth birthday at the Albatross Restaurant.

9

He presided over a reunion of his regular companions, who all praised his elegant appearance and lauded his black outfit, which served as a counterpoint to the white that had begun to lay siege to his head.

"Today your food and drinks are on my tab," he told them, raising a glass to toast their health.

They thrust their heads toward him like hungry draft horses reaching for fodder. "Does some occasion prompt this generous invitation?"

"No occasion!"

"No way! There must be some occasion!"

"I think you heard clearly what I said. There's no occasion!"

"Perhaps it's your birthday. Isn't that so?"

"Guys, I beg you! If you keep pestering me with these disquieting questions, I'll immediately withdraw my invitation, thus relieving all of us."

"No, no! Please don't do that!"

Si al-Tahir, who was known for his bright spirit and dark humor, commented, "Rest assured, dear Yunus: we will certainly drink and eat enough to send you home broke or even force you to pawn your elegant black suit and your shirt and shoes—every stitch of clothing you have on!"

They all burst out laughing.

He ordered grilled fish for them, salads, plates of spaghetti with seafood, and three bottles of Magon wine.

"This is the first round, friends, and the party lasts until midnight!"

Si al-Tahir cleared his throat again and said, "Listen, dear friends: anyone who renounces Yunus's amazing generosity tonight might just as well renounce paradise!"

Again, they laughed so loudly they couldn't hear the roar of the fretful sea.

Si al-Tahir, who was almost eighty but looked considerably younger, was seated opposite their host. He was always elegant, cheerful, and merry. He had many special qualities, and all reflected his expert knowledge of the country's traditions, spirit, and many factions. His words, which were carefully chosen and displayed a thorough knowledge of grammatical niceties and the fine points of proper Arabic, were free of any coarseness, affectation, obscenity, insipidness, or triteness. His remarks contained many radiant images, allusions, and clever references as well as some ingenious wordplay. Si al-Tahir adored classical Andalusian music, especially Malouf. He considered the *muwashshahat* to be some of the finest poetry Arabs had created. "They are innocent of overwrought eloquence and of the rigidity, dryness, and monotony of most poetry written in the desert, where there is no water or verdure, where life is harsh, and people's natures become coarse and their emotions desiccated. The *muwashshahat* sing with fluency and sweetness; a person responds to them and soars with his spirit into space, inebriated with life's light and delight.

You who sports the garden's rose on his cheek

And mimics the bamboo's stalk with his figure,

Who rebuffs a man with the sword you unsheathe,

And whose eyes are more incisive than the blades of his bravery.

All swords are trenchant when drawn,

But the cutting edge of your glance draws blood even in its scabbard.

If you wish to slay me, just do it,

For who would side with a slave against his master?"

Si al-Tahir's enthusiasm for *muwashshahat* could be attributed partly to his loyalty to his Andalusian heritage, of which he was proud. From youth to middle age, he had studied his genealogy and discovered that one of his ancestors was a major merchant in Granada before the Muslim Arabs were forced to leave Andalusia and scatter across the face of the earth in search of a refuge that would spare them the hardship of wandering. Si al-Tahir belonged to one of the oldest families in Neapolis, which he loved and preferred to all other cities. "When I'm away," he said, "I yearn for it like a babe longing for its mother's breast." Before his retirement,

Si al-Tahir had worked at the university for forty years as a professor of ancient history. Despite his vast knowledge of his field, all he written had been his dissertation on the age of Saint Augustine. His explanation was: "My sloth vanquished my knowledge. Besides, I can't bear to barricade myself in a room; life is always calling me to linger at its heart with all the others who are passionately devoted to it." Si al-Tahir had lived alone in a villa by the sea since his wife died about seven years earlier. He seemed extremely devoted to her memory because his face clouded over and his temper soured whenever he remembered her loss. His two married daughters, who worked in the French city of Lyons, visited him every summer. His older son, who was a bridge and highway engineer, lived and worked in Sousse. This son was married and had three children. His younger son, who had failed out of university, had succeeded in commerce and ran an electronics store in Neapolis. He was married and had a ten-year-old daughter with whom Si al-Tahir liked to walk through the city every Sunday morning.

Si al-Tahir spoke calmly, clearly enunciating his words and accentuating paragraph breaks. He was so reserved that his anger and reactions did not show. If he grew irritated, he would remain silent and leave without saying good-bye. He ate and drank deliberately. One of his drinking pals would down an entire bottle before he had emptied his first glass. Occasionally, however, he would challenge his health, age, and physician by consuming an entire bottle or more and partying until midnight. He was a vegetarian, although he ate fish. He had given up meat when he turned seventy. Si al-Tahir chose his companions carefully, and there was no place in his gatherings for bores, misers, failures, curiosity seekers, or men inflated with bogus arrogance. Always proud of Tunisia, he would declare that it was the best and most beautiful country in the world but that its citizens did not deserve it. He would frequently quote the statement of the Sufi Sidi Bel Hasan al-Shadhili: "If Tunisia were handed to us instead of its citizens, it would make an excellent home. They deny a benefactor's benefactions while praising every depravity."

When Si al-Tahir smiled—as at present—he resembled Anthony Quinn in his later years. He said he hadn't enjoyed life or savored its sweetness until he retired. Then he asked his companions, "Do you know why?"

Without waiting for a response, he continued in his entertaining way: "Excellent comrades, I was born the very year that a huge crisis afflicted the world. States were ruined and millions went hungry. Every country's condition became the opposite of the proverb 'fish eat fish, and he whose effort is weak fails.' Yes, excellent comrades, that crisis turned people into savage beasts that fought each other ferociously merely to survive. I spent my childhood watching my father exhaust himself daily to bring home enough to fend off one family's hunger. All this time, my grandmother kept ordering us to bar the door to prevent hungry Bedouins—who raided the city accompanied by whatever surviving livestock they had—from attacking us. Afterward, I learned that young women from our quarter and other areas were selling their lovely bodies to elderly merchants just to obtain a single loaf of bread. Yes, a single loaf of bread, Gentlemen! I also discovered that boys and adolescents were being sodomized at night in cemeteries, on the shore, and in other desolate locations, in exchange for a piece of meat, a hot pastry, or a handful of halva. When I turned ten, the World War flared up, and famine threatened us once more. We could no longer obtain basic supplies like sugar, salt, and coffee without huge effort. Fear spread throughout the entire country, and savagery and anarchy prevailed. We were no longer able to distinguish between the seasons, because all were dark, gloomy, and gritty. Calamities, pains, and funerals punctuated them. Wails and laments repeatedly resounded from homes every month—no—every week. The Jews, who were numerous back then, holed up in safe houses or fled elsewhere. Even Shlomo, the short, one-eyed, broad-faced man, who used to entertain us with curious tales he collected from the streets and markets, disappeared without a trace and didn't reappear again until the Allies entered the city—after the Germans left by sea for Sicily. For many weeks, one-eyed Shlomo kept yelling in the streets, 'Long live the Allies!' while waving British and American flags and wearing the Jewish star on his chest. This is how my childhood and adolescence passed. I was weighed down by the adults' problems, concerns, fears, sorrows, and pains. So I did not enjoy any of the mirth, delight, relaxation, or joie de vivre typically associated with that age. The adults may have regarded me with a sympathetic eye and thought to themselves, 'How unlucky you are! You were born in a difficult age. Now that you're grown, you live in a difficult age too!' When I turned twenty, the armed insurrection against colonial rule broke out, and young men my age forgot about girls, love, play, and similar topics to join the struggle. The homeland was our first and last true love; it deserved the sacrifice of our precious blood. I decided that the best sacrifice I could make for my country was to travel to Paris and continue my studies. When I arrived there, I didn't find the City of Light people had told me about when I was at al-Sadiqiya School. Instead, it was a gray city preoccupied with the serious disturbances and alarming apprehensions that preceded the collapse and dismemberment of France's colonial empire. We woke every day to some new report that confirmed this. Then the French army suffered a humiliating defeat in the Battle of Dien Bien Phu in what was known at the time as Indochina. In Algeria, the revolutionary war, which would continue for seven years, had begun, and French armies had started preparing to withdraw from other regions. Most of France's cultural elite—its writers, poets, and thinkers—were preoccupied by all this. The serious problems and political crises that France and the world faced in this postwar era, which also witnessed the appearance of new political maps and astonishing changes at multiple levels, were at the forefront of their concerns. They were constantly releasing new manifestoes to clarify their stance and ideas. Fierce battle flared up among them from time to time, and the flames would barely be extinguished before they reignited and became more ferocious than ever. I divided my time between the university, the library, and my small room in the student quarter on boulevard Jourdan. In that era, we North African students were subjected to searches and interrogations by the police because of the Algerian War of Independence. We were beaten on numerous occasions and insulted on the streets and in public places. Thus I can say I lived in Paris like a scared mouse in its hole. So, I didn't enjoy the city's lights, experience the thrilling adventures possible there, or score a single romance with a French blonde, contrary to my expectations when I was a student at al-Sadiqiya School. Therefore, once I graduated, I returned to Tunisia to work on my dissertation about the age of Saint Augustine. I was unable to defend it at the Sorbonne until three years after the end of the Algerian War of Independence. Then I was appointed a lecturer in ancient history at the University of Tunis. That era saw the birth of the new state but was difficult and nerve-racking because our country was plunged into the problems, concerns, and dangers of post-independence. Ignorance was widespread, and its consequences were dreadful. The country's citizens were coping with poverty and hunger along with false promises the new rulers made and the sacks of flour that America donated for propaganda. To console Tunisians, Bourguiba never stopped delivering speeches full of admonition and exhortation. He began by saluting his 'noble daughters and sons.' Then he would revisit past and present scenes from his lengthy saga of struggle—dwelling especially on the periods of incarceration and exile. He would break into sobs whenever he mentioned his mother, Fatouma. Men, women, and children would weep with him in cities, villages, and the countryside. After that he would wipe his eyes and recover his composure, severity, and sparkling leadership. He would call on his 'noble daughters and sons' to offer more sacrifices during the stage of the Great Jihad, as he called it, to build the new state. Then he would order them to use contraceptives to decrease the number of hungry mouths."

Si al-Tahir paused as if to catch his breath after this effort. For some moments, his mind floated away from his companions while he looked earnest and collected his thoughts and memories. Then he resumed his calm, deliberate monologue: "Back in those dark, stormy times, gentlemen, I married. I won't conceal from you that I discovered in matrimony the happiness and contentment I desired, although what was happening in the country spoiled them for me. Whipped up by the diverse ideological winds, strikes and protests proliferated both inside and outside the university, where students divided into factions and sects. Each group claimed to possess the truth and therefore fought every other group intensely and violently, thinking the others had no right to exist on the face of the earth! China's clients accused Moscow's champions of being revisionists and of betraying Marxist-Leninist principles and vice versa. Che Guevara's disciples came to the university sporting his image on their chests. Trotskyites smoked Galleon cigarettes and discussed the 'world revolution' that would guarantee the final victory of the proletariat and of socialism. Sympathizers with the Palestinian Revolution glorified skyjacking, Leila Khaled, and the Japanese activist Kōzō Okamoto. They also knew by heart the statements of George Habash. Fellow travelers of the Ba'ath Party and supporters of Gamal Abdel Nasser advocated 'a single Arab people with an eternal message.' Even Albania's president, who was known to only a few of the nation's citizens—with his wife, who as I recall was named Najma—had supporters at the university! All these little cliques, which fought each other, united against me! I was called a reactionary and backward, an agent, a traitor, and petit bourgeois because I taught a 'dead subject'—in other words, ancient history. According to these groups, I should have taught the history of the world's revolutions and the lives of their leaders, leaving Roman history to the archaeologists. My students repeatedly left me droning on alone in the classroom about Julius Caesar, Saint Augustine, or the Punic Wars as they rushed outside to chant, 'Death to reactionaries, death to the bourgeoisie, and death to imperialism!' Then I would be obliged to collect my lecture notes and return home, feeling frustrated and sad, trailed by the students' curses and insults: 'Cowardly agent! Gravedigger!' A student I didn't dare look at because she was so enchantingly beautiful told me angrily as she stormed out of the classroom, 'You're old. You ought to stay home. There's no place for you in today's world!' Me old? At the time I was forty-five. I raced home. Had it not been for the grace of God, a car would have run me down because I was totally oblivious to my surroundings. When I stood in front of the mirror, I saw I had become an old man!

"I turned fifty, and my circumstances became increasingly bad and crummy, while Arab wars, defeats, schisms, insurrections, calamities, diseases, and complexes multiplied. Whichever way you faced, you confronted ruins, conflagrations, and vanquished peoples awaiting a dubious liberation. During this period, the scene inside the university changed. The Maoists, revisionists, followers of Che Guevara, and the rest disappeared, only to reemerge as students with wan, rigid faces and unkempt beards, who called for holy jihad against 'unbelievers, atheists, and enemies of God and His Messenger among the Christians and Jews.' Now I was labeled a freethinker, an unbeliever, an agent of Christian evangelists—otherwise why would I consent to teach the history of pagans and crusaders and the life of Saint Augustine? If I were a Muslim who cared about his religion, I should teach the life of the Prophet and the glories of

Islam and introduce students to the mighty jihadis who had raised high the Prophet's banner in all areas of the earth, whether in China, India, Sicily, or Andalusia. As I approached the door of the classroom to deliver my lecture, a group of angry, raging, bearded students appeared before me. They waved the Qur'an in my face and began to shout, 'There's no place for Christian swine in our Islamic university!' In these circumstances, gentlemen, I reached retirement age. I left the capital and came to live with my wife in the house we built overlooking the sea. From that time, I have paid no attention to anything outside my personal world. I don't follow the news on television or the radio. I avoid anything that might spoil my peace of mind or upset me. Politics means nothing to me. I absolutely do not sit with anyone who might annoy me with its concerns, problems, vicissitudes, or storms. I pay no heed to what is happening or will happen to the Arabs. I've grown tired of all that. I wish to live out the remainder of my life the way I want and please. I listen to classical symphonies, Malouf music, and the songs of Fairuz, Saliha, Edith Piaf, Charles Aznavour, Brassens, Sinatra, Ella Fitzgerald, and Louis Armstrong. I walk along the beach on cold nights. I jot down my thoughts. I dance alone in the evening by candlelight, celebrating by myself. I reread extraordinary books like *The Confessions of Saint Augustine, A Thousand and One Nights, The Misers* by al-Jahiz, *Entertainment and Companionship* by al-Tawhidi, and Plato's *Symposium*. I watch new films that appeal to me or old ones I loved when I was young, especially westerns and the films of Charlie Chaplin and Buster Keaton, who make me laugh so loud the neighbors think I've gone mad. I sit on the balcony of my house to watch a beautiful sunset over the sea as I enjoy grilled sea bass, a Tunisian salad, and a glass of Magon. In summer, I like to spy on the beautiful girls who play and laugh on the sand. Occasionally I put a few books in my bag and head south to spend some days in the oases, where I grow even more focused on my own inner world. This is all I want, because happiness comes from simplicity, from being content with a little—like Sufis and ascetics. I think this is the best way to live in this world, which is imprisoned in a cage called globalization, a world so exhausted that it is no longer able to progress without major difficulty. Indeed, I find that it is drowning in the swamp of a civilization that has dominated it for numerous centuries and that has lost its human spark until it seems fated for self-destruction. I believe, therefore, distinguished gentlemen, that I never savored life's enjoyment and sweetness until I retired."

Farhat, who was seated to his right, was a scrawny fellow, and his eyes and cheeks were sunken. His features channeled the mournful, nineteenth-century Romantics, who thought death was overdue if they lived to be twenty and who welcomed it with satisfaction and open arms. His father had chosen this name for him because he was born the year the trade union leader Farhat Hached was assassinated—in the very same month. That happened on December 5, 1952—in other words, in the final years of the great ferment that preceded the announcement of independence. Although Farhat Hached had previously received serious death threats from the Main Rouge gang that colonists established to liquidate and terrorize national leaders, he had ignored them.

Early that morning Hached was driving his car on the road between the capital and the suburb of Radis, where he lived, when bullets struck various parts of his body. Even so, he managed to climb out of his vehicle, which had turned over. Soiled by his own blood, he stood on the road seeking help, but his attackers noticed and returned to complete their foul deed. The day he was assassinated was a black day for all Tunisians, who wept copiously for a man who repeated in all his speeches, "I love you, people!"

Farhat's father was one of those angered by Bourguiba's tilt to the West after independence. For this reason, he did not hesitate to join a group of soldiers and civilians plotting to assassinate the president. The conspiracy, however, was discovered in the final hours. Farhat said he was eight when his father was arrested. That occurred in the middle of the summer, one Monday morning when everyone in the family was still sound asleep. Then, suddenly, a great hullabaloo erupted, and they all woke up, terrified, to find themselves confronted by policemen, who were armed to the teeth. Trembling and teary-eyed, young Farhat watched the entire drama from start to finish: his father, still clad in pajamas, as stiff as a statue, was handcuffed; his mother, who was struggling to hold back her sobs; his brothers and sisters, who were devastated and stunned and seemed to be watching a clip from a horror film. The policemen turned the chairs and tables upside down, ripped open upholstery, emptied the armoires, scattered clothes around, smashed locked chests, climbed onto the roof, and then returned to search the kitchen, the pantry, and even the WC, looking for documents and incriminating evidence. After combing the house for about two hours, the police rushed away. Before Farhat's father disappeared with them, the boy heard him instruct his mother in a husky voice, "Take care of your sons and daughters, especially Farhat. He's the dearest to me and the apple of my eye!"

Some of the ringleaders of this rebellion against Bourguiba were executed; others were sentenced to life in prison. Farhat's father was sentenced to twenty years at hard labor. When he was finally released, he revealed that he and his comrades had been thrown into a cave dripping with water, where daylight never entered. Lice dined on their flesh, and mice cavorted around them, day and night. They relieved themselves in stinking, black buckets, and their lunch and supper consisted of nasty cold broth or dry bread dunked in salty water. If they complained about this diet, they were whipped until they blacked out. Then water was poured over their bodies, which were soiled with their own blood and ravaged by wounds.

A presidential pardon was issued after thirteen years of incarceration, so Farhat's father was released. The diseases that had ganged up on him during the many years he had spent in that black cave, however, soon finished him off. He departed from this world after enjoying only two years of freedom. Farhat intensely disliked any discussion of his father's tragedy and would merely comment, "I believe the bitterest and most atrocious punishment that can be meted out to a child is being prevented from seeing his father when he knows he's still alive."

Farhat rebuffed any inquiry about his private life. No one knew, for example, why he chose to live in Neapolis after being born and raised in Bizerte. Similarly, no one knew why he continually disappeared for many months at a time or what income allowed him to live without a job or career. No one knew either why he seemed averse to discussing women or love. Even so, once he became intoxicated, he would loosen up enough to say, "This puny body of mine entombs desires I have suppressed until they gave up the ghost. Others evaporated when I proved incapable of satisfying them." Every now and then Farhat would refer to three years he had spent in Paris, but without mentioning what he had done there. He may have enrolled in one of the universities. In any event, he did not devote much time to studying; he had preferred hanging out in the city's bars and patronizing its theaters and cultural circles. He may have attended lectures by Lacan at the Sorbonne because he cited Lacan's ideas and theories and discussed him and his works in exhaustive detail. What was certain was that in Paris he had acquired a sophisticated level of cultural literacy and a comprehensive knowledge of the French language and its literature. He enjoyed talking about obscure poets, writers, and philosophers. The thinkers he loved best were Pierre Abélard, who was castrated to punish him for loving his pupil Héloïse, and the Czech archbishop Josef Beran, who opposed the Communist regime. On the day of Beran's funeral, the police prohibited the sale of flowers in Prague. Yet the work Farhat liked best of all and could hardly stop praising was *Les Chants de Maldoror* by Lautréamont, whom he had discovered when he was twenty. (By now he was fifty.) He had translated the work into Arabic but continued to revise, rethink, and revisit his translation, adding new annotations to it. Smiling, he would say, "I would be the happiest man in this country if one day I were able to produce a translation that reflected the true genius of *Les Chants de Maldoror*." Then as humility softened his features, he would recite, almost in a whisper:

> May the heavens allow the reader, when he is emboldened and has temporarily become as ferocious as what he is reading, to find his path, which will be abrupt and wild, through the desolate swamps of these pages, which are somber and brimming with poison; because unless he brings to his reading a rigorous logic and the tension of a spirit that is at least equal to his mistrust, the lethal emissions of this book will dissolve his spirit like water dissolving sugar. It would not be good for the entire world to read the following pages; only a few can savor this bitter fruit without endangering themselves.[27]

Their third companion was Brando. His friends had called him that when he was young, and this nickname had quickly supplanted his given name until only a few people—mostly members of his tightly knit family—continued to call him Karim. People, including waiters in the coffeehouses and restaurants he frequented, generally preferred to call him Brando. His young friends had awarded him this name because of his passion—which approached veneration—for the famous American actor Marlon Brando. He admired other major actors like Orson Wells, Henry Fonda, Humphrey Bogart, Laurence Olivier, Al Pacino, Lee Marvin, and Robert Di Niro, but, according to him, Marlon Brando stood head and shoulders above them. Since he had seen this actor in the film version of *A Streetcar Named Desire*, he had persisted in collecting minor and major bits of information about his personal and public life and exceptional career. He had decorated his bedroom with pictures of Brando in different films he had starred in and for which he had won notable awards. When Marlon Brando died on April 3, 2004, he wept for the star more bitterly than for anyone else—even his father. Nowadays, when Brando the actor was mentioned in these gatherings, Karim would frown and then release a sigh that encompassed all the pains and sorrows the actor's death had caused him. He would whisper, "So far as I'm concerned, Marlon Brando wasn't just a great actor, he was a miraculous legend. No other twentieth-century artist compares to him!"

Karim worked for an insurance company in the capital but lived in Neapolis. On returning home, he would slip out of his business suit and head back to the street in jeans, T-shirt, and athletic shoes, or—in warm weather—dressed like a hippie. In winter, he wore a long black coat like that of a priest or herdsman. In the old knapsack he always carried he put French books he bought from used bookstores—detective stories by Agatha Christie and George Simenon and works by Edgar Allen Poe, Gogol, Chekov, and Borges. He acted as if there weren't any Arabic books. If someone asked why, he would reply, "The professors of my native tongue did everything they could to alienate me from it. All of them were humorless, potbellied, and empty-headed. On the other hand, my professors of French were like birds warbling in gardens in the spring. That's why I fell in love with their language and why I read the books I like in it. For me, reading is my second passion, after the cinema." In his thirties, Karim had married a girl with whom he was madly in love. According to him, she had reciprocated his love. Half a year after their wedding, however, this stormy love story came to a sudden end, in a way that he described as "hurtful and painful." Before this rupture, Samia—for that "was her name"—had been "grousing all the time" and precipitating fights and quarrels about the most trivial things, and her desires and demands had become limitless.

She wanted to furnish the apartment that they rented in El Menzah 6 of the capital in keeping with her extremely refined taste, and such furnishings required huge outlays of cash that their limited income could not support.

She also wanted to buy expensive dresses, perfumes, shoes, and jewelry that only women of the upper crust could afford.

She wanted to be as pampered as she had been in her parents' home.

She wanted to dine at least twice a week at fancy restaurants in La Goulette and Gamart.

Since she hated cooking, cleaning, and every other form of housework, she needed a maid.

She became hysterical if he wanted to drink a glass of wine or beer and attacked him furiously if he picked up a book. She would snatch it from him and toss it far away or tear it to shreds with the delight of someone taking revenge on an obdurate foe. In her opinion, the only people who read books were deadbeats, retards, wusses, and guys who ignored golden opportunities to "get a leg up." She also despised all the films he loved and forced him to watch cheesy romantic serials with her or other superficial, trite programing. In bed she exhibited amazing, weird proclivities, which Karim preferred not to discuss.

One fateful day, Karim quarreled with his boss at work and returned home early, sensing that some other misfortune awaited him. "I returned home as burdened with sorrows and worries as the clerk in Chekhov's story who dies of grief, in a chair, after spitting on his boss's bald head," he explained. When he opened the door, he stepped back, thunderstruck. Had he opened the door of the wrong apartment? Impossible! After living for six months in this apartment, which he had entered as a happy bridegroom, he could have found his way to it even in the dark or with his eyes closed. What was the matter then? He stepped inside with extreme caution, as if afraid of tumbling into an invisible abyss. Yes, he was in his conjugal flat, number 210, fourth floor, but it was totally bare. There was nothing in the kitchen, bathroom, living room, bedroom, guest room, or the small room used as an office—nothing—and the emptiness was oppressive and dreary. But what? His clothes were stacked in piles on the floor of the living room, along with his work shoes, his new pair of athletic shoes, his personal care items, and a few books he had hidden from his wife. At the entryway, he found a slip of paper on which Samia had written in her pathetic handwriting: "I've decided to leave you because I don't want to waste my life with a fool like you. Go to hell!" As night fell, he paced the empty flat like a man who finds himself imprisoned in a cramped cell, without knowing why. When he grew tired, he stretched out on the living room floor, where he lay smoking—eyes fixed on the ceiling—until dawn broke.

He commented about his marriage: "The bitterest and harshest trial of my life was my marriage to Samia. I never thought marriage could destroy a beautiful love story so quickly or hideously. That's why I'm astonished now whenever I meet a couple who are happy, even years after they wed. Oh, I admit my marriage was a grievous mistake. That's why I've decided to remain single to the end of my days. It's true that not being married is difficult, bitter, and annoying. All the same, it is far better than the headaches, problems, and destructive tempests of matrimony."

After falling silent momentarily, Karim smiled and opened his coffer of emotional secrets. "The decade of my life between twenty and thirty was a time of ebullient one-night stands. Back then, AIDS wasn't a concern, unlike now, and tens of thousands of female European tourists flocked to our country, starved for sex. Whether single, married, divorced, or widowed—they all wanted to experience Arab virility. So, it wasn't hard for me to perfect my French and improve my English and Italian. In one week, I would bed German, Scandinavian, Italian, English, and Dutch women, as well as other daughters of Jesus. Oh, I screwed so many women during that happy era! I would leave one only to find myself in the arms of another. I made love to them in their private rooms; by the swimming pool; on the beach at night, at dawn, and at sunset; in hotel gardens and restrooms. I would become thoroughly aroused when a woman slipped her hand beneath the table to open my pants and began to fondle me calmly while her husband sat beside her, eating, drinking, and laughing—oblivious and contented. She would continue to caress me until I ejaculated in her soft hand. After my divorce, I enjoyed sexual adventures with married and divorced women and then with students once the university opened in Neapolis. All the same, I wanted these relationships to remain temporary, with no strings attached. Now I'm over fifty, my hair has started to fall out, and wrinkles and furrows have begun to appear on my face. I won't hide the fact that I have started to rely on my imagination, using it to satisfy my sexual urges. I recall the most enjoyable moments of pleasure I have known in my previous sexual escapades or some of the extraordinary sex scenes from the films I love. Then I picture myself buck naked in bed with the most beautiful actresses in the world and do whatever I want and desire with them, my eyes shut tight, in my own bedroom. I admit my cell phone also affords me sexual enjoyment that has softened the loneliness of bachelorhood, melting its frost and icy chill. Thanks to my phone, I now have girlfriends in different regions of the country: southern women, coastal women, Kairouan women, Kefi women, Tabarka women, Béja women—students, civil servants, single, married, or divorced women. With them, I practice sex in an unprecedented manner and find in these cellular relationships a pleasure far superior to what I experienced face-to-face. Moreover, they only cost me the price of the call and don't, for example, oblige me to invite this or that woman to a restaurant, to offer her a gift, or to exhaust myself in writing her a phony love letter. I never tell these mobile girlfriends how old I am, and they all think I'm a young guy—I don't know why. Perhaps my mellow voice deceives them. In any case, they rely heavily on the imagination, as I do, and you all realize that the imagination can veil reality's ugliness and true condition." Then, closing his chest of emotional secrets, Karim quickly and deftly returned to his reality. "That's the truth, dear friends! I now feel that the only woman who has truly loved me and turned a blind eye to my misdeeds, errors, and transgressions, the only one who has penetrated the inner recesses of my spirit and heart, is my mother, may God preserve her for me. Even today she treats me like her little son who keeps her company in her solitude, now that my father has departed. My brothers and sisters left the family home to live their own lives. My divorce may have delighted her, and my eschewal of marriage may have gladdened her, since she wants me to remain by her side forever and a day. Now that she's over eighty and in failing health, she moves with great difficulty and only leaves the house to see the doctor. Her memory retains nothing but happy events. Painful occurrences never cross her mind. Almost every day she tells me the love story she experienced with my late father—how he wrote her love letters, which were moistened by his tears and marked by the kisses of a heart pierced by an arrow, to show the pain he suffered because of his love for her. She tells me how he threw flowers to her through her bedroom window that opened onto the street. Whenever she went with her mother to the public bath or market, he would trail after her from a distance, tossing her fiery kisses and displaying his eagerness to embrace her. She also recounts the details of a honeymoon trip they took to the capital and how its old markets enchanted her—Souk el Attarine with the perfumers, Souk el Blaghgia with the slipper makers, and Souk el Blat with the herbalists. The electric train that transported them from the capital to La Marsa also caught their fancy. She describes everything she saw, heard, encountered, and sensed in detail, including the fine atmosphere in the coffeehouse called el Safsaf. They took their honeymoon at summer's end, when the shore at La Marsa had begun to bid adieu to vacationers. Patrons of this coffeehouse were smoking water pipes and drinking tea with mint. They were all dapper, their white jubbahs were scented with cologne, and the men swapped jokes and wisecracks while listening to the songs of Umm Kulthum, Abdel Wahab, Sidi Ali al-Riahi, Saliha, and Cheikh El Afrit, who sang:

The days pass like a breeze
Through a windmill,
East, then west,
And never last.

"Yes, friends, days do pass as swiftly as wind through windmills. Life is short. When a man is twenty, he's proud of his youth and vitality and besotted with his elegance and grace. Then, suddenly, he finds himself confronted by old age's abyss, which opens before him a terrifying black pit like the mouth of a predatory beast preparing to swallow him whole. I won't conceal from you the constant panic I feel nowadays. What alarms me most is the coming of a day when my imagination fails me, when it will no longer assist me and shield me from time's evils, which are advancing toward me at an insane speed."

Their fourth drinking companion, Umar, came from the country of the Green Revolution. Si al-Tahir described him with terse eloquence as a "branch so desiccated it no longer aspires to sprout green leaves." With his frizzy hair, which resembled weeds that had burned and then become coated with dust, his wizened, brown body, his dull eyes that turned red when he drank, and his persistent hysteria that affected him even during his rare and brief periods of happiness, Umar actually did look as though he had resigned from life and no longer desired anything beyond permission to continue living in this manner—silent, neglected, and forgotten—until his final hour arrived.

Umar had lived in Neapolis for more than two years, although he visited his home country every two or three months to supply himself with what he needed to continue his exile, since life back in Libya was unbearable for him, especially after what he referred to as the Day of Unrest, because he had been one of its victims.

Umar's silence would last for days—even for weeks—but when he did speak he wouldn't stop until he had exhausted himself and his listeners. His father was a merchant who had lost his social status and a large part of his fortune following the Green Revolution, which had occurred when Umar was four. The people of this far-flung desert nation awoke to the news that their elderly, ascetic king—who loved to live in tents and hated pomp and palaces, who loved Sufi stories and epic tales of desert warriors, and who was deeply moved by Quranic recitations, religious songs, and dervish dhikr—had been deposed and replaced by angry young men who shouted loudly with fists raised in the air as they glorified something they called the Green Revolution. They criticized Jews and Christians as enemies of the Arabs and Muslims and promised everyone benefits across the board, perpetual happiness, freedom, justice, and equal rights. No one would be poor or oppressed any longer. In response to the fiery speeches of the youthful leader of that Green Revolution, massive throngs rushed into the streets and squares to salute and support him. Others hid in their homes, feeling deeply concerned and as glum as if they had lost both their parents. Umar's father was one of this latter group, and the small child, for the first time in his life, saw this dignified man, who had the lofty presence of a desert prince and who was his father, burst into tears in the presence of despondent family members as he repeated vehemently, "Everything is finished! Everything is finished!" Then he spent many months prostrate in bed, speaking only infrequently, eating but a little, and releasing one moan after another. The small child soon realized that the king's forced abdication was to blame. Therefore, he began to pray that some evil would befall the new rulers and implored God to restore the dear king to his throne so the boy's father would regain his dignity and prosperity would again fill their house, which had become as desolate as a haunted ruin. God, however, did not answer his prayers or heed his pleas. The leader of the Green Revolution quickly consolidated his grip over the country and its inhabitants. Those, like Umar's father, who secretly opposed him, lived in constant anxiety, since joy and contentment were foreign to them. Those who publicly rejected the new leader were thrown in prison, fled into exile, or disappeared without anyone ever learning their fate. Umar's family's neighbor, who was a prominent professor of English literature at the university and who belonged to a well-established family related to the deposed king, hanged himself in his bedroom after they confiscated his valuable library. Not a single day passed without the Green Revolution's leader acting in a way that demonstrated his tyranny, obstinacy, and brutality. No one shared in his rule. No one dared to disobey him, to criticize him, or to interfere—no matter how gently or suavely—with his many swift, contradictory, random, temperamental, weird, risible, and illogical decisions, which were as unruly as the sandstorms of his country's desert. Loyalty to him was the key to life. Those who refused him their fealty were destined to be killed and obliterated. The leader of the Green Revolution called for their bodies to be put on display, hung up in public squares, and shown on television during the primetime newscasts to serve as a lesson for anyone hiding behind a veil of bogus loyalty. He continued to call night and day on his supporters and spies, who were dispersed everywhere, to be on the alert and to be vigilant, in order to eradicate the remaining "stray dogs," "filthy rats," and "venomous vermin," until the country was cleansed of their evils and became a great power that awed the mighty of the world. The nation would ignore the puny people of the world because it could pulverize them in the wink of an eye. The child was so terrified that he no longer dared to recite his prayers and secret pleas for fear that he would be discovered and his tongue excised or his body suspended in Green Square, overlooking the sea. Like a child in some terrifying fairy tale, Umar grew up surrounded by yelling and chanting, operations of extermination and assassination, and threatening announcements and warnings. To liberate himself from everything that might interfere with his limitless and boundless ambitions, the leader of the Green Revolution accused his former comrades of conspiring against him and set about liquidating or removing them—without anyone raising a voice to find fault with this. After publishing a book that explained the teachings and principles of his Green Revolution, he summoned hundreds of translators to render it into the world's languages. He ordered the minister of culture and instruction to organize international conferences about the book. Experts and specialists in political science and economics, thinkers, scholars, authors, and poets were invited to these conferences—Arabs but especially foreigners. The "leader" was no longer satisfied with ruling one country with a fiery, iron fist; he aspired to be the leader and novice master for all revolutions on all continents and to advise oppressed peoples of their right to revolt against their iniquitous, tyrannical rulers. The world needed to listen to the new "messenger from the desert" and to esteem his words and deeds. Now his hand was reaching out to the Philippines and Thailand, to South America, to Ireland, to the "jungles" of Africa, to rebellious officers in neighboring countries, to Basque separatists, to the Palestinians, to the Tuareg—to gain helpers and advocates for his ideas and theories. To draw attention to himself, he issued secret orders to his agents and spies, and they organized terrorist operations hither and yon. They seized hostages, assassinated opponents to his rule, and kidnapped leading figures. They even blew up a plane over a British village with casualties in the hundreds! When the world's anger at the leader of the Green Revolution intensified and a great power dispatched its aircraft to bomb his residence, that retaliation only increased his conceit, violence, insanity, arrogance, and stubbornness. In the face of the calamities and ordeals that fell in waves upon the country because of this leader, Umar's father was afflicted with partial paralysis that made it impossible for him to move or speak. Shortly thereafter, as his eyes filled with tears, he died, and Umar took charge of what remained of his business ventures, adhering to the same principles he had observed since childhood. He limited his words and did not express an opinion on sensitive topics—and there were many. He did not frequent coffeehouses. He did not oppose government directives, even when they harmed his personal interests. He did not refuse to hang pictures of the leader on the walls of his business establishments. In fact, he hung them in his office to avoid raising the suspicions of the leader's men, who were planted everywhere. From time to time, he would travel to one of the neighboring countries "for a breath of fresh air," before returning to his monotonous, burdensome life. Despite criticisms directed at him in private and in public, Umar eschewed marriage, without providing any explanation. He secretly feared that marrying would bring him burdens he could not shoulder and that he would end up like his father. One Friday, he stayed home until evening—watching old Egyptian films, as he normally did on his weekly day off. Then he set out on a walk through the calm neighborhood where he lived. Policemen stopped him, however, and demanded his identity card. After examining it, they ordered him to climb into their Jeep. He obeyed silently, thinking they had made a mistake, which they would soon discover. Without interrogating him, however, they threw him in a putrid, gray cell into which many men were crammed. Gradually, he discovered among them blind men, cripples, beggars, frightened adolescents, and elderly men. One fellow, who really was an idiot with matted hair, bare feet, and a fetid smell, laughed hysterically and kept reciting as he clapped nervously, "Long live our virile leader, thanks to whom we live in ignominy."

He only stopped when he heard the guards' footsteps. Umar gradually grasped the reason for his arrest. A match between the two most famous soccer teams in the country had been held that day for the championship cup. The captain of one of the teams was the leader's son, who was famous for his boorishness, rashness, and constant nervousness. He would not hesitate to punish anyone who blocked one of his goals. His team naturally won that match and gained the cup. Then fans of the opposing team rioted in the streets of the capital, burning cars, shops, banks, and government and security offices. The army and the police had only been able to quell the wrath of those large multitudes with enormous effort. When the leader, who was secluded in his tent in the heart of the desert, was informed of what had happened, he ordered the arrest of the perpetrators of the incidents of what he called the Day of Turmoil and their prosecution. The mob, however, had dispersed, and the people left in the streets had no link to the unrest. Nevertheless, many of these hapless folks were marched off to prison to appease the leader and assuage his anger. Umar spent a month in that stinky cell. Then he and his cellmates were released once the leader issued a pardon for all those accused (falsely) in the incidents of the Day of Turmoil. Umar returned home devastated, hating himself and life. He met with his assistant, on whom he had relied since his father's time and to whom he had delegated the day-to-day management of his business affairs, and then headed to Neapolis for an "extended period of recuperation," as he liked to say.

At midnight, one after another of these drinking buddies departed. Yunus remained alone at the large table that bore witness—with its plates, empty bottles and glasses, and disorder—to their long, enjoyable evening. By 1:00 a.m., he was the only customer left in the restaurant. He paid the substantial bill and decided to return home on foot, along the shore. That would be the best way for him to begin his sixty-first year.

10

The waves' groans could have been the moans of harem women stimulated by caresses and kisses in sweet dreams to dance feverishly in expectation of intercourse's final intoxication. The world was still, and he felt alone in existence. According to Kierkegaard, "Life can only be understood backwards; but it must be lived forwards"; in other words, heading toward something that does not exist.[28] He was returning home, walking along the shore beneath a sky studded with stars. The future alarmed him because all he could envision was a bleak, desolate, thorny desert. The view back, though, was of an enjoyable, comforting expanse. There he was—sixty years ago—a baby his mother delivered him at dawn on a Thursday. Yes, she remembered that very well because it was the day of the weekly market in El Alaâ. While screaming in labor, she was able to hear the clamor of men exchanging morning greetings and preparing to head to the market. She also remembered that his father hosted a magnificent banquet and invited the village notables to celebrate the new baby. Her sister Salima, who was an expert cook, supervised the preparations. The guests ate couscous with *mislan*. They stayed up until late that night, enjoying panegyric songs, Sufi chanting, and Qur'anic recitations. The Qur'anic sura Yunus was recited more than once, because when his mother was pregnant with him, she had an amazing dream. She saw herself swimming in the sea—in her green wrap she wore to feasts and weddings. Around her waist, she had fastened a brilliantly colored sash. She was as light as a butterfly, and the sea was calm, blue, and as vast as the sky above. Her dream was truly amazing, since she had never seen the sea and tales that she had heard about it could not have created a clear image in her mind. She told her dream to her friend Dhahabiya, who was renowned for her skill and expertise in deciphering their riddles. She thought about it for a long time. When she failed to interpret it, she suggested that his mother head to Ammar, the teacher at the Qur'anic primary school. He was a thin man, who was said to resemble a scorched piece of firewood. Cross-eyed, he spoke extremely slowly—as if the words were imprisoned inside his chest and could only escape with difficulty. He pondered her dream silently, his brow furrowed, oblivious to her as she sat before him in the green cloak she had worn in her dream. Her heart was pounding quickly and powerfully. It was winter, and Kesra Mountain was covered with snow. A camel was wailing in the distance because they had slaughtered her calf to celebrate the ample olive harvest. Then Master Ammar cleared his throat and—with the slow diction for which he was renowned and beloved by the people of the village—began to tell her about a prophet called Yunus, who was a generous ascetic. "God sent him to his people, and he began to preach to them, counsel them, and guide them toward goodness, although none of them responded. When he gave up and left them, he was extremely angry, promising them a painful punishment that would befall them in three days. When he reached the sea, determined to quit his people for good, he boarded a ship bound for a distant land. He did so without realizing that God was displeased with him for lacking the patience it takes to deliver a divine message. For this reason, despair and hopelessness quickly spread to his soul for not properly performing the mission entrusted to him. Meanwhile, God granted the hearts of Jonah's people belief before He punished them. So, they repented, and the men, women, and children wept. They numbered precisely one hundred thousand, no more and no less. Meanwhile, a violent storm rocked the ship on which Prophet Yunus was a passenger. The waves raged high around it and began to toss the vessel about, threatening to drown the passengers. They considered this storm to be a sign that one of their fellow passengers had sinned. For this reason, they decided to throw the sinner into the sea, thinking this might decrease God's anger against them and that He would save them from imminent destruction. After discussing the matter, they drew arrows. Yunus picked the losing arrow, and they were amazed at that because he was renowned for his righteousness and veracity. Then they drew arrows twice more, but each time Yunus selected the losing arrow. So, he cast himself into the sea, where the whale swallowed him. God, however, directed that the whale should not harm His prophet. For three nights, Yunus was shaded by three degrees of darkness: the darkness of the whale's belly, the darkness of the sea, and the darkness of the night. This was a divine test for him. Afterward, the whale spat him out. Then Yunus stood naked and emaciated on the shore. Over his head grew a gourd plant with large, tender leaves that shaded him, and no flies or other insects would approach it.* The fruit of this plant can be eaten raw or cooked, together with its rind and seeds. It is beneficial in many ways. Once Prophet Yunus regained his health, God sent him back to his people. All of this was part of God's plan, may He be praised and exalted."

This strange story amazed Yunus's mother, who continued to gaze at Master Ammar with fascination, as if she were in the presence of an angel who had delivered her from darkness into the light. Master Ammar spoke again; he admitted he had not understood her dream well but advised her to name her baby Yunus, if it was a boy. Then he placed his hand on her belly and prayed for her and the Muslim community, hoping they would enjoy goodness, blessings, health, and happiness.

When she gave birth, the mother followed Master Ammar's advice and named her son Yunus.

Once he became conscious of the world around him, she liked to entertain him from time to time with the unique and amazing tale of the Prophet Yunus. This was the loveliest story he ever heard. When she finished, he would close his eyes to see himself first aboard a ship rocked by the waves, next in the whale's belly enveloped by the three types of darkness, and finally standing stark naked on the beach with a blessed gourd plant over his head, while his people stared at him, fascinated and astonished. When he was five and began to memorize the Qur'an, he was in a hurry to reach sura Yunus. With a speed that astonished the schoolmaster, he memorized the short suras and then started learning the longer ones. Whenever he finished one of the Qur'an's sixty sections, he would parade through the village with the slate on which he had written the revelatory

---

* Qur'an 37:146 As-Saffat (Rows).

verses with resin, decorating the center and margins with egg yolk. Then men and women would bless him and stroke his small head with their hands while praying for his success, by the grace of God, of His Messenger, and of the righteous saints.

After he finished memorizing sura Yunus, his heart overflowed with all the rapture of a voyager who has reached a verdant oasis where he hopes to rest after the hardships of a long trip. Whether he was alone on the footpaths, watching the sun set behind the hill, or wandering through the fields—his eyes moist with tears—he would repeat in a whisper: "If only a town had believed and benefited! Only the people of Yunus did. So, when they believed, we freed them from the punishment of ignominy in their worldly pursuits and allowed them to enjoy life for a time."*

Two years before her death, he brought his mother to the capital. Accompanied by his wife and their daughter Maryam, he took his mother to the seashore for the first time. That was at the harbor beach, early in the summer. They spent three hours there. When they were preparing to return, he asked her, "How did you find the sea?"

She smiled and replied, "Exactly like the sea I saw in the dream when I was pregnant with you!"

How he wished he might recall only happy memories—like Umm Karim. But these memories were threatened at any moment with annihilation by the weight of time. Rilke was wrong when he believed old age could be happy. No, it was hideous and unfair. The satirist Swift, who had created amazing worlds—after he was placed in a care facility that he had founded when he was younger—liked to stand before the mirror contemplating his face. Then he would yell with self-loathing, "What a miserable old man you are!"[29] Perhaps before long he would do that. Then he would fall over dead amid his defeats. The victories he had encouraged his soul to anticipate had never been achieved.

There was a commotion, and figures rushed toward him. He stopped walking only to find himself surrounded by a group of young men, all of them drunk. They were glowering, and sparks flew from their eyes.

* Qur'an 10:98 Yunus (Jonah).

"Didn't I tell you," one said in a harsh voice coarsened by rage and rancor, "he's one of those dogs!"

The others replied, "You're right!"

"Son of a bitch! He strolls along the beach in a fancy suit!"

"In fancy shoes too!"

"Yesterday, he and his brothers were picking up cigarette butts and eating crumbs. Today they've become the lords of the country!"

"They piss on us from dawn to dusk, and no one can punish them."

"Bastards! Thieves!"

"Crooks!"

"Sicilian Mafia!"

"Their sister, the whore, protects them and spoils them!"

"That vile stylist!"

"She's become the mistress of the country. She gives speeches, she commands, she appoints government ministers."

"Not to mention ambassadors, and she builds mansions and buys private planes!"

"Without any limits . . . as if buying children's toys."

"The hussy!"

"And her husband, the general, obeys her like a dog!"

"You suck him and her!"

"This wretch—what shall we do to him?"

"We'll fuck his mother and his sister."

He broke his silence and shouted at them, "Listen, guys!"

But they attacked him and began kicking him. They shouted gruffly, cursing and insulting him, spitting at him. Then they ripped his suit off and cast it into the sea. Blood flowed from him profusely, and he was about to pass out.

"Not so fast, fellows," he heard a young man say. "This isn't one of them!"

"How so?"

"I know this man!"

"Who is he?"

"He's that sad professor who sits in the Albatross Restaurant and prowls alone on the beach."

"Ah ... true ... true!"

"The poor man ... you've treated him badly."

"What shall we do now?"

"Let's scram! He's to blame for strolling on the beach in a fancy suit at this hour of the night!"

They fled. He remained on the cold sand where they had dumped him, unable to move. Pains and bruises covered every part of his body, and blood stained his face. With difficulty, he opened his eyes. The world was black: no sky, no sea. It seemed to him that he was falling into the deep, dark pit that had long terrified him in his nightmares. He remembered Abu Hayyan al-Tawhidi's words:

Life is short. Hours fly past. Motion is perpetual. Opportunities glitter brightly. When strings play music, they approach each other and then separate. As souls expire, they dissolve and catch fire.

Heinrich Böll Cottage
October 19, 2011

Glossary ◆ Notes

Glossary

Abd Allah al-Wansharishi (d. 1130): Disciple of Ibn Tumart.

Abd al-Qadir al-Jilani (or Gilani) (d. 1166): Muslim jurist, preacher, theologian, and founder of the Qadiri Sufi order.

Abdel Wahab, Mohammed (1902–91): Egyptian singer, composer, and actor.

Abdul Hamid II (1842–1918): Last Ottoman sultan of the Ottoman Empire; reigned 1876–1909.

Abélard, Pierre (1079–1142): French philosopher and theologian; castrated in 1117.

Adonis (b. 1930): Pen name of Ali Ahmed Said Esber, a distinguished contemporary Syrian poet.

Aghlabids: Dynasty of Arab emirs who ruled Algeria, Tunisia, and western Libya from 800 to 909 and Sicily from 827; they recognized the Abbasid caliphs in Baghdad.

Ahmad ibn Abi al-Diyaf, also Bin Diyaf (1804–74): Author of a multivolume *History of Tunisia* and of an *Epistle on Women*.

Alfonso VI (d. 1109): King of León and Castile.

Ali Ben Gh'dhahim (or Ghedhahem, etc.) (1814–67): Tunisian Berber tribal revolutionary leader.

Almohads: Twelfth- and thirteenth-century Muslim Berber dynasty that ruled Morocco and Andalusia.

Almoravids: Muslim Berber dynasty that ruled Morocco and Andalusia from 1062 to 1147.

Amor Abbada al-Ayari, Sidi: Nineteenth-century Sufi saint.

Apuleius: Born in present-day Algeria, died ca. 170; author of *The Golden Ass*.

Aroui, Abdel Aziz El (1898–1971): Tunisian journalist and broadcaster known for recounting folktales.

In these alphabetical listings, please ignore the initial definite article al-, el-, at-, etc.

217

al-Atrash, Farid (1910–71): Syrian-Egyptian singer, composer, and actor.

Awlad Majer Bedouins: Tunisian Berber tribe led by Ali Ben Gh'dhahim.

Ba'ath Party: Arab secular, socialist, nationalist political party founded in 1947; split in 1966 between Syrian and Iraqi Ba'athists.

Bab el Jalladin, Kairouan: Gate of the Leather Merchants.

al-Balawi, Abu Zamaʿa: A companion of the Prophet Muhammad; buried in Kairouan in 654.

Banu Hilal: Confederation of Arab tribes that migrated to North Africa and destroyed Kairouan in 1057.

Barrouta Well: Ancient, enclosed well built in 796 in Kairouan with a camel-powered waterwheel.

Ben Ali, Leïla (b. 1956): Wife and now widow of Tunisian president Zine El Abidine Ben Ali.

Ben Ali, Zine El Abidine Ben Ali (1936–2019): President of Tunisia from 1987 to 2001.

Beran, Josef (1888–1969): Czech Roman Catholic archbishop and then cardinal.

Bey: Title of rulers of Tunis before Tunisia's independence.

Bizerte War: Three-day crisis in July 1961 when Tunisia blockaded a French naval base; there were 630 Tunisian and 24 French fatalities.

Black Thursday: January 26, 1978, when mass labor union protests were suppressed, and many demonstrators were killed.

Bouvard et Pécuchet: Posthumously published satirical novel by Gustave Flaubert.

Bovary, Madame Emma: Character in the novel *Madame Bovary* by Gustave Flaubert.

Bouilhet, Louis-Hyacinthe (1821–69): French poet.

Boulus, Sargon (1944–2007): Important Iraqi poet of Assyrian heritage.

Bourguiba, Habib (1903–2000): Revolutionary leader, prime minister, and first president of independent Tunisia (1957–87).

Brassens, Georges (1921–81): French singer and songwriter.

Bread Revolt: Tunisian bread riots from December 29, 1983, to January 5, 1984; 150 killed.

burnous: A hooded cloak.

al-Burda: Famous, beloved poem in praise of the Prophet Muhammad.

al-Busiri (d. 1294): Berber Sufi poet.

Cave of the Patriarchs Massacre in Palestine: On February 25, 1994, Baruch Goldstein opened fire on Muslims praying in Hebron, killing 29 and wounding 125.

Céline, Louis-Ferdinand (aka Louis Ferdinand Destouches) (1894–1961): Controversial French author who affected a working-class style and was considered pro-fascist and anti-Semitic.

Cheikh El Afrit (1897–1939): Born Issim Israël Rozzio; a Jewish Tunisian singer.

Chott el-Djerid: Large salt lake in southern Tunisia.

Dala'il al-Khayrat: Collection of prayers for the Prophet Muhammad; written by al-Shadhili (d. 1465).

dhikr: Sufi chanting service.

dirham: Coin.

Eid: Muslim religious festival.

Eid al-Adha: Feast of the Sacrifice, commemoration of Abrahamic miracle; occurs during the pilgrimage month.

Fahmy, Hussein (b. 1940): Egyptian film and television actor.

Fairuz (Feyrouz, etc.) (b. 1934): Lebanese superstar vocalist.

Flaubert, Gustave (1821–80): Major French novelist; his *Dictionnaire des idées reçues* was published posthumously and translated to English as *Flaubert's Dictionary of Accepted Ideas*.

Foucault, Michel (1926–84): Influential French philosopher and theorist who taught in Tunisia from 1966 to 1968 while his lover did national service for France there.

Gaddafi (or Qaddafi), Muammar (d. 2011): Controversial and eccentric Libyan leader who toppled the monarchy in 1969; author of *The Green Book*.

Gaspar, Lorand (1925–2019): Born in what is today Romania, Gaspar was a Hungarian and French physician and poet who lived in Palestine and Tunisia.

Gelimer (480–553): The last German king of the Vandals in North Africa.

Germinal: French novel by Émile Zola about a strike by coal miners.

Giono, Jean (1895–1970): Pantheist, pacifist French novelist who often wrote about subsistence farmers in Provence.

The Golden Ass: Also translated as *The Metamorphoses*; an early novel by Apuleius.

Habash, George (1926–2008): Palestinian Christian founder of the Popular Front for the Liberation of Palestine.

Hached, Farhat (1914–52): Tunisian labor leader who was assassinated by a French colonist gang.

Hafez, Abdel Halim (1929–77): Major Egyptian singer and actor.

Hafsid sultans: Sunni Muslim Berber rulers of North Africa from western Libya to Algeria (1229–1574).

haik: North African full-body veil.

Halfaouine: Quarter of Tunis north of the Medina.

Hannibal (d. ca. 182 BCE): Carthaginian general during the Second Punic War.

Héloïse (d. 1164): Famous lover of Pierre Abélard, also a poet and composer.

Hosny, Soad (1943–2001): Egyptian film star.

Hoxha, Nexhmije (1921–2020): Albanian Communist politician, director of the Albanian Institute of Marxist-Leninist Studies, and wife of the Albanian Communist ruler Enver Hoxha; in 1993 she was sentenced to nine years in prison in Albania.

Husaynids: Tunisian dynasty of Beys ruling from 1705 to 1957.

Hussein, Taha (1889–1973): Pivotal Egyptian author, blind from the age of two.

Ibn Arabi, Muhyi al-Din (1165–1240): Andalusian Arab Muslim Sufi and poet.

Ibn al-Athir (1160–1233): Arabic language scholar.

Ibn Khaldun (1332–1406): Major Muslim historian and social scientist.

Ibn Tumart (d. ca. 1130): Muslim Berber reformer who founded the Almohad movement that eventually overthrew Almoravid rule.

iftar: A meal that breaks fasting; a literal "breakfast."

al-Jahiz, Abu Uthman Amr ibn Bahr (d. 868 or 869): A major Abbasid-era Arabic language author.

al-Jazuli, Muhammad (d. 1465): Sufi, Berber tribal leader; editor of litanies for the Prophet Muhammad.

Jemaa el-Fnaa Square: Major square in Marrakech.

El-Jerid: Semi-desert region of southwest Tunisia.

Jouini, Hédi (1909–90): Tunisian singer, instrumentalist, and composer.

jubbah: A man's robe.

Kemal, Yashar (or Yaşur) (1923–2015): Ethnic Kurdish author of Turkish novels.

Khaled, Amr (b. 1967): Popular Egyptian Muslim television preacher.

Khaled, Leila (b. 1944): Member of the Popular Front for the Liberation of Palestine; active as an aircraft hijacker from 1969 to 1970.

Khawarij, or Kharijis or Kharijites: Ancient, violent, sectarian splinter movement in Islam (657 to the present) represented today by the mild-mannered Ibadis.

khosrow or *khosrau*: Title for an ancient Iranian emperor.

Kitab al-Aghani: Massive compilation of lyrics and poems and information about medieval Arab poets and musicians by Abu al-Faraj al-Isfahani (897–ca. 972).

Kundera, Milan (b. 1929): Czech and French author of *The Unbearable Lightness of Being* and other works.

Lacan, Jacques (1901–81): French psychiatrist, psychoanalyst, and social theorist.

Lamti leather: From the Lamta clan of the Sanhaja Berbers.

Lautréamont, duc de: Pen name of Isidore Lucien Ducasse (1846–70), a French poet born in Uruguay; known for *Les Chants de Maldoror*.

Laylat al-Qadr: Night when the first verses of the Qur'an were revealed to Prophet Muhammad.

Lévy, Bernard-Henri (b. 1948): French public intellectual who was born in French Algeria.

Lutfi, Nadia (1937–2020): Egyptian film star.

al-Ma'arri, Abu al-'Ala' (973–1058): Major, blind, Syrian poet, author, and scholar.

Mahdi: Title for a Muslim latter-day savior.

Malouf, or ma'luf: Andalusian heritage type of music in Algeria, Tunisia, and Libya.

mamluk: A slave soldier.

al-Ma'mun (786–833): Important Abbasid caliph.

Mao Zedong, Chairman Mao (1893–1976): Chinese revolutionary; founder of the People's Republic of China; chairman of the Chinese Communist Party from 1949 to 1976.

Mahrez, Sidi: Patron saint of Tunis.

Abu Muhammad Mahrez ibn Khalaf: The Sidi Mahrez Mosque in the souk named for him was built in 1692.

Main Rouge, La: French terrorist group of colonists active in North Africa during the 1950s.

mislan: "A cut of lamb taken from the upper part of the sheep's hind legs. That piece of meat is considered a choice cut because it is tender, tasty, meaty and fat. It is cooked almost exclusively with couscous, and couscous *mislan* is cooked on special occasions, as a special treat, or in honor of special guests" (per Dr. Béchir Chourou, August 4, 2012).

Misers, The: Literary profiles of famous Arab misers, *Al-Bukhala'*, a book by al-Jahiz.

Msika, Habiba (1903–30): Tunisian Jewish sex symbol; also a singer, dancer, and actress.

Meursault: Main character in *The Stranger* by Albert Camus.

Montherlant, Henry de (1895–1972): French novelist and man of letters.

Mu'allaqāt: Important collection of pre-Islamic Arabi poems.

Muray, Philippe (1945–2006): French novelist and man of letters.

al-Mu'tamid ibn Abbad (1040–95): Last Taifa ruler of Seville.

al-Mutanabbi (d. 965): Major, medieval Arab poet who wrote many panegyrics.

muwashshahat (sing., *muwashshah*): A type of classical Arabi poem and its adaptation to music.

My Father Atop a Tree (*Abi Foq El Shagara*): Egyptian film released in 1969; last film of Abdel Halim Hafez.

Naama (Halima Echeikh) (b. 1936): Renowned Tunisian female vocalist.

Najma: See Hoxha, Nexhmije.

Nakba: The displacement of multitudes of Palestinians from their homeland.

Nasser, Gamal Abdel (1918–70): Charismatic Egyptian leader who was a leader of the 1952 overthrow of the Egyptian monarchy; second president of Egypt, from 1954 to 1970.

Neapolis: Nabeul, Tunisia: Classical name of this coastal city.

Nesin, Aziz (1915–95): Turkish writer; author of *Istanbul Boy*.

ojja: Tunisian omelet.

Okamoto, Kōzō (b. 1947): Member of the Japanese Red Army; a convert to Islam; imprisoned by Israel for his participation in the 1972 Lod Airport Massacre.

Oulaya (1936–90): Tunisian singer and actress.

Prévert, Jacques (1900–1977): Popular French poet.

Procopius: Sixth-century Byzantine historian.

al-Qaradawi, Shaykh Yusuf (b. 1926): Major, contemporary, Egyptian-born, Islamist-leaning, Islamic theologian and television preacher.

al-Qurtubi, Abu al-Abbas Ahmad ibn Rumayla (d. 1086): Pro-Sufi ascetic and friend of Ibn Abbad.

Rastignac: Character in the French novel *La Comédie humaine* by Honoré de Balzac.

Rênal, Madame: Character in the French novel *The Red and the Black* by Stendhal.

Riahi, Ali (Ali al-Riyahi) (1912–70): Singer-composer of Tunisia.

Roquentin, Antoine: Character in the French novel *La Nausée* by Jean-Paul Sartre.

Rumi, Jalal al-Din (1207–73): Major Persian-language poet, influential Sufi mystic, and founder of the Mevlevi Sufi Order.

Sabah (1927–2014): Lebanese superstar, singer, and actress.

Sahib al-Himar ("The Man with the Donkey") (d. 947): Medieval Tunisian revolutionary: Abu Yazid Mukallad ibn Kayrad al-Nukkari.

Sahnun (d. ca. 854): Maliki jurisprudent of Kairouan.

sahur: Last meal of the night before fasting begins during Ramadan.

Sa'id Aql (1911–2014): Lebanese poet and author.

Salammbô: Historical novel by Gustave Flaubert, set in Carthage in the third century BCE.

Saliha (1914–58): Tunisian singer.

Sand, George (1804–76): Pen name of the major French feminist novelist and critic Amantine Aurore Lucille Dupin.

Semlali, Hédi (1919–91): Tunisian actor and comedian.

Sentimental Education: Novel by Gustave Flaubert; published in 1869 as *L'Éducation sentimentale*.

Al-Shabaab: Present-day Somali militant Islamist group.

Shabbi, Abu al-Qasim al- (1909–34): Tunisian Romantic poet.

Shadhili, Sidi Belhassan al- (1196–1258): Abu al-Hasan al-Shadhili, Moroccan scholar and founder of the Shadhili Sufi Order.

Shapur II (309–79): Sasanian dynasty emperor of Iran.

Si, Sidi: An honorific; roughly *Mr.* or *sir.*

Sorel, Julien: Character in the French novel *The Red and the Black* by Stendhal.

Souk el Grana: An ancient market where various commodities are sold in Tunis.

al-Tabari (839–923): Important Qur'an commentator and major historian.

Taifa: Andalusian principalities that arose as the Umayyad caliphate faded; conquered by the Almoravids; the Taifas were independent principalities in al-Andalus (medieval Muslim Spain) during the eleventh through the thirteenth centuries. After they were conquered by Almoravids, they reemerged and then were conquered by the Almohads.

Al-Tamimi or Temimi, Youssef (1921–83): Tunisian singer known for his "manly voice."

tastira: Fried egg, tomatoes, and peppers served with fish.

al-Tawhidi, Abu Hayyan (d. 1023): Arabic language essayist and anthologist.

Al-Tha'alibi (d. 1038): Persian anthologist of and advocate for Arabic literature, best known for *Yatimat al-Dahr*, which includes poems by many Arab authors.

Tocqueville, Alexis de (1805–59): French diplomat, historian, and political scientist.

Trois Contes or *Three Tales*: A work by Gustave Flaubert.

Umm Kulthum (1904–75): Legendary Egyptian singer and actress.

Valjean, Jean: Character in the French novel *Les Misérables* by Victor Hugo.

wali: A Sufi saint, a "friend of God."

Yusuf ibn Tashfin (1009–1106): The most famous of the Almoravid kings and ruler of all of Morocco.

Yusuf Kahiya: Nineteenth-century Tunisian military officer.

Zarruq: Nineteenth-century Tunisian government official.

zawiya: A Sufi hostel or meeting house.

Zaynab al-Nafzawiya: Wealthy, influential Berber woman of the eleventh century; wife of Yusuf ibn Tashfin, an Almoravid ruler.

Zweig, Stefan (1881–1942): Prolific Austrian novelist and biographer who fled Nazi Germany and lived in Brazil.

Notes

1. Mon enfant, ma soeur,
   Songe à la douceur
   D'aller là-bas vivre ensemble!
   Aimer à loisir,
   Aimer et mourir
   Au pays qui te ressemble!
   Les soleils mouillés
   De ces ciels brouillés
   Pour mon esprit ont les charmes
   Si mystérieux
   De tes traîtres yeux,
   Brillant à travers leurs larmes
2. Homme libre, toujours tu chériras la mer!
   La mer est ton miroir; tu contemples ton âme
   Dans le déroulement infini de sa lame,
   Et ton esprit n'est pas un gouffre moins amer.
3. O douleur! ô douleur, le Temps mange la vie,
   Et l'obscur Ennemi qui nous ronge le coeur
   Du sang que nous perdons croît et se fortifie!
4. "Ulysses (1922)/Chapter 9," Wikipedia, https://en.wikisource.org/wiki/Ulysses
   _(1922)/Chapter_9, 204.
5. See, for example, chapter 20: "That to Think as a Philosopher is to Learn to Die," in *The Essays*, by Michel de Montaigne, trans. George B. Ives (New York: Heritage Press, 1946), I:116.
6. Raymond P. Scheindlin, *Form and Structure in the Poetry of al-Muʿtamid ibn ʿAbbad* (Leiden: E. J. Brill, 1974); see also https://upload.wikimedia.org/wikipedia/commons/thumb/6/63/T%C3%BAmulo_do_poeta_portugu%C3%AAs_%28nascido_em_Beja%29_Al-Mu%E2%80%99tamid.jpg/220px-T%C3%BAmulo_do_poeta_portugu%C3%AAs_%28nascido_em_Beja%29_Al-Mu%E2%80%99tamid.jpg.
7. Iʿtimad Arrumaikiyya in Abdullah al-Udhari, *Classical Poems by Arab Women* (London: Saqi Books, 1999), 196–97.

225

8. See Al-Mu'tamid Ibn 'Abbad, *Poesías: Antologia bilingüe*, ed. María Jesús Rubiera Mata (Madrid: Clásicos Hispano-Árabes Bilingües, 1982), 45, 78–79; and Mu'tamid, *The Poems of Mu'tamid, King of Seville*, trans. Dulcie Lawrence Smith (London: John Murray, 1915), https://archive.org/details/poemsofmutamidk00muta.

9. Hassouna Mosbahi has explained: "Abu Al-ABBAS AHMED IBN RUMAILA était un ascète proche des soufis, et était très proche de Ibn Abbad. Avant la célèbre bataille de Sagrajas en 1086, il avait raconté à Ibn Abbad, ainsi qu'à IBN TECHFINE qu'il avait vu le prophète Mohamed dans son rêve et que celui-ci leur avait garanti la victoire contre l'armée de Alfons 6. Il est mort en martyr dans cette bataille!"

10. Hassouna Mosbahi has suggested this French translation of the Arabic couplet:
Les grands malheurs se sont abattus sur moi
Et leurs épées ont déchiqueté mon corps sain en miettes!

11. Ahmad ibn Abi al-Diyaf, *Consult Them in the Matter: A Nineteenth-Century Islamic Argument for Constitutional Government: The Muqaddima (Introduction) to Ithaf ahl al-zaman bi akhbar muluk Tunis wa 'ahd al-aman (Presenting Contemporaries the History of the Rulers of Tunis and the Fundamental Pact)*, trans. L. Carl Brown (Fayetteville: Univ. of Arkansas Press, 2005).

12. Gustave Flaubert, *Salammbô*, trans. M. French Sheldon (London: Saxon & Co., 1886), 68–69.

13. "Barbara," in *Paroles*, by Jacques Prévert (Paris: Gallimard: le point du jour, 1949), 199.

14. C. G. Jung, *Memories, Dreams, Reflections*, ed. Aniela Jaffé, trans. Richard and Clara Winston (New York: Vintage, 1989), 238–43.

15. Jung, *Memories, Dreams, Reflections*, 242–43.

16. Women loved, respectively, by the Arab poet Qays (known as al-Majnun), the great Sufi theosophist and poet Muhi al-Din ibn Arabi, Dante, and the French poet Louis Aragon.

17. Mikhail Bulgakov, *Diaries and Selected Letters*, trans. Roger Cockrell (Richmond, UK: Alma Classics, 2013), 27.

18. Bulgakov, *Diaries and Selected Letters*, 27.

19. Bulgakov, 57.

20. Bulgakov, 59.

21. William Blake, "Vala: Night the Eighth," in *Selected Poems* (London: Penguin Classics, 2005), 215.

22. William Blake, excerpt from "The Four Zoas: Night the Eighth," in *The Complete Poetry and Prose of William Blake*, ed. David V. Erdman (Berkeley: Univ. of California Press, 1982), 385. See, for example, http://jacobboehmeonline.com/yahoo_site_admin /assets/docs/Zoas.14493358.pdf.

23. Pablo Neruda, "XVIII," from "Twenty Love Poems," in *The Poetry of Pablo Neruda*, ed. Ilan Stavans, trans. W. S. Merwin (New York: Farrar, Straus and Giroux, 2003), 18.

24. Jorge Luis Borges, "Flaubert and His Exemplary Destiny," in *Selected Non-Fictions*, ed. Eliot Weinberger (New York: Viking, 1999), 392.

25. See, for example, https://www.gutenberg.org/files/34327/34327-h/34327-h.htm, where this passage does not appear.

26. Federico García Lorca, "The Weeping," in *Thirty Spanish Poems of Love and Exile*, ed. Kenneth Rexroth (San Francisco: City Lights Books, 1968), 25.

27. Isidore Ducasse, Comte de Lautrémont, "Les Chants de Maldoror," in *Oeuvres Complètes* (Paris: Librairie José Corti, 1963), 123. This is the beginning of "Chant Premier": Plût au ciel que le lecteur, enhardi et devenu momentanément féroce comme ce qu'il lit, trouve, sans se désorienter, son chemin abrupt et sauvage, à travers les marécages désolés de ces pages sombres et pleines de poison; car, à moins qu'il n'apporte dans sa lecture une logique rigoureuse et une tension d'esprit égale au moins à sa défiance, les émanations mortelles de ce livre imbiberont son âme comme l'eau le sucre. Il n'est pas bon que tout le monde lise les pages qui vont suivre; quelques-uns seuls savoureront ce fruit amer sans danger.

28. Søren Kierkegaard, *Journals* (1843), IV A 164. See https://wist.info/kierkegaard-soren/35849/ and http://sorenkierkegaard.org/kierkegaard-links.html.

29. This story about Swift is found in Søren Kierkegaard, *Stages on Life's Way*, trans. Walter Lowrie (New York: Schocken Books, 1967), 191–92.

Hassouna Mosbahi was born in 1950 near Kairouan, Tunisia. He is a writer, literary critic, and poet, as well as a freelance journalist for Arab and German newspapers. He settled in Munich in 1985 and lived there until 2004. In 2005 Mosbahi returned to Tunisia for a time and has now settled there. In 2012 he wrote and lectured in the United States.

In addition to publishing many short stories, novels, and nonfiction works, Mosbahi has made a name for himself as a travel writer, biographer, and translator into Arabic—translating Samuel Beckett and Jean Genet, for example. His biography of Saint Augustine was published in Arabic in Tunisia in 2010.

A Tunisian Tale was his first novel to be published in English (2011). His short story "Paranoia" appeared in the *Brooklyn Rail* and his stories "Delirium in the Desert" and "Truman Capote" appeared on that journal's InTranslation website in September 2015. An excerpt from his 2020 novel, *La Nasbah fi al-Nahr Marratayn* (We Never Swim in the Same River Twice), appeared in *Banipal 69*.

William Maynard Hutchins has translated many works of Arabic literature into English, including *Return of the Spirit* by Tawfiq al-Hakim, *The Cairo Trilogy* by Naguib Mahfouz, and *The Fetishists* by Ibrahim al-Koni. His translation of *New Waw* by al-Koni won the ALTA National Prose Translation Award in 2015. A three-time National Endowment for the Arts Fellow, Hutchins's translations have appeared in *Banipal* and on *Words without Borders*, and elsewhere. He holds degrees from Yale University and the University of Chicago and has taught subjects ranging from English and Arabic to philosophy and religious studies at the Gerard School in Lebanon, the University of Ghana, the American University in Cairo, and Appalachian State University. His translation of *Return to Dar al-Basha* by the Tunisian author Hassan Nasr was published by Syracuse University Press in 2006.